Erica JAMES

An IDEAL HUSBAND

ONE PLACE. MANY STORIES

HQ
An imprint of HarperCollins*Publishers* Ltd
1 London Bridge Street
London SE1 9GF

www.harpercollins.co.uk

HarperCollins*Publishers*
Macken House, 39/40 Mayor Street Upper,
Dublin 1, D01 C9W8, Ireland

This paperback edition 2024

2

First published in Great Britain by
HQ, an imprint of HarperCollins*Publishers* Ltd 2024

Copyright © Erica James 2024

Erica James asserts the moral right to be
identified as the author of this work.
A catalogue record for this book is
available from the British Library.

ISBN: 9780008413835

MIX
Paper | Supporting
responsible forestry
FSC™ C007454

This book contains FSC™ certified paper and other controlled
sources to ensure responsible forest management.

For more information visit: www.harpercollins.co.uk/green

Printed and Bound in the UK using 100% Renewable Electricity at
CPI Group (UK) Ltd, Croydon, CR0 4YY

Praise for *An Ideal Husband*

'Wonderful on characterisation and family dynamics, and
done very deftly, with that wry humour of hers. I was
very entertained by her clever, tongue-in-cheek plotting.'
Marian Keyes

'Erica James explores the complexity of
family relationships with skill and sympathy
and her vividly drawn characters leap from
the page. I couldn't put it down!'
Sarah Morgan

'We're certain you're going to love it.'
Glamour

'So, so good… shades of dark and light in every character
which are gloriously done. A deliciously satisfying story.'
Cathy Kelly

'Erica James writes upliftingly and
humorously about family life.'
My Weekly

'So warm and kind in the face of betrayal.
I can highly recommend.'
Fern Britton

'This compelling family drama puts a spotlight
on how a family can evolve and re-invent itself…
Effortlessly elegant storytelling from Erica, as ever.'
Veronica Henry

'Erica James weaves a beautiful, humorous tale of
difficult family dynamics and self-discovery'
Woman's Own

For Samuel, and Edward and Ally, and
my grandest of grandchildren.

Chapter One

It was a perfect March day and spring had arrived in all its glorious splendour. Leaf buds were fattening on the hawthorn and cherry trees and in the glittery bright sunshine patches of buttery-yellow cowslips were shyly showing themselves in the grass verges. Daffodils were gaily bobbing their heads as though in time to some secret rhythm playing on the breeze.

Everywhere Louisa Langford looked as she drove home from the farm shop there was a sense of better things to come. Only a few months ago and she would have cheerfully declared it one of those days in which to rejoice and count one's many blessings. Now it took a little more effort on her part to do that, but she did it all the same because the alternative was she might end up howling at the moon like a vengeful madwoman.

So far, and in possession of an iron willed self-control, she had managed to avoid shaming herself by behaving like a lunatic. Friends and neighbours had offered shoulders to cry on and lavished swathes of sympathy on her, which was kind of them, but it wasn't what she needed. It was divorce she was going through, she wanted to tell them, not a terminal illness.

This was, she knew all too well, a typical character trait of hers, the desire to remain stoic in the face of excruciating bewilderment that this could have happened to her. Divorce was what happened to other people, not her. Not when she had truly believed that she and Kip had defied the odds, that they had done everything right to ensure that while the marriages of their friends and acquaintances sadly came unravelled, they were the lucky ones. How stupid she now felt for holding such a disgustingly smug and complacent view.

Every couple had their storms to weather and Louisa had taken pride in the fact that whatever had been flung at her and Kip, they had coped. When they'd had money problems, they'd tightened their belts and lived accordingly. When the children had been young and pushed them to the outer limits of their patience, they had gritted their teeth and dug deeper for further patience. Health problems and the death of their parents had all been an intrinsic part of family life and, as worrying and as upsetting as those events had been, they had pulled together as a couple and survived them. You could only do that if the foundations of your marriage were rock solid with love.

So what had gone wrong? That was what Louisa couldn't understand. Why, when they were on the verge of enjoying what other friends referred to as the 'golden years' of retirement, had Kip thrown it all away? And for what: a stupid, self-indulgent late mid-life crisis?

Nearly home now, she slowed her speed to round the bend of the tree-lined lane and was met with a sight that had her letting out a cry of shocked disbelief. There in the front garden of Charity Cottage, her home for over thirty years, was a for sale board. She had been gone for less than an hour, but in that short space of time somebody had come here and pounded a wooden post into the flowerbed. It might just as well have been hammered into her heart.

She drove through the gateposts and came to a stop on the gravelled driveway. Switching off the engine and willing herself to stay calm, she stepped out of the car, retrieved the shopping from the boot, and let herself in at the front door. Slamming the door shut with her foot, she carried the bags through to the kitchen. There she dumped them on the floor, not caring about smashing the eggs or bruising the fruit and vegetables she'd just bought. Sinking into the nearest chair, she took a long shuddering breath and let out a wail of despair. Her head in her hands, she wept at the injustice of it all. She wept too for the loss of the man she had loved – the man she still loved – but who she feared was in the process of making her hate him.

How could he do this to her?

How could he be so cruel?

Wasn't it bad enough that he'd left her for a girl younger than their own daughter?

Wasn't it bad enough that the girl had been their youngest son's ex-girlfriend?

But now this, forcing her from her beloved home. Had he become so ruthlessly fixed on carving out a new life for himself that he had lost every trace of compassion for how this would affect her?

Or was it a mistake? Had the for sale board been put up in the wrong place? Was that it? Was she working herself into state and thinking the worst for no real reason? Ever since the pandemic, for sale boards had sprung up like weeds in the area. Properties in Suffolk villages, particularly those with good rail links to London, had been selling at astronomical prices in the last few years. Her eldest son, Ashley, was an estate agent and he had benefited enormously from city folk rushing to live in the country. He had even sold a beautiful barn conversion in a nearby village to his sister and her husband after they'd decided country living would suit them and their young daughter better than London.

Wanting desperately to believe that the man to whom she had been married for nearly forty years would never behave so heartlessly towards her, Louisa clung to the hope that a quick telephone call would have this all sorted and the estate agent who had arranged to have the board put in her garden would apologise and send somebody to remove it. But by the sickening dread that was lodged in the pit of her stomach, she knew she was deceiving herself. Hadn't Kip said that there was a strong possibility they would have to sell the house so they could both move on, that financially they would both benefit from the sale? Her divorce lawyer had said as much too.

But naïvely Louisa had imagined that he would realise how much this would hurt her, and Kip would do the decent thing by letting her keep the house into which she had poured so much of herself. Everyone knew that it was a woman who made a house a home, that it was where a mother could nurture the family. It was women who made an emotional connection to a home; for men it was often little more than bricks and mortar, an investment to be cashed in at the appropriate time. Which was what Kip was now doing. He would doubtless claim that he needed to take this step so he could build himself a secure future with the new love of his life. Never mind what he was doing to his old family.

It was the thought of how Kip must have gone behind her back to put the house on the market that brought an abrupt end to her sobbing. Couldn't he at least have kept it in the family and asked Ashley to sell it? But of course not, that would have meant Ashley would have told her straight away what Kip was up to. Instead he must have secretly met with an estate agent here to have the house assessed and photographed at a time when he knew she wouldn't be around. Like last week when she was up in Harrogate. And what story had he given the agent, who would have been rubbing their hands at the prospect of selling one of the most attractive houses in the village of Ashbury St Clare?

'Oh, my wife is fully on board with selling up, we're divorcing but it's all very amicable,' he'd probably said, adding with a shrug, 'it's a shame, but just one of those things.' Louisa knew just how charmingly engaging and persuasive Kip could be. It was why everybody loved him.

So appalled was she at the idea that he could behave so duplicitously, Louisa sat in stunned shock at the table. She should have changed the locks, just as her sister had advised. But she had said no. She hadn't wanted to appear confrontational; Charity Cottage was still Kip's as much as it was hers. Damn fool her for being so trusting and gullible!

And damn fool her for thinking that Kip would never want to part with Charity Cottage, that if nothing else, it might be the one thing that would tempt him back. Hadn't he always joked that the only way he would ever leave was when he was carried out feet first inside a coffin? She could almost wish that he'd left her by dying rather than leaving her for another woman half her age.

Twenty minutes later and having pulled herself together, Louisa had organised for a locksmith to come later that afternoon to change the locks. She would have three extra sets of keys made up to give to the children, but no more would Kip be able to let himself in whenever he chose. She pictured him putting his key in the lock and the expression on his face when he realised what she had done. The thought should have brought her malicious pleasure, but it didn't. It made her feel hollowed out that it had come to this.

With the shopping put away she rang the young woman with the irritatingly upbeat voice who was acting on her behalf to ensure that a fair divorce settlement would be agreed. It still staggered her that Kip had initiated divorce proceedings with such indecent haste. But that was him all over; once he made a decision that was it, there was no going back.

The receptionist at the law firm who answered the phone to Louisa informed her that Ms Bailey was out of the office until Monday, but she could leave a message if she wanted. Louisa declined. What she wanted was for this nightmare not to be happening.

She then telephoned the estate agent whose for sale board had made such an unwelcome appearance in the front garden. Keeping her voice as level and as composed as she could, she made it clear that she'd had no prior knowledge of her husband's definite intent to put the house on the market, it had previously only been a possibility, and she was far from happy the way things had been done. She saw no point in demanding that the sign be removed; the house was a jointly owned asset, and although it would break her heart to leave it, she suspected it was a battle she would lose if she tried to fight the sale of it.

After ending the call, she then contemplated ringing one of her children but decided against it. Ashley and Angus would both be working, and Arabella would be busy with little Heidi.

In the weeks immediately after their father had made his shocking announcement on – of all days – Boxing Day that he wanted a divorce and was moving out to be with his absurdly young girlfriend, not only did the children call her at least twice a day, they visited her as often as they could.

Understandably, they were as shocked as she was by what their father had done and each in their different ways was still coming to terms with the situation. Anger seemed to be their number one emotion, especially for her youngest son, Angus. But then he had a lot to come to terms with: his father embarking on an affair with his ex-girlfriend.

Of the three children, Angus was the more self-contained and reserved one. His position within the family had not always been easy, as from a young age he'd had to accept that he would never be able to penetrate the close bond Arabella and Ashley shared as twins. Consequently, he tended to keep his emotions to himself.

To Louisa's knowledge he hadn't yet been able to bring himself to speak to his father since Boxing Day. She couldn't blame him for that.

To keep her mind from picking away at the raw hurt of Kip's latest act of betrayal, Louisa set to with peeling potatoes to make a fish pie with the cod and smoked haddock she'd bought at the farm shop. It was a favourite dish of the family, one that she had made for many years and which they would have for lunch tomorrow.

The children – she still thought of them that way, even though they were all in their thirties – were coming to spend the day with her. She wasn't planning on going to a lot of trouble; her days of spending hours cooking complicated meals were behind her, she really couldn't be bothered. But she would dress everything up by using the best crockery, which before had only been used for special occasions. Now she used it nearly all the time.

'Mum, you can't put those in the dishwasher,' her daughter had recently chided her, 'the gold will come off!'

'I don't care,' Louisa had said, ramming the plates into the dishwasher with a wilful excess of force. 'What does it matter? It's only a bit of china.' In the past Louisa had washed the dinner service – a wedding gift – by hand, treating it as though it were as delicate as a newborn baby.

When the fish pie was made and put in the fridge, and with an hour to go until the locksmith would arrive, Louisa made herself a mug of coffee and took it through to the timber-framed orangery which they'd had added on to the sitting room ten years ago. It was a beautifully bright and airy space and had instantly become Louisa's favourite room in the house. It was now where she spent most of her time. Before Kip had left her, her workshop had been confined to the box room at the top of the house, but since January she had brought everything downstairs and turned the orangery into her workshop.

It was here that she could lose herself in creating the miniatures which she sold under the name of *It's the Little Things* either through her Etsy shop or at the various doll's house fairs around the country. That was why she'd been in Harrogate last week; she had been at the Miniaturist Fair selling her miniature watercolours as well as a selection of hand-painted 12th scale furniture. She bought the furniture in kit form and put it together before decorating each item in tiny detail. She also bought pre-loved items on eBay to repaint. The work was intricate and immensely absorbing and by abandoning reality in favour of a perfectly controlled world, albeit a 12th scale world, it had enabled her to hang on to what was left of her sanity after Kip had left her.

But was that the source of the problem: had she spent too long focusing her attention on the minutiae of life – just as she had to concentrate on the tiny details of what she created – and lost sight of the bigger picture? Was that why she hadn't noticed her husband falling out of love with her and falling in love with somebody else?

Chapter Two

'Mum, I've just been told by a work colleague that there's a for sale board at the house. What the hell's going on?'

The vehemence of his words bounced back at Ashley in the confines of his car and he immediately regretted how he'd spoken. He'd sounded like he was blaming his mother and she was the last person who should be blamed. The person he should have rung was his father, because doubtless he was the one who had instructed Barston and Bright to put Charity Cottage on the market.

'I can assure you I had nothing to do with it,' his mother said.

He heard the hurt defensiveness in her voice and wished he'd spoken with more care. 'Of course, I didn't think you had,' he said more gently. 'When did the board appear?'

'It was there when I came back from the farm shop at about midday today. Can you imagine the shock I had when I drove home and saw it?'

Ashley could. 'And Dad hadn't mentioned anything to you before?' he asked. 'He hadn't warned you?'

'No. Other than some vague stuff a while ago that the house might have to be sold. But I never thought he'd go through with it. I thought he would at least leave me with my home. And the worst of it is that he did all this behind my back. He must have met with the estate agent here while I was away last week. I don't understand him, I really don't. Do you, Ashley?'

The anguish and confused disbelief in his mother's voice filled him with an impotent rage. 'No,' he said grimly, wanting very much to punch something very hard. 'I don't understand him any more. Shall I come over and see you? I'm on my way home, but I can easily call Caro and explain.'

'That's kind of you, darling, but you'll be here tomorrow, and we can discuss it then. Go home and enjoy your evening and give little Peggy a kiss from her Grammy.'

Knowing that Caro wanted him home early so she could go to her book group this evening, Ashley took his mother at her word and said goodbye. With a small stab of guilt, he was relieved not to have to spoil his wife's plans for the evening, but equally he felt guilty that his mother was facing this latest act of family sabotage alone.

That's how it felt to Ashley, as if his father was deliberately lobbing live hand grenades at them as a family and with each one that landed and exploded, another level of trust and love was lost. Putting the house on the market the way he had was the last straw. Although who knew, maybe there was worse to come.

Before Boxing Day, and when he last saw his father, Ashley had thought him one of the finest men he knew. Fair-minded, generous, always encouraging and supportive, open-minded and never judgemental, and always fun to be around; that was the man Ashley had known and admired. Yes, Dad had displayed occasional flashes of temper and irrational obstinacy, who didn't, but that aside Ashley would have described him as the perfect father, and the perfect husband too. He was what Ashley had aspired to be in his own marriage, but now he felt that he had been duped. Everything about his father had been a sham. He simply wasn't the man Ashley had believed him to be.

His father's choice of Barston and Bright, a rival estate agent, to sell Charity Cottage was a real kick in the guts for Ashley. If his old childhood home was ever going to be sold, then it should be

Taylor Marks who took on the job, and with Ashley as an associate partner at the helm. Not that he'd thought Mum would be forced to sell. He'd trusted his dad to have his finances sufficiently in order to live comfortably enough without breaking Mum's heart any more than it already was.

Or was it Zoe who had pushed him to take this step? Was she the one pulling the strings in their relationship?

When Angus had first brought Zoe home to meet the family last spring, Mum had gone out of her way to make his girlfriend feel welcome. Mum always wanted people to feel at ease and part of the family. She hated for anyone to feel uncomfortable or unwelcome.

At the time, and this wasn't with the benefit of hindsight, Ashley and his sister, Arabella, had discussed in private that they thought Zoe wasn't warming to the fuss that Mum made of her. But then Angus shared with them that Zoe wasn't used to a close-knit family like theirs. Her father had died when she was a child and then her mother had died a few years ago. Naturally, when Mum knew this, it made her want to lavish yet more affection on Zoe.

Five months after that first visit of Zoe's to Charity Cottage, Angus pitched up on his own for a family barbecue. He made out it was no big deal that Zoe had just dumped him, easy come, easy go, he'd said, but he'd got badly drunk that night and Mum had found him lying on the grass in the garden staring up at the sky as the rain came down. Mum never went into details about the conversation that had passed between them, but it was clear that Angus must have cared for Zoe a lot more than she did for him.

Fast forward to Boxing Day and Dad's shocking announcement, and when he'd sworn blind that he and Zoe hadn't started their affair while she was still seeing Angus. He'd said it as though that made everything okay, that that was a line they wouldn't have dreamt of crossing. Everything else was just fine.

Ashley didn't think he would ever forgive his father, who in one fell swoop had fractured them as a family. He'd broken Mum's heart, tainted the love both Ashley and Arabella felt for him and crushed Angus. His selfishness ensured that they would never be the same again. Every family occasion would now be different. Every family memory distorted.

Yet somehow Dad expected them to accept the new situation and move on. The child in Ashley – the boy who had idolised his father – wanted to do that, but his anger and disappointment, and his loyalty to Mum, wouldn't allow it. His wife, Caro, took the view that sooner or later they would have to accept the situation because otherwise it would only become a lot more difficult for them.

Caro spoke from experience. Her own parents had divorced when she was a child and after they realised the harm they were causing their two daughters with their arguing and petty disputes over whose turn it was to have the children, they sought counselling. From then on, they managed to put their own feelings aside so they could concentrate on their children's happiness. With that achieved they were both happier themselves and eventually found love with new partners. All four of them had come to Ashley and Caro's wedding and had seemed perfectly at ease with each other.

Ashley couldn't imagine anything remotely like that happening with his parents. How could Mum ever feel comfortable in Zoe's presence? For that matter, why the hell should she? And why should the family go along with it as though Dad had done nothing more than trade in his old car for a new one?

Grinding his teeth – something Caro said he'd started doing in his sleep these last few months – Ashley stopped at the temporary traffic lights on Chelstead High Street. The road was being dug up yet again, the second time in twelve months, and waiting impatiently for the lights to change, he drummed his fingers on the steering wheel. He supposed he should ring his brother and sister to discuss this latest news, but he decided it could wait.

With the lights now green, he drove on and made another decision. But as so often happened when he called his father, he was diverted to voicemail.

'Full disclosure, Dad,' he began, 'I didn't believe I could think any less of you, but then you go and do this, go behind Mum's back to sell the house from under her feet. And of all the agents you could have chosen, you appoint Barston and Bright who are not known as Bastard and Shite for nothing!'

He rang off and clamping his mouth shut, he ground his teeth. He didn't stop grinding them until he arrived home. Switching the engine off, he stared up at the detached house which he and Caro had moved into four years ago. He could remember their excitement that first night in their new home, surrounded by packing boxes and eating fish and chips and drinking Moët. Despite being exhausted, they'd made love and slept the sleep of the dead until woken in the morning by bright sunshine streaming in through the bedroom window that had no curtains.

They'd loved their new home, and with its weatherboarding and mellow brickwork, and what any estate agent worth their salt would describe as being a highly desirable individual property in a sought-after village, they had poured every spare moment they had into renovating and decorating it, making it theirs. But whatever pride and delight they'd derived from the months they'd spent knocking walls down, rebuilding and painting and tiling, putting in new flooring, and installing bi-fold doors to the kitchen, it all paled into insignificance when their daughter was born. In a heartbeat, the world changed for Ashley. Nothing mattered more to him than Caro and Peggy: they were his all.

They were also his Achilles heel. Life without them would be unbearable. That was why he could relate to the pain his mother was going through. All too easily he could imagine himself in his mother's place, losing the most important person in his life, and it terrified the hell out of him. Which made him hate his father all the more. Caro said that was an emotion that would ultimately be destructive and would do him no end of harm. Perhaps to their daughter as well. 'Hating your father indefinitely is not an option,' she'd warned him.

He was just about to push open the car door when his mobile rang. Caller ID showed that it was his father. His hand on the mobile, Ashley ignored it and let it ring. He suddenly didn't want to speak to him. In mutinous silence he stared at the screen and then when Missed Call appeared followed by a Voicemail alert, he listened to the message his father had left for him.

'Ashley, I know you're angry with me, but you must understand, I simply couldn't face your mother, that's why I did what I did. I know that makes me a coward but sometimes life makes cowards of us all. I'm sorry.'

'Sorry doesn't cut it, Dad,' Ashley muttered, shoving the mobile into his coat pocket. 'Not by a long way.'

His two-and-a-half-year-old daughter wearing her much-loved unicorn onesie came running towards him when he let himself in and she threw her arms around his knees with such force he almost toppled backwards.

'*Dada, dada!*' she squealed excitedly as he lifted her up and hugged her.

'*Peggy, Peggy!*' he responded, echoing the animated joy of her greeting.

Coming out of the kitchen, and still dressed in her work clothes, black trousers with a cream blouse, her tightly tied-back hair giving her a severe, and to him a very sexy look, Caro smiled at him. 'Somebody's pleased to see you,' she said, her voice low and teasing.

'Not as pleased as I am to see you two,' he said. Still holding Peggy, he went over to kiss his wife. Not on the cheek but on the mouth, and not just a peck, but a long, lingering kiss.

'Not that I'm complaining,' she said with a raised eyebrow, 'but what's that for?'

'Does there have to be a reason?'

'With you, Ashley, there's always a reason.'

'Then how about I love you?'

'As good a reason as any. Now hold the fort while I go upstairs and change for my evening out. How was your day, by the way?' she added as she moved towards the stairs.

He thought of his mother and how traumatic it was going to be in the coming months for her to leave the house she loved so much. There was no doubt that as a family they would pull together and help her all they could, and he'd personally do everything possible to find her the best house to buy, one that she could turn into a beautiful home just as she had with Charity Cottage, but it wouldn't be easy.

'Ashley?' said Caro in a quizzical tone, her hand on the newel post. 'Everything okay?'

'It can wait,' he said lightly. 'You go and change while Peggy and I catch up on her day at nursery before I give her a bath and put her to bed.'

Caro gave him a long hard stare. They knew one another well enough for her to know that whatever he had to say, he wouldn't share it until they were alone.

'I shall hold you to that,' she said before disappearing upstairs.

Chapter Three

All his life, well, for most of it, Christopher Langford had been known as Kip.

A boy at school had for some unknown reason given him the name of Kipper, which in turn had been abbreviated to Kip. As is so often the way with these things, the name stuck and before he knew it, it was as though he had always been called Kip, and always would be. Which was more or less how he had lived his entire life, living according to how other people perceived him and what their expectations or their needs of him were.

At a young age, and after a hit-and-run accident left his father confined to a wheelchair and his mother forced to take on the mantle of breadwinner, Kip had seen how a single moment in time could change a person's life for the worse and how it could fill them with bitter disappointment. He had hated the unfairness of it, that life could treat anyone – his father in particular – so badly and it set him on a lifelong course to try to make everything better for his parents. In time it was inevitable that he would want to do the same for others, to make their lives easier too.

The loss of his dad's pride, a man who had always believed it was his job to care for his family, had been terrible to witness. His mother did her best to stay strong and optimistic, working part-time as a telephonist for a large insurance company and doing dressmaking on the side, as well as caring for Kip and his father, but he saw the light slowly go out of her. So he did all that he could to bring that light back and to make both her and his father proud of him. Helping as much as he could at home, he studied hard at school too. He had a plan, and that was to earn enough to be able to make his parents' lives better, but more importantly, to make them happy.

Having previously set his sights on university, he suddenly changed tack and, much against his teachers' advice, left school at eighteen with an impressive set of O- and A-levels and applied for a job at a travel agent's office. For his first day in his new job, he turned up in a second-hand charcoal-coloured suit his mother had found at a jumble sale and which she'd altered to fit him, along with a pair of black brogues, which were two sizes too big for his feet and required him to wear two pairs of socks. His mother said they were handmade shoes and would therefore lend him an air of polished sophistication.

It turned out that the girls in the office joked behind his back that he looked more like an undertaker than a travel agent and after he'd heard them laughing about him he jazzed up his appearance with a red tie and matching silk handkerchief – more items his mother had sourced for him. Tall, with a thick head of hair that he swept to one side of his broad forehead, he was physically assured and looked older than his years and with his naturally persuasive manner combined with a hunger to do well, he was soon out-earning his colleagues.

Within six months he was promoted and before long he was transferred to the London office where he found he could do even better. There were no more second-hand suits or worn-before shoes for him, and that was despite sending money home to his parents back in High Wycombe. The streets of London weren't necessarily paved with gold back then in the early 1980s, but the opportunities were certainly golden. People had the travel bug and the more upmarket the holiday, the better the commission for him.

He was still in his twenties and had yet to visit the exotic holiday destinations he was selling, but he had the gift of the gab and having cast himself in the role of dream-maker, he could effortlessly sell stretches of bleached-white sand and azure blue skies all wrapped up in five-star luxury. If you couldn't sell that dream, then frankly you couldn't sell anything and didn't deserve to be in the business!

Many years on and he took the plunge to set up his own company called Uniquely You Villas. By this stage he had an in-depth understanding of the travel industry along with a network of specialists who were keen to work with him. His customers had one thing in common: they wanted to avoid the popular resorts where everybody else went and were prepared to pay for something special that was off the beaten track.

It was a massive risk, given that he was married by then with two young children – Arabella and Ashley – and he was still supporting his parents, but by leaving London and moving the family to Suffolk where their money would go further, he was able to set up an office with much lower overheads than if he'd stayed in London. The first year was a struggle, but with a great team around him, both on the ground in Corfu and in the office, he kept his nerve, determined to make a success of it; he wasn't a quitter by nature.

Which was why he had found it so hard to give up on his marriage, something he never thought he would do. Louisa didn't deserve the pain he was putting her through, but if she was really honest, she would admit that they had been drifting apart for some time. A relationship never came undone overnight, it was always over a period of time, a slow and steady decline, the stitches of a relationship worked loose by a series of niggling disappointments that on their own meant nothing, but when accumulated they meant everything.

He couldn't recall when he and Louisa had last done anything together, just the two of them, something for themselves and not for the children, or the grandchildren. He didn't begrudge doing anything for his family, but as he'd tried to explain to Louisa, somewhere along the way they had lost who they were, they were just Mum and Dad now.

'But that's who we've been nearly all our lives,' she'd said. 'Why feel that's such an awful thing after so long?'

There was no pain-free way to break it to a partner that you no longer loved them, and certainly Kip could have found a gentler way to go about it, to tell his wife why he couldn't carry on as they were, but he had been heartlessly blunt and told her the truth, that he loved somebody else. He'd been as brutal as he had to make her understand that there was no way back, no way to undo the decision he had made. For the first time in years, he wanted to be completely honest with her. He owed her that much. He had believed that in being straight with her he was getting the worst over with. Now he knew better. It had been the beginning of the pain.

When that moment came to tell Louisa he was leaving her, he'd sat her down and said that he had something important to tell her. It was Boxing Day evening, and the children and grandchildren had all left that morning after spending Christmas with them and selfishly he wanted to get on with starting his new life. It had been naïve of him, but he'd imagined that by making his announcement then, he would start the New Year without his decision hanging over him. He wanted it done. He wanted everything out in the open. But most of all he wanted the strain of living a double life over.

Perhaps in response to seeing the serious expression on his face, Louisa had jumped to the conclusion that it was something to do with the business. 'Is the recovery not going as well as you'd hoped?' she'd asked, 'I know the pandemic followed by the economy taking a—'

'It's nothing to do with the business,' he'd interrupted impatiently. Then without giving her a chance to come up with anything else, he'd said, 'I want a divorce.'

At first, she'd looked at him as though she didn't understand, and maybe she didn't. Once again, he seized the initiative.

'I'm in love with somebody else and I want to spend the rest of my life with her,' he'd said. 'And I know what you're thinking, that I must be having some kind of breakdown and have lost my senses, but I assure you, I know exactly what I'm doing and while I know the months ahead are going to be difficult, I promise not to make it any more painful than it already is for you.'

The well-rehearsed words had tumbled from him while the colour had drained from Louisa's face, her lips quivering, and the knuckles of her fingers bone white as she clenched her hands into tight fists. He'd wondered if she was going to do something totally uncharacteristic and hit him. He couldn't have blamed her if she had.

'Who is it?' she'd demanded, her voice barely audible. 'Somebody from the office?'

'It's Zoe. Zoe Pearson,' he'd added superfluously.

At that her eyes had widened, and she'd let out a laugh that bordered on hysteria. 'You mean you've been having an affair with your youngest son's ex-girlfriend?'

'I want you to know that she's not the reason I no longer love you,' he'd said firmly, not answering her question, 'but she is the reason I want a divorce. We've been seeing each other since August . . . after she'd finished with Angus.'

From then on, all attempts to discuss things rationally fell apart. Louisa leapt to her feet and through tearful sobs shouted at him to go. He didn't. Stupidly he thought he would be able to calm her down, to offer comfort and assurance that it wasn't the end of the world, that they could work things out amicably.

He'd been a fool to think it would be that simple. But the

trouble was he'd prepared his script for this moment so well he'd lost sight of the fact that Louisa had no such preparation and raw shock would fuel her reaction.

When she showed no sign of calming down, her emotional state escalating at an alarming rate, he accepted that his presence was only making her even more upset. So he'd gone upstairs, thrown some clothes into a suitcase, grabbed several files of paperwork and his passport and driven the six-mile journey to where Zoe lived.

Part way through the journey he'd had to stop as his vision was too blurred with tears to drive safely. His heart was hammering painfully in his chest too and the air seemed to have been sucked out of him. Trying to catch his breath, he'd told himself he'd done absolutely the right thing, Louisa just needed time to accept that for years now they'd been in what he regarded as a state of perpetual motion, constantly moving forward to the next stage, whatever it might be. It was what couples did when they didn't want to give themselves time to think if they were still moving in the right direction together, if their shared goals were still the same.

This was the thought that was with Kip now as in the white glare of the security lights of the car park in front of his office, he placed his laptop case behind the driver's seat of his car and slid in behind the wheel. Driving out from the business park, he had to remind himself to turn left and not right as he'd done for the last twelve years, since moving the company here from the centre of Bury St Edmunds when more spacious premises at a reasonable price became available.

Turning right would take him to Louisa.

Turning left took him to Zoe.

He hadn't meant to fall in love with Zoe, and even when he'd felt the attraction, he had fought it. Some would say he hadn't fought it hard enough, that he should have respected his marriage vows and put a stop to the direction in which he was willingly moving.

But when he'd been with her, he had felt something he hadn't experienced in a long time: the excitement of scorching desire and the feeling of being truly alive. He'd been sensible enough to acknowledge these were feelings not to be relied upon, they had no substance, they were not lasting. But very soon what he felt for Zoe was so much more than physical attraction. She made him feel young again, which he knew was a cringeworthy cliché, but she did, and he was only being honest. That's how he wanted his life to be now, full of honesty. For too long he'd known he didn't love his wife but had pretended he did, for the simple reason he didn't want to hurt her or the children.

He loved his sons and daughter and living now with the rift between him and them was as painful as he'd feared it would be. Every day he told himself that they just needed time to come to terms with the situation and to understand that it wouldn't have been fair to anyone for him to pretend that he still loved Louisa. She deserved better than that, and so did he.

And being with Zoe his life was infinitely better; it was as if through loving her he had rediscovered himself. Or maybe in loving her he had discovered his true self.

In the time before Zoe, he had merely been going through the motions of being married, of it being little more than an act of diligence. He could remember the exact moment when he'd first acknowledged a sense of discontent, it had been on the day of Ashley's marriage to Caro when he'd experienced an emotion that at the time he hadn't been proud of: it was envy. He'd put it down to some kind of male ego which had broken free, making him want to feel as alive and full of love and hope as his eldest son so obviously felt as he stood in front of the altar with his beautiful bride.

Something else Kip wasn't proud of was the way he'd gone about putting Charity Cottage on the market, and Ashley had had good reason earlier in the message he'd left on his mobile to be so cross with him. He'd acted with deplorable cowardice because he genuinely couldn't face Louisa. He knew what the house meant to her, but as one of their shared assets it had to be sold. He had previously discussed it with her in the vaguest of terms, that selling it might be necessary in the not-too-distant future when sorting out the finances. It had been a mistake on his part to underplay that possibility; he'd known all along that it would happen. He should have left it to his divorce lawyer to make the case on his behalf to sell the house, that it was an asset that had to be taken into account when dividing everything up.

He didn't want to be greedy; he was a fair man and if there was another way, he would let Louisa keep the house, but times had been tough ever since the pandemic and the subsequent economic situation, just as Louisa had referred to it on Boxing Day, had also hit him badly. Before Covid had all but destroyed the travel industry he had contemplated throwing in the towel and selling up for a stress-free retirement, which was what Louisa had been keen for him to do. That was no longer an option.

When he'd phoned Rob Shaw, his divorce lawyer, to let him know what he'd done in appointing Barston and Bright to sell the house, Rob had sucked in his breath. 'Okay, I'd have preferred it if you hadn't done that. That's going to give the other side every cause to accuse you of an overly aggressive act.'

'I jointly own the house,' Kip had said defensively. 'I had every right to let myself in and show the agent around.'

'We're in a negotiating situation,' Rob had said, 'and handing over any kind of advantage to the other side is a bad move.'

It pained Kip that Louise was referred to as 'the other side' but he knew that was lawyer-speak, that it helped to maintain a distance and keep things civil and impersonal. But how could the dismantling of two profoundly bound-together lives be anything but a deeply personal process?

As much as he wanted the process to be over, to be free and

moving forwards to his goal, there were occasional moments when he missed the familiarity of his old life. He wouldn't be human if he didn't feel that, surely? He likened those odd moments to how an amputee felt when a limb had been removed, the sensation of it still being there. That was how it felt to be away from Charity Cottage and his family, he couldn't help but feel the pull of it. But equally he couldn't resist the stronger magnetic pull of Zoe and the exhilarating new life she offered him. He still couldn't believe that she felt the same for him as he did for her.

Just thinking of being with Zoe that evening, of music playing in the background while they cooked their supper together – something he'd never really done with Louisa as the kitchen had been her domain and she had often accused him of being too messy to be trusted – caused him to smile and without intending to, he pressed his foot down on the accelerator to reach Zoe that much faster.

To have this second chance at this stage in his life made him the luckiest of men. Which was a haunting echo of what he'd said when Louisa had agreed to marry him all those years ago.

'I'll marry you on one condition,' she'd said.

'Name it,' he'd said, 'and I promise to do whatever it is if you'll make me the happiest and luckiest man alive and say yes.'

'I want you to give up smoking, and no pretending,' she'd added, 'no sneaking off for a sly smoke behind my back.'

He'd been an enthusiastic smoker back then, but such was his determination to claim Louisa as his wife, a girl whose very allure was her confidence and strength of character, as well as her independent nature, he agreed only too readily. It was a promise he kept; a cigarette never passed his lips again. It was worth it to be with this fantastic girl who possessed a fun and generous warmth, but also a wall of detached self-containment, which he took as a challenge to break down.

It was only nearly forty years later that he realised that as tantalisingly close as he'd come, he had never quite managed to break down that wall and have the whole of Louisa. He knew it sounded pathetic, but he'd felt excluded, as though he wasn't worthy of the whole of her. He'd wanted so much to believe that she needed him, but he came to suspect that she didn't. Not in the way that he'd wanted to feel needed.

Chapter Four

Saturday afternoon in the kitchen at Charity Cottage, and while her sister-in-law was clearing up the dining room following lunch, Arabella was filling the dishwasher.

Some of her earliest memories were of boisterous mealtimes with her family – plates being scraped, cutlery dropped, drinks spilled, and excitable voices raised to make themselves heard. 'You're noisier than a rookery of squabbling rooks!' Mum would say, but never with any heat, her emotions were always kept to a low simmer. Dad, on the other hand, would occasionally boil over and let rip at them, but once his anger was spent, it was gone and with no bad feelings left to linger.

If only that were true now, thought Arabella as she reflected with sadness on how the lingering effects of her father's selfish actions would be with them for ever. Nothing would be as it once was.

As her husband's second wife she had first-hand knowledge of the consequences of divorce and how nothing about it was ever in isolation. Giles had married his first wife when he'd been in his mid-twenties after she discovered she was pregnant, and because they thought they loved each other, and as brief as their relationship had been, they decided to get married. There were problems from the start, so Giles said, but they stuck at it for the sake of the child. Until, that was, he met Arabella. He didn't lie when they met, he made it clear that he was married with a young daughter but was planning to divorce his wife just as soon as the moment was right.

To lessen her guilt at what she was doing, involving herself with a married man, Arabella rewrote their relationship in her head and became virtually convinced of it. When she told her parents about Giles – an international tax lawyer – she said that he had already left his wife. Well, mentally he had, she told herself in an effort to neaten the edges of her relationship with him.

At no stage did Mum and Dad show any disapproval towards Giles; far from it, they welcomed him into the family with open arms as they did with everyone, but they did ask Arabella if she was sure she wanted to take on a man who already had a child. 'He's the man I want in my life,' she told them. 'I love him.'

As determined as she was to have Giles for herself, she had to wait patiently for him to go through with his divorce. They married just as soon as they could and now they had Heidi, their beautiful two-and-a-half-year-old daughter. As Arabella often told herself, all good things come to those who wait.

Giles hadn't come with them today, he had gone instead to Ely to take his daughter out for the day, something he did as regularly as he could. Lexi was twelve now and made sporadic visits to stay with them. Her visits were invariably a challenge for Arabella, but one she was determined to meet and with as much good grace as she could muster. Not easy these days as Lexi seemed to have hit what was euphemistically called a 'difficult age'. Bloody awkward, in other words! But at least the girl seemed genuinely fond of her half-sister. In turn, Heidi adored Lexi.

Given her own experience of falling in love with what might be considered as forbidden fruit, Arabella knew that she should feel more sympathetic towards her father, but she couldn't bring herself to do that. It was obscene, not to say embarrassing, what he'd done, leaving Mum for Zoe who was even younger than Arabella!

And now he was breaking Mum's heart even more by forcing her to leave Charity Cottage. It seemed that he only cared about himself and to hell with anyone else and their feelings. Didn't he know how much this would hurt, not just Mum, but them all as a family, their childhood home being sold? Yes, it would have to be sold one day, way off in the future, but not like this in this disgusting money-grabbing manner.

With the last of the pots and pans placed in the dishwasher, Arabella set it going and stood for a moment to look out of the window at the garden. Over by the old woodshed, her brother Angus was chopping logs for the fire. She watched him swing the axe high above his head before bringing it down on the log with an easy, fluid swing. Bending, he picked up the chopped wood, tossed it into a large wicker basket and then began the process again on another log. He looked like he was in a world of his own, but what, Arabella wondered, was going through his head with each rise and fall of the axe? He was taciturn at the best of times, but lately he'd been quieter still.

Coming into her line of vision now was Ashley with the lawn-mower. Mum had never been one for 'primping' the garden in the way Dad would have liked. He'd favoured a bowling green lawn with perfect stripes and precisely cut edges, everything neat and tidy, but Mum had preferred the more naturalistic approach – 'lazy gardening', as she liked to refer to the way she allowed everything to grow wild and abundant.

Arabella's gaze moved from watching Ashley as he emptied the grass box from the mower onto the compost heap and then settled on her mother at the far end of the garden where amongst the daffodils, and in the glittery bright March sunshine, she was hunkered down to be on the same level as her two granddaughters who were standing either side of her and staring up into the flowering forsythia to where she was pointing. Arabella could tell from the body language of the two little girls that they were fascinated by what they were looking at. They loved being with their grandmother and always behaved so well for her, probably because she gave them her undivided attention, but then she had been a teacher and had a knack for making everything interesting to children.

Even today when she was still reeling from the shock yesterday of finding the for sale board in the front garden, Mum hadn't let it stop her entertaining Heidi and Peggy. To look at her playing with them, you'd think she was perfectly happy, that she didn't have a care in the world.

Around the lunch table the girls had provided a welcome diversion from the topic of conversation that had gone on before, namely was there anything that could be done to prevent Dad from forcing through the sale of Charity Cottage? Could one of them convince him to act with more compassion, and if so, which one of them should try? 'I vote Arabella should be the one to do it,' Ashley had said.

'Me?' she'd replied.

'You're the obvious choice,' he'd insisted. 'You've always been able to twist him around your little finger.'

'I hate to correct you, Ashley,' Angus had muttered caustically, 'but there's a new kid on the block doing that now, and her name's Zoe.'

It had saddened Arabella to hear her younger brother sound so sharp and bitter, but she didn't blame him. Who would when your girlfriend dumps you to start sleeping with your own father? They didn't know for sure that this was true, and Dad had denied it when accused of it, but Arabella knew that it was what Angus believed, which had to be so humiliating.

Ever since this whole sorry mess had begun, she had been overwhelmed with the need to protect Angus, something she had never felt when they were growing up. Back then she'd bossed him about or deliberately excluded him from anything she and Ashley had wanted to do on their own. Pondering on how unnecessarily cruel children could be, she watched Heidi and Peggy run over to the Wendy house which Mum had built for the girls last autumn. Dad had promised to do it but had never got around to it. Too busy falling in love with Zoe, no doubt!

At the sight of the girls pushing open the door of the Wendy house and going inside – Mum having painted the interior as an *homage* to Beatrix Potter – Arabella hoped that as cousins they would always be friends and never behave meanly towards each other. Or to any future siblings who might come along.

Arabella was very keen to have another child, but Giles was resistant, he said he was perfectly happy as they were. 'Aren't you happy as we are?' he'd asked her. 'You, me, Heidi and Lexi?' She'd told him she was, but it was a lie; her mind, body and soul were crying out for another child.

Another movement in the garden caught her eye: it was Caro shaking out the tablecloth from the dining room which the girls had managed to cover with squashed peas and carrots and daubs of fish pie as well as smears of strawberry ice cream.

Arabella doubted that her coolly efficient sister-in-law would have a second child. Following Peggy's birth, a few months after Heidi was born, and as soon as her maternity leave was over, Caro had returned to work in the HR department of a large health care provider in Stowmarket. Arabella had no plans to return to work in the immediate future, not when she hoped to have another baby, but she had the distinct feeling that Caro disapproved of her being a stay-at-home mother, as though she wasn't quite pulling her weight.

When she and Giles had made the decision to leave London and move to Suffolk, Heidi had been a year old, and the move had made perfect sense for them as a family. With Giles's law firm still supporting hybrid working, he was all for the move as, much against his wishes, his ex-wife had recently moved from Watford to Ely to be near her sister. Being just a short drive away from her parents and her twin brother was a big plus for Arabella too.

Coming in through the door that led to the utility room, Caro interrupted Arabella's meandering thoughts. 'I've put the tablecloth in the washing machine,' she said. 'It beats me why Louisa bothers with one when the children visit, they always make such a mess.'

Privately Arabella agreed that tablecloths and small children were not an ideal mix, but she couldn't help but defend her mother. 'I know what you mean,' she said, 'but it's a distraction for Mum, you know, making everything nice for us.'

'Are you going to wash those?' Caro asked, inclining her head towards the wineglasses that were partially hidden by a large pottery jug of tulips. 'If so, I'll dry.'

That was another thing about her sister-in-law that irritated Arabella, the way Caro could so easily undermine her and make her feel as though she didn't know what she was doing. She wanted to say that of course she was going to wash the glasses, she wasn't some kind of slacker that left a job half done, but holding her tongue, she ran the hot tap and filled the sink while to the left of her Caro selected a tea towel from the three hanging on the rail of the Aga.

'So how do you think she is?'

'Who, Mum?' asked Arabella.

'Who else?'

'Hard to say really, she hides her emotions so well. Almost four months on from Dad leaving her and destroying us as a family, I think she was just beginning to get over the shock, but after yesterday and finding that for sale board in the garden, it's doubtless set her back.'

'You don't think that's a bit over the top, saying Kip's destroyed the family?'

'But it is what he's done. His selfishness has consequences for us all, we're all affected.'

31

'Only if you make it that way.'

Arabella counted to five as she rinsed a wineglass under the tap. Very carefully, she said, 'I doubt Ashley sees it like that.'

'You're right, he doesn't, and really he should. Taking sides isn't going to help anyone.'

'I think that as reasonable as you believe that to be, now isn't the time to be so objective.'

'I disagree. If you shield Louisa by constantly cosseting her with a pity-party, it will only weaken her. It will make her dependent on you all instead of her learning to stand on her own two feet. But that's just my opinion. Take it or leave it.'

I'll bloody well leave it, thank you very much! thought Arabella. 'We're doing what feels right for Mum,' she said firmly.

'Or what feels right for yourselves?'

Unnerved as she so often was in Caro's company, Arabella forced a light-hearted laugh. 'Goodness, it must be marvellous to be you and have all the answers.'

Caro gave a short laugh too. 'I assure you I don't, but I'm not afraid to ask difficult questions. I would say though, and I've thought this all along, that it would be a mistake to sugar-coat the situation too much for your mother. The reality is that she has to start looking to the future and deciding what she wants for herself. Who knows, leaving here might be for the best, a chance for her to put her creative resourcefulness to good use in making a new home for herself.'

How easy Caro made it sound. 'Probably what Mum wants,' Arabella said, rinsing another glass under the hot tap, 'is for Dad to realise he's made a terrible mistake and come back so that life can return to normal.'

'I think that's highly unlikely ever to happen. She and the rest of you would all treat him differently and he'd know it. He'd be constantly on edge. He'd feel totally diminished.'

But it would be better than this, Arabella thought miserably. She missed her father. She missed his reassuring presence and the familiarity of her parents being here together, of everything being just as it was. Just how it should be.

'I hope you don't mind me saying this,' said Caro, picking up a glass from the draining board to dry, 'but I'd have thought you of all people would understand.'

Confused, Arabella looked at her sister-in-law. 'What do you mean?'

'Well, Giles left his wife to be with you, didn't he?'

'It wasn't the same at all. His marriage was already over when we met.'

'Oh, but Ashley told me—' Caro's words ground to a rapid stop and she glanced away as if regretting what she'd been about to say.

A bolt of alarm ran through Arabella. Her twin brother was the only person who knew the truth of her relationship with Giles, but surely he wouldn't have broken his promise and told Caro? 'What's Ashley told you?' she demanded.

'Don't look so worried, it really doesn't matter that he confided in me. I know that it's not something you want to be made known and I wouldn't dream of telling anyone. But you know, if we could predict exactly when and with whom we fall in love, life would be a lot more straightforward, wouldn't it?'

Chapter Five

Back at his flat in Borehamwood that Saturday evening, Angus kicked off his shoes and, without switching on the lights, he helped himself to a beer from the fridge and went and stood at the glass doors that led onto the small balcony with its less than enthralling view of the car park. It was almost dark now and the lights of the town in the distance glinted with what he thought was false cheer. He'd bought the flat in the New Year, seeing its blank walls and laminated wood floors as giving him a fresh start. His old flat contained too many memories of Zoe.

The location suited him perfectly. It was a twenty-five-minute journey by train to St Pancras and his office and was well placed for the M25. His work as a technology consultant took him all over the country and really the flat was no more than a base. A base he had yet to make a proper home, the blank walls were still blank, and he hadn't yet found the time to buy any rugs.

For the last six months he'd been alternating between working from home and the office in London and travelling up to Sheffield to oversee the installation of a new software system for a massive distribution hub. The project had hit snag after snag but had finally concluded yesterday and he'd driven back late last night glad it was behind him. After Easter he'd be assigned to what he hoped would be a more straightforward engagement, that of updating a software system for a relatively small company on the outskirts of

Cambridge that made 3D printers. Usually when he was away, he stayed in a hotel, invariably as featureless as his flat, but working in Cambridge would mean that he would be able to drive over to Suffolk to see his mother more often.

Swallowing a mouthful of satisfyingly cold beer, he contemplated the day spent with his family.

His family *minus* Dad.

That's how it would always be now.

The empty chair.

The missing person.

And no matter how often he told himself he wasn't to blame, he couldn't shake off the guilt that this was down to him: he was the one who had brought Zoe into their midst. If he'd never met her, Mum and Dad would still be together.

He was by nature intrinsically rational and clear-headed, which was why he did the job he did, he could analyse the strengths and weaknesses of a company and through meticulous attention to detail, find ways to improve and turn things around. But his brain could not compute what had possessed his father to leave Mum for Zoe. Nothing about it made sense.

What repulsed him most and made him feel physically sick if he dwelt on it too much was the thought that Zoe had alternated between sleeping with him and his father. The pair of them had denied that had ever happened, and with what to his mind was an unconvincing act of shocked outrage. But then they would deny it, wouldn't they? Who could ever admit to something so messed up?

That denial had taken place the last time he had spoken to his father and since then he'd ignored any subsequent attempt at contact from him. Zoe had messaged Angus too, but he'd blocked her. There was nothing she could say that he wanted to hear. Yet whatever angry humiliation Angus felt, it had to be a fraction of what his mother was going through.

Last summer he had believed himself to be falling in love with

Zoe, he'd even begun to imagine a future with her. He'd enjoyed her *laissez-faire* attitude to life and the fact that she valued her own space as much as he did his. They seemed very much in tune with each other. Apart from how she viewed his family.

With both of her parents now dead and having no brothers and sisters of her own, Zoe's background was very different to his. After the first time he'd taken her home to Charity Cottage, which had coincided with a gathering of the hordes, she had asked him if he didn't feel swamped by his family. 'Don't take this the wrong way,' she'd said, 'but don't you feel swallowed up by them all, as though they take away part of who you are when you're all together?'

He'd laughed. 'I've always been something of a third wheel being the younger brother to twins, but no, we're all individuals in our own right, it's not like we're joined at the hip. But we do stick together, that's how we've always been.'

On successive visits home with Zoe, he'd tried to observe his family through objective eyes, to see if she had a point, but all he saw was what he'd always seen, everyone laughing and joking and having a great time. Maybe Mum had overdone the fuss factor with Zoe in welcoming her into the family, but that was just how she was. But he could understand that to someone who didn't have a family, meeting his *en masse* might be a bit overwhelming and take some getting used to.

As his feelings steadily grew for Zoe, he had the uneasy suspicion that exponentially she was withdrawing from their relationship. Then in the first week of August, not long after his thirty-third birthday and after ten months as a couple, she dumped him. No reason given. No explanation. Only some half-baked apology that had bordered on the meaningless 'it's not you, it's me' cliché.

The beer bottle now empty and darkness complete, he drew the curtains and crossed the open-plan space to the kitchen area. He switched on the under lights, rinsed out the bottle and put it into the recycling bin, then he set about making himself some cheese on toast.

He ate his supper with his laptop in front of him and brought his expenses spreadsheet up to date. He was part way through it when he became aware of a faraway beeping. He'd been so absorbed in what he was doing he didn't know if the noise had been going for some time, or if it had only just started. He was about to go and look out of the window to see if it was a car alarm going off when the doorbell buzzed.

It was a few minutes after ten, so not exactly the typical time for a social call. He went to see who it was and found an attractive girl smiling back at him. She was wearing a pair of those Ugg boots his sister liked to wear with black leggings and a baggy sweatshirt with Hokusai's *Great Wave* on the front.

'Hey, I'm sorry to bother you,' she said, 'but I don't suppose you have any double A batteries do you, only the smoke alarm in my flat is going off.' She gave a short laugh. 'And not because the place is on fire,' she added. 'In case you're wondering.'

'That's good to know,' he said with an amused smile. 'I'll go and see what I have. How many do you need?'

'Just two, please.'

He went back to the kitchen and pulled out the drawer where he kept a selection of basic DIY tools, along with a roll of parcel tape, a ball of string and an assortment of batteries.

'Here you go,' he said when he returned to the girl who had remained where she was on the threshold of his flat. 'Do you want me to come and put them in for you?'

'No, no, I can manage, thank you.'

'I didn't mean to imply that you couldn't,' he said, suddenly mindful of the myriad ways it was possible to cause offence. He'd had to do a questionnaire at work for HR recently which had been designed to flush out any unconscious bias and unintentional prejudice. He hadn't exactly passed with flying colours, but then no one had, it later transpired.

'I know you didn't,' she said cheerfully, 'you were just being thoughtful. By the way, I'm the neighbour who moved into the flat below you earlier in the week. I hope my playing hasn't annoyed you too much. Or the sound of the smoke alarm tonight.'

Angus hadn't known that the flat below him on the ground floor had even changed hands. 'I've been away,' he said. 'What do you play?' he asked, curious.

'The tuba and the drums.'

Nothing could have surprised him more. 'Really?'

'I'm joking!' she said with a laugh. 'I play the cello and it's usually the first thing I like to do when I get home from work. And now you're probably thinking I'm going to be one of those nightmare neighbours keeping you awake all hours. Anyway, sorry to have interrupted you. But thanks for these,' she said, brandishing the batteries he'd given her. 'You're a life-saver.' Then with a quick flash of a smile, she turned, and with a swiftness that made her ponytail flick round to catch her in the face, she made for the stairs.

He closed the door with the sensation that his new neighbour had appeared with all the force of that famous wave emblazoned on her sweatshirt.

Back in the kitchen and seeing the open drawer where he'd found the batteries, he thought of his father. The reason for that was because when Angus and his brother and sister had been children, Dad had called them his Triple As. Mum had chosen the names Arabella and Ashley and then Dad, to complete the set as he liked to joke, picked Angus for their third and last child.

With an abrupt burst of anger, Angus slammed the drawer shut, not wanting to think of his father.

He opened another bottle of beer and, finishing off the last of his cheese on toast, he noticed that the smoke alarm had gone quiet in the flat below him.

Chapter Six

Sunday morning and while Kip went to fetch a thick wodge of old-fashioned newspaper print for the day, something she had yet to wean him off in favour of reading the paper online, Zoe Pearson lay in bed listening to the nearby church bells ringing.

She was not what you'd call an early-morning person. Unlike Kip who was always awake at some unearthly hour, even at the weekend and, when he deemed it safe to do so, he would wake her with her first cup of coffee of the day. He made it using the machine he'd bought a few days after he'd moved in and it was a far superior model to the cheap one she'd had. She had to admit it made a better cup of coffee too. She had teased him about the extra space the device took up in her small kitchen which had made him anxious that he had transgressed by assuming she wouldn't object to him moving things around in her kitchen to accommodate it. It was an example of them both finding their feet, of establishing the ground rules for their living together.

During their affair Kip had never kept more than a toothbrush here but now the modest cottage she had inherited three years ago after her mother died from breast cancer was home to a lot more of his things.

'I'm sorry to clutter up your lovely cottage,' Kip had said when she'd helped him unload his belongings from his car.

'I don't mind,' she'd assured him, 'honestly.'

She did a lot of that, reassuring this exceptional man who had stolen her heart that all that mattered was their love for each other. So what if the place wasn't as tidy as they'd both like, it was nothing compared to the chaos Kip had brought on himself to be with her.

She hadn't asked him to leave his wife, she would never have done that. She'd told him that she'd been happy to keep things as they were because the snatches of time they spent together meant the world to her. When he was with her, she didn't feel as if she was competing for his attention, he was there because he wanted to be with her, to give her his all.

She refused to feel guilty about their relationship because if Kip had been happy in his marriage, he would not have looked twice at her. If her lack of guilt made her a bad person in the eyes of other people, then so be it. If she had learnt anything from her mother's painfully slow death and all the lives lost to Covid, it was that you owed it to yourself to make the most of the life you had, as who knew when it might end?

On Boxing Day, and quite unexpectedly, Kip had showed up on her doorstep with an overnight bag and looking like he'd been battered by a storm. 'I've left my wife,' he'd said, before she'd even shut the front door behind him.

Neither of them had slept much that night. They'd talked and talked and made love and then talked some more.

'I know I should have warned you what I was going to do, but I was afraid you'd talk me out of it. You are happy I'm here with you, aren't you?' he'd asked in the darkness when they'd finally switched off the light.

'Oh yes, happier than I ever thought I'd be.'

'And the age thing, you don't think you'll—'

'What age thing?' she'd cut in, silencing him with a kiss. 'I've told you before, there's no age barrier if you're comfortable with a person. So if you don't mind, not another word.'

Mentally and physically exhausted, they'd fallen asleep wrapped in each other's arms.

In the morning and while eating breakfast in bed, conscious of the enormity of what Kip had done and what it meant for them both, she had told him to be honest with her. 'Have you woken up with any regret because if you have, you must say. You must be truthful with me.'

'I'm exactly where I want to be,' he'd said, 'and that's with you.'

In the days and weeks that followed, and as relieved as Kip said he was to have told his wife the truth, Zoe knew that he was in pain. He'd tipped his life upside down for her, and she couldn't have loved him more for the enormous sacrifice he'd made. Nobody had ever declared themselves so utterly and wholeheartedly in love with her. But then she had never really gone looking for that kind of commitment or affirmation.

She was thirty-four and from as young as she could remember, she had wanted to be independent and not have anyone making demands of her. She very much believed in creating her own happiness, and not being dependent on anybody else to make her happy. That's why she had been content with what she'd had with Kip when they'd been seeing each other in secret, she hadn't expected more from him. Sometimes they had discussed what it might be like to be together more often and without the worry of anybody seeing him with her, but to Zoe it had been purely hypothetical, like discussing what you might do if you won the lottery.

Of course, she hadn't planned to have an affair with a married man, never mind the sixty-four-year-old father of an ex-boyfriend, but often the best things in life are never planned. Yet as happily in love as she was, Zoe wasn't deluding herself when it came to the landslide of emotions Kip's family would be going through. But wasn't it better that Kip and his family lived more honestly with one another? Did his children want him to stay married and be miserable, just to keep the status quo that suited them? Wasn't that a far worse act of selfishness than what she and Kip had set in motion?

She fully acknowledged that they had acted selfishly and if blame had to be apportioned, she would accept that she had acted out of selfish desire for him. Wasn't that what everyone did when they fell in love, they thought only of themselves and the person they loved and wanted?

What she'd felt for Angus, as kind and thoughtful as he'd been, it hadn't compared to the seismic sexual attraction she had experienced with Kip. It had consumed her and left her reeling that this man could have such an effect on her. When all was said and done, Kip was just a man – a man with a head, two arms and two legs, just like any other man. But to her the sum of his parts was so much more.

The first time she'd met him at Charity Cottage when Angus had taken her to meet his family, he had been a typically genial host with a pleasing ease about him, and an eagerness to make those around him comfortable. With his wide smile and thick, grey-streaked hair and well-clipped beard, he was undoubtedly an attractive man and reminded her a little of Pierce Brosnan. An old wedding photograph of him with Louisa had revealed him to have been exceptionally good-looking in his younger days. Quite the catch.

Her observations at that point had been entirely objective, especially so as there had been a lot to take in that day, mostly knowing that she was under the spotlight and being scrutinised by Angus's family. There was also the noise and chaos of two toddlers running about the place and the continuous sense of momentum, of no one sitting or standing still or wanting just to be quiet in their own skin. After a rowdy lunch when everyone seemed to be talking at once, they'd gone for a walk – a spare pair of boots had been found for her – and strolling through the village they had encountered various neighbours who all wanted to stop and chat and admire the grandchildren as well as be introduced to Angus's new girlfriend. It had been like something out of a rom-com film and had the village been covered with a blanket of sparkling artificial snow the image would have been complete.

When it had been time to leave and she and Angus had been waved off and feeling assaulted by the noise and energy of Angus's family, Zoe had closed her eyes in silent relief.

Since the age of six, when her father had died, it had just been Zoe and her mother. Mum had been a librarian and when she took early retirement (Zoe was living in London by then), she moved from Colchester to a small village in Suffolk with two pubs and a community shop. In the circumstances, Zoe and her mother should have been closer, but they were as stubborn and as headstrong as each other and frequently butted up against one another, whether it was the clothes Zoe wore, or the friends she hung out with and the lack of application she put towards her studies and her future. She didn't exactly go off the rails, but there was a time at uni when she could have worked harder and partied less.

Subsequent visits to Charity Cottage with Angus were not that different to the first. There weren't as many questions thrown at her, but it was always a family gathering of some sort which in turn meant noise and mayhem. Louisa tried so hard to make Zoe feel a part of the family, but with each nudge of kindness, Zoe felt herself pulling away. She simply wasn't used to that intensity of consideration. She felt suffocated by it.

And then in early July, six months after they'd started seeing each other, Angus added to that sensation of being smothered when she realised he was falling in love with her. It was like a light switch being flicked off; suddenly she no longer wanted to be with him, not if he was thinking they had a long-term future together.

That was when she decided to do what she'd been thinking about for some time; she would leave London and her job and move to Suffolk. She already had the cottage her mother had left her, all she had to do was find a new job. Which she did in surprisingly quick time and all without a word to Angus. When everything was finalised, she broke it to him that it was over between them. She blamed herself, that she wasn't as committed to the relationship as he was. She even tried saying that she suspected she was incapable of truly connecting with anyone and so it would be better that he found somebody more deserving of his love than she was.

She believed that was an end to it, that her brush with the Langfords was behind her. But she couldn't have been more wrong.

A week later she started her new job at the Vista Recruitment Agency on the outskirts of Bury St Edmunds. The company was situated in an out-of-town business park and on her first morning, just as she was locking her car, her gaze fell on a well-dressed man just getting out of a white Mercedes. He was wearing ivory-coloured chinos with an open-necked pale-blue shirt and there was something familiar about him, but she couldn't think what.

But as he locked his car and turned towards her she recognised who it was: it was Angus's father. There was no avoiding each other and in a stilted exchange, he expressed surprise at seeing her. She explained about her leaving London and her new job with the recruitment agency and in return he pointed to a double-fronted office unit and said that's where his company, Uniquely You Villas, was situated. Then without missing a beat he'd expressed how sorry he'd been to hear that she and Angus had split up.

Then for a long awkward moment they just stared at each other, as if waiting for the other to say something more. But not knowing what more there was to say, she'd said goodbye and got on with her day.

From her desk she had a clear view across the courtyard to Kip's office and thinking of their brief chat earlier she wondered what, beneath that polite and affable manner of his, he really thought of her. Did he hate her for upsetting his youngest son? She supposed so.

And what were the chances that she should end up working on the same business park as him? It had never crossed her mind, not for a single second, that his office could be here. But would she have looked for a job somewhere else if she had known he would be here? No, she wouldn't have. She had done nothing wrong. She had simply parted ways with a boyfriend, as she had done several times before Angus; she had done nothing to be ashamed of.

Later that morning, Phoebe, who had been assigned to help her settle in, suggested they went to the on-site café to fetch coffee for the small team which Zoe was now a part of. And who should she find herself standing behind in the queue, but Kip. He acknowledged her with a nod but didn't say anything. The fact that he was queueing for his own coffee and that he hadn't sent some minion to fetch it raised him a notch in her estimation.

He was there again at lunchtime when she joined the queue on her own and was once more standing directly behind him. She gave him a nervous smile. 'Well, this isn't awkward at all, is it?' she said.

'I guess we're going to have to find a way not to feel awkward,' he replied.

'Would it help to clear the air?' she asked. 'You know, you say whatever you feel you need to say in defence of your son. I'd quite understand.'

He frowned. 'I don't think Angus would thank me for doing that, he's always been more than capable of fighting his own battles. And speaking impartially,' he went on after the briefest of pauses, 'some relationships work out and some don't, some simply run their course. It's just the way it goes.'

She had been prepared for disapproval and reproach, or at best, a coolness, but Zoe detected none of that in his manner towards her. Which came as a relief, given that from now on they would probably be bumping into each other on a daily basis.

They were at the front of the queue now and standing side by side, they selected what they wanted to eat from the two women who ran the café, paid for their drinks and sandwiches and then when Zoe turned to look for a table, she realised there was only the one left, over in the far corner by the window.

Kip made the same realisation in the exact same moment. 'You have the table,' he said. 'I'll take my lunch back to my office.'

'We can share if you like,' she said.

He hesitated. She couldn't say why exactly, but she didn't want him to say no. But odds on, he would, if only out of politeness, or if he had the strong need to get away from her as fast as he could.

But he didn't say no. 'Okay,' he said, 'if you're sure you don't mind sharing.'

Initially the conversation revolved around the quality of their bacon and avocado sandwiches and how fortunate they were to have the on-site café as the nearest other place to eat was a ten-minute car drive away. Before long though, they were chatting more easily, and Zoe found herself enjoying his company. He was clearly well known at the business park as every now and then someone would spot him and ask how he was or enquire how business was going. It was the usual kind of playful office-life banter. But when Kip spoke directly to Zoe, she noticed he was more measured and totally focused on listening to what she had to say, especially when she explained about her decision to leave London and move permanently to Suffolk.

'I sometimes think how nice it would be to up sticks from Charity Cottage and live somewhere new,' he said. The admission surprised her, he'd appeared so settled and perfectly at one amongst his family in that beautiful rambling old house.

As the days went by, they had a few more lunchtime chats like that, pondering on life's what-ifs and maybes, and then something changed between them, and she noticed how much they laughed when they met up in the café. He made her laugh so much one day over some silly story about a goat found relaxing on a sun lounger at one of the holiday properties Uniquely You Villas managed on Corfu that she snorted into her cappuccino and blew a blob of frothy milk across the table. He'd laughed nearly as much as she had at that and then went on to say the worst of it was, the following day the goat returned with the rest of the herd, bringing with it a barrel of Metaxa brandy.

'I don't believe a word of it,' she'd said, wiping her mouth with a paper napkin.

'Okay, maybe the last bit was an embellishment too far,' he'd admitted with a grin. It was a grin that from nowhere did something totally unexpected to her; it made her stomach flip and her breath catch in her throat. That evening when she was at home, she told herself that she had imagined it, but she knew she hadn't. She then told herself that whatever it was she'd felt, it was totally inappropriate. But she didn't care if it was or not, she knew what she'd felt, and she wanted to experience it again.

Which was why, when she saw him a few weeks later in the car park just as she was about to drive home and he asked if she would like to go for a drink, she agreed all too readily. She didn't need to question his motives, or hers, because there was now no denying what was going on between them.

There was also no denying how attractive she found Kip and the sexual thrill she experienced whenever she thought of him. Which was a lot. She thought of his eyes and how they seemed to look deep into her soul when he looked at her. She thought of his hands and how they might feel on her skin. She thought about that smiling mouth of his and how much she had begun to fantasise about placing her lips against his. She tried berating herself for acting like a silly teenage girl experiencing her first crush, but the feelings wouldn't go away. After analysing what it was that she felt about him, she decided the appeal lay in the abundance of self-assurance he possessed.

The following week after that first drink together she invited him to her cottage. They didn't make love that evening, that happened the next time he visited, and it was like nothing she had previously experienced. It was more than a physical coming together, so much more. It was, she realised, just what she had been waiting for all her adult life, that moment when she made a genuine connection with someone.

From downstairs she heard the front door opening and shutting and back from the shop with his Sunday newspaper, Kip called up to her in that humorous way he did, 'Honey, I'm home!'

She smiled happily and wondered if life could ever be better than this.

Chapter Seven

'It's as though I no longer have any say over my life and I just have to go along with the decisions that are being made for me.'

'It only seems like that because you're allowing yourself to feel as though you have no part to play. Kip has decided how he wants to live his life and now you must do the same.'

'But I was happy with my life!' Louisa shouted back at her sister's implacable, not to say thoroughly exasperating manner and her insinuation that all Louisa needed to do was pull herself together. 'Why should I have to change because Kip has?' she demanded. 'Almost every day some new change or mandate is forced upon me and without anyone asking if that's what I would like. I've become an irrelevance. No, worse than that, a nuisance, I'm nothing but a nuisance that has to be got rid of!'

'Again,' said her sister, 'you're allowing yourself to feel that way.'

'But it *is* how I feel! How could I feel any different?'

'That's what I'm trying to explain to you; as hard as it is, you have to rise to the challenge. You need to accept that Kip no longer wants to be married to you and as a result you are facing a new future. So, what's it to be, a helpless Louisa who wants everyone to feel sorry for her, or a courageous Louisa who is going to take control of her life and view this as an opportunity?'

Gripping the mobile in her hand, Louisa pursed her lips. She was thankful that Stephanie was not in the same room as otherwise she might have been tempted to throw the device at her. 'Could you sound any more dismissive of what I'm going through?'

'I've given you months of full-on sympathetic support, now it's time to move on to the next stage of support, which is a lot more robust. You need to accept where you are and toughen up.'

'Is this coming from a bargain-priced self-help book you happened upon in a charity shop by any chance?' Louisa snapped sarcastically at her sister. She was sick of being told what she must and must not do and of the incessant advice people were determined to give her, most of it well-intentioned, but it was so wearing to be on the receiving end of it.

It was exhausting too having the roles reversed with her children. When they were with her on Saturday, they were tripping over themselves to help, and to assure her that they'd be right there at her side with whatever guidance and advice she needed in selling the house. As their mother her life had been dominated by caring for and shielding the family, but now the rules had changed, and she was the target of their care and protection. They treated her as if she might break if they raised their voices or said the wrong thing. There was little jollity to their visits, no irreverent jokes or lively chatter, they were now behaving like anxious grown-ups, perhaps aware for the first time just how easily lives could be dramatically altered.

Being in the garden with her granddaughters had been a welcome respite from the strain of her children's excess of care. Peggy and Heidi treated her in exactly the way they always had, they wanted one hundred per cent of her attention, and it had been a joy to give them that. It gave her time and space to forget how angry she was.

The house had felt very quiet after the family had gone, but at the same time it had been a relief to sink into a chair and close her eyes and hear nothing but the rhythmic tick of the grandfather clock in the hall. Having recalibrated herself she had then made herself a drink and got to work on a miniature portrait she had been commissioned to paint. While she had concentrated on applying delicate brushstrokes of paint to faithfully reproduce the client's pet dog, it had given her breathing space from thinking about Kip and the future.

First thing on Monday morning she had spoken with the divorce lawyer acting on her behalf about the situation with the house, hoping that the woman who was supposed to be 'on her side' would be thoroughly appalled at Kip's under-handedness and would take immediate steps to put a stop to it going any further.

But Megan Bailey had merely tutted and then in her maddeningly upbeat and efficient voice had said, 'Sadly, we knew this would be an inevitable consequence, and while I disapprove of the way things have been done, I'm afraid it doesn't change anything; the house does have to be sold as, unless you have a secret stash of funds you haven't told me about, you can't buy out your husband's share of the property.'

Deflated by the exchange, Louisa had swallowed back her disappointment and rung off, only then for the telephone to ring. It was a woman from Barston and Bright calling to say she had good news – she had four couples all champing at the bit to view Charity Cottage. This was the first form of direct contact Louisa had received from the agent and furious at the flippant insensitivity of the woman's manner, and in the politest voice she could muster, Louisa had said that viewings would be impossible for that week. She gave no reason and didn't give the agent the chance to pursue the conversation any further. It was a small moment of power and heaven only knew she could do with more of such moments.

That was four days ago and predictably Kip had tried contacting her, wanting to know why she wasn't allowing anyone to view the house. In response to the messages he'd left on the answerphone and her voicemail, she had replied with a curt text saying that it wasn't convenient.

'Why isn't it?' he'd replied within seconds, as though he'd been waiting for her text and had pounced on it.

She hadn't answered his question. Let him stew, she'd thought.

'This is basic advice I'm giving you,' her sister said, bringing her back to the present, 'and I wouldn't be saying any of it to you if it weren't true. You'll only start feeling you have control over the situation when you roll up your sleeves and try calling some of the shots yourself. You need to be proactive, not reactive.'

Louisa was tempted to tell her sister that she had been proactive by not allowing anyone to view the house that week, but she suspected that Stephanie would see through it, that she would accuse Louisa of merely putting something off, of sticking her fingers in her ears and singing la-la-la to herself. And maybe she was.

'Why don't you give yourself a break and come and stay with us?' Stephanie then asked.

Normally Louisa enjoyed spending time in Norfolk with her sister and her husband and going for long walks along the beach at Hunstanton, but the thought now of being away from Charity Cottage horrified her, as if it might not still be here when she returned. 'I can't,' she said.

'Can't or won't?'

'I'm busy with my work,' Louisa replied.

'How about a long weekend?' Stephanie negotiated. 'Surely you can give yourself a few days off. It would do you good to get away and maybe it would help to give you a fresh perspective.'

'I went up to Harrogate and look what happened in my absence. No, I'm better staying put, and besides, if people are going to start viewing the house, I want to be here to make sure they're not prying where they shouldn't.'

'Have you actually given any thought to where you might like to live? Have you looked at any properties online? Imagining yourself somewhere new might be the first step in helping you to move on.'

Louisa's daughter-in-law had said much the same thing last Saturday. Never slow in offering her opinion, Caro had perhaps been the only one brave enough to say the words aloud. The others were probably thinking it but were biding their time before saying anything. But then as Arabella had remarked, they were still coming to terms with losing their childhood home. Ashley had then said that if it would help, he'd start looking for her. 'Might it be less painful for you if I do, Mum?' he'd asked gently. 'I'd be happy to do that for you.'

The coward in her had wanted to say there was no hurry, but she knew that the wheels were already turning. She also knew that this was something she had to do herself.

When she'd ended the call with her sister, she pulled on her fleece, grabbed her keys, and set off for a brisk walk. An angry stomp, more like. She needed to vent, to work off some of the carefully managed fury that had been building during her conversation with her sister.

What was so galling was that every word of advice from Stephanie was not just well-meant but was spot on. Just as she'd been proved right about changing the locks. If Louisa had done that, Kip wouldn't have been able to ride roughshod over her. She'd been a fool.

The question was, for how long had she been a fool? Had there been a series of red flags which she'd missed because she hadn't been paying sufficient attention? Even if she had, would she have realised the extent of Kip's unhappiness? But what could she have done? Paid him more attention? Initiated sex more often? And why did women always blame themselves, especially when it came to sex? If he'd been bored or wanted more excitement, or for their lives to go in a new direction, why hadn't he ever said?

The only conclusion she could draw from that was that he'd been bored specifically with her and she could have done everything she could to please him, but it still wouldn't have helped.

He'd said that they'd become lost being just 'Mum and Dad' and 'Grammy and Grando' but she didn't really understand what he meant by that. Who did he want to be? Was that the big difference between them – she had been happy with being who she was, and she certainly hadn't ever been bored, she hadn't had time for that. She wouldn't have thought Kip had had the luxury of time to be bored either.

Or had it been the thought of retirement that had scared him? Had he worried that he couldn't see who he would be once his working life was behind him? Was an affair simply his way of proving that he was still in the prime of his life with plenty to offer?

She had never been one of those women who'd analysed who or what she was; she'd always been too busy for that. From the moment the twins were born her every minute was spoken for. It was an exhausting and chaotic period, non-stop feeding, snatching what sleep she could and keeping the house relatively tidy and the washing machine and tumble drier constantly filled and emptied. To be fair, Kip had pitched in when he could, but he'd had his hands full with setting up the new company. And then Angus had arrived and, while he was a beautifully compliant and placid baby, three children under the age of four was still a monumental challenge.

It was a challenge she'd enjoyed though. She'd taken immense pride in the fact that she'd kept all the plates spinning and could even juggle a few balls at the same time. Her friends marvelled at everything she did, especially when she organised a group for stressed-out mothers of twins as well as helping with the toddler group in the village. When the twins started at the village school, she became involved there too, going in to help with the infants and their reading and when all three children were at school, she accepted an offer to work part-time there. She'd put her teaching career on hold to have the children but now it was time to pick up where she'd left off.

That was when Stephanie, who prided herself on never dusting or ironing her children's clothes, her husband's too if she could get away with it, warned her to be careful with all that she took on. 'Nobody likes a martyr, Louisa, or a show-off.'

Stung by her sister's remark, Louisa had gone on the defensive. 'I'm neither of those two things,' she'd remonstrated. 'Do I ever complain about anything? And why should it be a problem that I like to do everything to the best of my ability?'

'Now don't get on your high horse,' Stephanie had said. 'It's just that by being so perfect, you undermine the rest of us. And martyrs never complain, that's the definition of a martyr.'

While it was true that her sister's observation had given her cause to think, it didn't change her, not really. She tried to adopt a more relaxed attitude, to let the housework go and to take on less responsibility, but she soon reverted to her old ways. It was who she was, it simply wasn't in her nature to be idle. When she retired from teaching, she threw herself into the world of miniatures, something until then she had only dabbled in; now it took up nearly all her time.

But had that desire to be so organised and busy and in control been her downfall? Was that what Kip had wanted to escape from, to be recklessly out of control?

The late afternoon light was fading now and having marched all the way around the village and across the fields where the mild spring air was sweet with new growth and the birds were singing, she retraced her steps to go home.

The angry stomp had gone from her feet, and she was less furious with her sister, and herself. Of course she should be looking for somewhere new to live, and while it was kind of Ashley to say he'd do that for her, if she were to take back control of her life, she had to find her own new home. It would be an important step towards building a new future for herself.

With this newfound acceptance came the sensation that she'd been jerked wide awake and suddenly she was galvanised, ready to stride into the unknown with the same level of commitment and determination she'd always shown for a new challenge. What was more, she owed it to her family to hold her head up high and move on.

She reached home in a considerably more positive frame of mind than when she'd set off, only to find a familiar car parked on the driveway and an even more familiar figure trying to let himself in at the front door.

Chapter Eight

Kip held up his bunch of keys. 'You've changed the lock,' he said, unable to disguise the peevish disbelief in his voice.

'How clever of you to notice.'

'I suppose it's to pay me back, isn't it?'

'No, it's to stop you coming and going as you please. I think I'm entitled to my privacy, that should at least be something you can't take from me.'

He pushed his keys into his trouser pocket and tried to diffuse his annoyance that he'd been locked out of his own house. He was annoyed too that he hadn't anticipated Louisa doing this. But if he was to achieve anything by finishing work early and coming here to speak to her, he had to respect her need to lash out at him and contain his own reaction to it. At all costs he must remain calm and not lose his temper.

'I'm sorry,' he said. 'I know it was wrong what I did, meeting with the agent here while you were away, but I knew how difficult it would be for you and that you'd try to put it off. I was trying to make things less painful for you,' he added, even though he knew it was a blatant lie.

'Well, that's all right then,' she said, 'so long as it's all been for my benefit, and you had no choice but to go sneaking around behind my back. You seem to be making a habit of that.'

'Please,' he said, seeing somebody walking by the other side of the low beech hedge, 'can we have this conversation inside?'

'And if I said I didn't want to talk to you, that you're the last person I want to talk to?'

'I'd say that I understood. But as difficult as it is, Louisa, we do need to talk. We need to straighten things out.'

'I thought the solicitors were doing that for us.'

'Look, I know you're cross with me, maybe you even hate me, but it would be so much better all round if we could deal with things more . . .'

'What? Amicably? Graciously? Cordially?' she said when he hesitated over which word to use, and which wouldn't sound too simplistic.

'All of those things,' he said, 'but really as two people who have shared a life together and still care about the family we've created. Don't we owe ourselves that much?'

She stared at him with an expression of withering contempt. He'd never seen her look like that before and it chilled him to the bone. As strong and as capable as Louisa had always been, there had been an ever-present reassuring gentleness to her. That was gone to him now and had been replaced with a cold hardness he didn't recognise. He recognised though that he was responsible for the change in her and it added to his guilt.

'Oh, what the hell,' she muttered. 'Come in and let's get this over with.'

He followed her round to the back of the house. When she'd unlocked the utility room door, she removed her fleece and hung it on the coat rack. He didn't have a jacket or coat to remove so he could have gone on ahead, but he didn't, he waited for her and then fell in step behind her.

Everything looked so familiar to him in the kitchen. There were tulips in a pottery jug on the windowsill, a vase of daffodils on the table, photos of the family pinned randomly to the noticeboard above the bookcase that was full of cookery books, the collection of Fortnum & Mason tea caddies by the kettle, the hand towels hanging on the chrome rail of the Aga tucked into the brick surround with its colourful tiles, the oak beams that were decorated with dried flowers and decorative china plates, and the slightly uneven floor of glazed bricks that was so typical of a five-hundred-year-old Suffolk cottage. It was the usual colourful jumble that looked and smelled the same, but it didn't feel the same. The atmosphere was different. It felt oppressive and unwelcoming. Or maybe it was just him feeling out of kilter amongst so much familiarity and knowing that his wife, whom he had hurt so badly, was standing a few feet away from him and looking like she wished there was an ocean of distance between them.

When he'd been here the other week with the estate agent, he hadn't felt like this, but then he'd been acting the part of agreeable client whose marriage had very sadly come to an end.

But being here with Louisa and feeling the animosity coming off her, he was forced to acknowledge just how cruelly he'd treated her, and as he felt his emotions sliding, wishing he could turn back the clock, he had to steel himself. It was too late. He couldn't undo the harm he'd done. There was no going back, not when he'd be doing it out of pity. But more importantly he didn't want to return to the life he'd once had. He wanted to be with Zoe.

'What is it you want to talk about?' Louisa asked.

'Shall we sit down?' he replied, indicating the table and pulling out a chair – the chair which the children had designated years ago as 'Dad's chair'. But Louisa didn't join him. She moved even further away and positioned herself by the Aga, forcing him from where he was sitting to twist round to face her. There was an unnatural tightness to her, and her gaze was clear and strong. Unnervingly so.

Regarding her across the kitchen and trying to see through the outer shell of the angry woman she had every right to be, he could still glimpse the woman she'd been when they were young and just starting out in life together. She had been everything he had wanted in a wife, loving and supportive, intelligent and independent, and full of enthusiasm for everything they hoped to achieve as a couple. She had been beautiful in a completely unconscious way, and he had genuinely believed he had found the only woman he could ever truly love.

She was just as beautiful now, he found himself thinking. Older yes, and a little thickened out, as he was too, but she still possessed an elegant radiance that would be the envy of many younger women. She had never needed to watch her weight or go to a gym to stay in shape. Her one and only vice, she'd liked to say, were the regular trips to the hairdresser to maintain the honey-gold colour which mother nature had given her in her youth and which age threatened to turn grey. Back in her twenties and thirties she'd worn her hair long, but for years now she'd had it cut into a sleek bob that was level with her jawline.

'I want to talk about the house,' he said, forcing his thoughts back in line. 'I know what a wrench it will be for you to leave, Louisa, but we do need to sell it if we're to make the most of our shared assets and live comfortably in the way we both deserve. I know it's not what you ever thought would happen, I certainly didn't, but it has happened and so we have to deal with—'

'Spare me the overly rehearsed homily,' she interrupted, 'I couldn't be less interested, especially when you say things like *we need* and *we have to*. This is not about me and what I want, it's about *you* and what *you* want. Now answer me this: what precisely do I get out of this divorce?'

He stared at her. 'In what respect?'

'In respect of my financial situation. I want to know what sort of house I can afford to buy, otherwise how will I be able to look forward to this exciting new life you've so generously bestowed upon me?'

Flinching at the sarcasm coming at him, and even though he knew he shouldn't, he went on the attack with some of his own. 'That's a hypothetical question, since you're refusing to allow anyone to view the house so there's no chance of it being sold and either of us moving on.'

'It was only for this week,' she said. 'The gawpers and time-wasters can come by the coachload from Monday onwards.'

He frowned. 'So you were just being awkward this week, is that it?'

'I was asserting my right to do things at my own pace. Which you might like to consider when it comes to any future dealings between us and our solicitors. Now please, answer my question.'

'I can't. Not really. Everything has to be put into the pot and then divided up and—'

'A ballpark figure,' she snapped. 'Surely you can give me that? Doubtless you know already what you'll be able to afford for when you and Zoe set up home together, which means you'll know what will be left over for me? I assume I'll have a half share of the proceeds from the sale of our house, but what about the rest – our savings, the shares, and the business. Bearing in mind, of course, all the years I contributed to the mortgage and how I helped shore things up during the pandemic with what I'd inherited from my parents.'

'For which I am and always will be extremely grateful,' he said. 'You know how much I appreciated that.' Inwardly he sighed; what Louisa could never understand was how beholden to her that had made him feel. He had hated taking the money from her, but it had been the only way to keep Uniquely You Villas afloat.

'Had I known what you were going to do a few years down the line, I would have let you go to the wall,' she said.

'And that would have hurt both of us,' he replied evenly.

'But it's all right to hurt me now?'

'I didn't ever mean to hurt you, Louisa.'

'But you have, and you can't expect me to behave as amenably as you so obviously want me to. In time I might forgive you, but that's a long way off. Now if you've said all you came to say, and if you've satisfied yourself that I'm going to play nicely and let people view the house, I think you should go.'

He stood up at her dismissal. He had hoped for so much more in coming here to speak to Louisa. He'd foolishly thought that a face-to-face conversation would help, that she would see he was still Kip, still the father of their children, and that he was only trying to make the end of their marriage easier for them both. But he'd miscalculated. She had put a protective barrier around herself, and nothing was going to penetrate it.

Chapter Nine

Saturday morning, and while Caro was in the shower, Ashley was downstairs in the kitchen having breakfast with Peggy.

His two-and-a-half-year-old daughter's attention was firmly fixed on the iPad screen in front of her as she absently chewed on small squares of Marmite toast. She was watching an episode of *Cocomelon*, a brightly coloured animation that never failed to induce in her a trance-like state of absorbed concentration. It was oddly hypnotic, even addictive because more than once Ashley had found himself staring at the screen in a state of mesmerised inertia. He might well need to resort to watching it later today as a form of escape. Or deep sedation.

It was the end of May, the Spring Bank Holiday weekend, and having worked the last three Saturdays in a row, he was off for this one. 'Any problems,' he'd told his staff who would be in the office today, 'you can always call me.' He almost hoped they would, that there would be a major problem which only he could resolve; it would mean he would escape today's outing.

Caro would be furious if that happened, as would Arabella. Peggy would also be disappointed at being denied a day at the beach. In the last few days her imagined trip to the seaside had taken on epic proportions in her young febrile mind. Her rapidly developing vocabulary now included an assortment of beach-related words, mostly acquired from a picture book that featured

Peppa Pig going on holiday to the seaside. Ashley had the sinking feeling that the day could only ever be a disappointment, that the beach at Aldeburgh couldn't live up to her expectations. And from his own perspective, he dreaded the day because it was going to be the first time that they would be together as a family.

And by family, he meant this new hybrid family his father had created.

Understandably Angus had turned down the invitation. 'No way!' he'd said savagely. 'No way am I playing happy families with my ex-girlfriend and Dad! Who do they think I am, the bloody poster boy for forgive and forget?'

When Dad had invited them all to go over to Aldeburgh to spend the day with him and Zoe, Ashley hadn't told Caro about it. He'd called his sister first and asked what she thought they should do. 'Do you think we should say no for Mum's sake?' he'd asked.

At the time Arabella had still been cross with him for telling Caro that Giles hadn't been separated from his wife when they'd started their relationship.

'You swore you'd never tell anyone,' she'd hissed at him when they'd been at Mum's that Saturday after Dad had put the house on the market. 'You promised!'

Embarrassed that he'd been caught out, and disappointed that his wife had given him away, he'd apologised and said that he hadn't meant to, but he'd let it slip one day when Caro had asked him if he really believed Arabella's story about Giles being a free man when she met him.

'You should have lied,' Arabella had said.

'You know I'm rubbish at doing that,' he'd said. 'My face always gives me away.'

As, no doubt, it would today, he thought. For Peggy's sake he wanted to pretend that there was absolutely nothing unusual about Grando having replaced Grammy with a new 'friend' – he couldn't bring himself to say girlfriend. Nor could he contemplate

Zoe ever being his stepmother. For the love of God, how was that ever going to work? Not that marriage, to his knowledge, had ever been mentioned.

According to Caro he was over-complicating matters, since it wasn't necessary to pin labels on people. 'Just see them as Kip and Zoe.'

Which was perhaps easy for Caro to do as she grew up calling her parents and step-parents by their Christian names. But for Ashley, his parents had always been Mum and Dad, and always would be.

Arabella had taken the view that they should accept Dad's invitation as sooner or later they were going to have to see him with Zoe, that is unless they wanted to lose their father.

The next big question was whether they told their mother what they were doing.

'Of course you do!' Caro had said. 'Honestly, you and Arabella are being such children over this. Your mum is quite strong enough to accept that your father is still your father and as such it's perfectly normal that you should want to see him.'

But I don't, thought Ashley miserably, *I really don't want to see him. Not like this.*

He turned to look at Peggy in her high chair next to him. She was still staring intently at the screen in front of her, her head of silky blonde hair bobbing along to 'Row Row Row Your Boat'. Her chin had a buttery smear of Marmite on it and using his finger, he wiped it away, then sucked his finger clean. She flicked her eyes towards him and gave him one of her specially heart-melting smiles. Then pushing her empty plate towards him, she said, 'More toast!'

'More toast, *please*,' he said automatically.

'More toast, *peeese*,' she echoed, her gaze now back on the screen.

Over by the toaster, and topping up his mug of coffee, he thought how awful it would be if when she was older, his precious daughter didn't want to see him. It was beyond his comprehension. And not something he would ever allow to happen.

From upstairs he could hear his wife using the hairdryer. Her long blonde hair, which Peggy had inherited, was the first thing he'd noticed about Caro when they'd met in Corfu. He'd been on holiday with a bunch of friends staying in one of the properties managed by Uniquely You Villas. The villa was in Agios Stefanos and one night while they were enjoying dinner in the harbour at a popular taverna to celebrate his thirtieth birthday, a group of girls arrived. They made the sort of arrival that was hard to ignore – three eye-catchingly attractive girls dressed to the max, and clearly enjoying the attention of the waiter as he showed them to a table parallel to where Ashley and his friends were sitting. There was only one blonde amongst the trio of girls and Ashley found he couldn't take his eyes off her. She was wearing a short figure-hugging dress that showed off her long tanned legs and his friends soon noticed they'd lost his attention and started teasing him in voices plenty loud enough to alert the girl in question. She gave him a cool look and to his complete surprise, as his face reddened, her lips curved into a smile. He hadn't expected that. Perhaps she hadn't either. He'd assumed she would regard him and his rowdy mates as beneath her attention. But apparently not.

By the end of the evening, they were all sitting around the one table, and arranging to take a boat out together in the morning as a group. Which they did. They puttered further down the coast and after swimming in a quiet bay, they pushed on further to have lunch at a taverna which Ashley knew well. He'd been holidaying in Corfu for years, originally with his family, and then with friends. But that holiday was easily the best. He fell in love that week and had been in love with Caro ever since.

Fourteen months later she had relocated to be with him in Suffolk, and they were planning to marry. There was a straightforwardness about her which he found immensely appealing, and he knew when she said something that she meant it. When she'd first said that she loved him, he hadn't doubted for a moment that she did. Not because he was arrogant enough to think that of course she would, but because there was no falsehood to her, no obfuscation. He liked that she saw things so clearly and was always the voice of reason. Just occasionally he might not see things the way she did, and there had been times when her candour was misplaced and a little clumsy, but he wouldn't have her any other way. She kept him balanced, and he liked to think that he did the same for her.

Spreading butter and then Marmite onto Peggy's toast and cutting it into squares, he took it over to the table where she was still held spellbound by the figures moving about on the screen in front of her. Going back to the worktop, he drank his coffee and wondered about ringing his mother.

She knew that they were going to Aldeburgh today, Caro had of course been right that they should tell her. 'I'd sooner have the truth than lies,' Mum had said when Ashley told her. 'I've had quite enough lies from your father.'

On the face of it, Mum seemed to have turned a corner. She was actively house-hunting and regularly reported back to Ashley about the properties she had either viewed or was going to view. So far nothing had come remotely close to what she wanted, not even the ones he was selling. Ashley hoped that she wasn't being overly picky. Although he couldn't blame her if she was. It was a massive readjustment she was having to make and so it was hugely important to her to find a home that wouldn't feel too much of a retrograde step. He kept a close eye on the property market himself, checking numerous times a day for anything new, but Mum seemed to have a good handle on the situation and so he backed off, not wanting to appear as though he was interfering.

There had been a steady stream of viewers to Charity Cottage and two offers made, both of which were well below the asking price. It was a classic Barston and Bright trick. They were known for encouraging buyers to under offer and then persuading the vendor that it was a fair price in the hope of a quick and easy sale. The less work they had to do, the better. They liked a rapid turnaround in properties and didn't care how they achieved it. Nor did they really give much thought to client care, all that mattered to them was the easy sale and the commission earned.

He'd told his mother not to accept any offer without speaking to him first. 'You'll be the first to know, darling,' she'd said with a smile that had more than a hint of mild forbearance to it, as though she were humouring him. He knew the look of old, he'd been on the receiving end of it many a time as a child when he'd denied all knowledge of some wrongdoing but she'd known all along that he was the one who'd smashed a pane of glass with a football; or when he'd tried to convince her he'd done all his homework.

Remembering that Angus was going to be with Mum for the weekend, he decided not to ring her. Instead, he checked in with Arabella. He wanted to make sure they arrived in Aldeburgh at the same time and more importantly, he wanted to work out some kind of strategy with her for keeping the day with Dad and Zoe as neutral and conflict-free as possible. Because as far as he could see it had all the potential to blow up in their faces at any moment.

He'd just picked up his mobile when it rang in his hand.

It was Arabella.

'I thought I'd give you a quick call to see what time you plan to arrive at destination nightmare and how we're going to handle things,' she said.

That was twins for you, he thought with a smile, weirdly telepathic and totally in tune with each other.

Chapter Ten

Sometimes Arabella felt she just couldn't win.

She had thought she was doing the right thing offering to sit in the back of the car with Heidi so Giles's daughter could sit in the front with him. It was another example of her bending over backwards to accommodate Lexi.

The girl had been staying with them for her half-term break while her mother and new boyfriend were on holiday in Majorca. Arabella had done her best to entertain Lexi while Giles was at work, but there had been moments when she'd been seriously out of her depth and close to losing her temper. The girl had started speaking with an annoyingly lofty pretentiousness, as if it was her greatest misfortune to be surrounded by simpletons. Her phrase of choice was 'I'm dying, I'm literally dying of boredom.' *Well, join the club*, Arabella wanted to say each time the phrase was given another airing, *because I'm bored of hearing your constant grumbling*.

The only good thing was that Heidi was so besotted with her big half-sister and in fairness, when Lexi wasn't complaining or messing about on the mobile Giles had surprised her with and for which she'd been nagging him for months, she did play with Heidi. Which was why Heidi had been grizzling ever since they'd set off from home for Aldeburgh; she'd wanted Lexi to sit with her, not her boring old mother. Lexi had made a half-hearted offer to switch seats, but Giles had said she should stay where she was in the front as it was important that Heidi learnt that she couldn't always have her own way.

The day could only go from bad to worse, Arabella thought now as she tried to distract Heidi with a small packet of raisins. Her daughter regarded the opened packet with shrewd scepticism, as if seeing it for what it was, a blatant bribe to keep her quiet. She gave another shuddery grizzle, just to prove there was still plenty more in the tank, and took the packet. After she'd popped a raisin into her mouth, she fell quiet, and Arabella relaxed, breathing a long inward sigh of relief.

But instead of having to focus on her daughter, she was now left with nothing to divert her attention from thinking how the day might unfold. She still felt incredibly angry with her father and would give anything for him to wake up one morning and realise that what he was doing was just so wrong. Apart from anything, it was embarrassing him being with Zoe who was so much younger than him. Nothing would convince Arabella that it was real love between them. It was lust combined with some sort of crazy fear of ageing. He just wanted to feel young again.

As her brothers had suggested, she had rung their father to try and convince him that that this *thing* with Zoe had no chance of lasting because it wasn't real, and that there was no way he could think she could ever replace Mum. But it hadn't worked.

'You have no idea of the depth of my feelings for Zoe,' Dad had said with a terse severity that shook her, 'so please don't lecture me on what is real and not real. I know you won't want to hear this, but what wasn't real was my relationship with your mother. It used to be, but then it became just two people living in the same house propped up by the past and with nothing to look forward to, just more of the same pretence.'

She had expected him to sound contrite, or at least awkwardly embarrassed that they were having the conversation. Moreover, she had wanted to have the upper hand and play on his conscience, maybe make him squirm in the hope that it would bring it home to him how others would view his relationship with a girl so much younger than he was. But he was resolute in his defence of Zoe and his feelings for her. Never had Arabella felt so distant from him.

'So you've been pretending all these years that your children and grandchildren matter to you?' she accused him. 'We've been nothing but props to you, is that it? And you couldn't look to the future and share in our happiness? Wasn't that enough?'

'That's the thing about when you're young,' he'd said. 'You think your own happiness is sufficient to make everyone else happy.'

At that she'd fired a low shot at him. 'Then maybe you'd better ask Zoe about that, seeing how bloody young she is!'

'I know you're still cross and upset, Arabella,' he'd said in a carefully measured voice, 'but don't you want me to be happy, and for your mother to find happiness with somebody new, somebody more worthy of her love than me?'

Without answering him, she'd ended the call, claiming that Heidi was crying and needed her. He'd rung the next day to say that if he'd been too frank with her, he was sorry, but essentially what he'd said was the truth. She'd let him say what he wanted to say and made no attempt to agree or disagree. The next time he was in touch it was to invite them all for lunch in Aldeburgh where he and Zoe were staying for the Bank Holiday weekend. She'd tried to wriggle out of it by saying Lexi would be with them, to which he'd said, 'Bring her too, I'd like to see her. I'm sure Zoe would too.'

It would have been more acceptable if he hadn't added Zoe's name into the exchange, but Arabella swallowed back the objection and said she would check with Giles to see how he felt about it.

'Of course, I don't mind,' her husband had said that evening when he was home from work. 'Why would I?'

'If you have to ask that, then you don't understand.'

'No, I don't,' he'd said.

From the front of the car, Arabella could hear Lexi asking Giles if he thought Grando Kip and Zoe would get married.

'I have no idea,' Giles said quietly, as though not wanting Arabella to hear.

'Shall I ask him?' asked Lexi.

'Perhaps not, sweetheart,' Giles said, his gaze meeting Arabella's in the rear-view mirror.

Arabella turned away. She thought how Mum and Dad, right from the very first time they had met Lexi, had been so good at making her feel part of the family. They hadn't forced any kind of a grandparent role or title on her, and it was Lexi herself who had decided she would call them Grandma Louisa and Grando Kip.

All credit to Mum, she had been great and had always found some special way to entertain and include Lexi. She had taught her how to make miniature doll's house food with polymer clay, modelling it and then baking it in the oven before painting and then varnishing it.

Lexi had always enjoyed those times at Charity Cottage, but then this week when Arabella had taken Heidi and Lexi to see Mum, Lexi had said she didn't want to mess about with modelling clay and paint, it was *boring*. Then to Arabella's horror, she had asked Mum if she was sad that Grando Kip had left her.

'Yes,' Mum had answered her. 'Very sad.'

Then with a sly look at Arabella, Lexi had said, 'My mum was sad when Dad left her, so I expect she knows just how you feel.'

For twelve years of age, the girl was as cunning and as knowing as they came. When Arabella had told Giles about the comment his daughter had made, he'd said that it was probably true and there was no point in kidding themselves that it wasn't. He'd kissed Arabella and hugged her. 'You have to stop being so sensitive,' he'd said. 'Lexi's just going through an inevitable phase of figuring everything out, and in her own way. It'll all be okay in the end. Just you see.'

Arabella wanted to believe him, she really did, but she felt horribly stung by what Lexi had said and was convinced it had been a nasty dig at her. The girl never aimed a blow like that at Giles, only Arabella, as though her father had played no part in ending his marriage, and it was entirely Arabella's fault.

She also wanted to believe that she wasn't making the same mistake as Lexi, but undeniably there was a part of her that really did want to heap all the blame onto Zoe for wrecking her parents' marriage. That way she could still believe in Dad. He could still be the father she'd always loved and wanted to go on loving, he'd just made the mistake of being taken in by some girl who had a thing for older men.

Once more her thoughts turned to what lay ahead, and imagining seeing her father all loved-up with Zoe made her insides turn into a roiling cauldron of angry apprehension. How on earth would she be able to conceal her real feelings? Ashley was adamant that their strategy was to behave in a civilised manner and under no circumstances should they cause a scene in front of the children. 'For their sake,' he'd said, 'we must keep a lid on our emotions and just focus on getting through the day, even if that means playing this absurd version of Happy Families.'

Chapter Eleven

Shell House was situated at the end of a smart little row of prettily painted cottages in varying shades of pastel that resembled a Neapolitan ice cream. The holiday cottage was owned by Iona, an old friend of Zoe's mother who had offered Zoe the chance to use it for the Bank Holiday weekend. She hadn't hesitated to take up the offer.

'But I thought we might grab a last-minute booking for a city break in Rome or Paris, or maybe snatch a few days in one of the villas in Corfu if a cancellation came up,' Kip had said when she'd told him where they were going. 'Wouldn't you prefer that? A beautiful hotel with a side order of romantic five-star luxury?' he'd added.

'No,' she'd said firmly. 'Flaunting a romantic weekend away in an expensive hotel wouldn't play well with your family, or even be fair to your wife. Better she thinks we're braving the worst of the elements which the North Sea can throw at us.'

'She needn't know where we're going.'

'But she will know. I guarantee it.' That was when Zoe had told Kip that it was time for peace to be properly brokered with his family.

'You don't think it's too soon?' he'd queried, his face clouded with uncertainty when she'd explained what she had in mind.

'It's five months since you left Louisa, that's plenty of time for everyone to adjust to our being together.'

Now, as Zoe laid the table in the small, sheltered garden at the back of the house, and with the ever-present chorus of discordant seagulls setting the scene for a seaside lunch, some of her earlier confidence that she could pull this off – reuniting Kip's family and proving to them that she genuinely made their father happy – was seeping away from her. The reality of having Arabella and Ashley here with their partners and children, plus Lexi, was beginning to dawn on her. What if it was a disaster and caused an even greater rift between Kip and his family? Would he blame her? Would he—

No! she told herself. No doubts. Show an ounce of doubt today and that would give them the advantage. This had been her way of taking the initiative and to show Arabella, Ashley and Angus that she meant business, that she simply wasn't prepared to let them go on hurting Kip. To that end, she had to play her part with total conviction; she had to be composed, confident, and caring. Once they saw with their own eyes how much happier Kip was since he'd begun his new life with her, they would understand that she wasn't the enemy, that she only wanted the very best for him.

Until now Kip had never pressed his children to spend time with him and Zoe. Once or twice he'd seen Ashley and Arabella individually, but not his youngest son. Angus still refused even to speak to him. Kip had claimed that the softly-softly approach was the way to go, but as far as she could see that had got them nowhere fast. That was why she had taken things into her own hands and insisted he invite his family to spend the day with them in Aldeburgh and on what could be seen as neutral territory.

To help make the day go as well as she wanted it to, after breakfast Zoe had gone across the road to the beach and gathered a bucket of shells and another of stones for Peggy and Heidi to paint. In advance of the weekend, she had bought a set of child-friendly paints so the two girls, maybe with Lexi's help, could amuse themselves by decorating the stones. Let nobody accuse her of not trying! She also had a few other fun activities planned for the children. Paddling on the beach was an obvious one, along with a trip to the ice-cream parlour and there was also the Scallop Shell sculpture to see, which the children could scramble over, if they wanted to. And just a short drive away there was Thorpeness to visit, if they needed yet more distraction, and where they could feed the ducks and swans.

She had thought of going the extra mile today and cooking lunch, but that would have been counterproductive because she didn't like cooking, so wasn't much good at it. The last thing she wanted was Kip's children comparing her cooking ability with their mother's. Zoe remembered all too well the magnificent meals Louisa had made for her family. Kip had suggested they buy some fresh fish from one of the fishermen's huts on the beach and he make use of the barbecue that was in the garden. Of the two of them, he was probably the better cook, and that wasn't saying much, but ever the one for compromise, Zoe had said they'd have fish and chips in the garden. What could be more appropriate than that in Aldeburgh, where reputedly there was the best fish and chip shop in the country?

'An excellent idea!' he'd said, suddenly taking her in his arms and performing a jaunty tango with her in the galley-style kitchen where they'd been having the conversation. 'The girl's a genius!'

'I'm glad you think so,' she'd said, laughing joyfully.

Tilting her backwards, he'd kissed her. 'Did I ever tell you how much I loved you?'

'Just once or twice,' she'd said.

He did that sometimes, surprised her by doing something completely unexpected and making her feel absurdly happy.

The table set, and above the persistent noise of screeching seagulls, she heard music coming from inside the house. It was Van

Morrison, a particular favourite of Kip's. She occasionally teased him that she'd have to update his taste in music and bit by bit she was introducing him to more of what she liked. She wasn't convinced he really enjoyed Taylor Swift, Billie Eilish, or even Ed Sheeran, but he gamely listened to it when they were in the car together, although she sensed he was only doing it to please her. He did a lot of that. As she did with him. Being together meant they were daily discovering so much about each other and continuously adapting.

'Glass of rosé?' said Kip, coming out to the small garden.

'Something to oil the wheels?' she said with a raised eyebrow and taking the proffered glass.

'Possibly.'

'Are you very nervous?' she asked, watching him take a gulp of his wine.

'Do I look it?'

Yes, she thought, *you look terrible*. But keeping that to herself, she leant in and kissed his cheek. 'It'll be fine. What's the worst that can happen?'

Chapter Twelve

For the last two hours Angus had been helping his mother clear out the attic and the hall was now home to a messy pile of useless junk. One dusty old box contained nothing but old football boots and another was crammed full of rolled-up artwork which he and his brother and sister had painted, probably while at junior school. 'All very sweet, Mum,' he'd said to her, 'that our priceless masterpieces have been kept, but since nobody looks at the daubs, what's the point in keeping them?'

'Because that kind of thing is always special to a parent.'

'I hate to point out the obvious, but if it's that special it shouldn't be in the attic.'

She'd tutted at that and proposed they took a break. They were now in the kitchen having coffee and a slice of fruitcake and Angus had just offered to take the junk to the tip.

'You don't think we should give the others a chance to go through it?' his mother asked.

Leaning back against the sink, he shook his head. 'Why? What's the point in giving them the chance to pick over the bones of a bunch of stuff they didn't even know was up in the attic? Better just to dump it all.'

His mother smiled. 'You've never been one for sentimentality, have you?'

'I can't see that it helps. Certainly not in a situation like this.'

'So, you won't be sad when the house is sold?'

He drank some more of his coffee before saying, 'I'll be sad for you, Mum, that things have turned out this way.'

'Don't be. Not when I'm doing my best to be so annoyingly positive.'

'Even more reason then,' he said with a smile, 'for me to load up the car and pay the tip a visit. Why run the risk of having to drag a load of rubbish to the next house, especially when it's going to be—'

'It's okay,' she said, when he stopped himself short, 'you can say that it's going to be a lot smaller than here, I'm not going to crumble at hearing the words out loud. I know it's a downsize move, I've come to terms with that.'

'I was going to say your next house will be more modest.'

'Boils down to the same thing,' she said with a shrug.

He drank some of his coffee and chewed on another mouthful of cake. 'What time did you say we need to leave here to go and look at this mystery house you refuse to tell me anything about?'

She looked at the clock on the wall, then back at him. 'We need to set off in half an hour, that should give us plenty of time to find the place and check out the surrounding area.'

'Look at you sounding like a pro.'

'I feel like a pro what with all the houses I've looked at.'

'And not one of them felt right? Not even a hint of potential?'

She tutted. 'Please don't start sounding like your brother. I'm convinced he thinks I'm being overly fussy and that I must lower my sights and compromise. But I don't want to be forced into settling on something which will only make me miserable.'

'Of all people I'm sure Ashley wouldn't want you to settle. He knows perfectly well that it's important you find a house that will feel like a home to you. Or one that makes you feel you could turn it into a home.'

Their coffee and cake finished, his mother gathered up the

mugs and plates and had just put them in the dishwasher when the telephone on the dresser rang. Leaving her to answer it, Angus went out to the hall to make a start on loading up his car with the boxes of attic junk. With a bit of luck he could shift it later when they were back from the viewing.

It was good that Mum was being as positive as she was, but he was glad he was here and able to be useful. They had neither of them said very much about Ashley and Arabella spending the day over in Aldeburgh with Dad and Zoe, but what was there to say anyway? No doubt they'd hear how it went at some point.

While working in Cambridge, Angus had spent quite a bit of time in the last month with their mother. He'd even gone with her to look at a few houses. 'Can you see me living here?' she had said to him of one uninspiring property.

'It's not what I think that counts,' he'd said carefully, 'what does is whether or not you can see yourself living here.'

It turned out that she couldn't, just as he'd thought.

For some reason she had been strangely reticent to give him any information about the house they were viewing today, which was why he'd referred to it as the mystery house. She hadn't even told him where it was. 'I want you to have a completely open mind,' she'd said over dinner last night. 'No pre-judgement. No thinking I must have lost the plot.'

Even if he did think she had, he would keep it to himself. Sometimes when a person had a massive unwanted change forced upon them, behaving completely out of character was a way to alleviate the pain of the shock. He couldn't personally lay claim to that pearl of wisdom, it had come from someone whom he was really enjoying getting to know.

The morning after his neighbour from downstairs had knocked on his door to ask if he had any batteries for her smoke alarm, he had gone out for a run and returned to find a bottle of wine by the door of his flat. Attached to the neck of the bottle was a note with the words *Thank you!* written on it. There was no name, no indication who had left it there, other than the assumption that he would know.

In the evenings that followed when he was home and not working away, he found himself paying more attention to the music coming from beneath his apartment and as the weather warmed, he would open the door onto the balcony and enjoy a beer while listening to the mellow sound of the cello floating up on the balmy evening air.

Then one evening, having been away for a few days in Cambridge, he came home anticipating listening to the sound of his neighbour's playing but was disappointed to be greeted with silence. There wasn't any music the following evening either or the next. He missed it and wondered if his neighbour was away, or maybe too ill to play. More likely, he reasoned, she was simply taking a break because surely even the most dedicated musician liked time off from their instrument.

A couple of days later he bumped into her on the ground floor of their block of flats when he was setting off to drive up to Cambridge.

'Hi!' she said, 'did you find the wine I left for you?'

'Yes,' he answered. 'There was no need. Really.'

'Perhaps not, but a good deed should never go unrewarded. Or unpunished!' she added with a laugh. 'Although I hope the wine didn't give you a punishing headache.'

'It didn't. In fact, I still haven't opened it. I don't suppose—' He broke off abruptly, suddenly doubtful it was a good idea what he'd been about to suggest. It was an idea that had nudged at him ever since he'd found the bottle.

'Don't suppose what?' she asked, smiling back at him.

He suspected she was one of those naturally very smiley people. He also suspected that she knew exactly what he'd been on the verge of saying. And why the hell shouldn't he, he thought? It was only a glass of wine he was going to suggest. 'I haven't heard you playing your cello recently,' he said, changing tack.

'I've been away. The quartet I play with had a booking for a wedding down in Dorset and afterwards I took the opportunity to go and stay with some friends for a couple of days. I expect you enjoyed the peace and quiet while I was gone.'

'Actually, I missed hearing you play.'

'You did?' Her face seemed to light up at his admission.

'Yes. So, are you a professional musician, then?' he asked.

'Sadly not, I'm merely a part-time cello for hire – weddings, birthdays, corporate dos, you know the kind of thing. By day I'm a paralegal assistant.' She glanced at the overnight bag in his hand and the leather satchel slung over his shoulder. 'Going somewhere?'

'Cambridge. For work.'

'I'd better not keep you then.'

He placed his hand on the door to push it open, but hesitated. 'Perhaps when I'm back we could have a drink,' he said. 'Maybe crack open that bottle of wine you gave me?'

'Sure,' she said. 'I'd like that.'

'How about Saturday evening, is that any good for you?'

'I'll make certain it is.'

'Good, I'll see you then.'

He had the door open and was almost outside when once more he turned around. 'I suppose it wouldn't be a bad idea to introduce ourselves, would it?'

Again the big smile on her face. 'I'm Cécile,' she said, 'but everyone calls me CeeCee.'

'And I'm Angus, and rather boringly everyone calls me Angus,' he added with a half-smile.'

He drove up to Cambridge thinking that for the first time in ages he had something nice to look forward to. *It's just a drink,* he cautioned himself, *a drink and that's all.*

But when Saturday evening came, they ended up in his flat having a Thai takeaway and chatting long into the night. Maybe it was the combination of wine and the beers he'd consumed, and feeling relaxed in CeeCee's company, but he'd told her about his parents splitting up and his father declaring himself in love with Angus's ex-girlfriend.

'Wow,' she'd exclaimed, 'that's a whole world of crazy hurt, isn't it?'

'Tell me about it,' he'd said grimly.

They arranged to meet again, this time to go for dinner at a nearby Indian restaurant, and then she invited him to a fund-raising concert she and her quartet were involved with. The concert was held inside a marquee in the grounds of a beautiful manor house in Northamptonshire and seated in the second row from the front of the audience Angus had a perfect view of CeeCee.

Observing her playing had an extraordinary effect on him. And to be clear, it had nothing to do with the sight of her fantastically long legs wrapped around her cello, and everything to do with how in awe of her he was. He sat there spellbound, watching the intensity of her facial expression as she moved the bow across the cello strings and how she swayed seemingly as one with her instrument. He was no classical music buff, but he recognised many of the pieces the quartet played from what he'd heard CeeCee practising. But seeing her play was another experience altogether, she was mesmerising. She often closed her eyes as though to lose herself in the music, and only once did she look directly at him while playing, whereas he couldn't take his eyes off her for the whole performance.

'You were amazing!' he said afterwards when the concert was over.

'I was okay,' she said, hitching the cello case onto her back. She had already refused his offer to carry it for her.

'We'll have to agree to disagree on that,' he said in response to her modesty. 'I thought you were brilliant.'

'Then I have a lot to teach you about music,' she'd said.

The next time they saw each other it was to go out for another meal. That was the evening she asked him if he was totally over his previous girlfriend.

'Yeah, of course, I am,' he'd said, 'why do you ask?'

'It's just that I'd hate to go any further with you – with *us* – if there's a chance you're still screwed up by what she did.'

'Is there an *us?*' he'd asked cautiously.

'Sure there is. There was an *us* the moment you opened your door to me. So answer the question, is this ex-girlfriend of yours, who might end up as your stepmother, still an issue?'

He had to admit that she was right to ask the question because until then he hadn't felt like taking the risk when it came to pursuing another relationship with anyone new. There was also the small but not insignificant matter of him not having met anyone he'd considered worth the risk.

'I was upset,' he said, 'but I was never screwed up by it. At least I don't think I was. But the long-term consequences of what my ex and my father have done has the potential to screw us all up as a family. Not just me. And that makes me angry.'

'Not too angry, I hope. How's your mother coping?'

'Pretty well in the circumstances.'

'The mother of a friend of mine went through a divorce, and her way of coping was to step out of the box she'd always been in and reinvent herself. She gave up her well-paid job in the City and went to live in the Outer Hebrides. She now runs a wildlife project up there.'

'Very laudable, but I don't see my mother doing something like that. Apart from anything else, she wouldn't want to put any distance between herself and her grandchildren. She dotes on them. But tell me some more about there being an *us*. What does that actually mean?'

Smiling across the table at him, CeeCee said, 'Oh, I think you're smart enough to know exactly what it means. That's if you're up for it.'

He returned the smile. 'Like you said, there was an *us* from the moment I opened the door to you.' The funny thing was, it was true; he'd known it from the get-go, even if he'd tried to kid himself otherwise.

'Something amusing you, Angus?'

He was in his mother's car and on their way to view the house which she'd been so secretive about. 'I was recalling a recent conversation with someone,' he said.

'Somebody special?'

He shot her a quick sideways glance, but her gaze was fixed on the road ahead, her hands at their customary ten-to-two position on the steering wheel.

'Possibly,' he said casually. He hadn't as yet told his mother, or his brother and sister, that he was seeing anyone. He had wanted to keep CeeCee to himself, he hadn't been ready for his family to leap to any conclusions. He just wanted to enjoy the moment without a big thing being made of him having 'moved on'.

'What's her name?'

'*Mum!*'

'That's a strange name for a girl. Unless she has a child.'

'Ha ha, funny you.'

Now his mother did look at him. 'I can tell you have met someone; I can see it in your face, and the way you look at your mobile so often. But I do understand how you like to compartmentalise your life. You've always kept yourself ever so slightly at arm's distance from people, and that's okay, we're all different and like to do things our own way.'

Bemused, he said, 'Where's all this coming from, Mum?'

'I've been thinking a lot recently about what makes us uniquely who we are.'

'Any conclusions reached?'

'Only in as much as this time last year I would probably have known exactly who and what I was, but I'm floundering now. So much of my identity was wrapped up in being a wife and mother, but your father has somehow made that seem meaningless, as though I valued it too much.'

'That's letting Dad's selfish actions eclipse all that you've achieved, because as far as I can see, as well as being a brilliantly supportive wife and mother you've been a highly regarded teacher, an excellent grandmother and now you're a respected miniature maker.'

'But is that really who I am?'

'Do any of us really know who or what we are?'

'Well, and this might surprise you, but I've decided it might be time to embrace a new me.' Then with a sudden smile she slowed the car and pointed at a for sale board on the righthand side of the road. 'We must be nearly there,' she said brightly. 'Now I want you to do something for me. I want you to close your eyes and keep them closed until I say you can open them.

'And this is not at all weird, Mum,' he said.

'Go on,' she said, 'humour me.'

'Okay,' he replied, 'if I must.'

'And no looking until I say.'

To prove he was willing to play along with her, he covered his eyes with his hands and wondered what on earth she was up to. What kind of house was it that she had made an appointment to see? Was it a wreck of a place that she imagined doing up as a creative challenge?

If the scratching noise he could hear was anything to go by they were now on a narrow single-track lane with hedges brushing against the sides of the car. The track was rutted in places, and they slowly bumped along and then picked up a bit of speed on a much smoother surface of road before coming to a stop and the engine being switched off.

'You can open your eyes now.'

He did as his mother said, and there, looming above them, was the last thing he expected to see. 'It's a windmill!' he said, and with all the wonder of a small child.

'Yes,' she said. 'And it could be *my* windmill.

He stared up at it, and then looked at his mother and saw the happy excitement on her face. 'Cool,' he said. 'Let's go and see it.'

Chapter Thirteen

'What am I supposed to call you now?' asked Lexi.

'Call me Zoe, like you did before when we met last year.'

'Not *Grandma* Zoe, then?'

There was an awkward silence around the table, followed by a laugh from Zoe. But it was Kip who answered the question.

'I think Zoe will do just fine,' he said smoothly. 'How are your vegetarian sausages?'

Lexi pulled a face at him. 'They smell funny.'

'Perhaps they're comedy sausages.'

She gave him a scornful look. 'What do you mean?'

'They crack jokes,' he said with a light-hearted chuckle. 'That's why they're funny.'

The girl's look of scorn intensified and, making it clear she wasn't going to eat the offending items, she pushed them to the edge of the plate. Shrivelling inside, Kip wished he'd kept his mouth shut.

'Aren't you even going to try the sausages?' this was from Arabella, who looked as miserable as Kip felt.

'I just said they smell funny, didn't I, so why would I want to make myself puke by eating something that is so minging?'

'Lexi, there's no need to be so rude,' Arabella said.

'I'm not being rude, I'm being honest. What's wrong with that?'

'It's okay, sweetheart,' Giles intervened, 'you don't have to eat anything you don't want to. Just eat the chips.'

'But they'll make me fat. *And* give me spots.' She gave the plate a dismissive shove with her hand, bumping it against the vase of flowers Zoe had put there earlier – flowers which Ashley and Caro had brought with them. The girl then pulled out a mobile phone from her pocket.

'We had an agreement,' said Arabella. 'Never at the table.'

Lexi puffed out her cheeks and rolled her eyes, but she made no attempt to put away the phone. 'What else am I going to do to stop myself from dying of boredom here?'

'How about we make an exception for today?' suggested Giles. 'Nobody would mind, would they?' he asked the rest of them.

There were murmurs of assent, probably because they'd all be glad of the peace, and wishing this nightmarish day was over, Kip drank deeply from his wine glass. He was knocking back far more wine than was sensible, but it was the only way he could keep the worst of his nervousness at bay. He regretted now agreeing to Zoe's idea that they invite the family here for the day; it was too soon. They were all still too angry to be at ease with him and Zoe. But then as she'd said, when would it ever be right? They had to try at least.

It had been fine initially when everyone had arrived, they'd been able to hide behind Peggy and Heidi's giddy excitement at being somewhere new. Oblivious to the tension amongst the rest of them, the two girls had raced about exploring the house and then the small garden, squealing and chasing each other with happy abandon like a couple of puppies. They had created the perfect icebreaker while drinks were offered, and the proposal was then made that Ashley and Giles would go with Kip to fetch lunch from the fish and chip shop in the High Street. That was when Lexi put in her two penn'orth and said she would go with them to choose her own lunch because she was vegetarian, and she couldn't possibly eat fish.

'It's a recent thing,' Arabella had said to Kip. 'Probably no more than a passing fad. I should have warned you in advance, but I forgot.'

'It's not a *thing*,' Lexi had corrected her. 'Or a passing fad. It's a *belief* that it's wrong to eat meat of any kind. It's child abuse to make me eat anything I don't want to!'

It was obvious that Arabella now had her hands full with her stepdaughter who, at the age of twelve, and dressed like an under-age member of a girl band in a short denim skirt and skimpy top that showed her midriff, was on the cusp of entering the twilight zone of adolescence. The last time Kip had seen Lexi she had been a perfectly normal child, but in the intervening months she had undergone a dramatic change. He didn't want to be critical of Giles, but it was as clear as daylight that his son-in-law needed to man up and support his wife a hell of a lot more than he was currently doing if he wanted to avoid problems between them as a couple.

It was also clear to Kip that Lexi was using his relationship with Zoe to get at Arabella. The father in him wanted to protect his daughter, and the lover in him wanted very much to defend Zoe against this child who was intent on stirring up trouble.

Realising that his glass was empty, again, and once more adopting a cheery tone, he said, 'Who's for more wine or beer, or a soft drink? What about you girls,' he added, looking at his granddaughters, 'would you like some more apple juice? Or maybe some fizzy water?'

Peggy waved a big chip at him, '*Feeezy* water!'

Heidi shook her head, but then nodded.

'Is that a yes?' he asked her.

She smiled back at him revealing two rows of perfectly straight milk teeth and then reached for her plastic beaker cup. 'Feeezy for me! *Feezy, feezy, feezy!*'

Everyone laughed which made the girls giggle and, pushing himself to his feet to go and fetch the drinks, Kip silently thanked his granddaughters for bringing some much-needed levity to the lunch.

'I'll give you a hand,' offered Caro. She took the plastic cups from the girls and followed Kip into the kitchen.

'How are you bearing up?' she enquired when they were inside and out of earshot from everybody else.

'Oh, you know,' he said lightly, 'not too badly in the circumstances. I could do without Lexi's sly comments.'

'Ignore her, she's just asserting herself. She's at that age when she's full of snark, and she's found a button which she's going to keep on pressing until she grows bored of it.'

'I don't mind so much for myself, but I mind immensely for Arabella and Zoe. I won't have them upset by a stroppy child trying to cause trouble.'

'They're old enough to stick up for themselves, it's not your place to do it for them.'

Passing her a bottle of fizzy water from the fridge, and opening another bottle of rosé, Kip gave Caro a grateful smile. He had always been fond of his daughter-in-law and had known from the start of Ashley's relationship with her that she would be good for him.

Seeing Caro as his ally, and knowing that she could always be trusted upon to be honest, Kip said, 'Do you suppose today was a mistake, that it was too soon?'

The two plastic cups now filled, Caro looked at him. 'No I don't. It's five months now since you left Louisa and it's time for everyone to accept the situation and get on with it. And look, we're all here today, aren't we, so that's a step in the right direction. You have to be pleased with that, surely?'

'I'd be happier if Angus was here too. I don't want to lose him.'

'You won't. He just needs to accept this wasn't about him and Zoe, it was about *you* and Zoe.'

Kip sighed. 'I don't think he will ever see it that way. He's convinced Zoe cheated on him with me, but it didn't happen like that. It really didn't.'

'I could try talking to him if you like.'

He shook his head. 'That's kind of you, but I think it would be better to wait for when he's ready to talk to me face-to-face. I shan't give up on him. I'll never do that.'

'In that case you must be patient. Patient with them all in fact. And with Louisa.'

He put a hand to Caro's arm. 'You're a very wise young woman,' he said, 'and I'm a lucky man to have you as my daughter-in-law.'

He picked up the tray of drinks and they were back outside in the garden just in time to hear Lexi say, 'Zoe, can I ask you something?'

Zoe and Ashley were hunkered down on the ground with Peggy and Heidi supervising the girls as they painted the stones Zoe had collected from the beach. 'Of course,' she said, smiling back at Lexi.

'I was just wondering,' the girl said slowly – deliberately slowly as if making sure that she had everyone's attention – 'don't you think it was a bad thing what you did, stealing Grando Kip from Grandma Louisa?'

Kip banged the tray down very hard on the table, anything to shock this girl into behaving better. He threw a look in Giles's direction, hoping that he'd step in and reprimand his daughter, but he wasn't meeting Kip's gaze.

'Arabella stole Dad from my mum,' Lexi continued, 'so she would know just how Grandma Louisa must be feeling.'

'That's enough, Lexi!' hissed Arabella. 'I did not steal your father away from your mother.'

'That's not what Mum says. She says that you—'

'Giles,' implored Arabella, 'for God's sake, tell her to be quiet.'

'Lexi, sweetheart, now's not the time. Let's talk about this later. When we're alone.'

'Why?'

'Because it's private.'

Lexi rolled her eyes and, muttering something about them all being boring, she returned her attention to the mobile in her hands.

Kip could have snatched it from her grasp and hurled it down on the flagstones, then ground it underfoot. He wouldn't have believed he could feel such animosity towards a child, but he did. He felt angry with Giles too for allowing his daughter to be so rude to Zoe.

Chapter Fourteen

Louisa could not have been more charmed by Melbury Mill.

The converted windmill was minus its sails, but she loved everything about it, the quirky rooms with their curving walls, the random scattering of windows, the unevenness of the wooden floors to the upper levels, the delightful cosiness of the ingeniously created accommodation, and the cleverly added kitchen and dining extension. But best of all, she loved the room on the fourth floor, right at the top of the brick-built mill. With its 360-degree views, it was beautifully light and airy and would be perfect as a workshop. There were glass doors that opened onto a wooden balcony, and it was there that Louisa and Angus were now standing.

She hardly dared voice her opinion for fear of her son telling her that she would be mad to consider buying this place. Maybe she was a bit mad, but this was the first property she'd viewed to which she'd experienced an emotional connection. The funny thing was, she'd known that the windmill existed in the village of Melbury St Mary, but not once had she thought of it as somebody's home. The village was a few miles from the market town of Chelstead, which she could see in the distance on the other side of the River Stour, so it would be handy for the shops and better still she would be that much closer to where Ashley and Caro lived. The thought that this quirky mill could be her new home gave her a pleasurable thrill of excitement.

'Come on then,' she said to Angus, 'do your worst, tell me I must be out of my mind to think of living here. On my own. And at my age. And all the other reasons why I shouldn't do it.'

He slowly turned round to face her; his intelligent eyes fixed on hers, his expression thoughtful. No, not thoughtful, solemn, very solemn as though he knew he was about to prick her bubble of happiness and was seeking the kindest way to go about it. She braced herself, ready to defend her position.

'It's great,' he said, 'and certainly a novel place to live.'

'But?'

He shook his head. 'No but.'

'Are you sure? You're not going to hint that I should be considering something with fewer stairs, something a little more conventional?'

'Why would I say any of that?'

'Because ever since yesterday morning when I saw the mill on the agent's website, I've asked myself those very same questions.' She breathed in deeply. 'There comes a point in one's life when one is made to feel one has to be sensible and practical and plan for when—'

'Oh, to hell with being sensible and practical!' Angus interrupted. 'You've had years of being sensible and practical, why not go a bit crazy and have some fun, and surprise people into the bargain? If it were me, I'd buy this place in a heartbeat.'

'Thank you,' she said, giving him a hug.

'What for?'

'For not accusing me of losing the plot, and I suppose, for giving me permission.'

'Mum, you don't need permission to do something. You're allowed to do what the hell you want.'

'What a quaint notion,' she said with a smile. 'You know perfectly well that my every move and choice is now being fully monitored.'

'Not by me, but I can't speak for Arabella and Ashley.'

'Precisely. I doubt very much that Ashley will approve of what to him will seem a very harebrained scheme, buying a converted windmill. Anyway, we'd better go downstairs and find the agent.'

And therein lay another reason for Ashley to disapprove of her interest in this property, the selling agent was Barston and Bright, the one selling Charity Cottage.

They found the estate agent in the kitchen tapping away at the screen of her iPad.

'What do you think, Mrs Langford?' she asked, in an overly cheerful voice, 'can you see yourself living here? The views from the top are quite something, aren't they?'

'It's certainly the most interesting property I've seen so far,' Louisa replied, going over to the Aga which was the same colour as the one at Charity Cottage, only bigger. 'And if I'm honest, I could be tempted to take things further and make an offer. But to do that I need you to find a buyer for my house and one who is going to make a decent offer, not one that is insultingly below the asking price. If you can do that, you might be able to tie up two sales in one easy step. If I were you, I'd go back to that last couple who offered on mine and see if you can squeeze some more out of them.'

Louisa could see from the woman's steady gaze she was reassessing her. The last time they had met, Louisa had not been entirely herself, she'd still been reeling from the shock of Kip going behind her back to sell Charity Cottage. But now she was a very different woman, a woman determined to take back control of her life.

'Leave it with me,' the agent said with a brittle smile. 'Meanwhile,' she added, glancing at her iPad, 'I've just had a request from the office for a couple to view Charity Cottage later today. Would that work for you?'

'It certainly would.'

*

Louisa drove them away from Melbury Mill with a lightness of heart she hadn't felt in a long time. Even if nothing came of today's viewing, it proved to her that there was life after Kip, and life after Charity Cottage. The fact that she was able to articulate this sentiment, if only in her head, proved that she was moving in the right direction.

She would never understand what provoked her husband to do what he had, but she had decided there was no point in trying to make sense of it. All that mattered was that she didn't let his actions ruin the rest of her life. Angus had to accept the same for himself too, otherwise his future could be blighted.

'You'll have to get rid of a lot of furniture if you do buy the mill,' said Angus, beside her. He was looking at his mobile phone, checking out the property details on the agent's website.

'I will anyway, wherever I move to. There again, your father might want some of it.' She let a moment pass between them before saying, 'Have you spoken to him recently?'

'No.'

'Are you going to?'

'I don't have anything to say to him.'

'I'm sure that's not true. I would imagine you have any amount of stuff you'd like to say.'

Angus grunted. 'What good would it do if I did?'

'You won't know unless you try. But I think the sooner you get everything off your chest, the better. For you and your dad, because whatever happens, he'll always be your father.'

'I don't need anyone like that in my life. Nobody does.'

'But what if talking to him might help you to be less . . .' she hesitated.

'Less what?' he said.

'Less angry about him.'

He sighed. 'Drop it, Mum.'

'Fair enough,' she said lightly.

They were almost home when Angus's mobile buzzed. Louisa saw him look at the message and then she saw a hint of a smile touch his lips as he typed a reply.

Definitely someone special, she thought. She was happy for him. It meant that he was hopefully consigning Zoe to the past. Although if she and Kip stayed the course the girl would never be completely in the past; Zoe was very much part of the present and their future.

But would they stay the course? It was hard to imagine anything more unlikely.

Louisa wondered how it was going over in Aldeburgh.

Chapter Fifteen

The day had been an unmitigated disaster and Arabella had spent most of it rigid with impotent anger at Lexi's appalling behaviour. The worst of it was the wretched girl had seemed to enjoy every moment of the tension she had created, especially between Arabella and Giles.

Once they were home from Aldeburgh, Arabella had tried to speak to Giles on his own. 'Not now,' he'd muttered when she'd cornered him in the kitchen, which had only made her angrier still. But what with Heidi acting up because she'd slept all the way home in the car and was then refusing to go to bed, and Lexi asking her father to help with some homework she had to do during her half-term break, Arabella could do nothing other than stew in her furious resentment that her husband hadn't dealt more firmly with his daughter. Or shown Arabella the support she deserved.

But now at nearly ten o'clock, and with Heidi finally asleep and Lexi upstairs in bed, she would hold her tongue no more. From the look of Giles, as she handed him a glass of merlot, he knew it too.

'Please don't blow this out of all proportion,' he said, before she'd said anything. 'Lexi apologised to me while you were upstairs with Heidi, she knows she went too far today, but she didn't mean it.'

'Oh, Giles, how can you be so blind? She meant every vindictive and nasty word of what she said. What's more, I swear she's determined to cause trouble between us.'

'Don't talk nonsense, she's a child! This is her way of reacting to her mother going away with a new boyfriend. That's all it is.'

'Is that what she told you?'

'I didn't need her to tell me, it's perfectly obvious what's going on with her. She's angry and upset that Jen has somebody new in her life. Surely you can see that?'

'No, what I can see is that she takes pleasure in undermining me and you do nothing to back me up. How do you think I felt today being demeaned the way I was in front of everyone? And what about my father, weren't you at all ashamed that your daughter embarrassed him the way she did?'

'Of course I wasn't ashamed,' he said as though it was the stupidest thing he'd ever heard. 'I was more bothered about containing the situation rather than escalating it. If I'd told Lexi off, she would have been upset and humiliated.'

'But it was all right for me to feel upset and humiliated?'

'You're an adult and should be able to handle these things without overreacting. And to be honest, I don't see why you're suddenly so concerned about your father's feelings. You haven't given a toss about upsetting him since he left your mother.'

'Hey,' she said, 'whatever I feel about my father has nothing whatsoever to do with your daughter and if you can't see that, then I give up.'

He took a long swallow of wine, followed by another, but Arabella put her untouched glass on the worktop; she didn't think she could force a drop down her throat, which was tight with angry frustration. She couldn't believe that Giles was refusing to accept that he needed to do more when it came to Lexi and that somehow the onus was all on her to be more understanding.

Then, thinking of what he'd said about Lexi playing up because she was jealous of her mother having a new boyfriend and going off on holiday with him, an unsettling thought occurred to Arabella.

'Just as a matter of interest,' she said, 'how do you feel about Jen having a new man in her life?'

Giles looked at her with a frown. 'What's that supposed to mean?'

'It's a simple enough question, isn't it?'

He puffed his cheeks out dismissively. 'What, you're implying I'm backing my daughter because like her, I must be upset that my ex-wife is happy with somebody else?'

'I didn't say any of that.'

'Then why ask such an ludicrous question when it has no bearing on the matter?'

'Maybe it does, but you haven't processed the thought yet?'

'Really, Arabella,' he said with a sigh and then a more conciliatory tone, 'you're making so much more of this than is necessary. I know hardly anything about this man, other than his name is Luke and that Jen likes him enough to go on holiday with him.'

'Has Lexi said anything about him? I did try asking her, but she said it was none of my business.'

'She has a point.'

'Not if it affects her behaviour towards me,' Arabella said fiercely. 'Not if it ends up making me miserable because I'm somehow made to look like the wicked stepmother while you walk around with a shining golden halo over your head!'

Her voice had risen sharply in volume and afraid that her emotions would get the better of her and betray just how close she was to losing it, she turned her back on Giles. She would not cry. She would not be that pathetic! It was bad enough that she felt so inadequate that she couldn't be the perfect stepmother to Lexi. Why did it have to be so hard? And why didn't Giles appreciate the effort it took, or understand how demoralising it was to feel that no matter what she did, she was destined to fail? Marrying the man she loved wasn't meant to be like this! All she wanted was to be a good wife and a good mother. And to have another baby! Was that really too much to ask?

Feeling the gentle pressure of hands lifting her hair and then warm lips pressing against her neck, and just where Giles knew it would have the most effect, her body went limp and from nowhere a torrent of molten-hot desire flooded through her. He turned her around so that she was facing him and met her lips with his own.

'I'm sorry,' he said, 'please don't be upset. As I've said before, it's just a phase she's going through. It's challenging, I know, but you have to remember she's just a child.'

'I do understand that,' she said. 'It's just so exhausting. I hate the way it reduces me to being a failure.'

'That's not true. You're a wonderful mother to Heidi. The absolute best. But what you need to bear in mind is that whatever you feel for Heidi, I feel exactly the same for Lexi. She means the world to me, so that inevitably means I'll defend her even when I know that she's on shaky ground. Wouldn't you be the same with Heidi?'

'Yes,' she said, wanting him to kiss her again. Wanting the physical craving for and the satisfaction of his body to wipe away the conflict of the day and her shattered emotions. Pressing herself against him, she could feel that he felt the same way too.

It was only later, after they'd had frantic, fast sex right there in the kitchen, paying no heed to the risk of Lexi or Heidi walking in on them, that Arabella thought of the way Giles had spoken about his daughter.

'. . . *whatever you feel for Heidi, I feel exactly the same for Lexi.*'
Shouldn't he have said, '*Whatever* we *feel for Heidi*'?

Chapter Sixteen

'I'm sorry,' Zoe said. 'I ruined the weekend for us, didn't I?'

'I told you before, it wasn't you,' said Kip, his hand squeezing hers as they trudged along the shingle on the beach. 'It was Lexi. She was hellbent on causing trouble and it was not so much for our benefit, but for Arabella's.'

They had covered the topic of yesterday's disastrous lunch many times over already, and no matter what Kip said, Zoe still blamed herself. She had been so sure that she could pull it off, that she could gather his family together for an enjoyable meal in a relaxed setting, and on neutral ground, and it would pave the way towards accepting the new life Kip wanted for himself. If they loved him, she'd thought, surely they could accept that? But all her careful planning had backfired. And all because of that devious little brat, Lexi.

If only the girl hadn't come, things might have gone a lot better. Yes, there would have been awkwardness, even a few jibes made, nothing though that couldn't have been diffused, but Lexi had been a toxic presence amongst them. The worst moment was when Lexi, probably bored with not being the centre of attention, and refusing to eat anything other than the apple which Zoe had produced for her, had asked if Kip and Zoe planned to marry. In the deathly hush that followed, coupled with the look of total horror on Ashley's face and a choking noise from Arabella, Kip's knee had jiggled next to hers beneath the table. Zoe had rested her hand on his leg to still him. 'No, Lexi,' she'd said, 'of course we don't plan to marry, we're quite happy as we are. Isn't that right, Kip?'

'Absolutely,' he'd said, putting his arm around her shoulders and smiling almost as grimly as she was.

Now, and deciding she could no longer ignore whatever it was that had worked its way into her shoe, Zoe suggested they sit down so she could deal with it.

As she slipped off her trainer and found the offending stone that was no bigger than a grain of rice, she reflected on how often in life that happened, the silliest or least significant of things could irritate or spoil something.

Observing Kip as he stared out at the depressingly grey sky which in turn made the sea look just as depressingly grey, she wondered what he was thinking. He looked so serious, so lost in thought. Had yesterday been too much of a reality check for him? Had the awkwardness between him and his children caused him to regret the path he'd chosen?

As though suddenly aware that she was looking at him, he turned his head.

'You okay?' she murmured, hooking her hand through the crook of his elbow.

'I'm fine,' he said.

'It's just that you looked so thoughtful.'

'I was thinking about something you said yesterday. Are you very against the idea of us marrying?'

Surprised at the question, she frowned. 'I don't think that was what I did actually say.'

'But you implied it. So are you against it?'

He was looking at her in a strange way and she was suddenly wary of giving the wrong answer. 'Is this a proposal?' she said with a light-hearted laugh.

'Would it be unwelcome, if it was?'

'I would have thought that you of all people would be the last person to be talking about marriage.'

'Because I'm still married?'

'Well, there is that.'

'And when I'm divorced, how would you feel then about marriage? To me specifically, in case you need clarification.'

'I think that's a conversation for another time,' she said, unhooking her arm from his and picking up a smooth white stone from in front of her.

'I'll take that as a no, then,' he said flatly.

She hurled the stone towards the sea. It fell well short of the target. 'What's brought this on, Kip?' she asked.

It was a few seconds before he spoke. 'It was the look on Ashley's face when Lexi raised the subject. He looked as though it was the most disgusting thing he'd ever heard.'

'And you want to prove to him how wrong he is, is that it?'

'Would it be very shallow of me to say yes?' Kip answered, his eyes fixed on hers again and his mouth curving into a slow wide and very sexy smile that was slightly turned up at one end. It had the inexplicable effect, just as it had many times before, of making her heart clench with love for him.

No other man had ever had the same effect on her, that with one look, or one small smile, her emotions could feel so exposed. It was what love did to you, she now understood: it could both empower you yet at the same time make you hopelessly vulnerable. Loving someone meant that you had to live with the constant fear of losing them and as never before, Zoe felt that now with Kip. In a crazily short space of time, this wonderfully extraordinary man had become her world, and she would do everything she could not to lose him.

'About as shallow as it gets,' she said softly. 'But I still love you.'

His smile widened further still, and her heart clenched some more. 'I'm a lucky man,' he said.

'I keep telling you that,' she said with a smile, relieved that whatever had just passed between them had been dealt with. 'And now,' she said, springing to her feet, 'what I want more than anything in the whole world is a Mr Whippy double 99 with extra sprinkles.'

Laughing, he hauled himself to his feet and holding hands, they made their way along the shingly beach, back towards the centre of Aldeburgh. But with every step they took, Zoe queried her reaction to Kip's question about marriage. Why had it caused her to react the way she had when she loved him as profoundly as she did? Was it because he had raised the matter for all the wrong reasons?

She would have to watch that, that he didn't succumb to the need to prove to his family how much he loved her. As far as she was concerned, she already had all the proof she needed.

Chapter Seventeen

It was now the end of July and Ashley still couldn't believe that his mother was going through with buying Melbury Mill.

He had hoped the moment of madness would pass, that common sense would prevail, and she'd realise that it was far from practical, but it hadn't, and with Charity Cottage now sold subject to contract, it was, to quote Mum, all systems go. A surveyor was due to make a detailed inspection of the mill this week and Ashley hoped that the report would flag up so many problems it would set the alarm bells ringing and his mother would back out of the purchase.

It still rankled with him that his brother had known about the mill from day one and hadn't seen fit to share it with him and Arabella straight away. Mum had only come clean a few weeks ago when she and Dad had accepted a realistic offer on Charity Cottage and in turn, she had made an offer on the mill.

'I asked Angus to keep quiet about it until it was more definite,' she had explained to Ashley, 'so don't go blaming him for something I asked him to do.'

'But why did you keep us in the dark?'

'Because I knew you wouldn't approve and would try to dissuade me from taking it any further.'

And with good reason, Ashley had thought. But he'd refrained from saying what he'd wanted to in the hope that Mum would realise for herself that it simply wasn't practical what she'd apparently set her heart on.

'You're frowning and gritting your teeth again,' Caro said.

Looking up from his laptop and over to where his wife was pushing Peggy on the garden swing, Ashley forced his facial muscles to relax. In the last few weeks Caro frequently complained that he was waking her in the night with the noise of him grinding his teeth. He blamed his father entirely for that, and as futile as the hope now seemed, he still wanted him to realise the folly of what he was doing and ask Mum to forgive him.

He'd said as much to his mother, and she'd sighed wearily. 'Darling,' she'd said, 'even if he did change his mind about Zoe, I couldn't take him back, not after what he's done. How could I ever trust him again?'

For some reason that had saddened Ashley immensely, that after so many years of his parents being together their marriage could end so easily.

'I really should have installed a worry jar,' Caro said, as he shut his laptop and went to join her and Peggy. 'If I'd made you put a pound in it for every time you frowned, I'd be clad from head to toe in Prada and Armani.'

'And very beautiful you'd look too,' he said as Peggy raised her arms and demanded to be lifted out of the swing seat. 'No question about it,' he said, following the forthright instruction, 'our daughter takes after you, direct and to the point at all times.'

Caro smiled, 'It will stand her in good stead.' Then as Peggy went running across the lawn to play in the sandpit, she called after to her: 'Five minutes and then its bath-time, little missy.'

'No bath!' Peggy responded, shaking her head vigorously and stamping her foot. 'No bath!'

'Which one of us is going to have that tussle this evening?' asked Caro.

'I'll do it,' said Ashley. This was a recent thing, Peggy deciding for no real reason that the bath was a place of great torment and to be avoided at all costs.

'Don't you have work to do?' said Caro. 'That's what you were doing at the table, after all.'

'It was only emails; they can wait.'

'So what were you frowning about this time?'

'The same as before, Mum buying that ridiculous windmill.'

'But can't you see how happy it's making her, the idea of living somewhere so different?'

'All I can see is the recklessness of the enterprise. She won't have any neighbours on the doorstep as she currently has, and she'll have to use the car if she needs anything from the shops.'

'There'll be a handful of neighbours a short walk away and she has to drive to the shops as it is, and there's always online shopping, so what's the big deal?'

He sighed. 'You know what the big deal is. She should be thinking more about the future and living in something that's more, well, you know.'

'Age appropriate?' Caro said with a raised eyebrow. 'A nice little retirement home, is that what you'd have her live in?'

'Now you're being silly. I know Mum's not old, but give it a few more years, and being on her own, who knows how things will be for her? I just want to know that she's going to be okay.'

'Of course you do, we all do, but who's to say she'll remain on her own? She might meet somebody, maybe even remarry?'

He groaned. 'I can't even begin to consider that.'

'Well, you should. Also, your mother might enjoy living in the mill for a year or two and then move again. Why not let her indulge this need of hers to do something out of character? She's been pigeonholed as wife and mother all these years, now she's going to stretch her wings and be a different person, if only to try it on for size. I would imagine that's precisely what your father is doing.'

'But I don't want her, or Dad for that matter, to be different people, which I know makes me sound selfish and pathetic.'

'It makes you sound like a son who cares very much about his mother, so not selfish or pathetic at all. But try thinking of it this way: Louisa let you fly the nest when the time came, now it's your turn to do the same for her. It really is what a good son should do.'

He smiled. 'All right, you've laid it on thick enough for me to get the message.'

'Good. Now I have something else to tell you.'

'Go on,' he said guardedly.

'You know we're going to the village quiz night tomorrow evening?'

'Yes.'

'Well, I've invited your father and Zoe to join us.'

He tightened his jaw and clamped his teeth together. But then checking himself, he relaxed his jaw. 'How did that come about?' he said.

'I texted Kip this morning. No, don't look like that, Ashley, he's your father and I decided it was time we reached out to him. And it'll be fun. You remember what fun is, don't you?'

'I believe that was what our day over in Aldeburgh back in May was supposed to be, a fun family day, and look how that worked out.'

'Yes, but then we had Lexi stirring the pot.' She gave him a wry smile and kissed his cheek. 'Now why don't you bath your daughter while I make a start on supper?'

He'd just turned to go and give Peggy the bad news when his mobile rang on the table where he'd left it with his laptop.

It was his sister. 'Hi Arabella,' he said, 'how's tricks?'

'A bit tricksy if I'm honest. Any chance I can see you tomorrow, maybe during your lunch break?'

'What's wrong?'

'I'll tell you tomorrow. Shall I come to your office in Chelstead?'

'No, I have two appointments in Lavenham with half an hour between them around midday, can you meet me there at twelve-thirty for a coffee?'

'Yes.'

'And can you at least put my mind at rest that it's nothing serious?'

'It's . . . it's nothing serious,' she said.

He knew his sister too well for her to hide the anxiety in her voice, but he didn't push it.

Chapter Eighteen

'Are you absolutely certain?'

'Thanks for doubting me.'

Ashley frowned. 'You know what I mean, is there any chance you might just be a bit late?'

'I'm one hundred per cent certain,' Arabella asserted, after taking a sip of her green tea. 'I did a test two days ago, followed by another yesterday morning. Not that I needed to, I know my body and am hypersensitive to any changes.'

'Okay then, but are you sure Giles is going to react in the way you think he will?'

Before answering her brother, Arabella waited for a noisy motorbike to pass where they were sitting at a table on the pavement outside Tatum's Teahouse in Lavenham. 'Giles has always made it very clear that he didn't want any more children,' she said. 'Only last month he started talking about making an appointment to have a vasectomy, that's how against having another child he is, and the worst of it is, I know he's going to accuse me of deliberately getting pregnant because he knows how much I wanted another baby.'

Ashley looked at her over the rim of his raised coffee cup. 'And did you?' he asked quietly.

She wanted to scream '*No, of course not! How could you ask such a thing?*' But this was her brother asking the question, her twin brother. She couldn't lie to him. 'I . . . I might have done,' she murmured guiltily.

'Okay,' he said slowly, 'in that case I can see why you might feel anxious about Giles's reaction. Is this something you'd been planning for a while?'

'Yes,' she admitted. 'And I'm not going to tell him the truth if that's what you're thinking. That's never going to happen. Not ever.'

'So, you'll lie to him?' Ashley said with a frown.

'I'll have to, and please don't judge me, anything but that.'

'I'm not judging you.'

She tutted, seeing him trying hard to keep his expression neutral and failing; shock and disappointment was written all over his face. 'Remember, I can always tell when you're lying.'

He smiled faintly. 'Yeah,' he said, 'my ugly mug always gives me away. But I'm not so much judging as wondering how you'll cope with lying to Giles and living with the consequences. What do you plan to tell him?'

Arabella thought back to when she was pretty sure conception had taken place. It was the evening they'd returned from Aldeburgh and after Lexi had been such a pain. 'I'm going to say that I forgot to take my contraceptive pill that Bank Holiday weekend because I'd been so wound up by Lexi's awful behaviour when she'd been staying with us.'

Ashley's eyes widened. 'You're going to blame his daughter? Do you think that's wise?'

'Look, I'm not going to blame her outright, I'm not that stupid, but come on, her exasperating presence that week might well have genuinely made me forget. She was a contributing factor, you could say.'

'I hate to say it, but while in your head that probably sounds perfectly reasonable, I doubt Giles will see it that way.'

'He'll have to accept it because that's my story and I'm sticking to it. And if he's going to accuse me of not being responsible enough to take the pill when I should have, I'll say he should have been the one to take care of that side of things.'

'But he trusted you to do it, Bells.'

Hearing her brother use the old nickname that he and he alone called her brought her up short. He rarely used the name, and only ever when he was concerned about her. 'I know that,' she said, 'and I know too that I've acted selfishly, but isn't the same true of Giles, that by denying me the chance to have another child, he was being even more selfish?'

'There is some truth in that, but I'd say that line of argument will be a hard sell.'

'Not to me it isn't,' she said resolutely, thinking that Giles's recent behaviour had made her feel she was wholly justified in her deviousness.

Things had been distinctly tense between them lately, caused once more by Lexi. Not directly, but she was definitely part of the problem in that she had been staying with them again as it was the school holidays. When her visit was over Giles had taken her back to Ely to her mother and for some reason he had stayed there for ages instead of driving home straight away as he usually did. His ex-wife had apparently offered him supper and he'd felt it rude to say no, especially as Jen was feeling down after just splitting up with her boyfriend. Anxious that he hadn't come home, and it was getting late, Arabella had texted Giles several times to ask where he was and if he was okay. He hadn't responded to any of her messages. By the time she'd heard his car pull onto the drive just after eleven o'clock and having imagined any number of dreadful scenarios as to why he hadn't replied to her, her relief that he was all right was superseded by the need to let rip. 'You've spent more time talking with your bloody ex-wife than you have with me this weekend!' she'd blasted at him.

He'd accused her of being irrational and told her to calm down or she'd risk waking Heidi. His patronising tone had made her angrier still and she'd told him he could sleep in the spare room. Breakfast the next morning had been a tetchy affair with them both doing their best to appear normal in front of Heidi. When he'd returned from work that evening, he presented her with a bunch of flowers and an apology. Which in turn extracted an apology from her.

But before the flowers were even dead another row had blown up between them after Giles had spent the best part of an evening talking on FaceTime with Lexi and his ex-wife. 'Perish the thought you'd spend time chatting with me,' she'd muttered when he'd put down his mobile.

'And perish the thought you'd ever show any consideration for my ex-wife who's going through a tough time.'

'She sounded all right from what I could hear.'

'She was putting on a brave face for Lexi's sake.'

From there it quickly spiralled into Arabella questioning why he was always so quick to defend and support Jen when he could never do the same for her.

'When are you going to tell Giles?' Ashley asked, breaking into her thoughts. 'Because you can only hide your pregnancy for so long. Better surely to bite the bullet and get it over with, and who knows, maybe he'll surprise you and himself, and will be delighted with the news.'

She shook her head. 'I really can't see that happening. Not when . . . ' she hesitated before going on, but acknowledging there was no point in not being completely honest with her brother, it was why she had asked to meet him in the first place. 'Ashley,' she said, 'if I tell you something, will you promise to keep it to yourself? No telling Caro, not like you did before about Giles and—'

He raised a hand to stop her. 'Just tell me. I don't have long before I have to go.'

'Not until you've promised you won't tell Caro about any of this conversation. I mean *any* of it.'

'Okay, I promise, and if I could hold back time, I would,' he said, pushing at his suit jacket sleeve to look at his watch.

'Hey, no need to sound so snappy with me, I get enough of that at home.'

The expression on his face instantly changed and drawing his brows together, he gave her a pained and very searching look.

So she told him how awful it had been with Giles these last few weeks: the rows and angry accusations.

'Is it serious, the problems you're having?' he asked when she finished.

'I don't know, it feels bad, so maybe it is serious. Or maybe I'm making it worse than it really is.'

'What's your main concern?'

Arabella chewed on her lip and took a breath. 'I'm scared he might be having second thoughts about his ex-wife, that he could be rekindling things with her.'

'No,' Ashley said adamantly. 'You're wrong, he loves you, and he loves Heidi. He's not going to do anything to spoil that.'

'But he already is. He keeps putting Lexi and Jen before Heidi and me.'

'No, I think that's your take on it right now. Don't be cross with me, but have you thought that being pregnant might be doing all sorts of crazy stuff to your hormones and that could be affecting your judgement?'

'I'll take that from you, but not from anybody else.'

'And?'

'And what?'

'Do you think you could be suffering from a hormonal overload? I know Caro went a little—' He paused, then continued, 'Let's just say she wasn't herself for much of the pregnancy, and immediately after Peggy was born she was less than her customary logical self.'

116

Arabella knew that her brother was understating what his wife had gone through. In private he had admitted to Arabella that Caro had a touch of the dreaded 'baby blues' but there was nothing to worry about. It was a confidence Arabella kept, but Mum had guessed there was something more serious going on. Any approach she made to try and help though was firmly turned down by Caro.

In contrast, Arabella had grabbed with both hands any help that was offered when she'd had Heidi and thankfully she hadn't encountered any problems. Her pregnancy had also been plain sailing all the way and compared to Caro, who had spent an inordinate amount of time reading up on the perils and pitfalls of pregnancy and motherhood, Arabella had done the bare minimum. Once or twice Giles had questioned if she thought she was fully prepared, and thinking about that now, she wondered if he had been comparing her to his ex-wife. Had Jen studied everything there was to know on the subject like Caro had?

No, she told herself, no comparing herself to Giles's ex-wife! It was bad enough that she frequently compared herself to Caro, and found herself wanting, but to do the same with her husband's first wife had to be the path to total madness.

'Anybody there?'

Once more Ashley's voice broke into her thoughts. 'Sorry,' she said, 'I went down a rabbit hole there for a minute.'

'While you climb back out of that hole, I'm going to have to love you and leave you, I'm due at my next appointment in ten minutes.' He was rummaging in the inside pocket of his suit jacket for his wallet to pay for their drinks.

'Put your wallet away,' she said. 'I'll pay. But before you race off, I have a question for you. Are you and Caro going to have another child?'

'No,' he said simply.

'Is that a joint decision?'

'Of course it is.' He was on his feet now, ready to go. 'I wouldn't want Caro to go through again what she experienced after Peggy was born,' he added.

He leaned in to kiss Arabella's cheek. 'Tell Giles about the baby and then get on with celebrating your good news. After all, having another baby was what you wanted, wasn't it?'

Arabella left soon after Ashley and after calling in at the chemist, she crossed over the road to go to the children's clothes shop to see if there was anything nice for Heidi. There was, and there was also a cute sleep suit for a newborn baby. She bought both items, reminding herself of what Ashley had said, that she must celebrate the fact that she was having another baby, and that it really was just what she wanted. Somehow, she would win Giles round, and everything would be all right again.

She had just reversed out of the space where she'd parked the car when her mobile rang. It was her mother. 'Hi Mum,' she said, 'everything okay?'

'Yes, we've been having a lovely time playing in the garden. Heidi's had her lunch and is now down for her nap.'

'Thank you for having her, especially as it was such short notice. I know how busy you are.'

'Nonsense, I'm never too busy to look after my two grandchildren.'

Make that three, thought Arabella with a smile. 'I'll be with you in about twenty-five minutes.'

'There's no hurry. But there's something I just wanted to run by you, you can think about it while you're driving here.'

Alarmed at what her mother might be about to say, Arabella held her breath. Ever since Mum had announced that she was buying a converted windmill to live in and had then taken them all to see it, Arabella and Ashley had had a collective sense of *Uh-oh, what next*?

'How do you feel about a family holiday?' her mother asked. 'Any chance you're free the first week in September?'

'Wow, this is all a bit sudden, isn't it?'

'It's called spontaneity, something I'm very keen to foster. So what do you think? It could be fun, us all going away together, like the old days, but in a different way, obviously.'

'Where are you thinking?'

'I'll tell you when you're here.'

Chapter Nineteen

'I know what she's doing,' said Kip, bending down to tie the laces of his deck shoes. 'She's trying to recreate the past when we all went on family holidays together.'

Looking at him in the reflection of the mirror where she was brushing her hair, Zoe frowned. 'What does it matter if that's what she's doing?'

'Because it's her way of getting back at me, of alienating me further from the family.'

'I think you're overreacting. We both know she loves nothing better than to have everyone around her so she can fuss over them. Arranging a holiday just means she can go all out with her Queen Bee compulsion.'

Feeling as though he were being rebuked, but at the same time perversely annoyed at the criticism Zoe had just levelled at Louisa, Kip tugged sharply on one of the shoelaces only for it to snap. *'Shit!'* he muttered under his breath.

With nothing else for it, he changed his shoes and braced himself for the evening ahead, hoping that an evening with Ashley and Caro was not going to turn into a disagreeable session of attack and defend. He was tired of justifying himself. Or more precisely, he was tired of being constantly on the back foot as though he still had to convince his family that he knew what he was doing. He'd never been surer about a thing when he'd fallen in love with Zoe and walked away from his marriage, but that had been the easy part; everything since had been an uphill struggle. Had he been naïve to imagine it would be otherwise?

And was Zoe's comment about Louisa having a Queen Bee compulsion justified? He'd never thought of his wife in that way before, but did Zoe have a point? Better to believe that, he thought, than to become paranoid that Louisa was trying to alienate him from their children. Besides, she'd never been nasty or vindictive, it simply wasn't in her nature. But then who knew how a person would behave when seriously tested? Look how cold and severe she'd been towards him that day in the kitchen at Charity Cottage when he'd discovered she'd changed the locks. That had clearly been a vengeful act on her behalf, a way to prove a point with him.

As for this madcap scheme of hers to live in a windmill, what on earth had possessed her? He'd been genuinely lost for words when she'd told him about it on the telephone. They'd just agreed to accept the offer made on Charity Cottage and curious to know what her plans were, he'd asked if she had found somewhere new to live.

'I thought that would surprise you,' she'd said when she'd told him about Melbury Mill.

'It certainly has,' he'd said.

The satisfied tone in her voice had stayed with him for several days afterwards.

Zoe offered to drive them to Ashley and Caro's so he could enjoy a drink at the pub where the quiz was taking place.

They had only been in the car a short time when Kip realised that Zoe wasn't her usual self. She was quieter than normal, and seemingly preoccupied. Was she anxious about spending the evening with Ashley and Caro?

Or was he to blame? Had he annoyed her with his earlier crankiness after ringing his daughter for what had been yet another stilted attempt at conversation, only to learn that Louisa was in the process of rounding them all up for a family holiday? He'd felt peevishly out of sorts, knowing that traditionally this had always been something that he planned. He was the one, after all, who ran a holiday company!

If Zoe was annoyed by his poor mood, he needed to sort himself out. He mustn't allow anything so trivial to spoil their happiness. It was what he'd vowed when he'd moved in with her, that no matter the challenges they faced, nothing would harm the strength of their love for each other.

But it wasn't just that Zoe was quieter than usual that bothered him, there had also been that uncharacteristically sharp Queen Bee comment she'd made about Louisa. He couldn't recall another time when Zoe had been remotely rude about his wife.

He decided rather than avoid the issue, he should tackle it. 'Everything all right, Zoe?' he enquired.

She flicked him a sidelong glance. 'Yes,' she said, 'why do you ask?'

'No special reason, other than you seem as though you have something on your mind. Are you worried about being with Caro and Ashley this evening? I wouldn't blame you if you were.'

'I'm fine,' she said lightly. 'Caro's okay, more than okay; I like her. She doesn't judge me. Or us for that matter.'

'And Ashley, how do you feel about him?'

Her gaze flicked briefly again to meet his. 'I'm getting there, but it's hard knowing that he'd sooner I didn't exist and that you were still with your wife.'

'He just needs time.'

'It's been seven months, Kip, how much time does he need?'

It was a good question and one he couldn't answer and as Zoe kept her eyes on the road ahead and fell quiet again, he had the nagging feeling that whatever was troubling her had nothing to do with this evening. It was something else. But he let it go, concerned that if he dug too deep, he might hear something he didn't want to hear, like she was having second thoughts about their being together.

The one person who was most definitely her customary self was his granddaughter, Peggy. She had been allowed to stay up to say hello before being left with the babysitter and the grown-ups going off for their 'fun evening', as Ashley kept referring to their night out at the village pub.

But before they could go, Peggy was eager to show off her vast collection of plushies to Zoe. Children were always so much better at accepting change than adults, and Kip was grateful for the little girl's readiness to accommodate Zoe as his other half. An expression he wouldn't dream of using in front of Zoe. He knew better than that. She was a person in her own right, not an appendage to him, as she herself would be quick to point out. He and Louisa had always seen themselves as two halves that made a whole. Though it would be true to say that he had seen himself as the driving force, the one who made the big decisions. That wasn't how it was in his relationship with Zoe. If anything, he deferred to her because he wanted to be sure that she had no doubts about the rightness of their relationship.

With Louisa, he had enjoyed the luxury of never doubting her love for him. He knew that sounded arrogant, but it had only struck him recently that this was the case because everything with Zoe was so different. In contrast he had less certainty with Zoe and felt he had to earn her love. He understood now that longevity and familiarity had made him complacent with Louisa, but with Zoe he must never be anything but constantly on his toes. On the one hand it excited him, but it also made him vulnerable and that was a phenomenon that was new to him.

It had been a stupid mistake on his part when they'd been in Aldeburgh and he'd asked what she thought of them marrying;

he'd been in too much of a hurry to move things along. That had been a typical trait of the old Kip, wanting to control a situation and bend it to his will. The new Kip had to learn to take a step back and allow Zoe to dictate the pace. But he couldn't ignore how disappointed he'd felt at her reply. He wasn't used to being thwarted.

Quiz night at the Cap and Feather was a popular event and whoever had set the questions had been determined to test them to the full. Kip held his own when it came to geography and world affairs, but anything to do with popular culture in the last twenty years he left to the others. The picture round of so-called celebrities was their undoing; they'd only managed to get one right out of ten.

'That's the worst we've ever done,' declared Caro when the points had been totted up and they found they'd come equal fifth with the group around the table nearest them.

'Better not invite us again,' Kip joked, 'we've clearly bought you bad luck.'

'Nonsense,' said Caro. 'It's been fun, hasn't it, Ashley?'

'Yes,' he said, but not really sounding like he meant it as he drank from his beer glass.

'It was kind of you to invite us,' said Zoe.

'Yes,' agreed Kip, 'it was a kind thought and one we both appreciate. By the way, I spoke to Arabella earlier and she told me the latest news.'

'What news?' queried Ashley, his expression suddenly alert.

'That your mum is planning a holiday with you all.'

'Oh, that,' said Ashley.

'Going somewhere nice?'

'They'd hardly be going somewhere horrible,' said Zoe with a smile.

Kip laughed. 'Of course not. So where are you off to?'

'Nothing's planned as yet,' said Ashley. 'We're still at the stage of deciding on a week when we're all free.'

'That was one of the reasons we gave up on family holidays,' said Kip. 'It became impossible for everyone to agree on a mutual date to go away together.'

'Given the circumstances, I think we'll make the extra effort for Mum and nail down a date without too much of a problem.'

Ouch, thought Kip, but then he probably deserved that low blow from Ashley. He should have left well alone, but his pride and curiosity had got the better of him. It was irrational, but he regretted that he hadn't taken the initiative himself and proposed a family holiday. Although after the spectacular failure of Aldeburgh, who in their right mind would want to risk a repeat of that? He took another long and determined swallow of his drink. Was this how it was always going to be, him on the outside looking in, and his children punishing him for what they saw as his betrayal?

'You know what would be nice,' he said, forcing himself to sound upbeat, 'is if you'd come for dinner with us one evening.' Too late he realised that it wasn't his place to extend the invitation; it was Zoe's, since it was her house where they lived. He shot her an anxious glance and to his relief she echoed his suggestion.

'Yes,' she said, 'we'd love to have you over. Kip can do the honours and cook.'

At that Ashley let out a laugh. 'You, Dad?'

'Hey, don't mock, I'm on a steep learning curve, Zoe's giving me a complete overhaul, turning me into a thoroughly modern domestic man.'

'Only because I hate cooking and one of us has to do it and I don't see why it should be me.'

'Bravo to the pair of you,' said Caro. 'I shall expect great things from you, Kip.'

'No promises on the quality of what I cook, but I'll do my best not to let the side down.'

*

'Well, that went better than I thought it would,' he remarked when Zoe was driving them home. 'I really believe we're getting there now.'

'Maybe,' she murmured.

Once again Kip was struck by what appeared to be a change in Zoe's manner. In front of Caro and Ashley she had seemed more like her usual self, but now they were alone once more, she seemed preoccupied again.

'I hate to be a bore and repeat something I said earlier, but is everything all right, Zoe?' he asked.

In the semi-darkness of the car, he saw her purse her lips. 'I'll tell you when we're home,' she said.

'Can't you tell me now?'

'No,' she said with a firmness that brooked no argument.

If he'd been concerned before, now he was consumed with the very worst fear that Zoe was going to finish with him. His instinct was to push until Zoe put him out of his misery. *Just get it over with*, he wanted to say. But he didn't and it took all of his willpower to remain quiet until she pulled up outside her cottage.

As soon as they were through the front door, she said, 'I think you're going to need a stiff drink for what I'm about to tell you.' Without waiting for a response, she led the way to the small kitchen, switching on lights as they went. She opened the cupboard where she kept a selection of spirits and, taking out a bottle of whisky, she poured a generous amount into a tumbler and handed it to him.

'Take a sip,' she instructed.

'I'd sooner wait until you've—'

'No,' she interrupted, 'take a sip. A large one. You're going to need it.'

'Aren't you having one?'

She shook her head. 'Go on, drink it.'

Stubbornly, he refused. 'If you're about to tell me it's over between us, a glass of whisky is hardly going to soften the blow.'

126

'That's not what I'm going to say,' she said. 'The thing is, I'm pregnant.'

He stared at her, shocked. This had been the furthest thing from his mind. He tried to say what he imagined she would want him to say, but the power of speech was failing him. What the hell could he say? The longer he grappled for the right words, the more she would know the truth of his feelings, that a baby was the last thing he wanted at the age he was. Finally, he said, 'Are you sure?'

'Yes. I can see from the look on your face that you're as shocked as I was when I did the test.'

Putting the untouched glass of whisky on the countertop behind him, he said, 'How do you feel about a baby?'

She swallowed. 'I don't know. How do you feel?'

Careful, he warned himself, all too aware of the lethal minefield with which he was suddenly confronted. Surely, she had to know how he felt, that he was appalled at the prospect of going through all that again – the sleepless nights, the enormous responsibility, the rigour of a life thoroughly upended by a small human being that had the power to force the world to revolve around it. Yes, he was being utterly selfish, but who wouldn't be in his shoes? Being a grandfather was fine, he could lavish love and attention on Heidi and Peggy and then walk away. But fatherhood all over again, no, it was unthinkable.

'Judging from that silence, I assume the thought of a baby horrifies you.'

'No,' he lied. 'It's . . . it's just that we're still . . . '

'In the early stages of our relationship,' she finished for him. 'I get it. I really do.'

'How long have you known?'

'I did the test three days ago.'

'Why didn't you say anything before now?'

'Does it make any difference?'

'No. Yes! Of course it does, we're in this together.'

'No,' she said. '*We* are not in this together. This is *my* decision.'

'What do you mean?'

'I haven't made up my mind what I'm going to do.'

'Whether to keep it or not? Is that what you mean?'

'Yes,' she said simply. 'I won't be persuaded either way. I need to know that you understand that and that you'll respect whatever my decision is.'

Now he did reach for the glass and downed the whisky in one.

Chapter Twenty

When Angus pulled onto the drive of Charity Cottage that warm Friday evening in the middle of August, there was a Model S Tesla parked alongside his mother's car. He wondered if it belonged to the people who were buying the house. Mum had mentioned on the phone last night that they might be calling in today to take some measurements. Apparently, they were cash buyers and were pushing to exchange contracts as soon as possible, and as luck would have it, the owner of Melbury Mill had already moved out and so there was no long chain involved. From what Mum said, the conveyancing solicitors were confident they'd have things buttoned up by the end of September, if not sooner. Which had stymied Mum's plans for them all to go on holiday together. Fortunately, they hadn't got as far as booking anything, so no money had been lost.

'They're a lovely couple,' Mum had said of the couple buying Charity Cottage, 'and I'm so glad they're the ones who will be living here; they have grandchildren who will love exploring the garden. I'd have hated it if it had been people I didn't like buying our house and who I thought wouldn't look after it.'

Which was such a typical Mum comment. What did it matter if the new people living at Charity Cottage were nice or not? It wasn't as if they were going to be her new best friends.

But that appeared to be the very scenario Angus walked into

when he carried his overnight bag round to the back of the house and found what looked like a drinks party in full swing in the garden.

'Angus, you're early!' his mother greeted him and with what looked like a large glass jug of Pimm's in her hands. Around the table were seated two people he didn't recognise, presumably the buyers, along with the Wallaces and the Paulsons who lived either side of Charity Cottage. Everyone smiled at him.

'Come and say hello to the Cartwrights, who will be the new owners,' Mum said. 'This is Rosalyn and this is Dominic.'

'And Louisa thought we should meet our new neighbours,' added Delia Wallace, as though needing to clarify why they were there too.

Going over to say hello, Angus then indicated the house. 'I'll just go and ditch my bag and come back out to join you.'

'Yes, do,' said his mother who was now passing round a dish of nuts, crisps and olives, ever the genial host. 'There's beer in the fridge if you'd rather have that,' she added.

Upstairs in his old bedroom and where he had been intermittently staying while working on the project in Cambridge, Angus swapped his work clothes for jeans and a T-shirt. He stood at the window and looked down onto the garden and thought that only Mum could turn what started out as her worst nightmare, being forced to sell Charity Cottage, into something upbeat and fun.

The party came to an end shortly after he'd joined the group, and then once they were alone he and his mother sat down at the table in the garden with a Chinese takeaway he'd just been to fetch.

'You did like the Cartwrights, didn't you?' she asked him.

'They seemed perfectly fine,' he said, amused that she thought it was so important he should approve of the new owners for Charity Cottage.

'I thought it would be a good idea to introduce them to a few neighbours, you know, to help them to fit in with village life here.'

'I bet they're already thinking that you'll be a hard act to follow.'

'What a strange thing to say.'

'Not at all. You'll be much missed. Over the years you've made your mark here in a very positive way.' Time was Angus would have said the same of his father, but now his father had made his mark in a very different way; now he was the adulterous husband who traded in his wife for his son's ex-girlfriend.

As though reading his mind, his mother said, 'I know you hate me asking this question every time I see you, but have you spoken to your father yet?'

She was right, it did irritate him, mostly because he knew he could never give her the answer she wanted. But on this occasion, he could. 'I have actually,' he said.

Her face brightened. 'Really?'

'But it doesn't mean we've swept everything under the proverbial rug and kissed and made up while playing a round of Happy Dysfunctional Families.'

His mother tutted. 'You shouldn't be so cynical, Angus.'

'Why,' he said with a laugh, 'will the wind change, and I'll be stuck this way for ever, just as you used to say when I was a child, and I pulled a face?'

'If it becomes a habit that you can't shake off, then yes. Was it a productive conversation you had with him?'

Angus thought back to the awkward conversation which he had unwillingly instigated on the phone. 'Hard to say,' he replied. 'He sounded odd. Certainly not like a man who was living the dream.'

'Understandable perhaps,' she said with a small shrug, 'because as much as he's wanted to clear the air with you, he's probably still hugely embarrassed.'

Angus shook his head. 'He didn't sound embarrassed, more, kind of . . . deflated. Yes, that's what it was, he was deflated. Whereas the last time I spoke to him, back in January, he'd sounded defiant and quite able to justify what he'd done.'

'Do you suppose that things aren't going as well as they once were? Is there trouble in paradise, do you think?'

Angus laughed. 'Is that wishful thinking on your part, Mum?' he asked. 'Hoping that a nasty bolt of reality has finally kicked in?'

'Would you think badly of me if it was?'

'Not a bit. I think you've been unbelievably magnanimous. Most wives would have wanted to wreak havoc and revenge. I know I did on your behalf.'

'In my head I wanted to a million times over, but, oh, I don't know, I thought it better to try and hang on to what little dignity I still had.'

'You always told us to be the bigger person whenever we got into fights as children. I could never really manage it; I wanted to be the victor, which didn't necessarily mean that would be the bigger person.'

'Is that why you wouldn't speak to your father?'

'I suppose so, but it went deeper than that. I think I'd convinced myself that by refusing to speak to him I was hurting him in the only way I could. It was the one form of revenge I could exact. Which sounds petty, I know.'

'Not petty at all. You had every right to feel aggrieved.'

'Not as much as you, and you're the one who's been affected the most.' Helping his mother to more rice and some for himself, followed by a spoonful Szechuan beef, he said, 'How satisfied would you feel if Dad's relationship failed with Zoe? Would it change anything for you?'

'I'd be lying if I said there wouldn't be a moment of *schadenfreude*, but then I'd think of the utter waste of his selfish actions and there'd be no sense of satisfaction. Instead, I've forced myself to contemplate just how unhappy your dad must have been to jettison the life we had. And why did I never know he was so miserable? There isn't one single moment I can pinpoint and say, yes, that was when it all began to fall apart. But equally I understand that some relationships simply drift in the wrong direction, yet it never occurred to me that that was happening to us.' She paused to eat something before continuing. 'What pains me the most is that I've always believed myself to be extremely observant and accommodating of other people's feelings, of wanting those around me to be happy, and I failed to spot that in your father. Was I too busy caring about everybody else to see what was right under my nose?'

This wasn't the first time Angus had heard his mother reproaching herself for what Dad had done. 'We none of us saw it coming,' he said, 'so ease up on the blame-game. Anyway, two can play at that game, because I could shoulder all the blame since I was the one who brought Zoe into our family.'

She tutted. 'We both know that's complete nonsense.' Then in a sudden change of direction with the conversation, although Angus could see the link, she said, 'How are things between you and CeeCee?'

'Good,' he replied.

'Just good, or *very* good?'

He smiled. 'Exceptionally good, I'd say.'

She smiled back at him. 'Good enough to risk bringing her home for me to meet? Are you at that stage yet?'

'Define what you mean by "at that stage"?'

'You know perfectly well what I mean. You deserve somebody who makes you happy and I have a feeling CeeCee does that.'

'On what evidence do you base that opinion?'

'I've seen a change in you these last few months. You seem more content.'

Intrigued, he said, 'Did I seem that way with Zoe?'

'No. I'd say with Zoe you were on edge. Well, that was when I saw you together. You didn't seem able to relax fully.'

All these months on he could see that his mother was right. He had been so keen for Zoe to fit into the family while all the time knowing that she felt like a square peg in a round hole amongst them. Now he felt the opposite way, he knew that CeeCee would fit in perfectly with his family, yet something was holding him back from introducing her to them, as though it might tempt fate.

When they'd finished their meal and the coffee was made, his mother pushed two small cellophane-wrapped packages across the table, 'Let's see what pearls of wisdom our fortune cookies have in store for us.'

He did as she said, tore off the wrapping and cracked open the brittle cookie. '*A lifetime of happiness lies ahead for you,*' he read aloud from the curled-up piece of paper.

'*A fresh start will put you on your way,*' his mother read from hers.

'Well, there we are,' he said as he poured their coffee from the cafetiere, 'everything neatly sorted for us.'

She smiled. 'Speaking for myself, I'm hoping that a fresh start is exactly what lies ahead for me.'

'Will you miss this very much?' he asked, casting his gaze around the garden that in the darkness was now illuminated with diamond-bright solar-powered lights laced through the branches of the trees and bushes.

'I imagine I will,' she said, 'but I'm forcing myself to concentrate on what I shall do with my new home. It's the future I must think of, not the past. I've decided something very important, that regret is like a favourite old cracked vase, it should be chucked out and not kept in the back of the cupboard for sentimental reasons.'

Angus wondered if his father had reached the same conclusion, and that was why it had been so easy for him to walk away from his marriage. Perhaps it had been nothing more than habit and sentiment that had kept him from leaving years ago.

'What's the programme of events for tomorrow then?' he asked, not wanting to dwell on his father any more than he already had. 'When do they all arrive?'

'Eleven o'clock-ish. I'm under strict orders from your sister that I have to vacate the kitchen and live entirely for pleasure for the rest of the day.'

'Quite right too,' he said, knowing that Arabella was in charge of tomorrow's birthday celebrations for their mother. 'Obviously with this being Mum's first birthday without Dad,' she'd said, 'we need to make a great fuss of her.'

Angus had proposed a fancy meal out somewhere, but his suggestion had been rejected as not being ideal with Heidi and Peggy running amok. Also, Caro was on a mission to potty train Peggy and so puddles, or worse, were to be expected, and it was better for accidents to happen at Charity Cottage than a smart restaurant.

There had been something about his sister's manner when she'd called him that had rung a faint alarm bell for him. She'd sounded snappier than usual and not at all inclined to chat. Perhaps she was just tired and under pressure with having Giles's daughter staying with them again. He'd heard on the family grapevine that Lexi was going through an awkward phase and had caused no end of trouble when they'd all gone over to Aldeburgh for the day. He hoped there wouldn't be any problems tomorrow when she was here.

Later that night when he'd just settled himself in bed, his mobile rang with a FaceTime call. He didn't need to check who it was; he knew it would be CeeCee. He put in his earbuds and picked up the phone.

'Hiya,' he said when he saw her smiling face looking back at him, 'how was the concert this evening?' Ever since he'd first attended one of the events she played at, he'd gone to as many as he could. He loved watching her play.

'It went pretty well,' she said.

'Coming from you I'll interpret that as it went brilliantly, and the audience gave you a ten-minute standing ovation.'

'Is that your totally unbiased opinion based on years of expert music appreciation?'

'It's my totally *biased* opinion based on thinking you're the sexiest cello player that ever placed a cello between—'

'Keep it clean, Crazy Fan-Boy!'

He smiled. 'You don't exactly make it easy for me,' he said.

'Can I help it that I'm so wildly irresistible to you?'

'And so staggeringly modest.'

'Yeah, that too. So how's it going there with your mother? Is she looking forward to her birthday tomorrow? And is everything going well with the house sale?'

He provided a brief run-down on the evening and about finding the buyers looking comfortably at home in the garden.

'That all sounds good to me,' she commented. 'But why am I detecting what sounds suspiciously like a cadence of uncertainty in your voice?'

Trust a musician to say something like that, he thought. She was right though. While his mouth was opening and shutting an inner voice was shouting at him: *Ask her! Just ask her! What's the worst that could happen?*

'Tick-tock,' she said, 'I'm waiting for an answer.'

'My mother was asking when she was going to meet you,' he blurted out.

There was a pause. Then: 'Was she now?'

'Not to sound too pushy, but is that something you might consider?'

'More to the point, is this something you'd like me to do?'

'I . . . I think so.'

'Hey,' she said, pointing a finger at him on the screen, 'you're not selling this to me, but I do understand why; you need to know that there's zero chance of me running off with some random member of your family like your ex did. But the thing is, why would I trade my Fan-Boy for some inferior being?'

He smiled at her. 'You know what, I think that's the nicest thing you've ever said to me.'

'What, nicer than when I said you kissed better than Darren Jones?'

'Easily better than that, as I don't think you'd set the bar all that high, seeing as you were both in primary school at the time.'

'Wow, that's pretty dismissive of one of my most treasured memories. So what about my comment that you were hotter in bed than Ryan Gosling?'

'I hate to say it but that doesn't count either as it only ever happened in your imagination.'

'Hah! Shred a girl's dreams to pieces why don't you? And on that note, I shall say goodnight as I have an early start tomorrow morning.'

Remembering that she was playing at a wedding in the Cotswolds the next day, he said, 'Good luck with tomorrow, I hope the guests appreciate your amazing playing.'

'They'll all be so busy getting drunk they won't notice a boring old quartet in the corner of the marquee playing Mozart and Vivaldi.'

'I'd notice you for sure.'

She blew him a kiss. 'And I'd notice you too.'

When she'd disappeared from the screen in his hand, and still smiling as he removed the earbuds from his ears, Angus allowed himself to think that maybe he and CeeCee had indeed just reached that *next stage*. And it felt good. Very good.

Chapter Twenty-One

The day had started extra early for Louisa.

Birthday or not, she had a long list of commissions to fulfil and what with the house move and the never-ending stream of depressing communications from the divorce lawyers to deal with, which always left her feeling depleted, she was behind with her work. But this morning, waking just after five and while Angus was fast asleep, she'd managed to complete a set of 12th scale Rococo-style dining room furniture for a customer. She had enjoyed the intricate detail of the work and she hoped the customer would be as pleased with it as she was. First thing on Monday morning she would put it all in the post, along with the sweet little cushion she had made yesterday morning, the silk fabric of which she had painted with blowsy roses.

In her bedroom now, and having changed into the new mint-green linen dress she had treated herself to the other day in Long Melford, and put her hair in order, she looked at her reflection in the full-length mirror. *Not bad for sixty-three*, she thought, *and let's face it, it could be a lot worse*. While she had endeavoured to keep her weight down as middle age and the menopause had approached and had taken reasonably good care of her skin, she had never been particularly vain, seeing it as a thief of her valuable time, time that could be so much better spent.

Had that been a factor in Kip's attention being drawn to a much younger woman? When compared to Louisa's ageing body, had Zoe's unlined complexion and youthful pertness been too tempting for him to pass over? What man could resist, she imagined Kip saying, what man wouldn't seize the opportunity if given the same chance?

All these months since Kip had left her, she had fought hard not to let her mind dwell on comparing herself to Zoe, and today of all days, on her birthday when another year was added to the tally, she refused to give in to it. She'd always believed that age was a natural process and nothing to be ashamed of, and she wasn't about to change that view just because Kip had done what he had. She was better than that. Well, that's what she told herself as she went through to the en-suite bathroom to use the magnifying mirror – another cursed reminder of her age. Leaning in close, she applied a few brushes of mascara, some lipstick and a dab of blusher to each cheek.

Party time, she thought, spraying perfume to her neck and wrists. As much as she was looking forward to the day, she couldn't ignore the niggling feeling that all was not as it should be with Arabella. She could always tell when her children were anxious or hiding something, and for a while now she had been aware that her daughter was not herself. She said things which she then forgot she'd said or flew off the handle for no real reason. Louisa had tentatively asked if everything was all right: this was after Arabella had forgotten to collect Heidi at the time she'd said she would. Ordinarily Louisa wouldn't mind, but she'd promised to complete an order for a customer and couldn't get on with it while Heidi was with her. In response to Louisa asking if anything was wrong, Arabella had said petulantly, 'If it's too much trouble looking after Heidi, you only have to say.' Probably at the shocked expression on Louisa's face, Arabella had immediately apologised and explained that she had barely slept the night before.

At the sound of the doorbell, Angus, who had only surfaced

half an hour ago, called up from downstairs that he'd see to it. Louisa added a necklace of chunky beads and a matching bracelet to her outfit and then thought better of it – her children often teased her about her taste in Flintstone jewellery. Maybe the more elegant – much safer – option was her old pearl necklace. But Kip had bought the necklace for her, and she couldn't bear to wear something that reminded her of him.

Her costume jewellery would do very well, she decided; it was her birthday after all, so she could wear what she wanted. What was more, her granddaughters loved it when she wore some of her quirkier things, especially if she let them try on the necklaces or bracelets.

Dear little Heidi and Peggy, she thought with great fondness, how they never failed to lift her spirits. There was never any judgement from them, just unconditional love, and just like Angus, they never questioned her. No doubt the subject of her buying Melbury Mill would come up again in conversation today. Ashley had done his best to talk her out of it, but she wasn't having it. Her mind, she had told both him and Arabella, was made up. And if it was an act of madness on her part, she thought now as she went downstairs as the doorbell rang again, so be it. She was tired of safe options, she wanted to shake things up, be a little reckless!

Her birthday lunch was held in the garden and while the menfolk had taken charge of the barbecue, Arabella and Caro had organised the salads and laid the table, leaving Louisa and the children to decorate the garden with bunting and balloons. Lexi had been reluctant to join in, perhaps seeing it as too childish for her to be involved with.

Now, as Ashley placed a plate of chicken wings on the table, along with another of steaks, Lexi groaned. 'I don't know how you can eat that stuff,' she said. 'You know it's basically child abuse forcing children to eat meat, don't you?'

'Nobody's forcing you to eat meat,' said Arabella tightly.

'But you're forcing Heidi to eat it, aren't you?' Lexi replied.

'She likes it.'

'She wouldn't if she knew what it really was.'

'I'm sure she'll make her own choice when she's older,' intervened Louisa amiably, 'just as you have, Lexi. Now can I pass you some of this melon and feta salad Caro has made?'

'Is it vegan cheese?'

'No,' said Caro.

'Then I can't eat it.'

'How about you pick out the cheese and leave it to one side of your plate?' her father suggested.

Lexi pulled a face. 'But it's contaminated.'

'Why don't you try the coleslaw or the potato salad I made specially for you?' asked Arabella, cutting up one of the steaks and placing the pieces on Heidi's plate. 'Neither of those have anything bad in them.'

'I've told you before, I don't like coleslaw. It's yucky. And *duh*, mayonnaise isn't vegan for your information.'

'It is when I went to the trouble to buy a jar of vegan mayo,' said Arabella, glancing at Giles for back-up and finding none.

'I still don't want it.'

'Bread then,' said Angus, passing the basket of soft rolls towards the girl. Out of all of them, he was the least used to children, and he looked rather like he was tempted to hurl the basket of bread at the ungracious girl.

With a sigh, Lexi took a roll and examined it suspiciously.

With everybody's plates now loaded up, apart from Lexi's, and glasses refilled with wine, beer and soft drinks, the meal was finally under way and a silence fell on the group as they tucked in.

It only lasted a short while before Lexi was off again grumbling about the smell of cooked meat making her feel sick.

Nobody responded.

'I said the smell is making me want to puke,' she repeated.

'We heard you the first time,' said Arabella, once more seeking support from Giles.

'Sweetheart,' he said mildly, 'just let everyone enjoy their meal.'

'But it's not fair when it's making me feel unwell; it's proper minging.'

'I'll tell you what isn't fair,' said Arabella, 'is us having to put up with your constant griping. It's my mum's birthday and all you've done is complain.'

In the awkward hush that followed, Lexi looked at her father. 'Are you going to let her talk to me like that? She's always having a go at me. She's nothing but a bully.'

'She didn't mean it, love,' said Giles, 'it was just—'

'I did mean it,' cut in Arabella. 'I meant every word! I'm sick to the back teeth of her constant grumbling and I'm sick of you never sticking up for me!'

At the sight of Peggy and Heidi's anxious faces, and fearing that there might be no way back from this, Louisa said, 'Let's all calm down, shall we?'

'I'm sorry, Mum,' said Arabella, tears filling her eyes, 'but I've been pushed as far as I'm ever going to be pushed.' She suddenly sprang from her seat and hurried towards the house.

'No,' said Louisa as Ashley, always the first to rush to his twin sister's aid, rose from his chair, 'I'll go.' Giles, she noted as she hastened after her daughter, made only a pathetically half-hearted attempt to stand. Honestly, what was the matter with that man!

She found Arabella on the window seat on the upstairs landing. Her head was buried in her hands, and she was the picture of abject misery.

'I'm sorry, Mum,' she sobbed as Louisa sat next to her, 'I've spoilt the day for you, haven't I? I wanted everything to be so perfect for you after all that you've been through.'

'Darling, you haven't ruined the day. What's more, you only

142

said what most of us were thinking. But my goodness, that girl would test the patience of a saint right now.'

'I should have kept quiet, I know I should, but she won't stop goading me. She's relentless. I can't do anything right in her eyes. Whatever I do is wrong. She's a malevolent monster!' At that Arabella sobbed even harder.

With her arms around her distressed daughter, Louisa let her cry out the worst of her misery. 'It's a phase,' she said, searching in vain for something positive and placating to say when Arabella's sobs eventually subsided. 'Lexi's at that tricky time in her young life when she's confused and angry about everything.'

'If only Giles would do more to help,' Arabella mumbled. 'He lets her get away with murder.'

'I daresay he finds himself between a rock and a hard place, but I agree he could do more to support you.'

'He's going to have to help an awful lot more before too long.'

'What do you mean?'

'I'm pregnant.'

'Oh darling, that's wonderful!' Louisa exclaimed. And it explained everything, she thought, relieved at last to know what had caused the change in her daughter. She really should have guessed.

'It's not wonderful, Mum. Not when Giles is going to be so furious.'

'Why on earth would he be furious about a little brother or sister for Heidi?'

'He's been adamant since forever that he didn't want any more children.'

'Lots of husbands say that, but he'll change his mind when you tell him. Of course he will. How many weeks are you?'

'Ten.'

'And you've kept this to yourself all this time?'

Arabella sniffed and sat up straight. 'I told Ashley a couple of weeks ago.'

Louisa smiled and pushed at a lock of Arabella's hair and tucked it behind her ear. 'Better Giles doesn't know that. He'll need to think he's the first to know.'

That was the moment when they both turned at the sound of creaking. There, almost at the top of the stairs, were Giles and Lexi, and judging by the expressions on their faces, they had both overheard, if not all, then the last bit of the conversation. The most crucial bit at any rate. And then Lexi spun around and charged back down the way she'd just come, leaving her father standing alone on the stairs.

Giving Arabella's arm a gentle reassuring squeeze, Louise stood up. 'I'd better leave you two to talk,' she murmured.

She edged past her son-in-law. 'I'll go and see if I can find Lexi,' she said. 'I expect she's gone back out to the garden to join the others.'

Just as Louisa had comforted her daughter, she wanted to do the same for Lexi, to reassure the child that even though her father and stepmother were having another baby, it wouldn't mean he would love her any less.

But when she went downstairs and out to the garden through the dining room French doors, there was no sign of Lexi and the party seemed to have dispersed, with only Angus and Ashley still sitting at the table.

Chapter Twenty-Two

'Go on then,' said Arabella, 'just get on with being mad at me for telling Ashley before you that I'm pregnant.'

An incredulous expression on his face as he looked down at her where she was still sitting on the landing window seat, Giles shook his head. 'Don't you mean telling Ashley *and* your mother before me?'

'I'm sorry,' she said.

'What, sorry that you've been caught out? But that's not my priority right now,' he went on, not giving her a chance to reply. 'I'm far more interested in knowing how you became pregnant in the first place.'

Arabella held her nerve and tilted her head back to look up him and meet his eye. 'What a thing to say, you know perfectly well how these things work.'

'Don't insult my intelligence, you know that's not what I meant. We'd decided that there would be no more children. You knew I didn't want any more, we'd discussed it repeatedly that another child was out of the question. You knew, and yet here we are.'

'Yes,' she said coolly, 'here we are.'

'Did you do it deliberately?'

The severity of his bluntness shouldn't have surprised her, but it did. Before she had taken the test and discovered she was pregnant, Arabella had pictured this moment many times in her head, how she would break the news to Giles that she was expecting another baby. She had imagined winning him round with an Oscar-worthy performance of helpless disbelief that something like that could have happened to her – *to them* – when every day she religiously took the very pill to prevent it. But the carefully rehearsed scene of her imagination wasn't going to plan, and instead of being able to put on a show of tearful distress to prove she was as shocked as her husband was, all she felt was angry hostility towards him that he could stand in judgement of her. Fair enough he was essentially accusing her of the very thing she had done, but what gave him the right to do that? Everything about his antagonistic manner totally legitimised what she said next.

'No,' she said with as much blistering indignation as she could summon, 'and how could you ever think that?'

'Then tell me how it happened.'

This was the tricky bit and she had wanted to word it so very carefully, just as Ashley had warned, but now she didn't give a damn. 'It was when Lexi came to stay during that half-term break in May, when your ex-wife was away on holiday. I'd had a hell of a few days thanks to Lexi's awful behaviour, and I tripped up some days with taking my pill and then,' she took a breath, 'there was that night in the kitchen when we came back after that disastrous day in Aldeburgh, and I suppose—'

He raised his hands to stop her from continuing. 'You're seriously blaming Lexi for this? You're making out it's her fault?'

'Of course not, it's nobody's fault. But those are the circumstances which have led to this happening.' She tried a more placatory tone. 'I know this isn't what you wanted,' she said, reaching up to him to pull him down to sit on the window seat with her, 'but surely it won't be so bad having another baby? Maybe it will be a boy, wouldn't you like a son?'

He resisted her attempt to make him sit down and remained stubbornly where he was, still looking down at her, his hands clenched either side of him. 'It doesn't matter whether it's a boy or girl, I didn't want any more children,' he said flatly. 'We were complete as we were.'

You might have been, she thought, deciding to stand up so she didn't feel at such a disadvantage, *but I wasn't*. 'Life doesn't always go as we plan it,' she said, 'so there's nothing else for it but to accept the situation and get on with it.'

He stared at her. 'Have you ever wondered why my daughter feels so awkward around you?' he interrupted.

Without thinking Arabella said, 'Well, this should be interesting.'

'There's no need to be sarcastic.'

'Equally there's no need for you to lecture me!' she fired back, all trace of her earlier conciliatory tone gone.

'I'm not, I'm merely trying to explain why you rub Lexi up the wrong way. It's because you're always on her case. You can never let her have her say on something, you're forever correcting her or rubbishing her opinions. You might not agree with them, but you could at least respect her right to hold those views.'

'I only say what I do when she's being rude to me, or members of my family, and would it kill you just once to take my side and not hers?'

'I would if I thought it was necessary or the right thing to do. Out in the garden just now you humiliated her in front of everyone, so of course she was going to retaliate. Sometimes I think you forget that she's only a child.'

'But couldn't you see how rude she was being? Are you really that blind to the way she treats me, and my family for that matter? There wasn't one person round that table during lunch, apart from you, who didn't feel the same as I did. We were supposed to be celebrating my mother's birthday, but somehow Lexi made it all about her.'

'You see, there you go again, exaggerating the situation and criticising her behaviour. And I'm not blind; I could see that you were upset, which was why I asked Lexi to come with me to apologise to you. That's why we were on the stairs and overheard what we did.'

'That was good of you to persuade her to apologise,' Arabella conceded. Until now it hadn't occurred to her why Giles and his daughter had been there; all she'd been aware of was that he'd just caught her telling Mum that she was pregnant.

'Maybe *you* could apologise to Lexi,' he said, his voice softer now.

Never! Arabella wanted to shout. *Never in a million years!* But in a clearing of her mind, she suddenly saw an opportunity, that if demeaning herself by saying sorry to Lexi would help to win Giles round about the baby, then so be it. There were times when you just had to swallow your pride, and this was one of them.

'Of course I will,' she said, 'and I'm sorry for reacting the way I did at the table. I'm probably strung out with hormones right now.'

He nodded. 'We'll speak about that later.'

For the first time since she had discovered she was pregnant she felt the weight of worrying about sharing the news with Giles ever so slightly lift from her. It was going to be okay. Just as Ashley had said. They were over the worst.

But she was wrong.

When they went downstairs there was an almighty commotion kicking off. Everyone was crowded into the orangery and at the centre of the mêlée was Lexi, red-faced and staring sullenly back at them all. Both Heidi and Peggy were crying their hearts out. Ashley had Peggy in his arms and was trying to soothe her, and Heidi, on seeing Arabella, ran pell-mell at her.

When Lexi saw her father, she pushed past Arabella and threw herself at him. 'Tell them, Dad, that I'm not a liar! I've told them what happened, but they won't believe me. They're blaming me!'

'What on earth is going on?' he demanded above the cacophony of noise as his daughter clung to him.

'There seems to have been an accident of some sort,' said Louisa.

'What kind of accident?' asked Arabella, lifting Heidi up. And then she saw it. On her mother's worktable, a set of beautifully painted miniature furniture lay in shattered pieces.

'I saw them do it!' cried Lexi. 'It was Heidi and Peggy who broke the stupid bits of furniture. Why would I do it?'

'I'm sorry, Lexi, but that's simply not true,' said Caro. 'I saw you in here on your own when I took Peggy to the toilet. She hasn't been out of my sight for a single minute the whole time we've been here, so I know she couldn't have had anything to do with this.'

Coming from her sister-in-law, the most rational and infuriatingly fair-minded of people, Arabella didn't doubt Caro's assertion for a second.

'It's you who's lying!' wailed Lexi, her face buried in her father's chest. 'Why would I do it?'

'That's a very good question,' said Angus from where he was standing next to Mum and looking at the remains of what must have taken her so long to create.

'And why would you be so cruel as to blame Peggy and Heidi?' asked Ashley. 'Just look at the state of them thanks to you.'

'That's enough,' said Giles. 'You're not going to interrogate my daughter and upset her any more than you have already.'

'She did it because she's angry at knowing that I'm pregnant,' announced Arabella.

'I didn't!' screeched Lexi. 'I couldn't care less if you're having another stupid baby. Why would I?'

Arabella was about to reply when Giles silenced her with a severe look and her mother said, 'Come on everyone, I think we should all go back out to the garden.' Her voice was tight with what Arabella recognised as barely controlled emotion.

'And perhaps we should have your birthday cake,' suggested

Caro in an attempt to defuse the dangerously charged tension in the room.

'Good idea,' said Ashley. 'What do you think, Peggy, will you help Grammy blow out her candles? Heidi, you too?'

The two girls miraculously fell quiet. Then: *'Cake!'* they chorused together, turning to look at their grandmother who smiled at them encouragingly.

'I don't want any stupid cake,' said Lexi, emerging from her father's chest. 'I want to go. I want to go *now!*'

'Yes,' said Giles, 'I think we should. Arabella?' He looked at her for agreement. But she couldn't give it, and whatever the consequences of her decision would be, she didn't care.

'That's all right,' she said, clutching Heidi to her, 'you two go; I'll cadge a lift home with Ashley and Caro.'

'Are you sure?' he queried and in a tone that insinuated he thought she was making a big mistake.

'Perfectly sure, Giles.'

This was her mother's birthday, and she wasn't going to let Lexi spoil it any more than she had. Moreover, she wanted to get to the bottom of what had happened while she had been upstairs with Giles. 'Say goodbye to Daddy and Lexi,' she said to Heidi.

All cheerful smiles now, her tears forgotten, Heidi gave her father a dismissive wave of her hand. 'Bye, bye, Daddy.'

Chapter Twenty-Three

'It's important that we don't demonise the poor girl.'

'Mum, we're not demonising her, we're merely pointing out the obvious, that she's a gobby troublemaker from the Ninth Circle of Hell!'

'Now Angus, that's just the kind of thing we mustn't say, about Lexi, it's not at all helpful.'

'Oh Mum,' said Arabella, 'you're trying to be so generous and reasonable, but we all saw your face, you were devastated by what she'd done. All that beautiful painstaking work of yours trashed. It was an act of spite for which there is no excuse or forgiveness.'

'That's a little harsh, darling, shouldn't we try to understand why she did it and make allowances for her?'

'That's all well and good, Mum,' said Ashley, 'but don't expect me to make any allowances for her when she tried to lay the blame on Peggy and Heidi, that was bang out of order.'

He was still fuming on his mother's behalf for Lexi's act of wanton vandalism. Had Caro not witnessed what she had, the truth might never have been known. Lexi's spurious claim that she had seen Peggy and Heidi breaking the miniature furniture and that she had been trying to fix it when Caro had seen her, might have worked had Caro not known it for the lie it was and called her out on it. That was when Lexi had started shouting at Caro and attracted everyone's attention. When they'd all piled into the orangery, the devious girl had pointed at Peggy and Heidi and shoved the pieces of the broken furniture at them. 'Look what you did!' she'd yelled. Their little faces had dropped and then they'd burst into tears which, to all intents and purposes, seemed to confirm their guilt. But then Caro had spoken up.

So much for celebrating Mum's birthday, Ashley thought now as he watched his mother pass round slices of cake, the candles of which the girls had helped blow out with plenty of spitty-puff.

What disappointed him most about his brother-in-law was that once again Giles had made no effort to apologise for his daughter's conduct. It was as if he flatly refused to believe Lexi could ever do anything wrong, or that if she did, he would stand by her no matter what. But would Ashley do anything differently if Peggy ever behaved so badly? Was that the fate of a parent, forever destined to support the unsupportable? You saw it all the time with parents of terrorists; they always claimed that their offspring had been led astray, that it wasn't their fault that they'd bombed innocent men, women and children.

Not that he was seriously comparing a twelve-year-old-child to a terrorist. More likely Lexi was going through a stage of honing the art of being a total pain in the arse.

'All I'm saying, Arabella,' Ashley heard his wife suggesting, 'is that you and Giles, and his ex-wife too, should arrange to have some family therapy sessions, otherwise things could escalate, and you don't want that with a baby on the way, do you?'

'I'm not the one who needs therapy,' said Arabella defensively, 'it's bloody Lexi!'

'Bloody Lexi!' echoed Heidi, her grinning mouth full of cake and her cheeks smeared in buttercream.

'Naughty Mummy for saying that,' said Arabella, taking a paper napkin and wiping Heidi's face.

'Naughty Mummy,' Heidi said solemnly. 'And naughty Lexi.'

'Yes,' said her mother. 'Lexi was very naughty today. You mustn't ever do something like that. Or use bad words like Mummy just did.'

Her eyes wide, Heidi shook her head.

'Naughty bloody Lexi,' parroted Peggy next to Ashley. They all did their best not to laugh.

Seeing that his mother's champagne glass was empty, Ashley reached over and refilled it, followed by his wife's. Being pregnant, Arabella was eschewing alcohol, as was Angus, who, like him, would be driving home later.

'We should raise our glasses to you, Arabella,' said their mother. 'To you and the new baby!'

'Thanks, Mum,' she said, as they all chinked their glasses together, 'I just wish my news hadn't been announced the way it was.'

'Well, not to worry, we'll just have to put this day behind us and look to the future.'

Ashley had to admire his mother's steadfast attempts always to look on the bright side and to make everyone feel more positive about a situation, but surely even she had to admit that thanks to Giles and Lexi the future for Arabella might not be as rosy as she'd like it to be.

Their bodies now rebooted with an overload of birthday cake sugar, Peggy and Heidi persuaded Angus to play hide and seek with them. With an admirable show of enthusiasm, he entered into the spirit of the game and soon had the girls squealing with delight each time he 'chanced' upon their hiding places. Their ability to conceal themselves was as hopeless as their ability to keep themselves from giggling while Angus in true pantomime style pondered where on earth they could be, asking the rest of them if they had seen Peggy and Heidi, to which they replied, 'No, they seem to have vanished.'

Just as Ashley was thinking that it was good to see his brother happier than he'd been in a while, and wondering what had caused the change in him, Caro returned to the subject of family therapy sessions for Arabella.

'I can't see Giles agreeing to the idea,' Arabella said. 'In his mind his daughter never does anything wrong. Somehow he'll probably find a way to say it's understandable that she lashed out in the way she did, immediately after overhearing that I'm going to have another baby. That's if he even accepts the truth of what she did. But she has to learn that she can't go around smashing things up just because she's upset.'

'Perhaps that's what a counsellor could help with,' said Caro. 'For the three of you.'

Perhaps not wanting to hear any more about family therapy sessions, Arabella had declined Ashley's offer of a lift with them, but instead had asked Angus to drop her off on his return to Borehamwood.

'Given Giles's less than delighted reaction to being a father again,' said Caro, 'do you think Arabella deliberately got herself pregnant?'

'What a question!' Ashley replied, checking in the rear-view mirror that their daughter was asleep. She had nodded off just minutes after leaving Charity Cottage. She was in her pyjamas and hopefully they'd be able to lift her out of her car seat and slip her straight into bed when they arrived home.

'I wouldn't put it past her,' said Caro, 'and let's face it, she wouldn't be the first woman to do that.'

'Would you do it?'

'Who knows? If I wanted something desperately enough I might. But luckily for you, I don't want another child, so you can rest easy, I won't be springing any surprises on you.'

Relieved that she hadn't pressed him about Arabella and he'd be forced to lie, he glanced at her and smiled. 'I'm glad to hear that.'

'Do you like Giles?' she then asked, 'And before you answer, be honest, don't say what you think you should because he's your brother-in-law.'

'He's certainly gone down in my estimation after today,' Ashley replied.

Caro tutted. 'Not quite what I asked.'

'Okay, I admit it, he's not my favourite person. He's hard to get to know properly and he never really throws himself into a family get-together in the way my sister would probably like.'

'She might say the same of me. Giles and I are outsiders, after all.'

Ashley was shocked at her words. 'You're not an outsider. Why would you say that?'

'It's the reality of marrying into another family. Don't you feel the same way with mine?'

'I've never really thought about it before. But have you ever felt as though you've been deliberately kept on the outside of, or on the sidelines of my family?'

'Your sister has never really warmed to me, has she?'

'But have you ever warmed to her?' he asked.

Caro had the grace to laugh. 'Touché. We're chalk and cheese and apart from me being married to her twin, there's not much else the two of us have in common.'

'There's Peggy and Heidi?' he suggested. 'They're like twin sisters they get on so well together. And come to think of it, you and I are pretty much chalk and cheese, aren't we?'

She laughed again. 'I could never have married anyone who was the same as me, that would have been a disaster. Aren't all the best marriages based on couples who bring out the best in the other by being different?'

'The old chestnut of yin and yang?'

'Yes, you complement me perfectly and I'd like to think I do the same for you. We don't choose who we fall in love with, it just happens and if it's genuine we love unconditionally, faults and all. It's why you're able to love me, you accept me as I am and hopefully not as you'd like me to be.'

He smiled. 'True. Then why isn't it the same for you and my sister? Why can't you accept her for how she is and love her the way I do?'

'For the simple reason I haven't fallen *in* love with her. We're merely forced into each other's orbit because of you.'

'So, you tolerate her because you're in love with me?'

'And she tolerates me for the very same reason because she loves you and wants you to be happy. Which is what we do with Giles. We tolerate him because he's married to Arabella. It's called compromise for the sake of family accord.'

And it's dishonest, thought Ashley. But did all families accept that the only way to get on was to live with a degree of dishonesty and compromise? Was it naïve to think that there was any such thing as a family truly honest and fully in step with itself?

They were very nearly home when Caro said, 'Are you at all envious of Arabella having another child?'

'No, why would you think I would be?'

'Just a hunch, you being twins and all that.'

'I think that's taking the twin thing to extreme.'

'But it's nice that Peggy and Heidi are the same age, isn't it?'

'Yes, it is. So what are you saying, you'd like another child to be more or less the same age as Arabella's next one so they have one another to play with?'

'Not when it means going through another difficult labour and then suffering postnatal depression. No, the idea fills me with absolute horror.'

'There's no reason why that would happen to you again,' he said tentatively.

'Says the man who won't be the one going through it.'

Admittedly he hadn't suffered the agony of childbirth, but he had lived with the bleakness of those early months of Peggy's life.

It should have been a joyful time for them both, but he had felt so miserably helpless and had lived every day in fear that he had lost his wife to the debilitating depression that consumed her. So no, no matter how appealing the thought of another child was, he would not put Caro through that a second time.

When he hadn't responded to her comment, she placed a hand on his forearm. 'You don't mind, do you?' she asked softly, the vulnerability in her voice catching him off guard and filling him with protective love for her. This was the Caro nobody else saw. The defenceless Caro who wrongly believed she had failed and could never forgive herself for not being the naturally proficient mother she had assumed she would be after having Peggy. Everything else in life, she had taken in her stride and mastered, but early motherhood had challenged her in ways she had simply not anticipated.

'No,' he said, glancing at her and then in the rear-view mirror again at Peggy, 'we're perfect just as we are, the three of us.'

Chapter Twenty-Four

With her head on his lap, Angus was gently stroking CeeCee's forehead, paying particular attention to her temples to try and ease her headache. He had done this for her several times before and she said his hands had more healing power in them than any painkillers on the market.

They were in her flat and on the table in front of the sofa where they were sitting were two plates, and all that remained of the large slice of birthday cake Mum had given him were a few crumbs. 'I've cut you a slice big enough for you and CeeCee when you get home,' she'd whispered, respecting that he was still reluctant to share anything about his girlfriend with his brother and sister. He knew it was far from normal behaviour, this desire of his to keep his personal life under wraps, but after a day like today he had even more reason to keep CeeCee to himself. Why expose her to any of that? Although it had to be said, she was showing plenty of interest in the events of his brief time in Suffolk.

'That's one screwed-up kid,' she'd just said when he'd told her about Lexi and the way she'd carried on. 'How did your mum react?'

'Once she was over the initial shock it was business as usual, she went into full *we must find a way to be more understanding* mode.' He had begun to wonder if his mother wasn't just a bit too compassionate sometimes, too concerned with empathising with other people and their feelings. Was it a way to avoid confronting her own?

'Go on,' CeeCee murmured after he'd fallen quiet, and his fingers had come to a stop either side of her eyes which were still closed, 'tell me what happened next, when you drove your sister home.'

'Why do you want to know?'

'I want to know what her pathetic husband said or did.'

Until today Angus hadn't really given his brother-in-law much thought. Other than the guy being married to Arabella, Angus had had little reason to have an opinion on Giles one way or another. Some might say his indifference was a cop-out, that of course he had to have an opinion. But often that was what he did, he took a person at face value and simply accepted them for who and what they were.

'I'm waiting,' prompted CeeCee, her eyes now open. 'What did happen when you dropped Arabella and her daughter off?'

'Why are you so fascinated by my family?' he asked.

'Because it's so unlike mine.'

'You mean we're a freak show?'

She smiled. 'Not the words I'd use, but you have to agree, your family is definitely rich in drama, there always seems to be something crazy going on.'

'Until recently I'd have said we were just an ordinary family.'

'No such thing. All families are different and fall out with each other at some point.'

'You've just implied yours is the exception.'

'Okay, smart arse, we'll get to mine another time.'

Smiling, he ran a forefinger lightly across her lips and she shivered just in the way he knew she would. They'd spent enough time exploring one another's bodies to know where and what the flash points were.

'Don't distract me,' she said, 'finish your story.'

'Nothing happened,' he said, his finger still playing across her lips. 'Giles's car wasn't on the drive when we got there.'

'Was that a disappointment to you, were you spoiling to be your sister's fierce defender?'

'I wouldn't put it quite like that, but I did plan to go in with her, just in case.'

'My hero!' she said, putting a hand to her heart. 'But in case of what precisely?'

'Sounds silly but I felt the need to stand up for my sister. My mother as well. I wanted to let Giles know that he couldn't pretend his daughter hadn't done anything wrong, that he had to make amends and apologise to my mother, she deserved that at the very least. And before you say anything, I don't have some weird Oedipus complex going on that makes me rush to defend my mother.'

She laughed. 'I should hope not! I've had experience of that before, with a boyfriend who when he climaxed called me Mummy. It was very off-putting.'

'You're kidding?'

'I wish I was. He was an oboist.'

'You say that as if it explains everything.'

'It does. Trust me, oboists are the most neurotic of the orchestra, it's all that fiddling they have to do with their reeds. Understandably, that was a relationship that was never going to work out. So where had your brother-in-law gone?'

Angus loved how CeeCee flitted about in a conversation, yet somehow never lost track or focus. 'Arabella reckoned he'd driven Lexi home to her mother,' he said.

'And he didn't text to say that was what he was doing?'

'Seemingly not. Which doesn't bode well.'

'I guess not. Will you contact your sister to make sure she's all right?'

'If she needs help or advice, Ashley is the one she'll turn to. It's always been that way, them being twins.'

'You've never said before, but do they look very alike?'

'No. In fact, they have no more than a passing resemblance to each other, but they're close, very close. She told Ashley she was pregnant before she told anyone else, even before Giles.'

'But as close as they are, there's no harm in you stepping up a gear and changing things, is there? Your sister might appreciate some extra brotherly support.'

That seemed unlikely to Angus since Arabella had never turned to him for help before, but was that because she'd never needed to? And maybe because he'd always taken things at face value, assuming that his help wouldn't be welcome, or that there wasn't anything wrong. He'd certainly missed that there was anything wrong with his father and that he'd been having an affair with Zoe.

Pushing his family from his thoughts, he looked down at CeeCee's long-limbed body lying stretched out on the sofa with him, her eyes closed again and her lips slightly parted as he continued to caress her face. She had a beautiful face and one he loved to look at. She'd told him that her sherry-coloured eyes, her long nose and wide cheekbones came from her French mother, and that her height and musical talent was from her father. 'I'd describe that as a perfect combination all round,' he'd said.

'Oh, I'm far from perfect,' she'd replied, showing him her left hand and the fingertips that were covered in calluses – her *grisly calluses* as she called them. 'All I need is to start growing hair on my palms and I'll be mistaken for a troll,' she'd joked.

'The price of being a brilliant cellist,' he'd said, kissing each of her fingers.

'You've gone quiet on me again,' she said, interrupting his thoughts and looking up at him. 'What were you thinking of?'

'The truth?'

'Nah, tell me a whopping great fib and see if I fall for it!'

He laughed, both at her teasing response and the way her face was rarely anything but aglow with the sheer joy of living. When he was in her company there was never any danger of taking himself too seriously. She was quite literally a breath of fresh air in his life.

'I was thinking how perfect you are,' he said, adding, 'even with your grisly calluses.'

'Oh, he gives with one hand and takes with the other!'

'Talking of hands, and my healing hands in particular, are you feeling any better?'

'Much better,' she said, lifting herself up so she could kiss him on the mouth. 'Shall we go to bed now?'

He didn't need asking twice and easing her off his lap, he got to his feet and scooping her up in his arms, much to her amusement, he carried her through to her bedroom.

It was the perfect end to a less than perfect day.

Chapter Twenty-Five

With the sound of church bells ringing, Zoe stood at the open bedroom window that looked out over the clay-tiled rooftops of the village and breathed in deeply to clear away the last vestiges of morning sickness. While Kip was out buying his weekly fix of Sunday newspaper print, she had just spent the last ten unedifying minutes in the bathroom bent over the loo.

But as she took in another restorative gulp of fresh air at the window, the milky smell of mown lawn from when Kip had cut the grass last night was almost enough to send her hurtling in the direction of the bathroom again. She moved away from the window to dress and thankfully the threat passed.

Normally Zoe would cut the grass, but in the light of her recent seismic news, Kip had rushed to do the job himself. He claimed it was nothing to do with her being pregnant and more about him doing his fair share of the chores around the house, but Zoe knew that he was lying to her, and not just about his keenness to cut the grass. She knew it in his every inhale and his every exhale of breath. Try as he might, and he did try, he simply could not conceal the truth from her that he was in a perpetual state of anxious shock and very likely a large dose of denial.

In the weeks since she had told him she was pregnant things had changed between them. It wasn't what they said, but what they didn't say that was causing the tension. Kip was endlessly judicious with his comments that he was happy to wait for her to reach a decision about the baby and whatever it was, he would respect it. He tiptoed around her, or even avoided her by saying he had work to do of an evening and that being the middle of August, it was the height of the holiday season and there was an infinite number of problems to deal with. When they travelled to work together, usually in his car, she was as guilty as he was during their commute together at sidestepping the subject.

She knew that if she challenged him, he would say that he was giving her space. Space in which to make the biggest decision of her life.

But that was another lie from him. She suspected his part in the creation of this growing distance between them was because he hated not being the one to decide the future for them. She couldn't think badly of him for that. How could she when she had claimed the right unilaterally to determine their future? *Her* future.

Her pregnancy was now in its tenth week, and she still hadn't decided what she was going to do. Some days she believed she had reached the end of what seemed an endlessly long tunnel of dark confusion and knew exactly what she was going to do. But then she would wake the next morning assailed by a ferocious bout of nausea and that would have the instant effect of clouding any clarity of thought she'd previously had.

Her head dictated that going ahead with the baby would be a disaster; Kip was too old to be a father all over again. He hadn't said as much, but then he didn't need to, she had seen the raw shock on his face that night when she'd told him she was pregnant.

Yet her heart, or maybe her rampant hormones, said a baby would strengthen their relationship, and maybe, just maybe, this would be her only chance of motherhood. Did she really want to sacrifice that chance? But if she kept the baby and lost Kip because he couldn't face bringing up another child at his time in life, how could she bear it?

The one thing she knew for sure was that she had to be responsible for making the decision. She could not allow herself to be influenced. If she were to spend the rest of her life regretting what she chose to do now, then she had to be able to say it had been her choice and hers alone.

And all the while the clock was ticking. If she carried on much longer with this see-sawing indecisiveness it would be too late, and perhaps that was the solution, to keep on vacillating until the decision was made for her.

But that wasn't her style. She had never dithered over anything in her life. If she wanted something she grabbed it with both hands. Just as she had with Kip. When she had realised she was in love with him, nothing on earth would have made her give him up.

Did Kip feel the same way about her, would he go through with being a father again so he didn't lose her? Because if he loved her as much as he said he did, he would support her, wouldn't he, so what was she worrying about?

She sighed with irritable exasperation. This was the conversation she had with herself at least twenty times a day, and all because of a moment of carelessness that weekend in Aldeburgh when she had forgotten to pack her contraceptive pills and had taken a risky chance. She had done it because Kip had been so low and vulnerable after his family's visit to spend the day with them and making love with him, as much to assuage her guilt for putting him in the situation he was, had been her way of proving to him that the sacrifice he'd made was worth it.

Now she was responsible for expecting his child. A child she was convinced he didn't want.

Chapter Twenty-Six

Melbury Mill, Mill Lane, Melbury St Mary was officially Louisa's new address.

It was the third week of September and she'd moved in five days ago and despite the many packing boxes she had yet to deal with, and some of the items of furniture she had brought with her and which she now realised would never fit or look right, she felt cosily at home.

By virtue of its shape, the mill felt as though it literally wrapped itself around her in a welcoming embrace and with each day that came and went, she learnt something new about the characterful building, such as which of the steps on the stairs creaked the most, when and why the plumbing clanked, or how when the wind blew in a certain direction there was a low moaning sound that could be heard from within the structure. It was a wistful note and sometimes she fancied the mill was softly singing to her.

The weather had been beautifully warm and sunny ever since she'd moved in and had added to her overall sense of wellbeing. Today had been no different; the sun had shone all day and this afternoon in her workroom at the top of the mill, and which she referred to as her eyrie, it was so warm she'd had to open the doors onto the wooden balcony while she sat at her crafting bench.

This was the first opportunity she'd had since the upheaval of the move, and all the preparations for it, to do any of her miniature work. Early that morning she had carefully unpacked her collection of materials, magnifying lamps, tools, brushes and paints and, putting them in place ready for use, she had awarded herself the pleasure of a few hours to tackle one of her commissions. It was a 12th scale armoire decorated in an oriental style with a black background and landscape scenes painted in rich gold. With an undercoat of paint now applied, she sat back in her chair and turned towards the open glass doors through which blew a pleasingly cool breeze.

From where she was sitting, she had a stunning view of the surrounding countryside, including the River Stour. Gazing at it, she followed its winding path until it skirted the market town of Chelstead with its handsome wool church standing tall and proud, and then it was lost in the distance amongst the dense trees.

There was a metaphor there somewhere, she thought, something along the lines of a life with all its hopes and dreams being like a river, meandering this way and that only then for it to vanish as though it had never existed.

This time last year she would never have dreamt that her life could have changed so dramatically. Some days she woke up still trying to grasp what had happened and where it had gone wrong and railed at the unfairness and waste of it all. But then there were the days when she accepted what had happened and took comfort in knowing that compared to so many she was lucky. What did she have to complain about? She was in good health, had a roof over her head, food to eat, the love of her family to rely on, and would be reasonably financially secure when the divorce was finalised.

Tearing her gaze away from the view, a view she didn't think she would ever tire of, she decided she had earned herself a cup of tea and a piece of shortbread. One of the many things she planned to do was to have a kettle up here in her eyrie, along with a small fridge; it would save her trekking down to the kitchen on the ground floor every time she wanted a drink. She could cope perfectly well with the stairs, in spite of what Ashley might think, but it would be more convenient to be able to make herself a drink in situ. Apart from anything else, she liked the idea of being self-contained in her work space. That was something she was learning now, that she had total autonomy over any decision she wanted to make. She didn't have to confer with Kip, there was no negotiating or compromising to be done.

Which was something Louisa suspected poor Arabella was having to do a lot of with Giles. A month had passed since Louisa's birthday. Lexi had eventually sent an apologetic text to her, and Louisa had wanted to think well of it, but she couldn't. The message had been too cursory and probably sent under duress, but rather than make a fuss she had let it go. Probably that was the best one could expect these days from a twelve-year-old girl who doubtless viewed a handwritten note as hopelessly old-fashioned and unnecessary.

As for the baby Arabella was expecting, she had sworn them all to secrecy. 'I don't want anyone else knowing about it yet,' she'd explained to Louisa.

'What about your father, don't you want him to know?'

'No, not until I know Giles is more receptive to the idea. I owe him that much.'

And what about Giles, Louisa had wanted to say, didn't he owe Arabella something, like his support and commitment to making her happy? But she'd held her tongue, again, not wanting to make things any worse than they already were. Whatever issues Arabella and Giles had to deal with, they needed to resolve them on their own without any interference, as well-meaning as it would be, from Louisa or anyone else.

Making her way down the creaking stairs and poking her head into each room as she passed, Louisa mentally added yet more jobs to the never-ending list of things she had to do. Later she would hang some more pictures, just to get them unwrapped and off the floor. She had let Kip have the bulk of their larger-sized paintings as they wouldn't fit here with the curving nature of the walls. She had been surprised how easy it had been to part with everything that she had known wouldn't fit in her new home, seeing them as just things.

In the weeks before Charity Cottage was sold and while she was packing up what she wanted to take with her, Kip visited several times to select what he wanted to keep and put into storage. Apparently, he and Zoe hadn't even started to look for a new home together. During each of his visits Louisa had thought there was something different about him. Previously he had been so sure of himself and his belief that if only she would admit it to herself, she would realise their marriage had died years ago, and that she would then understand that this was for the best. He had almost made it sound like he was doing her a favour! But there was none of that about him when he'd stared at the packing boxes she had already filled in the dining room and sitting room. Was it only then that he understood the reality of his actions, that nearly forty years of a shared life was in the process of being dismantled thanks to him?

Pleased with yourself? she had wanted to say, as he stood self-consciously in the hall after choosing the things he wanted and putting what fitted in his car. There wasn't much that he'd wanted, possibly because he didn't want it tainting his wonderful new life. Or had Zoe laid down the law and warned him against filling their new home with anything connected to Louisa?

The garage at Charity Cottage had been very much Kip's domain and Louisa had insisted that he should be the one to take on the job of clearing it. He duly arranged for a skip and spent a day filling it and then sweeping the garage clean. She had offered to make him a sandwich and when he'd sat at the kitchen table, she'd been struck by how tired and visibly older he looked. She'd wondered if the strain of a young lover was taking its toll on him.

Once or twice the old her – the Louisa who had loved and cared about Kip – had wanted to ask if he was feeling all right, but she couldn't bring herself to be that person in his company. One day she might manage it, but not yet.

The main topic of conversation between them had been about the divorce, which in Louisa's opinion was going at an absurdly slow rate. She just wanted it over; she was sick of the emails and letters and the endless back and forth which the solicitors seemed so keen to prolong and over the slightest of minor details. It wore her down with each communication she received as it meant she had to stop what she was doing and respond.

She took the last few steps down into the kitchen, just as the grandfather clock she'd brought with her struck the hour. This was the largest room of the mill by virtue of it being on the ground floor and having the widest diameter of the building; it also had the addition of a glass-roofed extension which provided a light-flooded family area that was big enough for a sofa and two armchairs in front of a log-burning stove. It was here in this beautiful area on the ground floor that she imagined spending most of her time when she wasn't in her eyrie.

She filled the kettle, put it on the Aga and while she waited for it to boil, she opened the cupboard where she had put the mugs and then lifted the lid on a tin of homemade shortbread. It had been a gift from her nearest neighbours and delivered by the sweetest elderly gentleman.

'My wife's done a bit of baking for you,' he'd said after introducing himself as Jim-from-up-the-road. 'It's a small welcome gift to wish you all the best in your new home. And there's a card for you too,' he'd added, passing her an envelope. 'Maggie's written down the name of a handyman we use, along with our telephone, just in case you need any help with anything.'

'Oh, how very kind of you and your wife, please thank her,' Louisa had said, touched at the couple's thoughtfulness. She had invited him in, but he had held back, saying he had a hard day's graft ahead of him at his allotment. He'd then turned to toddle off down the lane, but not before saying he'd bring her a bag of runner beans and tomatoes if they'd be of any use.

Louisa had added the card to the many she had received from friends and family and which she'd hung up around the kitchen with a length of string.

She looked at those cards now and experienced a wave of happy gratitude for all the good wishes she'd received, and the offers of help.

All three of her children had helped on the day of the move, whether that was packing, cleaning or making drinks for the team of removal men who did such an excellent job for her. Giles hadn't been able to help as he'd had a work commitment he couldn't get out of and Caro's contribution to the day was to look after Peggy and Heidi and then bring the girls over in the evening to see Grammy's new home. With everyone there it had been quite a squash, what with all the packing boxes and jumble of furniture that hadn't yet been properly put in place, but her granddaughters had enjoyed exploring and had loved the quirky little bedroom with its sloping walls and tiny window which Louisa said would be theirs when they next stayed with her. As efficient as ever, Caro had brought a celebratory bottle of champagne as well as a large lasagne and a salad and when they'd sat down around the table in the kitchen to eat, it had felt like home already to Louisa.

The tea now made, she carried the mug and piece of shortbread back upstairs and went out onto the balcony of her eyrie where she had placed two garden chairs and a small round table. In the short space of time she had lived here, she had come to love this spot and whenever she took a break from unpacking it was where she liked to sit and enjoy the view.

Her gaze once again following the winding path of the River Stour, she suddenly found herself thinking that it was going to be all right. She had made the right decision and was going to be happy.

She was done with regrets.

She was done with dwelling on Kip and what had led to this moment.

No more would she think of the past, it was the present and future that mattered now. A few months ago, the future had seemed a very daunting far-off place which she had no desire to visit, but now she welcomed it and was ready for all it might bring her.

Chapter Twenty-Seven

'I can never say anything right, can I? Whatever I say or do, it's not enough, or let alone right in your opinion.'

'For God's sake, Arabella, give it a rest why don't you? It's been a long day and I'm not in the mood for another of your tantrums.'

'*Tantrums!*' she exploded, staring in disbelief at Giles through a cloud of steam where she was furiously ironing one of his shirts. 'I dare to speak and you call it a tantrum?'

'What else would you call it when the minute I walk through the door you immediately launch into a tirade of criticism and ridiculous accusations that are completely groundless?'

'And you never give me the benefit of the doubt or even stop to think why I say the things I do. What am I supposed to think when yet again I spend the evening alone while you're with Jen and Lexi?'

'You know full well I went there after work today to take Lexi for her appointment with the orthodontist.'

'Why couldn't Jen do that on her own?'

'For the simple reason Lexi wanted me there with her as well as her mother. Can you not understand that as her father I want to do these things for Lexi? I want to be more than just a part-time presence in her life.'

'But you don't mind being a part-time presence in my life or Heidi's!'

'That's an absurd exaggeration and you know it.'

'All I know is that you said you'd be home by seven and here it is almost ten o'clock because you fancied having supper with your ex-wife. If I didn't know better, I'd say you prefer spending time with Jen and Lexi than you do with Heidi and me.'

'If you think that's true, then perhaps you should reflect on why that might be.'

'You admit it! You do want to be with them more than me!'

'With the way you're constantly banging on anyone would.'

This was too much for Arabella. 'In that case, why don't you just go? Go and be with Jen and your bitch of a daughter because I've had enough of being lumbered with the role of wicked stepmother and useless second wife who can never do anything right! But ask yourself this, if Jen's so bloody perfect, why the hell did you leave her for me?'

For the first time since their argument had kicked off within seconds of Giles arriving back, he fell silent and stared unblinkingly at Arabella. In the silence that followed she heard her words replaying in her head and her insides shrivelled and the blood in her veins ran icy-cold. What had she just done?

'I didn't mean that,' she murmured anxiously, a quiver in her voice.

Still staring grimly back at her, his eyes as hard as the granite worktop against which he was leaning, Giles said, 'Oh, I think you meant it. I think you've wanted to say that for some time.'

'No,' she said, 'it's just that . . . ' Her words tailed off and she put the iron down, playing for time.

'Just what precisely?' he prompted, shoving his hands deep into the pockets of his suit trousers.

'It's the feeling that your loyalties are divided and that no matter what, you'll always put Lexi before me. Can you not see how that makes me feel, knowing that you'll always take her side? I swear that if she told you black was white and white was black, you'd believe it.'

'We've been over this God knows how many times,' he snapped, 'and what you refuse to accept is that Lexi is just a child. I'll concede that she's going through a difficult phase, but Jen says she's no trouble with her, so I'm afraid the reality is the problem lies with you.'

The iron at Arabella's side gave a sudden and noisy hiss and for Giles that seemed to bring about an end to the conversation. He moved away from where he'd been standing and shutting the door after him, he left Arabella standing there alone in the kitchen in a steamy cloud of impotent injustice. How could he remain so stubbornly blind to the truth? Could he not hear the absurdity of what he claimed that somehow all this was her fault?

For a few minutes longer she continued with the task in hand, ironing Giles's work shirt. But it did nothing to settle her mind, quite the opposite and out of sheer petty spite, she stopped moving the iron and instead pressed it against the cuff of the sleeve and kept it there.

Then just as she caught the smell of scorching cotton, she heard footsteps approaching. The door opened and Giles appeared. He had changed into jeans and a polo shirt and was holding a bag and a suit carrier.

'I think it's better if we have some time apart.'

She gaped at him. 'You can't be serious.'

'I am.'

'But why?'

'You just told me in no uncertain terms to go.'

'But I explained that I didn't mean what I said. It was just in the heat of the moment.'

'No, I think it's the first time in ages that you've been truly honest with me. And unless you intend to set the ironing board alight, you should move the iron.'

With the acrid smell of burning now filling her nostrils, Arabella snatched up the iron to reveal a smoking blackened patch. Not only was Giles's shirt ruined but so was the fabric of the ironing board cover.

'Is that another heat of the moment thing?' he said, observing her in that odd way he sometimes did, of angling his head to the left as though his vision was better from his right eye. She had always found this curious habit of his rather endearing, regarding it as being uniquely him, but now she was seized with the impression that he was looking down his nose at her, that he was sneering at her.

That feeling, combined with the sarcasm in his voice, made her thump the iron into place at the end of the board. 'How on earth has it taken me so long to realise how cold-hearted you could be?' she said. 'Although I suppose you leaving your first wife the way you did should have warned me. I should have guessed that if you could do that to her, you could do the same to me one day.'

'I left Jen because I loved you,' he said.

'And now? Do you still love me?'

'Don't ask me that.'

'Why not?'

'Because I don't know the answer.'

She gasped at his response, wishing she could start the evening over, before she'd got so worked up about how late he'd come home. 'But Giles, what am I going to tell Heidi in the morning?'

'I'm sure you'll think of something.'

'You can't do this.'

He hitched the suit carrier over his shoulder. 'It's for the best. I need time to think.'

'What's there to think about?'

'You shouldn't have said what you did about Lexi.'

'I'm sorry.'

'I doubt that's true.'

She swallowed. 'Where will you go?'

'I'll find somewhere.'

She stared at him, willing herself not to say the words, but she couldn't *not* say them. 'To Jen's, I suppose?'

'If you need to contact me,' he said, not bothering to react to her assertion, 'you have my mobile number.'

Frozen with shocked disbelief, she watched him walk away and then listened to the sound of the front door shutting.

Was this the end of her marriage? Was she now going to be in the same position as her mother, except she would be a single parent with two young children?

She remembered Mum saying of Dad that she didn't understand where the man she'd married had gone. 'He looks just the same,' Mum had said, 'but he's no longer Kip. Not the Kip I've always known.'

This was exactly what Arabella felt about Giles. The man with whom she had fallen in love was not the man who had just walked out on her. What had gone wrong between them? Was it really all Lexi's fault as Arabella believed?

Or had Arabella been distracted by the girl and missed what was really going on with Giles?

What she knew with certainty was that he was on his way back to Ely to be with his ex-wife, and that hurt more than anything.

Had Giles ever really loved her? Arabella was forced to wonder. Or had she been nothing more than an affair that had got out of hand and which he'd regretted ever since?

Was this her punishment for stealing another woman's husband?

Chapter Twenty-Eight

'It's your sister,' Caro said, holding up his ringing mobile for him to take.

In the bathroom and just out of the shower, Ashley tightened the towel around his waist and took the mobile from his wife. It was gone eleven o'clock and for Arabella to be ringing at this late hour, it had to be serious. He could tell from the worried expression on Caro's face as she got back into bed that she must have thought the same.

When he heard the tearful distress in Arabella's voice, he knew something truly awful had happened. She was crying so much he could scarcely make out what she was saying. After he'd asked her to take a breath and start again, the full shock of what she was trying to say became clear.

'Do you want me to come over?' he asked, already moving towards the chest of drawers for some clean clothes.

'No. Yes. Would you? But it's late.'

'It doesn't matter; I'll be with you shortly. Just hang in there. Giles is just making a stand, that's all it will be. You've had a row and things have got out of hand.'

'I think it's more than that,' she said with a gulping sob. 'A lot more.'

After he'd rung off, he turned to Caro. 'It's Giles,' he said, 'he's gone, says they need to have some time apart.'

'How much time apart?'

'I don't know,' Ashley said, pulling on a pair of boxer shorts followed by a T-shirt. 'You don't mind me going, do you?' he asked, grabbing his jeans.

'Of course not. Arabella needs you. Stay the night with her if you feel you have to. But promise me you won't drive too fast to be with her.'

With one leg in his jeans and the other poised, he said, 'I promise. And thanks for understanding.'

Arabella as good as fell into his arms when she opened the door to him. Ashley had never seen her in such a state, and he knew he'd done the right thing in coming.

'You should have seen and heard Giles,' she said, when he had her settled in a chair in the kitchen and he'd put the kettle on. 'His manner was so cold; it was as though he hated me. I can't believe he could do this. Walk out and not give any clue as to when he'll be back. What am I supposed to tell Heidi? And yes, I know I shouldn't have said what I did about Lexi, but I did apologise, only he wouldn't have it.'

'What *did* you say?' Ashley asked when she paused for breath and blew her nose.

'I called her something I shouldn't have.'

'What?'

'A bitch. Because that's what she is!'

'Oh, Bells,' he said softly, 'you shouldn't have said that. Imagine how you'd feel if somebody said that about Heidi?'

'Don't you think I know that!' she wailed. 'But I lost it and the words just came out. He had the nerve to claim that Lexi is no trouble when she's with her mother, therefore it must be me who's to blame for her dreadful behaviour. It's always my fault. *Always*.'

When Ashley had their drinks made, he chose his next words

with care. 'Things couldn't go on as they were,' he said, 'something had to happen so that the problem could be resolved.'

She looked at him with puffy, bloodshot eyes. 'But how? What can be done?'

'Well, there's no avoiding that you've reached a crunch point and you both now need to do something about it.' He held up a hand to stop his sister from interrupting him. 'Giles must face up to what has happened here tonight and what provoked it. He must also acknowledge the part he's played. You need to do that as well, Bells, as painful as that might be.'

As though he hadn't spoken, Arabella said, 'The worst of it is I know he's gone to his ex-wife. I see Jen's hand in all this; she's never given up on wanting him back.'

'You don't know that. Not for sure.'

She cradled the mug of tea in her hands and took a sip. Then: 'Would you speak to Giles? Maybe you could talk some sense into him.'

'I was going to suggest that. But we need to let the situation cool before I contact him. There's always the chance he'll wake in the morning and realise he's overreacted. Then he'll come home because he loves you and Heidi and, of course, there's the baby to think about.'

'He left his first wife and child, didn't he?'

'Yes, but he knows only too well the consequences of that decision, so he won't make that mistake a second time.'

'Are you saying it was a mistake him leaving Jen to be with me?'

'I'm sorry, I didn't mean it like that. What I meant was that with one failed marriage behind him, he's unlikely to let history repeat itself.' Not if the man has any sense, thought Ashley, hoping to God that he was right.

'What's happening to us?' Arabella asked after she'd taken another sip of her tea.

'What do you mean?'

'Our family is breaking up. First Dad leaving Mum, and now Giles is leaving me.'

'Giles hasn't left you, he's merely making a point, an overly dramatic point, but he'll be back and then you two will have to sort things out. Maybe, as Caro suggested, you should seek professional help. I know you didn't like the idea of it, but if it helps to resolve the difficulties you're having as a family, then wouldn't that be a good thing?'

His sister's lower lip trembled. 'But what if he's gone for good? How am I going to cope on my own with Heidi and a baby?'

'There's nothing to be gained in dwelling on a worst-case scenario.' A thought then occurred to Ashley. 'You know who the perfect person might be to talk to Giles, someone who he would regard as being fairly objective, and that's Caro.'

Arabella gave him a doubtful look. 'She might take Giles's side and agree with him that I've behaved unreasonably.'

'I promise you, she doesn't think that. But if it would help, it's worth a try, isn't it? What do you have to lose?'

Later, when he was sure Arabella was feeling calmer and likely to sleep, he drove home with the promise that he would call her first thing in the morning.

It was gone three when he let himself in. He crept upstairs and looked in on Peggy and found her sleeping on her front with her bottom sticking up in the air. Smiling, he kissed her lightly on the back of her head and tiptoed away. In the room next door, Caro was also fast asleep and lying on her side, her hair partially falling across her cheek. He undressed in the bathroom and then slid as silently and carefully as he could into the bed next to Caro.

She stirred. 'How'd it go?' she asked.

'Go back to sleep, I'll tell you everything in the morning.'

Mumbling something incomprehensible, she reached for his arm to place it protectively over her. He willingly moved in closer and thought as he often did there wasn't anything he wouldn't do to keep his wife and child safe. If only Giles felt the same way about Arabella and Heidi. But perhaps his true loyalty lay with his first family and was that the real problem? If so, the time ahead for Arabella was going to be the hardest of her life and she would need all the support the family could give her.

Chapter Twenty-Nine

'Kip, come and sit down.'

From where he was cleaning the lawnmower after cutting the grass, Kip glanced over his shoulder to see Zoe placing a tray of drinks on the glass-topped table on the patio. 'Give me five minutes and I'll join you,' he called to her.

He was in no hurry to stop what he was doing as judging by the serious expression on Zoe's face, and the nervous edge to her voice, this was the moment he had been dreading, and, he suspected, the moment she had also been dreading. Playing for time, he brushed at the blades of the lawnmower, seeking out every bit of grass he could find, before putting the mower away in the shed.

Last weekend he had emptied everything out of the shed and reorganised it, installing shelves and rows of handy hooks from which he hung the selection of garden tools that had belonged to Zoe's mother, and which previously had been stored any old how. It had been yet another job to keep himself busy, another distraction from worrying about the future. Just a few months ago and the future had seemed such a glorious prospect, an exciting adventure to enjoy with Zoe, but now the future looked a very different destination.

'Your beer's getting warm,' he heard Zoe call out to him.

The coward in him wanted to remain in the semi-darkness of the shed and its safe treacly warmth. It reminded him of when he'd been a child and before his father had been invalided and when he'd spent hours in his potting shed cleaning and oiling his gardening tools with linseed oil. A strong wave of poignant nostalgia sweeping over Kip, he wondered what the hell his parents would make of him now.

Both Mum and Dad had been very fond of Louisa, although initially his mother had been concerned this latest girlfriend he'd brought home to meet them was a bit posh and out of his league.

He'd met Louisa in a bar in Covent Garden where she was waiting for a date who never turned up. Kip had noticed her when she'd walked in – early twenties, like him, tall, elegantly dressed, long hair reaching beyond her shoulders, and looking confidently around her as she'd sat on a stool at the bar and ordered a drink. But that confidence had ebbed away with each glance she made at her watch and each time she looked towards the door whenever it opened.

Kip had been there with a group of friends from work, and having sussed the situation, and seeing that the attractive girl was now picking up her handbag and presumably preparing to leave, he went over and asked if he could buy her a drink.

'You've been watching me, haven't you?' she said. Her tone was accusatory as though he'd had no right to observe her.

'Yes,' he said with an honesty he hoped would appeal to her. 'But then it was hard not to, a gorgeous girl like you sitting alone at a bar.'

She'd rolled her eyes. Cool, assessing eyes that were an arresting combination of blue and violet. Much later, when he knew her better, he learned from her that the colour was called gentian blue.

But staring into those eyes that night in the bar, he wasn't about to give up; he was known for his charm and getting what he wanted. 'Whoever the man is who was supposed to meet you here tonight,' he said, 'he's a fool for not showing up. So, what'll it be, another Cinzano and lemonade?'

She gave him a long appraising stare. 'How did you know that's what I'd already had?'

'An educated guess,' he'd said. He'd actually seen the bottles from which the barman had poured her drink. But a little subterfuge was no bad thing when it came to winning a girl round, and he very much wanted to win this girl round and impress her. 'Maybe you'd prefer dinner?' he tried. 'I know a lovely little trattoria just around the corner. They do the best ravioli.'

'Are you sure about that, that it is the best?'

'How about we put it to the test? My name's Kip, by the way.'

'What an unlikely name.'

'I'll explain about it over dinner.'

That was the moment when he'd been rewarded with a smile. A smile that led to an evening in his favourite trattoria with its red-and-white chequered tablecloths, shelves of Chianti and dishes of ravioli which she agreed really was excellent.

Once they were established as a couple, she introduced him to her parents. Her father was a finance director of a large engineering company, and the family, with their two grown-up daughters, lived an enviably comfortable lifestyle with two cars on the drive of a large detached modern house in Hertford, and holidayed every year in either Bordeaux and Tuscany. Before giving up work to have children, Louisa's mother had been a ceramicist and it was from her, so Louisa claimed, that she had inherited her artistic talent. They were exactly Kip's target audience for the travel company he dreamt of one day running.

But as faultlessly polite as Guy and Justine Nicholson always were towards Kip, he couldn't be free of the suspicion that his prospects and intentions towards their elder daughter were constantly under review. Although once they were married and the years passed, their opinion of him steadily improved, especially when the children came along. That he had contributed to creating three perfect grandchildren raised his stock considerably.

No prizes for guessing what they'd think of him now.

'Kip?'

Startled, he spun round to see Zoe staring in at him through the open door of the shed.

'Are you going to hide in here for the rest of the evening?'

'I wasn't hiding,' he lied.

'Whatever you were doing, can you stop it and come and sit with me, please? We need to talk.'

This was it, he thought with a sinking feeling. 'I'll just go in and wash my hands,' he said, squeezing past her, 'then I'll be right with you. Anything you need from the kitchen? Maybe something to go with our drinks? How about some of those salted almonds you like?'

'And a plate of procrastination crisps while you're about it,' he heard her mutter as he hurried away.

That was the trouble, she knew exactly what was going on with him, that he had found these last weeks such a trial at not being part of the decision-making process, and that there had been numerous times when he had gone out of his way to avoid her. She had, he acknowledged, indulged him in allowing this obvious display of cowardice.

In the time since she'd told him she was pregnant he had experienced a range of emotions. Some days he imagined himself in the role of proud father, cradling his fourth newborn child and making plans for its future. But then other days he dreaded the thought of fatherhood at his age, which inevitably would force him to keep on working to provide for the child.

Resentment was an insidious thing, he'd discovered, it nestled deep within a person and slowly uncoiled itself like a poisonous snake ready to attack at the slightest provocation. It had slowly dawned on him that he'd resented being in a marriage when he no longer loved his wife and he resented the situation in which he now found himself – why in God's name should he be in this mess at his age when he should be looking forward to a relaxed and happy retirement, reaping the rewards of a lifetime of hard work? Now there would be no chance of him taking it easy if Zoe decided to go ahead with the pregnancy.

If she didn't go ahead with the pregnancy, he could imagine himself experiencing an enormous sense of relief, but in the next breath, and quite irrationally so, he grieved at the thought of a child of his not being given the chance to live. He had never really given the subject of abortion much thought before, other than the usual, that it was the woman's right to choose. Yet now that he was in the position he was – father to be, or not to be – he felt strongly that he should have an equal say in what happened.

But as his continuously changing sentiments proved, he was not capable of making the right decision. So he had no choice but to leave it to Zoe.

There was so much in his life now which he felt he had no control over and the worst of it was he was entirely responsible for that. It was weeks since he had spoken with any of his children. Not because they refused to speak to him, but because he hadn't been able to bring himself to ring them when he was in this state of limbo. Zoe had made him promise that her pregnancy was to be kept between the two of them until she'd decided what she would do. The thought of telling his children that they might have a half-brother or sister filled him with stultifying dread.

His hands washed and dried, a bowl for the salted almonds located, he went back outside to await his fate.

Their fate, he reminded himself. This wasn't just about him.

'I thought perhaps you were having trouble working the tap in there you were so long,' Zoe said when he sat down opposite her.

'No, I just couldn't find the nuts.'

'Oh, Kip,' she said with a gentle smile, 'you're such a shocking liar. Now have some of your beer and since you know exactly what I want to talk about, let's get on with it, shall we?'

Kip did as she said and downed several large swallows of beer.

'I know this hasn't been easy for you,' she said, 'and to be honest it hasn't been easy for me either. Had it been, I wouldn't have had any trouble in making up my mind.'

Now she paused to take a sip of whatever non-alcoholic drink she had poured herself. She hadn't touched alcohol as far as he knew since she'd known she was pregnant.

Putting the glass down, she said, 'I'm going to keep the baby. I appreciate that this is probably the last thing you wanted, so I'm giving you a get-out-of-jail card as you didn't sign up for a second family when you left your wife for me. Having a baby couldn't have been further from my thoughts when I fell in love with you, but now that the inconceivable has happened,' she paused to smile wryly at him, 'no pun intended, I'm certain I want this child.' She paused again. 'There, I've said my piece. Your turn now.'

The coiled snake of resentment in him gave a small violent twist of annoyance at the way she had given him permission to speak, but he cautioned himself to proceed with care. 'I won't deny that the last few weeks have been difficult,' he said, 'and you're right, this is not want what I anticipated for us, but—'

'But?'

He swallowed and strengthened his resolve to utter the words he knew he had to say. There could be no shirking his responsibility, he had to do his duty. Wasn't that how he'd always tried to live, doing the right thing? Not that having an affair had been the right thing to do to Louisa. No, he could not count that as an act of honourable duty. It pained him to admit that embarking on an affair with Zoe had been the first real selfishly reckless thing he'd done, and look where it had got him.

'But?' pressed Zoe?

'We're in this together,' he said. 'Of course we are.'

She gave him an intensely hard stare. 'There's no *of course* about it, Kip. Are you being completely honest with me, or just saying what you think you should say, or what you think I want you to say?'

He met her gaze. 'I'm being honest.'

'I hope so because there's no point in either of us pretending that this doesn't change things.'

'I know that,' he said, irked that she seemed to be treating him as an imbecile, as though he hadn't spent all these weeks thinking of what a child would mean for them. 'But let's face it,' he said lightly, 'of the two of us I'm more than qualified for the post as I have previous experience both as a father and a grandfather.'

'You're not applying for a job, Kip,' she said with a grimace.

'It was meant to be a joke. A poor effort, I'll concede.' Then suddenly desperate to remove himself from the conversation, he stood up abruptly. 'We should celebrate!' he announced. 'I'll go and put a bottle of fizz in the freezer, and we'll crack it open when it's cold enough.'

Frowning at him, she said, 'But I'm not touching alcohol.'

'A tiny drop won't hurt, will it?' He stopped himself just in time from blurting out that Louisa used to have an occasional drink and their children hadn't come to any harm, had they?

In the cramped kitchen, and with his back to the window, he let out his breath in one long exhalation and held his head in his hands. Until then he hadn't realised just what a performance he'd put on for Zoe's benefit and how it had taxed him. He felt light-headed and consumed with the need to fill his lungs with more air than was available where he stood. As the sensation gathered pace and ferocity, and his stomach churned, his heart raced as he broke out in a sweat.

It wasn't the first time this had happened to him. That day at Charity Cottage when he'd been clearing the garage something very similar had occurred, and also on Boxing Day when he'd broken the news to Louisa that he wanted a divorce. It felt far more severe today, more like he was suffering a heart attack. Which he knew he wasn't. He'd checked in with Dr Google, like everyone did these days, and his every symptom indicated that he was suffering with a panic attack. It was nothing to worry about. He just needed to relax and steady his breathing. It would pass.

Chapter Thirty

From his second-row seat in the auditorium, Angus watched the quartet playing the Prelude to Bach's Cello Suite No.1 in G Major. Accompanying CeeCee to as many of her gigs as he had, he knew that this piece heralded the interval. In fact, he'd heard it so often he could almost believe that he could play it himself.

Which was total rubbish, of course, even if, and as unlikely as it was, CeeCee had taken it upon herself to teach him to play the cello. With phenomenal patience she had advanced him to the dizzy heights of that well-known orchestral piece, 'Baa Baa Black Sheep'.

'I'm not a natural musician,' he'd remonstrated when she'd announced her intention to make a maestro of him. 'I'm a lost cause. Give up while you still have your sanity!'

'Nonsense,' she'd said, 'there is no such thing as a lost cause when it comes to music.' She had then embarked on a mission to convince him of her belief, which he had to admit, despite his ineptitude, was surprisingly good fun. She was constantly teasing him to be less buttoned-up and more open with his emotions because apparently it would help him to be a better musician. What was more, so she said, the better the musician he was, the more emotion he would feel and express. Music, she claimed, was the gift that kept on giving.

He didn't know if there was any truth in that, but his family was certainly the gift that kept on giving when it came to family drama. Two days ago, his mother had rung with the news that Giles had just walked out on Arabella, declaring they needed time apart. Angus had been surprised how angry he'd felt on his sister's behalf. He'd immediately called her to ask if there was anything he could do.

'Do you want me to go and thump some sense into that dumb husband of yours?' he'd asked.

'As tempting as that sounds, I don't think it would help,' she'd said. 'But thanks for the offer.'

'He'll soon realise he's made a mistake,' Angus had then said, aware that it was something of a platitude.

'That's what Ashley and Mum say, but I don't believe it. I'm convinced he now regrets leaving his first wife for me.' Arabella then told Angus what she'd blurted out about Lexi and how bitterly she regretted it. 'If only I hadn't lost my temper. I pushed him too far.'

Angus disagreed and said as much, but he didn't give full vent to what he really felt. In his opinion, Giles should have done a lot more to keep his daughter in order; that was at the heart of all this and unless the man could accept that, it was game over for their marriage.

Mum was very much of the view that nobody should be outright rude about Giles as it would make it harder for things to return to how they once were if he and Arabella did manage to work things out. 'He's a member of our family and because of Heidi and now the baby Arabella is expecting, he always will be.'

It was a typical example of Mum's habitual need to show a generous and forgiving nature, although she would be the first to say she hadn't managed it with Dad.

A restless movement on the part of the woman to Angus's left distracted him from his thoughts and the music. The woman was Madame Sabine Vernier-Crawley and she was CeeCee's mother. She had arrived from Provence yesterday on a sudden whim to stay with her daughter, and there was no doubting the resemblance between mother and daughter, in looks as well as manner. They both fizzed with energy, as though nothing could dampen their zest for life.

In her mother's company CeeCee, who at all times was referred to as Cécile by her mother, suddenly became more French than English – her flawless English accent was gone, and she was even more animated and expressive with her every gesture. Her father hadn't been able to make the trip due to attending an auction in Paris, and was, according to CeeCee, and despite having lived in France for nearly three decades, still as British as a hot-buttered crumpet.

'So, this is your handsome English boyfriend I have heard so much about!' CeeCee's mother had exclaimed when Angus had been introduced to her. Enveloping him in an embrace of silk and heady perfume, she'd insisted right away that he called her Sabine, and then turning to her daughter, had said, 'You told me he was attractive, Cécile, but you didn't say just how handsome he was.'

'*Maman*,' said her daughter, 'behave and don't embarrass Angus. Or me.'

Waving the reprimand aside, Sabine said, 'He has something of the stoic about him, that is probably the attraction. That and him being so tall and proud-looking. He is a modern-day Mr D'Arcy, yes, now I see why you are so fond of him!'

Laughing, CeeCee tutted and urged Angus to ignore her dreadful *maman*.

With loud enthusiastic clapping now breaking out and as the quartet stood to acknowledge the applause and then left the stage, CeeCee's mother took hold of his arm.

'A drink,' she said, 'I am desperate for a drink. As proud of my daughter's playing as I am, I need a large glass of wine to help me through the rest of the concert. Come, let us hurry so we are not at the back of the queue and forced to wait!'

In spite of the high heels she was wearing, she set off at an Olympic medal-winning speed, weaving her way through the other charity concert-goers with scant regard for whether Angus was keeping up with her or not. Being bigger, and less inclined to barge anyone out of his way, he wasn't as quick on his feet as she was, but he eventually caught up with her in the bar where she had already attracted the attention of a male member of the bar staff. Angus didn't doubt that she would never have any trouble catching the eye of someone when she wanted something. The same was true of CeeCee. They both had the same appealing allure which Angus called her superpower.

Their drinks in hand, Angus looked around the crowded bar and spied a quietish spot some distance away and made for it before anyone else did. Their territory seized, Sabine lifted her glass of red wine to his of water – he was their designated driver for the evening – and with a quick *'Santé!'* she put the glass to her lips.

'Is it okay?' he asked, anxious that the wine might fall well below her expectations.

'It's fine,' she said with an elaborate shrug. The same shrug he had seen CeeCee perform many a time. 'And your mineral water,' she enquired, 'that too is okay?'

He smiled. 'Yeah, it's okay.'

She smiled back at him. 'I know what you are thinking,' she said.

'You do?'

'That Cécile is just like me, I can see the recognition in your face whenever I do a certain gesture or say something in a particular way. Am I right?'

'Yes,' he said.

'So now you know just how Cécile will be when she's older, only she will be more beautiful. Tell me, Angus, who do you take after, your father or your mother?'

'My mother,' he said without having to think of his reply.

'In what way?'

That was not so easy to answer. 'It's probably my tendency to take people at face value,' he said at length.

'That is an admirable trait,' she said with a nod. 'Until one is proved wrong, of course. How are things between you and your father now? Cécile has told me all about him leaving your mother.'

There was no mistaking the association of thought she'd just made. 'Not brilliant,' he answered.

'There are few things worse than believing in a person only then to feel they've disappointed you and let you down,' she said, 'but you really shouldn't think too badly of your father. I speak from experience. My *papa* was repeatedly unfaithful to my dear *maman*, it simply wasn't in his nature to be faithful, but as angry as that made my *maman*, she still cared about him, right to the very end. As did I. Do you think your mother still cares for your father?'

'It's hard to say,' he responded, trying not to feel woefully gauche in the company of this alarmingly candid woman.

'The hurt will lessen with time,' she continued, 'especially if your mother takes a lover, which I strongly advise her to do. And the sooner the better. She will benefit from it marvellously.'

Knowing that he was blushing, that the last thing he wanted to imagine was his mother taking a lover, Angus lowered his gaze and gulped at his water.

'Cécile tells me that your mother has moved into a windmill,' Sabine carried on blithely. 'How very romantic that sounds.'

'It's certainly different,' he said, feeling they were now on less hazardous ground.

'And she's happy there?'

'Yes,' he said with more assurance. 'She loves it. She really does.'

'Which is good. It means that she is prepared to embark on a new adventure for herself. And what about you, Angus, are you the adventurous type?'

'I'd never really given it much thought.' He inwardly cringed at his answer; could he sound any more dull?

'Oh, but you should! Everyone should have an adventure in their life. You and Cécile should plan something together. Or maybe you could surprise her with one? Her father has always been very good at doing that for me.' She leaned in closer to Angus, her sherry-coloured eyes, wide and determined, just like CeeCee's, and pointed a well-manicured finger at him. 'Shall I tell you what our biggest regret for Cécile is?'

His heart plunged. Was he about to be warned off, to be told that he was their biggest regret, that he wasn't good enough for their only daughter? 'Go on,' he said warily.

'It's that she hasn't taken more risks in her life. She's played it too safe. Do you want to know why she didn't make music her full-time profession? She feared the risk involved, of being considered not quite good enough. Better, she decided, to play safe and settle for a boring day job and excel as an amateur in an insignificant quartet.'

'I don't think there's anything insignificant in what she's doing here this evening,' he said, quick to leap to CeeCee's defence, 'she's helping to raise much-needed funds for a children's charity.'

'Yes, yes, very laudable, but where is the adventure, where is the risk?'

Thinking that negotiating a conversation with CeeCee's mother was a huge risk in itself, Angus was saved from being put on the spot any further by the ringing of a bell alerting everyone to return to their seats.

Back in the small auditorium and with the lights lowered, the quartet reappeared to generous applause and began the second half of the concert with the third movement from Borodin's String Quartet No.2 which Angus knew was a favourite of CeeCee's. It had become a favourite of his too and all the while he listened to the music, letting it wash over him, he kept his gaze fixed on CeeCee. She had told him once that it was impossible for her to put into words the absolute beauty of this Borodin piece, that when she played it, she succumbed to a profound sense of peace, almost like an out-of-body experience. 'Alexander Borodin wrote the piece for his wife,' she had explained, 'just imagine how much he must have loved her to do that!'

Angus had never known anyone talk about music the way she did and looking at the intensity of the expression on her face now as she played in front of the audience, her eyes closed, and her body swaying as she moved the bow across the strings of the cello, he felt a great swell of aching pride that she was his girlfriend.

But it was more than that, so much more. It was, he knew, love that he felt for her. He felt it as surely as he felt the exquisite notes of music that were fluttering through his senses. It was an awakening he was experiencing, as though everything that had gone before was building to this moment.

All of these thoughts were completely new to him. He was by nature eloquently fluent in all things cogent and analytical and in contrast the language of love in all its profound mystery was as alien to him as the intricacies of Borodin's music had once been.

It was through this enlightening prism of self-awareness that he pondered on Sabine's assertion that everyone needed an adventure in their life. Was she right? And if so, what sort of adventure could he and CeeCee share together? But there again, he thought with a sudden smile, from the moment CeeCee had rung his doorbell that night back in March, he'd had the feeling of being on an amazing and unexpected adventure with her.

But a worrying thought then struck him. If being a part-time musician for CeeCee had been a safe, second-best choice, was he a safe, second-best boyfriend? Shouldn't she be with somebody a lot more exciting and as musically gifted as she was? Was that what her mother was hinting at?

Chapter Thirty-One

'Wow, you took a massive risk, didn't you? What if he'd said he didn't want to be a father again and ditched you?'

With forced nonchalance, as though it had been the easiest decision in the world to make, Zoe shrugged off the question from her work colleague. 'Oh, I knew it wouldn't come to that,' she lied, 'Kip loves me, end of.'

Having just eaten lunch, she and Phoebe were making the most of the late September sunshine before going back to their desks by going for a stroll around the grounds of the business park.

In the last few days, pregnancy had given Zoe an unexpected appetite for anything with a colossal carb count and now at just fifteen weeks, there was no denying the strain her waistbands were under. It wouldn't be long before she wouldn't be able to conceal her pregnancy, though there was the option of just letting people think she was gaining weight.

Kip was anxious to keep their baby news under wraps for a while yet as he wanted to break it personally to his family and in his own time. Zoe had no right to be annoyed by this, not after she had insisted he give her time to reach a decision as to what she wanted to do about the baby, but irrationally she *was* annoyed. In her mind, this had nothing to do with his old family, she and the baby were his new family and that's where Kip's loyalty should lie. He should be more worried about offending her, not them.

He was away in London for two days with some of his team at the Luxury Travel Show at Alexandra Palace, and from what he'd said it was an excuse for a lot of eating, drinking, and sharing of industry gossip. The pandemic had very nearly brought the travel industry to its knees and while many firms had gone under, the ones who'd survived – the comrades in arms – enjoyed meeting up at trade shows to relive the old glory days.

He had left the house early yesterday morning with what she was convinced was something of a spring in his step: maybe he was glad to be escaping, and to have the chance to think about something other than being a father once more. Not that he would ever admit to that. And not that she would ever wheedle such an admission from him; there was no need to compound the risk she had taken. Because as Phoebe had just suggested, it had been a hell of a risk on her part to take the unilateral decision to go ahead with the pregnancy.

As clearsighted as she now felt about the choice she had made, Zoe knew that Kip still had some catching up to do, which was understandable. It sounded calculating of her, but she had reasoned that her decision would test Kip's love for her. She had seen it as only fair on them both.

'I bet Kip was shocked though,' Phoebe said. 'He must have thought all that was behind him.'

'It was a shock to us both,' Zoe admitted, 'but he's delighted at the prospect of taking on the role of father again.' And echoing his own words, she added, 'After all, he's the more experienced of the two of us when it comes to babies, so he'll be a dab hand.'

'It's still going to be a big change for you both, isn't it?' Phoebe said, 'seeing as you haven't been a couple for that long and with him being so much, well you know, so much older than you. He's a granddad, isn't he?'

'He'll be a great dad,' Zoe said tightly, disliking the negative way Phoebe was talking and the way she was putting Kip down. Not a word had Phoebe ever said before about Kip and his age.

Full of regret now that she'd admitted to Phoebe that she was pregnant, especially as she knew Kip would be cross with her, she wished she could rewind to the moment when Phoebe had leant over her desk that morning and caught Zoe looking at a mother-and-baby website on her computer in the office.

'OMG, you're not, are you?' Phoebe had whispered excitedly.

It had seemed futile to lie and in a way, Zoe had wanted to share her news with a friend, with someone who wasn't a doctor or a midwife. And Phoebe was the one work colleague who Zoe considered a friend. She was actually the only new friend Zoe had made since making the move to Suffolk. Her relationship with Kip had been all-consuming and she simply hadn't felt the need to mix with either her old friends back in London or make new ones here. There was, given the age difference, the small matter of Kip and her old friends not necessarily being compatible. She hadn't cut them out of her life entirely, but she had certainly stepped away from them. A few had said she was mad hooking up with a man old enough to be her father, and one had criticised her for having an affair with a married man and for letting the sisterhood down with her dishonest behaviour. A friend no more, in Zoe's mind.

'When do you plan to let them know in the office?' Phoebe asked.

'Soon,' Zoe said. 'But I'll work for as long as I can.'

'I'll miss you. I suppose you won't come back after the baby is born, will you?'

Surprised at the assumption, Zoe frowned. 'Why do you say that?'

Phoebe smiled. 'You won't need to. Kip will be able to afford to keep you in the style you'd like to be accustomed to, surely?'

Zoe shook her head. 'Not with his divorce, he won't, and more to the point, I like working. I can't see myself stuck at home 24/7. And there's a creche here on site, so childcare won't be a problem.'

'My sister thought the same but when the time came, she didn't go back to work. She says she will eventually, but when both her kids are at school. Will you find out what sex the baby is when you have your first scan?'

'That's something I'll have to discuss with Kip,' Zoe said. 'That would have to be a joint decision.' In view of the autonomy she had previously insisted upon, she could imagine Kip saying, *Oh, so I get a say now, do I?*

In the last week or so, she'd been busy doing the things that most mothers-to-be would have done already – she'd seen a GP and midwife at the medical centre, and she had an appointment arranged for a scan. It suddenly felt very real now.

'Hey, you know what we should do,' Phoebe said, as they turned around and began retracing their steps back to the office, 'but only when you think it's the right time. We must organise a baby shower. What do you think?'

Zoe thought it a terrible idea. 'But who will we invite?'

'Tons of people. Your friends from London for starters. And then there's Katie and Jo in the office here, and ... ' She hesitated. 'Now don't take this the wrong way, but this might be the perfect olive branch for Kip's family, why not invite his daughter and daughter-in-law? Obviously not his wife, that would be a step too far.'

Zoe goggled at Phoebe. 'You can't be serious.'

'I'm being perfectly serious. Like I say, it's the ideal olive branch.'

'You haven't met any of his family. They hate me.' Even though she and Kip had enjoyed a relatively pain-free evening with Ashley and Caro at their village quiz night, the Curse of Aldeburgh still haunted Zoe when she thought of the Langfords *en masse*. Although in fairness, it had been Lexi who'd been the main troublemaker.

'They might hate you now,' Phoebe said, 'but throw a baby

into the mix, well, not literally, obviously, but they'll come round because your child is going to be a half-brother or sister to Kip's children. How could they not want to be involved?'

Cloud-cuckoo-land, thought Zoe, imagining putting the suggestion to Kip and visualising the absolute horror on his face. On her own face come to that.

Much later and having gone to bed early because she was falling asleep while watching the TV, she had no sooner switched off the lamp and laid her head on the pillow than she was wide awake, her mind racing at top speed.

Turning over in the bed, she rested a hand on the space where Kip should be. This was the first time they had spent a night apart since he'd moved in with her and it felt strange him not being here. She'd tried ringing him when she'd arrived home from work, but he hadn't answered. He was probably busy enjoying himself with his old pals. Would he tell any of them about her and his being a father again, maybe as a proud boast that he was in a relationship with a girl so much younger than him? Perhaps not, that wasn't his style; he wasn't the boasting sort.

She wouldn't have thought he was the cowardly sort either, but she sensed he was dragging his feet when it came to telling his family about the baby. Was he really so concerned about upsetting them? Weren't they grown-up enough to accept the situation, and that given Zoe's age, a baby might well have always been on the cards?

Kip had once said that as a parent you never stop wanting to protect your children, and she supposed that was what he was doing. But what would happen when their child was born, would it take second place to Kip's first family?

She thought again of that day in Aldeburgh and of Arabella's husband, Giles, and how he had taken his daughter's side, rather than his wife's. Just a few months ago and Zoe would never have allowed herself to dwell on such a thought, and for the simple reason she had felt one hundred per cent certain of Kip's love for her, that she came first for him and always would.

But now, and since she had fallen pregnant, the axis of their relationship had subtly tilted, and she was no longer so sure that she did come first. She was surprised how much that hurt.

Chapter Thirty-Two

Kip surfaced from the groggiest depths to the sound of a door softly shutting, followed soon after by water running. It took a few seconds for his brain to battle the thumping of a hammer drill going off inside his head in order to orientate himself.

He was not at home.

This was not his hotel room.

And . . . and he hadn't spent the night alone.

He scrambled out of bed, snatching up his clothes from where they'd landed, almost falling over in his haste to put as much on as would make him decent so he could make his escape.

It was not the act of a gentleman when he quietly closed the door after him and shot off down the corridor to his own room, socks and shoes in hand, but then he had not behaved in the manner of a gentleman in the last twelve hours.

Fumbling for his electronic key card to let himself in, he then slammed the door shut as though that would be enough to block out the shame of his actions.

Breathing hard, his mouth dry, and his head still pounding, he tried to compose himself. But he couldn't. It was such a pathetically sordid cliché what he'd done.

Tugging off the clothes he'd just put on and tossing them onto the bed in which he hadn't slept last night, he went through to the bathroom and turned on the shower. He dialled up the heat to as hot as he could bear and stood beneath the showerhead, his face tilted back to let the searing hot water scorch him to the point of pain.

When he could stand it no longer, he switched off the shower and in the steam-filled bathroom he grabbed a towel from the rail, rubbed at his stinging skin then tied it around his waist. Using another towel, he wiped the mirror above the basin and stared grimly at his reflection.

He wished he could say he was looking at a stranger, but he wasn't. This was who he really was. This was the real Christopher Langford, the man who had betrayed his wife by sleeping with Zoe, and now he was the man who had betrayed Zoe. He had known exactly what he was doing when he had said goodbye to his team – Ronan, Amanda and Lucy – who were all heading out for a final night on the town, telling them they didn't need an old codger like him holding them back, and that he would see them at breakfast in the morning before returning to Suffolk. Instead, he had gone to the hotel bar, as arranged, to have a drink with the woman who had been on a nearby stand at the show. One drink had led to several more, followed by dinner and then an invitation to her room.

It was a replay of something that he had very nearly done many years ago when Louisa had been so preoccupied with taking care of the twins and Angus, who was just three months old, that Kip had felt he scarcely registered on her radar. He wasn't making excuses for his behaviour, but at that time sex was the last thing on her mind and there he was alone with a beautiful Greek woman while in Corfu glad-handing existing villa owners, along with prospective ones whose properties he hoped to rent out to holidaymakers. As the ouzo had flowed, he had told himself that so long as Louisa never knew, what harm could it do? But right at the last moment, when he was about to take the woman back to his hotel room, he made his apologies. She had been very good about it, and said that if he changed his mind, he had her telephone number.

That near miss, as he'd referred to that shameful evening of temptation, haunted him for weeks and months after and to make amends he vowed he would be the best husband and father he could possibly be. He sometimes thought that that vow had been far more important to him than the ones he'd said in church when he and Louisa married.

But then Zoe had happened, and that vow had meant nothing. And now he had betrayed Zoe just as he'd betrayed his wife.

'What the hell is wrong with you?' he demanded of his reflection. 'You gave up everything for Zoe, and now you've done this! *Why?*'

He knew the answer all too well and it filled him with wild anger, making him slap both his hands down hard on the marble surround of the basin. Too late he realised he'd brought his left hand down on the water glass which contained his toothbrush and now it was smashed, and a shard of glass was embedded into his palm. For a moment he stared at it in fascinated horror, it seemed so improbable. When blood began to drip onto the marble and into the basin, he gritted his teeth and carefully removed the shard. Blood now flowing copiously, he used a face cloth to bind his hand as tightly as he could.

Going back into the bedroom, he hurriedly dressed and, taking the lift down to the ground floor, he asked the girl on reception if they had a first-aid kit. She took one look at the reddening face cloth he'd tied around his hand and disappeared through a door, returning seconds later with an older woman carrying a white box with a red cross on it. The woman took him away from the reception desk and over to a comfortable sitting area.

'I think you should go to A and E,' she said when he removed the face cloth.

'I'll be fine,' he said, trying not to grimace, 'and who knows how long I'd have to wait before I saw anyone at a hospital.'

She gave him a doubtful look and in exchange he offered up one of his most charming and persuasive smiles. God help him, it was the one he'd used so much last night. 'Please,' he said, 'if you could just do your best for me now, I'd be very grateful.'

She did as he asked and with surprising skill and efficiency.

'You've done this before, haven't you,' he said with another smile.

'Yes,' she replied. 'I was sent on a first-aid course recently; the management here insist on someone knowing what's what.'

'Well, I'm very grateful to you.'

'I still think you need stitches. You will see someone about it, won't you?'

'I will,' he said, rising to his feet. 'I promise.'

Another promise made, he thought while crossing the foyer to take the lift back up to his room. Letting himself in again, and after boiling the kettle to make some coffee, and registering that it wasn't yet eight o'clock, he downed two paracetamol to quell the throbbing pain in his hand as well as the pounding inside his skull.

He'd said he would have breakfast with his team, but he couldn't face them, or risk seeing the woman from last night, so he messaged them to say something had cropped up and that he was leaving earlier than planned.

Next, he texted Zoe. But he struggled to know what to say. Just as he hadn't known what to say when she'd called him before he'd gone to the bar for a drink last night. It had been easier to ignore her call because selfishly all he'd wanted was to be left alone, if only for a few hours, so he could lose himself in a world that was devoid of complication and where he didn't have to be responsible for anything, or anyone.

It was the fear of being a father all over again that was scaring the hell out of him. All that obligation again. Would there never be any let-up from it? A new life with Zoe was supposed to have been about a new chapter for him, one of carefree fun that saw him sauntering off into a golden sunset.

He didn't care if that made him sound selfish. It was selfish! But hadn't he earned the right to be selfish, to want something purely for himself? Ever since his father's accident he'd seen it as his duty to step up and take on the responsibility for others – for his parents first, then for Louisa and the children. There was also the business and all those he employed to think of, and for pity's sake, he even felt responsible for the customers who booked their holiday villas through his company, the homeowners too. Just once he'd like to feel the burden of his life lifted from his shoulders. Was that too much to ask?

He drank the rest of his coffee, cleaned his teeth, having first carefully put the broken water glass in the bin, and then sent a text to Zoe saying he still had a few things to wrap up in London, but he would be home late that afternoon, or early evening depending on the traffic. Before switching off his mobile so no one could contact him, he promised Zoe he'd keep her posted on when he'd be home.

More promises.

More lies.

With London and the M11 and Stansted airport behind him, he pulled into a drive-thru McDonalds in Braintree for more coffee and a burger. Having missed breakfast, he was now hungry. The palm of his hand was hurting too and so he swallowed another couple of paracetamol before setting off again.

Forty minutes later and he suddenly realised that he'd been so lost in his thoughts and on autopilot while driving that he was heading towards home . . . but it was the wrong home, it was Charity Cottage.

He could have found a turning off and performed a U-turn, but out of curiosity he pressed on. It had only been a few weeks since the house had been sold, but when he drew alongside it, he could see the new owners had already begun to put their mark on it. There was a decorator's van on the drive and two men in overalls were on ladders painting the top-floor windows. As ridiculous as it was, he took it as a personal slight, as though he was being accused of letting things slide and not caring enough. He drove on, not wanting to be spotted by any of the neighbours.

It seemed an age ago when he had dealt Louisa such a treacherous and hurtful blow by going behind her back and putting the house on the market. Had the boot been on the other foot, he would have gone ballistic. Louisa in contrast had been a model of constrained anger and hurt. Yes, she had changed the locks to prove a point with him, and had fired off the occasional salvo of sarcasm, but really she had let him off lightly. Another wife might well have wanted to exact hate-filled revenge and punish him more severely. But Louisa hadn't. She had somehow risen above the shock of what he'd done to her.

'Didn't I say Louisa was too good for you?'

The gently scolding voice belonged to his mother and as imagined as it was, it felt unbearably authentic, and he was suddenly overwhelmed with gut-wrenching shame. Both in the way he'd disgraced himself by cheating on Zoe last night and in the way he'd treated Louisa. Perhaps especially in the way he'd treated the woman to whom he'd been married for nearly forty years and who had loved and unquestioningly supported him through the good and the bad times.

With the familiar sensation of his heart quickening and the sense that the air was being sucked out of his lungs, making his chest feel as though it were about to collapse, he slowed the speed of the car and as soon as he was able to, he pulled over onto the side of the road and switched off the engine. Taking a paper bag out of the glove compartment, he put it to his mouth and breathed into it, his eyes closed the better to visualise his lungs slowly filling with air. Just as good old Dr Google had recommended.

When the attack had passed, he opened his eyes and as though hit by a moment of extreme clarity, he knew there was something he had to do.

He had no idea how it would be received, but it felt immensely important that he should do it, as though in some way it would help to alleviate the stress he was under and perhaps put an end to the panic attacks.

Chapter Thirty-Three

In her eyrie at the top of the mill, and with the aid of her craft lamp to help her achieve the extra-fine detail required, Louisa was putting the finishing touches to a pair of 12th scale Ming-style ginger urns. The glazed ceramic pots had started out as plain white, but were now a beautiful blend of yellows, pinks, greens and corals with flowers interspersed with Chinese dragons.

Working on the ginger urns for the last two hours had been a welcome distraction from what had arrived in the post that morning. Opening the envelope and seeing the words *Decree Nisi* had caused her to feel all over again the painful loss of her marriage. The piece of paper signalled that all the legal requirements had now been met and there was no reason for the divorce not to go ahead and the decree absolute issued. She had tried to convince herself that it was no more than a piece of paper with words written on it. She had known the decree nisi was imminent and what it would mean, and that it didn't change anything that wasn't already happening, so why allow herself to be upset?

Because it was impossible to detach herself from the shock she still felt at Kip's betrayal. To feel anything but pain and loss would make a mockery of the life they'd shared and all it had once meant. Her solicitor had warned her that there was a grieving process she had to go through with divorce and there were no time constraints put on it. It would take as long as it took.

Frustratingly it seemed to be a permanent state of affairs that, just as Louisa believed she was making positive strides into her new future and felt more in control of her situation, she suddenly found herself dragged back to the past. But as true as that was, she was aware that with each knock-back she experienced, such as today's post, she did eventually move forward with renewed strength and determination.

If she had learnt anything this last year, it was that it was foolish to presume anything in life. Sometimes she looked back on her old self almost with laughable scorn that she had been so complacent about her happiness, and the happiness of those she loved. And that included Kip.

Currently it was her daughter's happiness, or lack of it, that dominated much of her thoughts. Louisa had tried several times to ring her son-in-law but he had ignored her calls. According to Arabella he was adamant they needed more time apart to think about their relationship. Louisa feared that he had already made up his mind about it and it was only a matter of time before he set divorce proceedings in motion.

As a family she had believed they could not have been more welcoming to Giles and his daughter, but now he couldn't even be bothered to speak to any of them. Ashley had been convinced that Caro would be the one to whom he might speak, but even she had been ignored.

Perhaps it had been a mistake on their part to approach Giles, but how could they not? He was a member of the family – her son-in-law and father to her granddaughter, Heidi, as well as uncle to Peggy and brother-in-law to Ashley and Caro and Angus. He couldn't just be gone from their lives.

Her work finished on the ginger urns, and blotting the excess porcelain paint from the fine bristles of the brush she had been using, and the others she'd wrapped in clingfilm to stop them drying out, she switched off her craft lamp and went downstairs to the kitchen. She was just dipping the brushes into a jar of turpentine to clean them, when she heard a car door slamming followed by a ring at the doorbell. Wondering if it was somebody from the removal firm to collect the empty packing boxes that were piled up in the garage, she went to open the door.

Seeing Kip staring back at her couldn't have astonished her more.

'What's wrong with your hand?' she blurted out.

'It's nothing,' he said.

'It doesn't look nothing,' she said, noting that blood had seeped through the bandage wrapped around his hand.

'Can I come in?' he asked.

She hesitated; her instinct was to say no, she didn't want him in her new home, this was her space which had nothing to do with him.

'There's something I want to discuss with you,' he said when she didn't answer him.

'Is it about the decree nisi?' she asked. 'Presumably you've received your copy this morning.'

'I wouldn't know about that; I've just driven up from a trade fair at the Ally Pally.'

She recalled all the times in the past when she'd gone there with him to help set up the stand, to Olympia too. 'What is it you want to discuss?' she said.

'Please,' he replied, 'I know I'm probably the last person you want to see, but can we talk inside? It won't take long, I promise.'

Reluctantly she stepped aside to let him in and led the way to the kitchen where she indicated that he should sit at the table.

'It's good to see that it's made the move with you,' he remarked, tapping the old oak table that had been at the heart of their family life ever since they'd moved into Charity Cottage. 'How do you like living here?' he asked, glancing around. 'It looks like you've made it into a comfortable home for yourself already. But then you were always good at that.'

'That sounds very like you're patronising me.'

'That wasn't my intention.'

'Have you and Zoe decided where you're going to live?'

He shook his head. 'Not yet.'

'Why not? You were in a tearing hurry to oust me from our home, I assumed that was because you were desperate to buy something to impress your girlfriend.'

The sharpness of her words must have hit their target as he looked down at his bandaged hand, then back up at her, but hesitatingly so. 'I'm sorry that I made you feel that way,' he said. 'How are the children? I haven't spoken with them in a while.'

'Too busy to pick up the phone?'

He frowned at her obvious sarcasm, for which she wasn't about to apologise. 'No,' he said. 'There's a reason why, but I'll get to that in a moment. The thing is, I wanted to . . . well, I wanted to say that I'm sorry for turning your life upside down the way I have, and I do want you to know that I never meant to hurt you. I really didn't. You're the last person in the world who deserved to be treated the way I treated you.'

For the first time since Boxing Day last year, Louisa thought she detected something akin to genuine regret in his voice. Moving away from where she'd been standing, she went and sat down opposite him. 'It's not just me you've hurt,' she said less severely, 'it's our children too.'

'I know, and I'm not proud of that. But it's important to me that you know that my apology to you is sincere. If there was a way to make amends, I'd do it.'

Louisa couldn't help but think there was more to this unexpected visit than Kip merely wanting to apologise to her. Was it her forgiveness he wanted? Did he need her to absolve him of everything he'd done?

'So, tell me how the children are?' he said. 'The grandchildren too, I've missed seeing them all.'

Louisa contemplated Kip's face, a face she knew so well and had loved for so long. He'd been one of those lucky men who had aged well with the passing of years. With a broad forehead and strong jawline, he'd been blessed with a face that automatically inspired confidence and attracted admiring glances. He'd always dressed well too and that had added to his appeal. But sitting here at the table with him, she saw quite a different man. He seemed sadder. Less vibrant. Tired even. And unless she was imagining it, he was a touch greyer at the temples. Was it possible he regretted what he'd done and was that why he hadn't yet bought somewhere to live with Zoe? And just what should she tell him about the family? Arabella had made it plain that only those in the immediate circle of the family should know about Giles taking time out from their marriage. 'The more people who know what's going on,' she had said, 'the harder it will be for him to return.'

But no matter what Kip had done, thought Louisa as she observed him across the table, he was still family, he was still Arabella's father and always would be, and it felt only fair that he should know what was going on. So she told him.

'Did you see this coming?' he asked when she'd explained.

'You say that as though I could have done something to stop Giles.'

'Not at all. Do you think he'd been unhappy for some time?'

'You mean like you were?'

He flinched. 'I suppose so. Rarely are these things done on a sudden whim. Other than Lexi playing up and pushing Arabella to lose it with her, was there anything else going on between them?'

'I believe he's using the fact that she's pregnant as cause for—'

'Arabella's pregnant?' interrupted Kip. 'Why didn't anyone tell me?'

A part of Louisa wanted to say, *because being out of the loop is one of the consequences of you choosing Zoe over me and your children.*

215

But very calmly, she said, 'Arabella doesn't want it to be common knowledge, not when things are so up in the air.'

'But I'm her father. I should have been told.'

'I'm afraid that's something you'll have to discuss with Arabella. But if you'd been in touch, she might have shared her news with you.'

He looked suitably shamefaced at that. 'You're right,' he said. 'Of course you are. When is the baby due?'

'February.'

He blinked. 'That . . . that would mean she conceived around the end of May.'

Surprised how swiftly he'd made the calculation, Louisa nodded. 'Yes,' she said. 'I believe so.'

He blinked again and picked at the bloodstained bandage on his left hand. 'The thing is,' he murmured, 'and I'd rather you heard it from me, but Zoe is also expecting a baby next February.'

Louisa was tempted to laugh but was worried it might develop into an ugly burst of full-blown hysteria. 'Goodness,' she managed to say. 'Am I supposed to congratulate you?'

'I wouldn't expect that of you.'

'You don't sound very pleased, or are you trying to spare my feelings?'

'I'm trying to respect your feelings, but if I'm honest, I'm still in shock.'

'It wasn't planned?'

He shook his head.

'A father all over again,' she said quietly, understanding now the change in him. Clearly fatherhood second time around had not figured in his plans for his wonderful new life. She could actually pity him for the situation in which he now found himself.

'Cup of tea?' she offered.

Chapter Thirty-Four

'How did that make you feel?' the quietly spoken woman on the other side of the coffee table asked. 'When you learned that your father was having a child with his new partner?'

It was the first week of October and this was Arabella's first session with the couples therapist Giles had insisted they see in the hope it would sort out the mess of their marriage. Those were the actual words he'd used – *the mess of their marriage* – which Arabella was sure no therapist would ever employ. When she had opposed the idea of seeking help this way, he had forced her hand by saying her attitude proved that she wasn't as committed to resolving their difficulties as he was.

But here she was, forty minutes into the session and being asked how she felt about her father's girlfriend expecting a baby the same time as she was. *How the hell do you think it makes me feel?* she wanted to shout at the woman opposite her. 'I don't know,' she lied.

'Were you surprised, perhaps? Or maybe a little angry?'

Furious and shocked to my bloody core, more like it, thought Arabella. 'Why would I be angry?' she said, trying not to sound angry. 'It's up to my father what he does.'

'That doesn't preclude a reaction from you, does it?'

'But then why do you assume that my reaction might be one of anger?'

'So you're pleased for your father, then?'

As exasperated as she was, Arabella stifled the sigh of irritation she felt and reached for the glass of water on the table. She wished now she had never mentioned anything about her father to this frustratingly composed woman with her watchful gaze and unnaturally still demeanour. With her large-framed spectacles and thick tawny brown hair, she reminded Arabella of an owl that might at any minute scarily swivel its head 360 degrees. In contrast Arabella felt she was twitching like a hyperactive rabbit in her constant attempts to evade the questions being put to her, expecting every question to be a trap.

She'd fallen headlong into the first trap when she'd been asked to give a broad-stroke picture of her own family and inevitably one thing had led to another, including blurting out the latest news from her father, that Zoe was pregnant. Apparently, Dad had gone to see Mum and had asked her to tell them his news on his behalf, but she'd put her foot down and said it was his place to tell his children they were going to have a half-brother or sister.

He'd rung Arabella a few days ago and had sounded so different from the dad she'd always known, not at all as sure or upbeat as he used to be. But then she supposed she hadn't sounded anything like her normal self either when he'd told her about Zoe being pregnant. Disbelief, followed quickly by angry resentment coupled with Heidi throwing a tantrum at being given the wrong cup to drink from had made her tell her father that she didn't have time to talk.

'When would be a better time?' he'd asked, 'I want to know how things are between you and Giles. If there's anything I can do to help, just let me—'

She'd stopped him from going any further. 'Yes, because clearly you're an expert on marriage, aren't you?' Before he had a chance to reply, she'd ended the call and switched off her mobile.

'I'm neither pleased nor unpleased,' she said in answer to the owl-like woman who was staring at her and patiently waiting for a response. 'Like I say, it's up to my father what he does now.

I'm more concerned with saving my marriage, which is the only reason I'm here. I want you to tell me what I need to do to make things right.' *There*, she thought with satisfaction as she redirected the conversation to where it should have been.

The woman's face lost some of its impassiveness. 'That's not really my role.'

'So what is your role? Why am I even here if you're not going to provide answers?'

'My job is to enable *you* to find the answers.'

Which seemed about as credible as Giles ever owning his failure to see things from her perspective. Not for the first time Arabella wondered what he'd told this woman yesterday when he'd come for his initial session. The arrangement was they should have these two separate sessions to begin with and then the two of them would come together for the next one. Despite her cynicism, Arabella badly wanted to believe that it would work, that this woman would somehow find a way for them to communicate in the way they always used to and their relationship could go back to where it was before it all went horribly wrong.

In the weeks since Giles had moved out, supposedly to give them space in which to think, Arabella's emotions had been all over the place. One minute she'd be vowing she'd do whatever it took to make her marriage work, and the next she would be thinking that she didn't need Giles and he could sod off back to his precious first wife.

He had refused point blank to say where he was staying which left Arabella in no doubt that he was with Jen. Which made a complete mockery of these therapy sessions. Because if he was serious about making things work, he would move back in with Arabella. If not for her sake, then for poor little Heidi's sake. And was it any wonder that Heidi missed her father and had started being difficult and playing up?

She glanced over to the clock positioned between two hideously sentimental framed photographs, one of a cat peering out of a large flowerpot and the other of a wicker basket containing a bundle of kittens. Were these sickly images supposed to put clients at ease, to take the edge off their anxiety? If so, it wasn't working. On the upside, the clock indicated that Arabella only had another two minutes of this torture to endure.

The Owl also looked at the clock. 'There's something I'd like you to think about in the days before I see you and your husband together,' she said.

The session over, Arabella stomped down the narrow staircase of the Georgian building and when she emerged onto the street, the late afternoon October sky was leaden, and it was raining hard. With no umbrella, she set off at a fast pace to where she'd parked her car and by the time she'd unlocked it and was safely inside, the sky was darker still and she was drenched.

Drying her face with a tissue, she started the engine up and as soon as she was on her way to the supermarket before collecting Heidi from Mum's, she rang her brother.

He answered his mobile after three rings. 'How'd it go?' he asked.

'Before I say anything, you're not in the office, are you?'

'No, I'm on my way to pick up Peggy from nursery, Caro's working late. Did talking to someone objective help?'

'No. The woman seemed to be obsessed with our own family dynamics. She was especially keen on talking about Dad.'

'In what way?'

'My homework before Giles and I see her together is to explore how Dad fathering another child might affect me. Because guess what, my reaction is probably the same as Lexi's was to Giles being a father again.'

When Ashley didn't say anything, and as the rain came down harder still, Arabella flicked angrily at the wipers to make them go faster still. 'For God's sake, Ashley,' she then said, 'you don't agree with that, do you?'

'Well, we haven't exactly greeted his news with joyful enthusiasm, have we? It's not like we've rushed to congratulate him.'

'But we haven't gone around smashing things up like Lexi did.'

'That's because we're all grown-up and know that it's wrong. I'll be brutally honest with you, I felt angry enough to punch something, and I'll put money on Angus reacting in the same way.'

Arabella was so distracted by the frantic speed of the wipers and the worsening visibility because of the rain, she nearly didn't see that the car in front had come to a stop. She slammed the brakes on just in time, sending her handbag on the passenger seat flying into the footwell, at the same time letting out a choice expletive.

'You okay?' her brother asked.

'I'm fine,' she said, the traffic moving on now, 'just a useless driver in front of me.'

'You are using your mobile hands-free, aren't you?'

'Of course I am! But honestly, Ashley, I can't see how these sessions are going to help. It feels like I'm going to be permanently on the back foot having to defend myself.'

'You don't know that for sure. If the therapist is any good at her job, she'll try to encourage you and Giles to see things from a different perspective. This isn't just about you. Or for that matter, just about Giles. You both need to take full advantage of the help on offer so the two of you can put things right. That is what you want, isn't it?'

She was just thinking that her honest answer was that she no longer knew what it was she did want when there was suddenly no gap between her and the car in front. The grinding crash of glass and metal and the deafening explosion of the air bag hitting her in the chest and face knocked the breath out of her.

Her only thought was that she would now have to ring her mother to explain that she would be late collecting Heidi from her.

Chapter Thirty-Five

In a daze of jaw-dropping disbelief, Zoe stared at the image on the screen trying to make sense of what she was looking at, and what she'd just been told. She desperately wanted to hang on to the hope that the sonographer was joking, that any second she'd say, 'Aha, only teasing! It's just a little prank I like to play on expectant mothers.' It would be a pretty sick healthcare worker who played such a trick, but right now Zoe would happily take an inappropriate joke over the shock of truthful professionalism.

'Twins,' she murmured, hardly daring to say the word out loud. 'Are you absolutely sure?'

The woman who had squirted gloopy gunk over Zoe's swelling abdomen, and then guided the hand-held device over it and after what felt a very long time, had delivered the bombshell, said, 'Quite sure. Are there twins in the family?'

Zoe swallowed. 'No. I mean yes, in as much as my partner already has a twin son and daughter. But it never crossed my mind that I might . . . that he and I might have twins.'

'In the case of non-identical twins, the gene would have had to come from your mother,' the woman said. 'Twins from a single egg is different, of course, that's nothing to do with a gene being passed down.'

'So, this is just a random coincidence?'

'Yes, if there's no history of non-identical twins on your mother's

222

side of the family. Shall we take another look?' The woman smiled at Zoe and then resumed running the hand-held device over Zoe's abdomen, at the same time pointing to the screen and indicating two tiny heads, and a bunch of legs and arms. Although really it was hard for Zoe to pin down exactly what it was she was looking at. She certainly couldn't tell what sex the babies were, not that she had expected to with this being her first scan, even if it was later than when most first scans were carried out.

Kip was firmly against knowing the sex of the baby. 'Call me old-fashioned,' he'd said, 'but I'd prefer not to know.' Wanting to please him and suspecting that he was still upset that she'd locked him out of the decision-making process, and this was his small way of asserting himself, she had agreed that when the time came, she would go along with his preference.

She had done a fair bit of that in the last week or so, agreeing to his preferences, particularly after his return from the trade show in London. From the moment he was home he'd seemed on edge, one minute bending over backwards to make her feel special and then the next, withdrawn and preoccupied. He'd cut his hand while he'd been away, a clumsy accident with a glass, he'd said, and she often caught him staring into the distance absently picking at the plaster he'd used to replace the bandage which he'd arrived home with. She knew that he'd now told his children that she was pregnant and that he'd discovered Arabella was also expecting.

He made no secret of his annoyance and disappointment that he hadn't been told about that sooner and that his daughter's marriage was going through a shaky patch.

'I was deliberately kept out of the loop,' he'd repeatedly grumbled. To which there was no reassuring response Zoe could give. And there was definitely no point in reminding him that he'd deliberately kept his own news from them so he could hardly claim the moral high ground. It all meant that Zoe was constantly on her guard and constantly making allowances. She knew and accepted that it couldn't be easy for him, but it wasn't exactly a picnic for her either.

Yesterday, when he'd been driving them home from work, and in stony silence, she'd been worried enough to ask if he was okay, because unquestionably he wasn't. He'd said he was just tired. But when she asked him the same question again later that night as he was getting into bed and she was putting away his shirts which she'd ironed for him, he'd snapped at her. 'For God's sake, just leave me alone will you!'

Her immediate reaction – her totally unfiltered reaction – was to swing round from the wardrobe and let him have it. 'Hey,' she'd yelled, 'you might have spoken to your wife like that, but I'm not going to take that shit from you!'

Her words had sprung unbidden from her mouth and as Kip stared back at her with a shocked expression on his face, she'd realised that the outrage she'd expressed was a mere drop in the ocean of what had been simmering away inside her for some time.

He'd apologised and said he'd had one of those days and the last thing he needed was any more hassle at home.

'*Hassle?*' she'd flung at him, not believing for a second that his apology was genuine, not when he'd levelled a criticism at her in the same breath. 'Asking if you're okay is considered hassle, is it? Well, I shan't make that mistake again. And you can hang up your own shirts,' she'd said, tossing the last two she hadn't put away onto his side of the bed. 'Better still, you can iron them yourself from now on!'

'Don't be like that,' he'd placated.

'Like what? Walking on eggshells around you and then being accused of nagging because I'm concerned? Is that what you mean?'

'I didn't accuse you of nagging,' he'd said, out of bed now and picking up the shirts.

'It bloody well felt like it! And don't you dare patronise me by saying it's probably my hormones talking. Do that and you can sleep in the spare room!'

She had been at boiling point by this stage and beyond listening to any kind of reasoning he might offer. Which he didn't and it only made her feel even angrier. In a stew of silent reproach and resentment, she'd spent the night with her back to him. She had flinched exaggeratedly at his touch when he'd apologised again and attempted to kiss her goodnight. He'd then turned away from her. *Good*, she'd thought, *stay as far away from me as possible!*

In the morning, she'd woken to the smell of coffee being brewed downstairs. Not so long ago she would have welcomed that first cup of coffee of the day, but now the smell was enough to trigger a bout of morning sickness. She had just managed to overcome the urge to be sick when the door opened, and Kip appeared in his towelling robe carrying a breakfast tray for her.

'I behaved like a complete ass last night,' he said, setting the tray down on the empty side of the bed. 'Am I forgiven?' There was a small vase on the tray with a single pink rose in it. He must have gone out to the garden for it to add a gesture of sincerity to his apology.

The gesture, however well meant it was, annoyed her. It was self-indulgent of her, but she wasn't prepared yet to relinquish the sense of injustice that had kept her company for most of the night. It still bothered the hell out of her that he'd spoken to her the way he had. She would never have imagined he would do that, nor would she have imagined that she would react with so much anger and resentment. She had to wonder whether her hormones were to blame, even partially, or was there more to it than that, something much more serious? Whatever the reason, she knew she had to accept the olive branch Kip was offering her.

'That was our first fight,' she said, when he handed her the cup of weak tea he'd made for her, 'and it doesn't feel nice.'

'I agree,' he said, 'it doesn't feel nice. And for the record,

Louisa didn't take any nonsense from me either. She was never a doormat, and I don't expect you to be one either. I'm not that kind of a man.'

If only he hadn't said that about his wife, Zoe had thought later when he'd left for work. Why had he felt the need to bring her into the conversation? The disagreement had nothing to do with Louisa, it was about the two of them.

She had still been brooding on this when she was on her way to the hospital for her first scan. She had taken the day as holiday, and Kip, who hadn't been able to take the day off, was supposed to meet her at the hospital, but he hadn't shown up. Which was why she was here without him, lying on her back and receiving the news that she was expecting twins.

When she emerged from the ultrasound scan department, she took out her mobile which she'd switched to silent mode during her appointment. She was just thinking that Kip had better have a damned good excuse for why he hadn't been with her for this significant moment, when she saw that he had tried several times to ring her. There was a text too and in response to that, she put away her car keys, and her irritation that he had seemingly let her down. Following the hospital signs, she hurried in the direction of the A&E department.

Chapter Thirty-Six

It felt forever before somebody came and gave them any information about Arabella's condition and the longer the wait had gone on, the more Ashley feared the worst.

But thank God, and as bad as it was, the worst hadn't happened. Mum had been given permission to go and see Arabella and so that left Ashley and his father in the crowded waiting area hovering awkwardly around each other. They neither seemed to know what to say to the other. He was ashamed to think it, but there was a part of Ashley that wanted to blame his father for Arabella's accident because ever since he'd left Mum for Zoe, it was as if it had triggered a chain of events and nothing was as it should be.

His parents' marriage was gone.

Charity Cottage was gone.

Arabella's own marriage was in trouble.

And now this.

For something to do, and to stop his mind from going any further down the dangerous path of apportioning blame, Ashley went in search of more coffee from the vending machine. It didn't matter how awful the murky brown liquid was, it was a distraction from worrying, and of reliving that awful moment when mid-conversation with his sister, he'd heard the crunch of metal and glass and then the explosion of the airbag. A surge of adrenaline flooding through him, he'd shouted her name into his mobile in the hope of a response, a confirmation that she was okay and involved in nothing more serious than a tiresome shunt. But there had been nothing from her, not even a gasp or a groan. The silence had been unbearable.

Leaving his personal mobile free in case Arabella was able to call him back, he'd used his work mobile and rung the emergency services. But unable to provide the exact whereabouts of his sister, other than she had been heading out of Bury St Edmunds, he'd had to put his faith in somebody on the scene of the accident calling for an ambulance. He'd then rung Caro to explain that she would have to collect Peggy instead of him as he was on his way to the hospital. Caro had immediately offered to ring his mother and leave work to drive straight to Melbury Mill to take charge of Heidi before fetching Peggy so that Mum could go to the hospital as well. She also said she would contact Giles. 'What about Kip?' she'd asked. 'Shall I call him?'

'No, I'll do that when we know more,' Ashley had said. 'I might be overreacting and this might be nothing more than—'

'No,' she'd said firmly, 'your twin intuition has never let you down, I'll ring your father. Angus too.'

When Ashley had arrived at the A&E department nobody under his sister's name had been admitted. That continued to be the case until shortly after his mother appeared. No details were given to them, only that Arabella had been admitted and was now being attended to. It was an hour and a half later, and after Dad had shown up, that a doctor came and spoke to them. Arabella had been taken to the X-ray department and it had been confirmed that she had two cracked ribs, and a broken wrist. She also had lacerations to her face and what was going to be the most upsetting for her, there was a risk that she might lose the baby. She was bleeding, so the doctor said, and a scan was being arranged as soon as it could be done.

While waiting his turn in the queue for the vending machine,

Ashley's mobile vibrated. Taking it out of his pocket, he saw that it was Angus.

'Caro's just told me the news. What's the latest? Is she okay?'

Heartened to hear his brother's voice, Ashley brought him up to speed.

'I'm working down in Plymouth,' Angus then said, 'but I could be there late tonight if I set off now and get my foot down.'

The thought of his brother driving too fast and putting himself at unnecessary risk made Ashley say, 'No, stay where you are, and I'll keep you updated.'

'Are you sure?'

'Definitely, the last thing Mum needs is to worry about you having an accident as well.'

They ended the call, and carrying two paper cups of coffee, Ashley went to look for his father. If it were possible, the waiting area had suddenly become even busier and noisier, and wanting to escape the stiflingly chaotic atmosphere, Ashley suggested they take their drinks outside.

Running the gamut of smokers gathered around the entrance, they found an area in the shadowy dark behind a concrete pillar which afforded them some shelter from the wind that had picked up. At least it wasn't raining now.

'I spoke to Giles while you were fetching the drinks,' his father said, 'and he's on his way. Apparently, he's been in meetings all afternoon which is why it's taken Caro so long to reach him.'

'Did you tell him there's a risk Arabella might lose the baby?'

'I didn't think that was my place.'

'Whose place do you think it is?'

His father looked at him with a pained expression. 'That sounds like a very barbed remark.'

'I suppose it does. Because time was you wouldn't have doubted your place in the family, and now you—'

'And now I do,' he finished for Ashley. 'You really don't have to spell it out for me; I know all too well that I'm now regarded as being outside of the family, rather than at its centre. But just because I left your mother, it doesn't mean I stopped loving and caring for you children in the way that I always have, and always will.'

Ashley couldn't help himself, he felt ruthlessly compelled to drive home the point he wanted to make. Maybe it was because he needed to lash out, to break something irrevocably, in precisely the same way Lexi had wanted to destroy what she'd known to be precious. 'But with the path you've chosen, your loyalties are obviously divided now, aren't they, Dad?' he said.

His father shook his head. 'Not true. Right now, I should be with Zoe while she has her first scan. But I'm not with her, I'm here with you because I love my daughter and I put her first.'

And how was that going to go down with Zoe, thought Ashley.

Chapter Thirty-Seven

Kip drove away from the hospital with reluctance. He'd wanted to stay by his daughter's bedside watching protectively over her, but along with Louisa and Ashley, he had been told very kindly, but very firmly, that they should all go home now.

But home was the last place Kip wanted to be. He suspected he might be in big trouble with Zoe. There had been no response to his text that Arabella had been involved in a car accident and that he was on his way to the hospital so wouldn't be able to be with Zoe for the scan. He had hoped she would come and find him in the A&E department when her appointment was over, but she hadn't. Initially he'd wanted to think her staying away had been a mark of respect, that this was a family matter, and she felt her presence might be unwelcome. He'd sent her several more messages, but there had been nothing in return. Then just as he began to worry that maybe something had happened to her, Zoe sent him a text – *I'm at home*. He should have felt relieved that she was all right, but the terseness of the text provoked him. Where was the concern for Arabella? Where was the support for him when he'd been frantic with worry?

He was convinced that there could only be one reason for Zoe sending that message and it was because she was aggrieved at his not being with her for the scan. If he was right, she needed to accept that there were certain no-go areas in their relationship.

Louisa might not be his wife anymore, just as he'd told Ashley, but his children would always be his children, no matter what.

He parked behind Zoe's car on the road outside her cottage. There were lights on inside and with the curtains not yet drawn, a habit of Zoe's that always irritated him – he favoured pulling the curtains across to thwart passers-by from looking in – he could see straight into the sitting area and beyond to the kitchen at the back.

When he'd first moved in with Zoe he'd enjoyed the compact size of the cottage, but all these months on and it felt too small for them and as Zoe kept reminding him, with a baby on the way they really should be looking more seriously for somewhere bigger. But nothing they had seen online, or the few properties they'd viewed, had appealed to Kip. He had thought Louisa quite mad for buying that windmill, but secretly he was envious. Not of the mill itself, but of the creative freedom she must have experienced imagining it as her new home. Something like that would, of course, be totally impractical for him and Zoe, now that she was pregnant.

He favoured a property with character and some space around it, while Zoe wanted nothing older than Victorian, the more modern the better. To his surprise, and disappointment, she had said she wouldn't sell her cottage. 'That's ring-fenced,' she'd informed him.

'But it would add to our funds in buying something really nice,' he'd countered.

'I'll rent it out to put towards whatever mortgage payments we take on together,' she'd said, 'but I won't sell it.'

He wanted not to mind that she flatly refused to sell the cottage, but he did. He minded a lot. Did she want to hang on to it because she wanted an escape route should things not go as planned between them? It certainly didn't encourage him to take on the huge financial commitment that buying a new house would entail, not when divorce was having such a depleting effect on his resources.

But then wracked with guilt after what he'd done in London

at the trade show, he felt it was the least he could do to let Zoe keep her mother's cottage. Sometimes he'd wake in the night, his heart hammering in his chest and his body covered in sweat after dreaming that it wasn't Zoe lying in the bed next to him, but the woman he'd slept with. Once or twice, he'd wanted to confess his crime to Zoe, just to be rid of the guilt, but he couldn't bear the shame of such an admission to her.

He still didn't know how he could have done what he had when he loved Zoe. He hated himself for his betrayal, for being so pathetic that he had needed to do something so reprehensible. The cut to his hand, thankfully healing now, was a daily reminder to him of his deceit. Every time he looked at it, he was filled with regret, and not just for that shameful night, but regret that he hadn't taken charge of ensuring Zoe didn't fall pregnant. Regret too that he'd agreed to that awful weekend in Aldeburgh when conception had happened. It seemed to him that ever since then, a shadow had been cast over them and with each day that passed, the shadow had lengthened inexorably.

Still sitting in the car, he checked his mobile for work messages. He scrolled through the emails for anything that was urgent and decided they could all wait until the morning.

Out of the car, he let himself in with the key Zoe had given him when he'd moved in. He called to her. She didn't call back as she usually did and dumping his work things and overcoat at the foot of the stairs, he went in search of her.

He drew a blank downstairs and after plugging in his mobile in the kitchen to charge, he went upstairs. He found her in semi-darkness lying on the bed with a flannel draped across her forehead.

'Are you okay?' he asked. It was a stupid question; she obviously wasn't and all at once he was full of concern and was sorry for being so cross that she hadn't come to be with him at the hospital.

'It's just a headache,' she murmured.

'Have you taken anything?'

'No. I don't want to.' She moved a hand to her abdomen. 'It might be harmful. Tell me about Arabella. Is she all right?'

He went and sat on the edge of the bed and shared what he knew. 'They're keeping her in overnight, maybe tomorrow night as well,' he said. 'She'll be devastated if she does lose the baby.'

Zoe removed the flannel from her forehead and eased herself into a sitting position. 'I'm sorry.'

'So am I. We'll probably know more in the morning.' He found he suddenly had to clear his throat which had become tight with emotion as he recalled how upset Arabella had been when he'd left her. Then wanting to make amends for thinking badly of Zoe, he said, 'Shall I make you a cup of tea? Or what about something to eat? Have you eaten?'

'You haven't asked about the scan,' she said, ignoring her questions.

'I'm sorry, what with Arabella and then seeing you like this, I—'

'Please don't say you forgot.'

'I wasn't going to say that,' he said, affronted, 'I was going to say I was coming to it after I'd made sure there wasn't anything I could do to help you. Come on then, tell me everything.'

'Something else you haven't asked me is why I didn't go to the A and E department when I read your text.'

He looked at her, baffled. 'I assumed, knowing now that you weren't feeling well, that you just wanted to come home.'

'No,' she said flatly, 'that wasn't the reason. I did go, in fact, I rushed to be with you, to be by your side when I knew you'd be so worried. But then I saw you outside the A and E department with Ashley and I heard what you said, that your loyalty to your daughter effectively trumps whatever it is you feel for me. I heard you, Kip, so don't insult me by denying it.'

'I didn't see you,' he said lamely, aghast that she'd heard what she had. 'Why didn't you come and say something?'

'What, humiliate myself by letting you say to my face that I'll forever be second best, that your family will always come first?'

'You're being ridiculous,' he said. 'You're making something out of nothing. For God's sake, my daughter had just been in a car accident, and I was worried sick! How the hell could you expect me to make any choice other than the one I did?'

She stared at him with such coldness, he felt a chill run through him.

'You'll never do the unthinkable, will you?' she said.

'What?'

'Put me first. It's never going to happen, is it?'

He was shocked. 'You have no idea what you're saying,' he said. 'But I promise you, when the time comes and you're a parent, you'll know that there are some ties that you can never cut, and they will always make you behave in a particular way.'

'And how will you prioritise your new offspring? How low down the pecking order will they come?'

He was about to say again that she was being ridiculous when the words froze on his tongue. 'What do you mean by *they?*' he said.

She swung her legs round, pushing him out of the way so she could get off the bed. Looking down at him now, she said, 'If you'd been with me for the scan, you'd have seen for yourself that I'm expecting twins.'

He stared at her as yet another wave of shock swept through him. He swallowed. 'Twins,' he echoed.

'Yes,' she said. 'Perhaps now you'll answer my question. How low down the pecking order will *they* be in your priorities?'

'That's not how parenthood works,' he said, something hardening in the pit of his stomach as he too stood up.

'It clearly does because Arabella's husband has prioritised his first daughter over Heidi, hasn't he, and look what that's done to their relationship!'

'Stop!' he cried, 'this is nonsense!'

'It's not nonsense, it's the truth!'

Kip couldn't take any more of this. He'd endured enough emotional stress at the hospital worrying about his daughter without Zoe acting as though the world had to revolve around her. He suddenly needed air. Lots of it. His mouth was dry, and his head was spinning. The breath snatched out of his chest, he charged from the room and hurtled down the stairs, nearly stumbling such was his need to get away. He heard Zoe call after him.

'I suppose this means the honeymoon period is over for us.'

Chapter Thirty-Eight

Zoe didn't follow Kip down the stairs, instead she threw the damp flannel she'd been holding through the doorway and onto the landing. She was fully aware that it was a childishly petulant gesture, but she didn't care. She was all out of caring.

At the sound of the front door slamming, she went over to the bedroom window and saw Kip approaching his car in the street. With a blip of the locking system and a flash of lights, he flung himself behind the wheel and without bothering to put on his seatbelt, he drove off into the night. So that was his answer, was it, to run away?

Just as Giles had, she thought bitterly.

Her head throbbing ever more painfully, she snatched at the curtains and drew them across the window. Picking up the damp flannel from the landing floor, she took it through to the bathroom. There, she opened the cabinet above the basin and found some paracetamol. She'd previously checked online and read that it was safe to take, but she hadn't wanted to take any chances.

Bit late now for that, she thought, downing two of the pills with a gulp of water from the tap. She'd taken a colossal chance on Kip and look where that had got her.

That was the trouble with love, it never felt as though chance had anything to do with it. It was fate. It was destiny. It was meant to be. That was the spell that love cast over you. Until it went wrong. Then it felt like the stupidest risk you could ever take. Playing Russian roulette would come with less jeopardy!

Question was, where did they go from here?

She didn't have a clue. Right now, she needed to go downstairs and make herself something to eat. She had been too wound up earlier to contemplate eating and with the headache from hell which had started in the car coming home, she had lain on the bed and had tortured herself with replaying repeatedly what she'd overheard Kip saying to Ashley. *'I'm here with you because I love my daughter and I put her first.'*

She had gone to be with Kip with the best and purest of intentions, only then to hear those damning words coming out of his mouth. He and Ashley had been so focused on each other neither had spotted her and, unable to bring herself to take another step forward, she had slipped away. Why stay when she counted for so little? She had driven home brimming with righteous anger and a brewing headache.

In the kitchen and having scrambled some eggs and buttered a slice of toast, she sat down to eat. Such was her hunger she cleared the plate within minutes. Putting another slice of bread in the toaster, she thought with some irony that she wasn't eating for two now, but three.

The look on Kip's face when she'd broken the news to him that she was expecting twins would have been funny had it not been so serious. Fatherhood second time around had been a big enough shock for him, but twins, and she knew this with total conviction, was the end of not just their honeymoon period, but of their relationship. Everything had changed for the worse since she had taken that pregnancy test and seen that life-altering result. Or did it all start going wrong when Zoe first strayed into the Langford family's orbit and she began seeing Angus?

No sooner had she thought of Angus than she had a sudden longing for those simple days of when she had been in a relationship with him, and it had been so uncomplicated between them. But then he had scared her off by becoming too serious about her.

What a joke, she thought as the slice of toast popped up. Buttering it with a generous hand, then adding a hefty layer of peanut butter, she wondered if she was jinxed in some way and attracted bad luck. Or was she bad luck itself and anything she touched she destroyed? Look what she had done to the Langfords. She had turned his children against Kip and forced his wife to give up her beloved home.

And all for love.

Where was that love now? Had it been so fragile that it couldn't weather the first storm they encountered? Had Kip ever really loved her?

He had spoken so powerfully of her being his soulmate, of her setting him free from his tired old existence with all its constraints and the sense of duty he had borne all his life. She had, he said, given him the chance to live anew. She had got such a big kick out of knowing she had done that for him. It had been a massive turn-on too, being told that she'd set someone free to live their best life. How quickly though that best life had been revealed to be nothing but a mirage. She had been no more than a form of carefree escapism for Kip and now with twins on the way he doubtless saw himself as constrained as he'd ever been.

Her hunger satisfied, she boiled the kettle for a cup of tea. She'd just taken her first sip when she started at the shrill ring of a mobile. It was coming from the countertop where her mobile was charging. Except it wasn't hers, it was Kip's phone that was ringing. He must have left it there in his hurry to get away from her.

Thinking it might be important, something to do with Arabella, she went over to see if caller ID would show who was trying to contact Kip.

It was Angus and he certainly wouldn't want to speak to her.

But again, she thought of Arabella and knew that she should answer the phone.

'Oh,' he said, when she told him his father wasn't there. 'He was my last hope as I can't get hold of Mum or Ashley.'

An awkward pause then followed between them.

'I'm sorry about Arabella,' she said to break the silence, almost adding that she had just been thinking about him. In the circumstances she didn't think that would be a good idea.

'Is Dad at the hospital?' he asked without responding to her comment.

'No. He's . . . well, I don't know where he is.'

There was another lengthy silence, then Angus surprised her. 'So . . . er . . . how are you?'

She swallowed nervously. 'You know I'm pregnant, right?'

'Oh yeah, we all know you're pregnant.'

'You make it sound as though I did it deliberately.'

'It's no business of mine if you did or didn't.'

'But I didn't,' she said, wondering why on earth she was so keen to defend herself to him.

'Whatever you say, but I hope you're pleased with yourself for what you've done to my family.'

At the hostility in his voice, she felt a weight of sadness. 'Angus,' she said, 'I didn't make Kip do anything he didn't want to do.'

'But if you'd done the right thing and left well alone my parents would still be together.'

'But would they be happy?'

'They were before you split them up. But I guess your happiness is much more important to you than my mother's. Or anyone else's for that matter.'

It was hard to take his acrimony, especially given how things were between her and Kip now. She didn't want to fight with Angus. She didn't want to fight with anyone. 'I'm sorry, Angus,' she said. 'I'm sorry for making your mother so unhappy, and you

240

too. It seems I have a knack for hurting people. But if it makes you feel any better, life isn't exactly a bed of roses here for me.'

She heard Angus scoff at that. 'Is this the bit when you say you regret what you did and ask me to forgive you on behalf of my family?' he asked.

No, she thought, *it's the bit when I admit that I may have got it wrong and thoroughly screwed up my life*. 'I'm not looking for forgiveness from you,' she said, 'or sympathy.'

'Why would you think I would offer you either of those?'

'I don't. I . . . I don't know why I said that.' She suddenly felt dangerously close to being overwhelmed by the events of the day, realising that she did want sympathy, she wanted lots of it! She wanted someone to take her in their arms and tell her it was all going to be fine.

'Are you okay?'

'Not really,' she managed to say after taking a deep breath.

'Why, what's wrong?'

'Everything. Everything that could go wrong, has.'

'Anything in particular?'

'Why do you want to know, so you can revel in my misfortune?'

'That might be your MO, but it's not mine.'

'I'm sorry. It's just been a shitty kind of a day. But I'm well aware that your sister's had a far worse day, so really I have nothing to grumble about.'

'Except if my ears don't deceive me, you do want to have a grumble about your *shitty* day, so go right ahead and tell me what's wrong.'

Hearing Angus speak in that familiar arch way of his reminded her once more of when she and Angus had been a couple and of the straightforwardness of their time together, when life had been so steady and easy. Halcyon days, she thought with sadness.

'I found out today that I'm expecting twins,' she said, 'and I think . . . I think it's over between Kip and me. That's why he's not here. We had a row when he came home after being at the hospital and then he walked out on me.'

'What was the row about?'

'That his family is always going to come first.'

'It didn't feel that way when he chose you over Mum.'

'That was then. Now that I'm pregnant with a double load of trouble and responsibility, everything's changed. And I can't believe I'm having this conversation with you, Angus. You must hate me and would have every right to say I destroyed your parents' marriage and for no real reason if Kip and I split up for good.'

'Sounds like there's no need for me to say that when you've said it yourself. But do you really think it's over between you both?'

'Yes,' she said with frightening certainty. 'I'm no longer what your father thought he wanted.'

'But is he still what you wanted?'

Good question, she thought.

Chapter Thirty-Nine

In the hours since Louisa had left Arabella and arrived back at the mill, and in an effort to distract herself from worrying about her daughter, she had thrown herself into frenzy of activity by emptying the last remaining packing boxes which she hadn't yet dealt with.

Now at just gone ten o'clock and having realised she'd missed a call from Angus, even though she'd been listening out for her mobile in case the hospital rang, she messaged him. She waited for a reply and when there wasn't one, she poured herself a large gin and tonic and tipped some stuffed olives into a ramekin dish and went and sat by the log-burning stove in the hope of relaxing. But as comforting as the warmth of the flickering flames and the sound of spitting logs were, and as tired as she was, it was impossible for her to relax fully.

From the moment Ashley had rung her with the news that Arabella had been involved in a car accident while talking to him on her mobile, the adrenaline had not stopped pumping through her until she had actually seen her daughter. Knowing that she was alive, after that long unbearable wait for news, had made Louisa want to weep with relief.

But seeing her daughter lying in that hospital bed looking so hurt and vulnerable, then having to leave her there alone and not knowing if the baby was going to be all right, had been heartbreakingly difficult. They had just said their goodbyes, Kip being the first to leave, when Giles had shown up.

It might have been the accumulation of emotion Louisa had tried so hard to contain for Arabella's sake, but Giles's late appearance had the effect of making her want to have a go at him. Perhaps sensing that, Ashley had stepped in and after explaining what they knew, he'd led his brother-in-law over to the reception area to see if there was any chance of him being allowed to see his wife. There was some waiting around before the reply came back that it wouldn't be possible. Giles had kicked up a bit of a fuss at that but was then informed that it wasn't the medical staff who had refused to let him go up to the ward, but Arabella herself. Giles was guarded at the best of times, and it was hard to read his reaction, but he had to have been taken aback.

'She's obviously tired,' he'd said. 'If only I hadn't been working up in Nottingham, I could have got here sooner.'

'Oh please, save us your *if onlys* and your *could haves*,' Louisa had snapped at him, 'as though any of that would have made a difference!'

There was no difficulty in reading Giles's shocked reaction to that, and she was beyond caring how he might feel, she was also beyond always trying to say the right thing. Before Giles could respond or defend himself, Ashley intervened once more.

'Giles, I suggest you follow me home so you can see Heidi, although it's likely Caro will have put her to bed. You can have something to eat with us.'

Every family needs a peacemaker, Louisa reflected now as she sipped her gin and tonic while listening to the wind gusting outside. Normally that was her role, but tonight at the hospital, Ashley had been the one to take it on.

He'd called her from his car when she'd been driving home to make sure she was okay. He'd apologised for not inviting her to come back for supper as well, but he'd thought it best to keep her and Giles apart for the time being. 'Very wise of you,' she'd said.

She was on her feet, poker in hand to push another log into place when the doorbell rang. A quick glance at the grandfather clock told her it was half past ten. With the mill being at the end of the lane there could be no reason for anybody to be just passing by. Her grip tightened on the poker. But then she thought that maybe Angus had ignored his brother's advice to stay in Plymouth and had come anyway, and that was why he'd tried calling her.

She went to see if it was him but when she cautiously opened the door not only was she hit by a blast of cold wind, but she was stunned to see Kip standing in front of her and not Angus.

'What on earth are you doing here?' she asked. 'It's not Arabella, is it, there's not been a change for the worse, has there?'

'No, no, don't worry, I'm not here because of Arabella. Not directly at any rate. I hope that isn't for me,' he added, his gaze dropping to the poker in her hand.

'At this time of night, you can never be too careful,' she said.

'Very true. I know it's late, but may I come in?'

What choice did she have, she thought, closing the door after him. Once he was inside and he'd removed his overcoat, which she took from him and draped over the back of a chair, she watched him push a hand through his hair. He looked as exhausted as she felt, only more so.

'I don't wish to be rude,' she said, 'but why are you here, Kip?'

He rubbed at his face, dragging his skin down so roughly with his hands that his face appeared momentarily to resemble a grotesque mask.

'I know I have no right to bother you,' he said, 'but I couldn't think where else to go.'

'I'd have thought home with Zoe was the obvious place.'

'Yes, it should be, but I've been driving around for the last hour or so trying to think straight.' His eyes darted about the kitchen as though searching for something, then came to rest on the bottles of gin and tonic which she'd left out, along with the lemon which she'd sliced on the chopping board. 'I don't suppose I could have a drink, could I?' he asked. 'I haven't had anything since that foul coffee at the hospital.'

'What would you like?'

'A gin and tonic would hit the spot if you don't mind. I know it's more than I deserve.'

She rolled her eyes. 'Don't do that.'

'Don't do what?'

'Play the phoney I'm-not-worthy card. It's pitiful.'

'I'm sorry. But maybe it's how I feel.'

'Well, it won't wash with me. Take the poker and go and sit down by the fire while I mix you a drink. Then you can tell me what brings you to my door. Again,' she added, thinking that this was the second time in as many weeks that he'd paid her an unexpected visit.

His drink poured and her own glass topped up, she opened a bag of salted cashew nuts and joined him by the fire.

'By the way,' she said when she sat down, 'Giles turned up at the hospital shortly after you left.'

'He took his bloody time getting there.'

'Apparently he'd been in Nottingham.' She then told Kip what she'd said to their son-in-law.

'Good for you. I'd have said much the same, only not so politely. Which I'm all too aware makes me sound like a hypocrite, given how I've behaved and how you must consider me as the lowest of the low when it comes to husbands.'

'Look,' she said, exasperated that he seemed to be overplaying his hand, 'we've established you've been a bastard, so can we just leave it at that, and you stop looking for ways for me to contradict or exonerate you? Because it won't happen. As you've told me before, you did what you did, and this is where we are.

And I for one am doing my best to move on with my life, just as you frequently said I'd have to. I'm not interested in easing your guilty conscience.'

He had the grace to look shamefaced. 'I'm sorry, I was so insensitive when I kept telling you to accept things and move on.'

'Yes, it was insensitive of you, but I have accepted the new reality of my situation and I have got on with it. Sometimes I regret that I didn't kick up more of a fuss and make your life hell, but to fight you would have required more energy than I possessed.'

'It would have been completely out of character for you, too.'

She looked at him with a frown. 'What's that supposed to mean?'

'I mean that you were being the better person. You always were. You still are.'

'Some might say I'm too placid and too willing to accommodate other people's feelings to the detriment of my own.'

'And yet you didn't hold back with Giles this evening.'

'Trust me, I did. There was so much more I could have said.'

Taking a long swallow of his drink, Kip looked at her. 'Do you think there's any chance we can be friends?' he asked.

'Is that really so important to you?' she replied.

'Yes,' he said, 'it is.'

She didn't know what to say, so she said nothing. But with sadness she thought how not so long ago things would have been so different for them. They would have been consoling each other over their daughter's accident. They would have hugged and held hands at the hospital while they waited for somebody to tell them how Arabella was. They would have driven home to Charity Cottage, lain in bed together and given thanks that their daughter hadn't been more seriously hurt. But above all they would have been solidly united in their love and support for her. They could still be the latter, she thought, there was no reason why they couldn't join forces for their daughter's sake.

'Now tell me why you're here and not with Zoe,' she said, passing Kip the bowl of cashew nuts. 'Has she had enough of you already and kicked you out?'

'After today I think there's a very high probability of that happening. She's extremely angry with me. I was supposed to be with her while she was having her first scan this afternoon, but of course, I was with you in A and E.'

'She can surely understand the choice you made?'

'That wasn't the problem. You see, what I didn't realise was that she came to find me only then to overhear me talking to Ashley when I was explaining to him that my priorities would always be to put my children first, that nothing would ever alter that.'

Louisa pictured the scene and could appreciate what a slap in the face that would have felt to Zoe. 'That was unfortunate timing,' she said.

'She accused me of making her feel second best, of putting my family before her and that I was no better than Giles. And in a way, it's true, because how can it be otherwise?'

'Well, you've certainly got yourself into a mess, haven't you?'

'On top of all that, the scan revealed that Zoe is expecting twins.'

You poor devil, Louisa thought. 'Double trouble,' she murmured. 'Do you remember that's what you said when we were told we were expecting twins?'

He nodded. 'And you said it would be twice the joy. You always could see the positive side to something.'

It was true what he'd said, but it was also true that she'd been terrified at the prospect of having twins, yet she had refused to give in to the fear, or let others know how she really felt. It was how she'd always been, not so much a stiff upper lip, as adopting an air of make believe that everything was hunky-dory. Because that was what she wanted, everything to be perfect.

'You still haven't explained why you're here,' she said. 'I hope you're not expecting me to wave a magic wand and make everything better for you.'

'If only it were that simple,' he muttered.

Taking pity on him, she said, 'Kip, I can't solve this for you. My advice is for you to go back to Zoe and say you're sorry. Get down on your knees and beg her forgiveness if that's what it takes.'

'I'm not sure that I want her forgiveness.'

Louisa looked at him sternly. 'You'd better not be thinking of baling out on the poor girl. Do that and I'll lose all respect for you. As will your children.'

'But what if it's all a terrible mistake?'

'Then make sure it isn't. You played a part in creating those two babies; whatever happens, you're their father. You have a responsibility to them, and to Zoe.'

He looked crestfallen at her words. 'I can't go back to her tonight,' he said. 'It's too risky. We'll both end up saying things we'll later regret. Can I stay here tonight? I'll sleep on the sofa. Or the floor. Then we can go to the hospital together and see Arabella in the morning.'

'Visiting hours are from the afternoon onwards,' she said.

'Oh,' he said flatly. 'But please, can I stay? Just for tonight. I'll leave first thing.'

God help her, but Louisa said yes.

Chapter Forty

Visiting hours didn't start until the afternoon, but Giles had somehow sweet-talked the nursing staff into bending the rules so he could see Arabella this morning. Presumably they thought he would be the perfect person to console her and to share in the pain of their loss. They couldn't be more wrong.

She had been woken in the night by a sudden cramping pain in her stomach and she had known immediately that the worrying loss of blood following the accident, as slight as it was, had resulted in her miscarrying. Everything from then on as her precious baby had drained out of her had been a nightmarish blur. But now, now that she was back on the ward and despite how tired and how much pain she was in from her cracked ribs and her broken left wrist which had yet to be put in a cast, she felt her mind was crystal clear on one thing. And that was Giles.

'There's no point in making yourself too comfortable, you won't be staying long,' she said as he sat down by the side of her bed, having tried to kiss her, and then frowned when she'd rebuffed him.

'I know,' he said, 'I was told I could only have a few minutes with you. How are you feeling? I've been so worried about you.'

'Have you? Have you *really*?'

The frown on his unshaven face deepened, the lines around his eyes showing more marked. Since she'd last seen him, he'd had his hair cut. It was shorter than she liked. Perhaps it was how Jen liked it.

'I'd hoped you'd reply to my messages last night when I was with Ashley and Caro,' he said, 'just so I could sleep knowing you were okay and—'

She raised her right hand to stop him from going any further. 'I didn't reply because the only thing I wanted to say to you had to be done face-to-face. I want a divorce.'

His eyes opened wide, and he drew his well-defined brows together. 'Now isn't the time to make any important decisions,' he said. 'Not after what you've been through. You're upset about losing the baby, of course you are, that's understandable.'

'*Don't!*' she burst out loudly, causing the patient in the bed next to hers to look over. 'Don't you dare mention the baby,' she hissed. 'Your first thought must have been one of relief when you heard I'd lost it, and don't deny it.'

'Of course it wasn't, I'm not a monster! But, come on, Arabella, now really isn't the time for this conversation. You need to rest and—'

'Stop telling me what I need when you don't have the first idea how I'm feeling. Now is exactly the right time because it's now that I'm thinking straight, and I can see that you're not the man I thought I'd fallen in love with. I've seen the real you and I don't want to stay married to that man. I deserve better. If we stay married, I suspect you'll end up having an affair, just as you cheated on your first wife with me.'

The muscles in his jaw tightened. He opened his mouth to speak, but whatever he had to say, she didn't want to hear it.

'When I'm discharged from here,' she said, 'I don't want to find you at home. I want you gone.'

'Hold on, it's my home too. I'm the one who pays the mortgage.'

'And you're the one who was only too happy to leave it to take time out when you wanted to give us time to think. Well, guess what, I've done just that! And you can forget about any more couples therapy sessions. What were they for anyway, to turn me into an even bigger doormat so you could blame me for all the problems in our marriage?'

'Everything all right here?'

Arabella turned from Giles to see the nice nurse, the one who earlier had been so sweet to her, standing at the end of the bed with an enquiring look on her face. 'It's just that your voices can be heard by others,' she added discreetly.

'No, everything's not all right,' Arabella said. 'I'd like my husband to leave now. I'm tired.' She closed her eyes and twisted her head pointedly away from him.

'I'm sorry,' she heard him say to the nurse, 'I'm afraid I've exhausted her. Arabella, I'll come back later this evening when you're not feeling so tired.' To her irritation she then felt his lips press against the cheek he'd tried to kiss when he'd arrived.

When the sound of his footsteps had receded, and with her eyes still firmly shut, she drew the bedsheet up over her head.

Chapter Forty-One

Kip's whole being ached for his daughter. Her left wrist was now in a cast, and the cuts and bruises to her face stood out more vividly today. And as much as she tried to sound so bravely defiant, she seemed so very fragile. The worst of her suffering had to be caused by her losing the baby, and he knew there was nothing he could say or do that would ease her sadness. The first they'd known of her miscarrying was when she'd contacted Louisa early that morning. It was news they had both dreaded.

'If this is what you're sure you really want to do, you won't be on your own, love,' Kip said to Arabella, 'you'll have the family to help and support you. But shouldn't you wait until you're feeling stronger before making such a massive decision?'

'Please don't try to talk me out of this, Dad, I know what I'm doing. And anyway, you're a fine one to lecture me about divorce.'

He winced at that, but from the other side of the bed, Louisa said, 'I agree with your father, your body and mind are still in shock from the accident and losing the baby.'

'When you're home you might have a different perspective on things,' Kip tried, 'and more to the point, Giles might realise just how much you really mean to him.'

'I'm seeing things clearly now, Dad. Much more clearly than I ever have before.'

'But what if Giles promises to be more understanding when it comes to you and Lexi?' asked Louisa. 'If that's the root cause of most of your problems, surely that can be resolved?'

'Mum, do you really want me to stay in a marriage that is going to make me miserable?'

'But you were so in love with Giles, weren't you? You used to be so happy together.'

'And you and Dad were so in love with each other once upon a time, and happy too, but look at you now?'

Kip flinched again. 'Comparisons are never a good idea, sweetheart.'

'I don't see why not. You made the decision to end things with Mum because you weren't happy. I might not have agreed with what you did, but everyone deserves to be happy, don't they?'

But I'm not happy, thought Kip, seeing the wounded expression on Louisa's face, *I'm as miserable as hell right now, and I've never felt more alone.*

After staying the night with Louisa, Kip had gone with her to Ashley's to help with the childcare arrangements for Heidi. Louisa had been surprised that Kip wanted to help with their granddaughter, but the office was the last place he wanted to be. Not when there was the risk of running into Zoe. In his hurry and need to get away from her last night, he'd left his mobile on the kitchen worktop, so using Louisa's phone, he'd called his office to say he wouldn't be going in but if there were any emergencies he could be contacted on that number.

When they'd arrived at Ashley's, Caro had already left to drop Peggy off at nursery before going on to work. Giles had also left to go and see Arabella, even though it wasn't visiting hours until the afternoon, and Ashley was holding the fort with Heidi before he too needed to shoot off to his office. The trouble started several hours later when Giles returned from seeing Arabella and with a face like thunder, and without a word of thanks to them for looking after Heidi, he'd announced that he was taking her home with him.

'We're more than happy to look after her if you need to be at work,' Louisa had said. 'It'll be no trouble.'

'Your family isn't going to monopolise Heidi and turn her against me,' he'd exclaimed, 'she's my daughter!'

It was such a wildly irrational and hostile comment that it had triggered in Kip the strongest urge to defend Louisa, and his family. But before he could say anything, Louisa had beaten him to it.

'Giles,' she'd said in a calm but firm voice, 'I appreciate that things are not easy for you right now, but I can assure you nobody has any intention of monopolising your daughter or turning her against you. As a family we're just trying to do our best to help, so please don't ever talk to me like that again.'

Giles had made no effort to apologise and had scooped up Heidi from the sofa where she was watching *Paw Patrol*. She wasn't pleased at being uprooted and immediately made her feelings known and instead of defusing the situation – perhaps he was too rattled – Giles made it worse by raising his voice at her. Her plaintive cries then turned into a full-blown fire-engine wail of outrage and by the time her father had carried her as far as his BMW outside, she was red-faced and screaming, her legs kicking, her arms flailing. Kip had seen it all before with his own children at some point or other during their toddler years, a tantrum that had swept in from nowhere, but he'd never found it as distressing as he had in that moment. He'd felt so angry with Giles but had known it would make things worse to intervene.

It was only when he and Louisa had arrived at the hospital after lunch and when visiting hours had begun, that they learned from Arabella that she'd told Giles earlier that she wanted a divorce. While that might have explained Giles's foul mood, it did not excuse the way he'd spoken.

'I'm hoping to be discharged tomorrow,' he heard Arabella saying now, rousing him from his thoughts. 'I don't want to be stuck here away from Heidi for a minute longer than I have to be.'

'But you mustn't be in too much of a hurry to leave,' Louisa said. 'You must listen to what the doctor says.'

'I can't stand being here though,' Arabella pleaded, a chink in her defiance breaking through, 'I want to be at home with Heidi, I know I'll recover that much faster there.'

'Then let's plan for that, shall we?' Kip said to Louisa, sensing that what their daughter needed to hear was something positive to lift her spirits, even if later a doctor refused to have her discharged.

'Of course,' said Louisa. Then to Arabella, she said, 'How shall we work things? Do you want to come and stay with me so I can look after Heidi while you rest, or shall I move in with you? Although that might be awkward if Giles is around.'

'I've told him I don't want him there when I'm allowed home. Let's face it, he'd as good as left anyway.'

'He was in a very combative mood before we came here,' remarked Kip, 'so my guess is he'll have moved back in.'

At that Arabella grimaced and Louisa said, 'Well, we'll sort all that out should we need to, but I'd be happy to have you stay at the mill if that works best for you and Heidi.'

It was late afternoon when they said goodbye to Arabella and Kip drove them away from the hospital.

They'd only been on the road a short while when Louisa's mobile rang. It was Ashley wanting to know how Arabella was. She put her phone on speaker so Kip could join in with the conversation, a gesture he appreciated. Louisa then relayed what Arabella had told them, that she was set on divorcing Giles.

'I wish I could say I'm surprised,' Ashley said, 'but given how bad things have been between them lately, I'm not. Giles has made it very plain where his loyalties lie.'

'But I can't bear the thought of her going through the same emotional ordeal that I've had to—' As though registering how her words might sound to Kip, Louisa changed tack abruptly.

'Whatever the outcome, your father and I have said we'll support her all we can.'

Having then covered all there was to say, Ashley said that to save Louisa the job of ringing Angus to bring him up to speed, he'd do it himself.

When he'd rung off, Kip reflected on how loyal and supportive his children were, not just to each other, but to their mother. Perhaps especially to Louisa after what he'd done.

'We managed to get a lot right in our marriage, didn't we?' he said.

'In what way?'

'Our children,' he replied, glancing briefly in her direction. 'They really care about each other. That isn't always true of siblings, is it?'

'Yes,' she said, 'we have been lucky in that respect.'

He wanted to say it wasn't luck, that they, as loving parents, had set them the example that working together as a united team was always best. He didn't dare say the words though, not when Louisa would have every right to laugh in his face and accuse him of not caring a damn about their family, not when he could leave it the way he had. But he loved his children so much and he missed the easy relationship they'd once had. For that matter, he missed the relationship he'd once had with Louisa, the familiarity of everything they'd experienced together. Their marriage may have lacked excitement and passion in recent years, but there had been a lifetime's worth of dependable friendship.

They were only ten minutes from the village of Melbury St Mary when Louisa's mobile rang again. This time it was Angus. Once more she put the phone on speaker.

'Ashley's just given me the latest news,' he said. 'Arabella must be devastated.'

'She is,' Louisa said. 'Your father and I have spent most of the afternoon at the hospital with her. He's driving us back to my place now.'

'He's . . . he's there with you?'

Kip caught the surprise in his son's voice.

'Yes,' Louisa confirmed, 'and my phone is on speaker.'

There was a lengthy pause from Angus that made Kip wonder if his youngest son didn't want to continue the conversation knowing that he could hear every word. But what Angus said next totally threw him.

'Dad,' he said, 'I think you should know that I spoke to Zoe last night.'

Out of the corner of his eye, Kip was aware that Louisa was looking at him, probably as surprised as he was. 'How did that come about?' he asked evenly.

'That's not important,' Angus said, 'what is important is that she's under the impression that things are over between the two of you. Is that true? Because if so, considering she's pregnant with twins it doesn't cast you in a favourable light. To put it mildly.'

The last thing Kip needed was his youngest son stating the obvious and making him feel worse than he already did. 'The situation is not as black and white as you portray,' he said. He wanted to ask what had possessed Zoe to tell Angus what she had, but now wasn't the time. Not with Louisa sitting next to him, and not when it should be Arabella who was the focus of the conversation.

Perhaps thinking the same, Louisa said, 'Did your brother tell you that Arabella has told Giles she wants a divorce?'

'Yes. Which doesn't really surprise me after everything that's happened. Do you think she's up for a call from me?'

'I'm sure she'd love to hear from you. Just don't ring too late.'

'Will do. I'm driving back to Borehamwood now, maybe I'll visit her tomorrow if she's not discharged by then.'

'If you need somewhere to stay the night, you're more than welcome?'

'That would be cool. Thanks, Mum.'

When Angus rang off, Kip left the main road and drove slowly along the narrow lane to Louisa's new home, the hedgerows brushing against the sides of the car, the puddles created by yesterday's rain splashing up from the potholes.

'What are you going to do now?' she asked, when he came to a stop beside her car in front of the windmill and she'd leant forwards to pick up her handbag from the footwell.

'To be honest, I don't know.'

'That must be a first for you. You've always known what you wanted and known exactly how to go about getting it. You certainly knew that you wanted Zoe and not me, and you knew that you wanted a divorce and that Charity Cottage had to be sold. All of which you made happen.'

He let out a long sigh and bowed his head. 'The truth is I don't know anything anymore.'

It was an admission that was only partially true because one thing he did know was that he suddenly felt old. All these months of feeling young and full of vitality, as though he was in his twenties again and could take on the world, and now he felt as if he was running on empty.

'I would invite you in for a drink,' Louisa said, 'but I think you need to go home and make things right with Zoe.'

Home, he thought. Where exactly was that for him? He'd had a beautiful home – Charity Cottage – and he'd effectively burnt it to the ground. He raised his head and gazed up at the mill looming over him where the low afternoon sun glinted off the small windows. He thought of the warm comfortable kitchen in which he'd sat last night and he recalled how unexpectedly well he'd slept in the cosy bedroom with its curving walls. He had woken this morning with the childlike sensation that he didn't want to leave. He'd felt cocooned, safe from having to deal with any difficult decisions.

Never in his life had he been afraid to confront a situation and decide exactly what he wanted, and yes, he'd acted with selfish single-mindedness at times, just as Louisa had observed, if somewhat acerbically, but that ability now seemed to have deserted him.

'What if I can't make things right with Zoe?' he said, turning to look at Louisa. 'What if it's over between us?'

'Kip, I told you last night that I can't solve this for you. You need to find out what it is you both want.'

I want for the last year not to have happened, he thought grimly. *I want this nightmare to be over.*

Chapter Forty-Two

Using his mobile in the car, Angus had chatted with his sister for nearly thirty minutes during which time she had veered from total condemnation of Giles and her marriage to tearful regret about losing the baby. He could do nothing more than listen while letting her vent. He feared that for some time yet she would be caught in the same loop of bitter regret.

As soon as he'd said goodbye to Arabella, and with only twenty-five miles to go before he'd be back in Borehamwood, he'd then rung CeeCee in the hope that he might see her when he arrived home. They'd spoken late last night and knowing about his sister's accident, she'd asked straightaway how Arabella was. He told her everything that he now knew.

He'd then moved on to the next big topic of family news which he hadn't felt able to share last night. He'd felt too angry and if he were honest, too ashamed of his father to be able to talk about it. But not wanting to hide things from CeeCee, he now told her about his conversation with Zoe and subsequent brief exchange with his father that afternoon.

She let out a long whistle. 'So now your ex-girlfriend is expecting twins with your dad and he's probably going to dump her? He doesn't do things by halves, does he? I can't wait to meet him; he sounds a real peach of a guy.'

'Why would you want to meet him?' Angus asked.

'To see for myself what kind of man he is.'

'I'm not sure I want you to meet him.'

CeeCee's laughter filled the car. 'Are you worried I might fall for him like your ex did?'

'Not funny. Not in the slightest.'

'Hey, I'm just messing with you.'

'I seem to have a complete humour block when it comes to my dad. You can see that, surely?'

'I certainly can. But I hate to succumb to the use of a cliché, but you really do have to let it go. Unless you like holding on to a grudge; maybe it gives you pleasure.'

'It doesn't!'

'You sound angry.'

'I am. Because just as I thought I was coming round to accepting the situation, I then discover that he might be dumping Zoe. It's like all over again I'm asking the same question, who the hell is this man masquerading as my father?'

'Have you considered that he could be asking himself the very same question? And in any case, some might have expected you to feel that Zoe deserves what's happening to her. Unless, that is, you still have feelings for her. Do you, Angus? Do you feel protective towards Zoe, as though she really doesn't deserve to be treated so badly?'

'No!'

'Are you sure about that?'

'Look, in my book nobody deserves to be treated so callously.'

'That either makes you a very special kind of person for being so generous, or you're kidding yourself.'

'You sound like you've set yourself up as judge and jury of my feelings.'

'And now you're sounding defensive. Which means I must have touched a nerve.'

Angus chewed on his lower lip. This wasn't how he'd imagined the conversation going. Or maybe subconsciously that was why he hadn't told CeeCee about this last night when they'd spoken. Had he been afraid she might dig below the surface of his anger and find something he didn't want her to find? But what exactly? That he'd heard the misery in Zoe's voice and actually felt sorry for her and the mess in which she now found herself? But why did he not feel the same level of sympathy for his father, who clearly had not imagined his new future panning out like this?

'How would you rather I was,' he said to CeeCee, 'the type of person who holds a grudge on an ex and hopes revenge will come in the form of them living a miserable life for ever more, or the type who cares how somebody is treated?'

'The latter, of course. But I'd hate to think that you weren't being honest with me. You are being honest, aren't you, Angus, because I'd sooner you just came right out and said what you really feel.'

She'd said something similar after her mother's visit. 'Come on, out with it,' she'd said, 'what's on your mind? Did my mother give you the third degree and say something she shouldn't have?'

Wary of repeating exactly what Sabine had said about her daughter playing it safe and not taking a risk, he'd fudged his response by saying he'd been wondering if CeeCee wouldn't prefer a different sort of boyfriend, a musician perhaps. She'd laughed long and hard at that but then had stopped abruptly. 'Wow, you're serious, aren't you?'

'Yeah, kind of,' he'd admitted.

'Then don't give it another thought. Put a whole orchestra in front of me and guess what, you, with your unique way of playing "Baa Baa Black Sheep", would still win hands down!'

'You say the sweetest things,' he'd said.

'Always.'

'What I really feel,' he said now in answer to her question, 'is that somehow this conversation has become all about me, and I'd prefer it to be about *us* and if I'm going to see you this evening when I'm back.'

'But the *us* bit only works if you've sorted out the *me* part.'

'But I have,' he said. 'I promise you I know exactly what it is I want.'

'And what would that be, Fan Boy?'

Relieved to hear her customary teasing tone, he played along. 'I reckon you're smart enough to work it out for yourself.'

'In that case I'd say you're completely crazy about me.'

'True. And how do you feel about me?'

'Oh, that's dead easy, I love you.'

And just like that, she'd said the three most meaningful words a person could say to another.

'You still there, Fan Boy?'

He smiled to himself. 'Yes, I'm still here.'

'Well? When a girl declares herself, she expects more than a deafening silence in return.'

'I was enjoying the moment, and because when a guy is crazy about the girl who's just told him she loves him, he needs time to choose his next words with care.'

'And?'

'I'll tell you when I'm home.'

'Leave a girl hanging, why don't you?'

'I promise you it will be worth the wait.'

'Then you'd better get yourself here asap.'

He drove home with the biggest of smiles on his face.

Chapter Forty-Three

Zoe was lying on her bed with her hands laced together and resting on the swell of her abdomen. As tired as she was, she could not relax sufficiently to fall asleep.

She had left work early that afternoon giving the excuse that she was feeling unwell. It wasn't exactly a lie, because feeling sick with worry had to count, surely? It had been a mistake to go in to work in the first place, but she had thought being busy and carrying on as normal in the office would be the ideal distraction. It hadn't; it had made things worse for the simple reason the proximity to Kip's office was such a torment. Unable to concentrate, or stop herself from doing it, she'd kept staring out of the window to see if Kip's car was in the car park. Phoebe had picked up on how jittery she was and asked if she was okay.

'There isn't a problem with the baby, is there?' she'd whispered. 'You weren't given bad news yesterday when you had the scan, were you?'

Whispering back that maybe they should continue the conversation where nobody could hear them, Zoe had indicated they go and talk in the small kitchen area.

'The baby's fine,' Zoe had then said, 'in fact, they're both fine. I'm expecting twins.'

Phoebe had gasped. 'Wow, that's wild!

'That's one way of putting it,' Zoe had said.

'But it's not the end of the world, is it,' Phoebe had said brightly, 'not when you have Kip with all his years of experience on hand? Didn't you tell me that he already has twins? Hey, that's probably how it's happened, a genetic hand-me-down thing.'

Zoe hadn't been able to admit that there might not be any Kip on hand to help, her pride wouldn't let her reveal that this was the main reason for her being upset. 'No, it turns out that hereditary twins pass down the maternal line,' she'd said, 'not the paternal route.'

'So, it's just a case of insane chance then?'

'Something like that, yes.'

But nothing now felt as if chance was involved to Zoe. Now it felt like she had brought this on herself. If she hadn't embarked on an affair with a married man, she wouldn't be being punished the way she was, and if only she hadn't acted the way she had when Angus had wanted to move their relationship onto another level. What had she been so scared of? Hadn't she even conceded to herself that Angus was the nicest boyfriend she'd had, that he had fitted in around her life better than anyone else had, and for the simple reason he hadn't crowded her? Yet somehow none of that had been enough for her. She just couldn't be satisfied, could she? Or had it been too easy with Angus, too perfect and safe, too like the real thing to which she would have to commit? Was that why she had hit the self-destruct button?

And wasn't that what she had done now with Kip by blaming his family for coming between the two of them? She could so easily have avoided doing that if she'd wanted to, but she hadn't. So what the hell was wrong with her that she seemed determined to repeat what was so obviously a pattern of behaviour?

She had never told Kip this, or Angus for that matter, but no boyfriend had ever finished with her, she was always the one to pull the plug on a relationship. Invariably she had done it because she had found herself becoming too emotionally committed, and she would convince herself that it would hurt less if she was the one who walked away first. It was a control issue, of course. But it couldn't go on. She wasn't some hapless teenager or twenty-something-year-old who still wanted to pretend she was footloose and fancy free; those days were behind her now. She was an adult who, come the end of February next year, would be a mother to two children. Did she think she could walk away from them when she became too emotionally committed?

And did she really want to lose Kip? Even when the odds were so thoroughly stacked against them as a couple – the age difference and the fact he was a married man – they had been so wonderfully in love in their blissful bubble of happiness. But look how easily that bubble had burst when they'd encountered their first real problem.

That's what some of her friends in London had said would happen.

'Just wait until reality sets in,' one had said.

Another had warned: 'Wait until you wake up from this dreamland you've created for yourselves, then tell me you're still in love.'

The negativity from those friends had made Zoe even more determined to prove them wrong. But the thought that they might now be proved right was more than she could bear. She had to make it work with Kip. And not just for the sake of her pride, but for the sake of her unborn twins.

All she had to do was accept that she had to share Kip with his first family. That wasn't too much to accept, was it?

She was still asking herself this same question several hours later when she was downstairs giving in to the temptation of a small glass of red wine. Just the one wouldn't hurt, would it?

With a bottle selected from the rack, the screw top removed, and a glass filled, her moment to savour the taste of the wine, which until then she had denied herself since knowing she was pregnant, was interrupted by a knock at the front door.

'I'll be back,' she muttered to the glass as she put it down and went to see who was at the door.

'You could have used your key,' she said when she'd ushered Kip through to the kitchen. He was dressed in the clothes he'd been wearing yesterday – navy blue trousers and a blue-and-white check shirt – and presumably he'd spent the night with Ashley and Caro.

'In the circumstances I didn't think I should,' he said, sounding as awkward as he looked while switching his car keys from one hand to the other.

'Wine?' she said, proffering the bottle. 'I'd just decided to break the rules,' she added.

He nodded. 'Just a small one.'

She poured him a glass then watched him go over to where he'd left his mobile charging last night. He unplugged it, coiled the cable around his fingers and slipped it, and his mobile into his pocket.

'You look tired,' she observed.

'That's because I'm knackered. It's been a long day.'

She passed him his glass. 'How's Arabella?'

'Not good. She's had a miscarriage.'

'Oh Kip, I'm so sorry.'

'And she's decided to divorce Giles.'

Privately Zoe thought Arabella would be better off without a husband like Giles, but she decided now wasn't the time to air her opinion on the subject. Instead, she pointed to the sitting room. 'Shall we go and sit down?'

He nodded again.

'Make yourself comfortable while I draw the curtains,' she said. 'I know how you hate it when I leave them open.'

But when she'd done that and they were seated, she in her usual armchair which her mother had reupholstered many years ago and he at the farthest end of the sofa from her, comfortable was the last thing they looked.

'We both said a lot of regrettable things last night,' she began when it seemed unlikely that Kip was going to lead the conversation.

'Do you regret what *you* said?'

Something in his tone made her sit up straighter, as if she was under attack and would need to defend herself. 'Some of it, yes. What about you?'

He put his glass down very carefully on the coffee table in front of him and then turned to face her properly. 'I can't help but think that often things said in the heat of the moment are the most honest and revealing.'

She gulped at her wine. This wasn't what she wanted to hear. She had hoped for there to be more of a conciliatory mood between them so they could then apologise to each other and hit the reset button, but here was Kip giving the impression that an apology was the last thing he had in mind.

'Why did you tell Angus what you did last night when you answered my mobile?' he asked.

'I can't remember everything I said,' she replied evasively, not liking where this might be going.

'I'm surprised you said anything at all. But apparently you as good as told my son that I'd left you.'

She met his cool penetrating gaze with one of her own. 'Hadn't you? That's certainly how it felt to me. And for all of today when I didn't hear from you.'

'Is it what you want, for me to be gone?'

This was too much for Zoe. 'Oh, you'd love that, wouldn't you, me letting you off the hook so you can play the victim! Is that why you're here, to push me into giving you what you want?'

'I don't know what you mean.'

'Please don't play games, Kip, you checked out of this relationship the moment I told you I was pregnant.'

'That's not true.'

'It is, but you're too much of a coward to admit it.'

'If there's any truth in what you say,' he said after taking a long and very deliberate breath as though needing a moment to regroup his thoughts, 'it's down to you freezing me out, insisting that I had no right to voice my opinion about the pregnancy. How would you have reacted if it had been the other way around?'

'That's just the point,' she exclaimed, 'it can never be the other way around! So is that what this is about, my right to decide what happens to my body versus your right to decide for me?'

'Not at all. I'm saying that it should have been a two-way discussion; I should have been allowed to express how I felt about it.'

'Then why didn't you?'

'Because you made it clear I wasn't to influence you in any way, and I did my best to respect your wishes.'

'And I expect you were hoping that I'd make it easy for you by terminating the pregnancy, didn't you?'

'That's a dreadful thing to say.'

'Not when it's the truth. Can you honestly say you didn't secretly hope that I'd make the problem go away?'

His gaze slid from hers. But as cowardly as she thought he was being, she could not in all honesty blame him for wanting the problem to disappear so that they could carry on as they had been. She saw now that whatever dream they'd enjoyed or hoped to enjoy together it wasn't going to happen.

It probably had nothing to do with Kip prioritising his family over her, but everything to do with the decision she had made to go ahead with the pregnancy. There was no way back, that much was obvious. She thought of the way he'd methodically coiled that charging cable around his fingers, then slipped it and the phone into his pocket. He hadn't come here to put things right; he'd come to fetch his things and to tell her he was leaving.

He had been a fair-weather lover, in love with her only when it had suited him.

Chapter Forty-Four

Saturday morning and on the gloomiest of mid-November days Louisa was in Chelstead. After calling in at the Co-op for some ground nutmeg for the Christmas cake she planned to make at the weekend, and for some other bits and pieces which she'd promised to fetch for Arabella, she skirted around the church towards the car park where she'd left her car.

It was almost seven weeks since Arabella's accident and while Louisa knew that her daughter was making good progress physically – her ribs were healing well and the cast on her wrist had now been removed – the healing process for losing her much-wanted baby was understandably an altogether different matter.

On the day Arabella was discharged from hospital, Louisa had moved in to take care of her daughter and granddaughter. Giles had moved back in with his ex-wife and to all intents and purposes, it looked very much as if Arabella had been right with her recent suspicion that he had either rekindled his feelings for his first wife, or they had never really gone away.

Nobody knew better than Louisa that you didn't stop loving your partner overnight and as much as Arabella professed to being relieved to be shot of him, the reality had to be otherwise. Very likely she was using her anger with Giles to get her through the pain of losing the baby, but that was not a state of affairs that would do her any good long term. The time would come when she would have to mourn the end of her marriage. Just as Louisa was still trying to do. Some days, even now, she raged against the shocking recklessness of what Kip had done, but whenever she was in danger of letting her emotions have the better of her, she forced them back into line. Sometimes she wondered if she'd been too calm about the whole business, but the alternative, to lose control and go out of her mind with angry hurt and the desire for revenge was anathema to her. What use would that be when Arabella and Heidi needed her to be strong and reassuringly calm for them?

Last week Arabella decided it was time for Louisa to return to the mill. 'Mum, I need to learn to cope without you,' she'd said, 'or I'll become too reliant on you.'

'Your wrist has only just had the cast removed,' Louisa had countered, 'there's no hurry to rush things.'

'But I need to know that I can do it,' Arabella had said.

Louisa would be lying if she said she hadn't felt as though she were being dismissed – she had enjoyed being needed again, of playing a pivotal role in the life of her family – and it must have shown in her face.

'Oh, don't look like that,' Arabella had said. 'I'm more grateful than I can say for everything you've done for me. But I feel guilty that you had to miss the Miniature Fair over in Coventry, and that you haven't been able to keep up with your work. I know you're itching to do that, aren't you?'

'Not at all. You and Heidi are all that matter to me.'

'I can't go on being mollycoddled though,' Arabella had persisted. 'I have to find a way to organise myself and plan for the future. I have to take back control. Surely you of all people can understand that?'

Louisa could. Even so, she couldn't stop herself from saying that there was plenty of time for Arabella to plan for the future. 'I hate the idea of you coping alone when maybe you're not yet strong enough,' she'd said.

'There's only one way to find out if I am strong enough and to discover if I really am my mother's daughter, and that's to try it,' Arabella had said.

As reluctant as she was to leave, Louisa had driven home to the mill filled with pride for her strong-minded daughter in wanting to prove that she could stand on her own two feet. The words – *to discover if I really am my mother's daughter* – had stayed with her for some days.

Of course, Louisa wasn't the only one to rally around Arabella, Ashley and Angus had also pitched in by helping her deal with the hellishly complicated business of the accident claim process and the insurance claim made against her. A courtesy car had been offered while the damage to Arabella's was being assessed for repair, and although it was an automatic, Ashley had advised against putting her wrist to the test just yet. Caro had helped too and had found Arabella an online support group through a friend of hers who had suffered a miscarriage, as well as another online group for women going through divorce with young children. It was so heartening that when the chips were down, the family was there to help and support.

Louisa had just passed the florist shop with its beautiful and highly fragrant display of potted chrysanthemums when she heard a cry from behind her. Turning round she saw that a girl had fallen over and the contents of one of her shopping bags had spilled across the pavement; a couple of oranges rolled right up to where Louisa stood. Picking up the oranges, Louisa rushed to help the girl to her feet. That's when she realised who it was.

It was Zoe, and she couldn't have looked more awkward.

Louisa took in her hugely swelling body and the very obvious impossibility of the buttons of her coat being done up. Remembering her own pregnancy with twins and how colossal she'd been and how she'd thought she would never be a normal-sized woman ever again, she said, 'Are you all right? You didn't hurt yourself, did you?'

'I'm okay. Tripping over has become something of a speciality for me,' Zoe said, 'on account of not being able to see my feet anymore.'

For the longest moment they stared uneasily at each other, until Zoe said, 'I'm sorry, this has to be horrendous for you, bumping into me like this when you must absolutely hate me.'

'I don't hate you.'

Zoe blinked. 'And now I don't know what else to say, so I'll just gather up my shopping and go.'

'Let me do it, it'll save you bending down.'

The shopping rounded up and noticing that the carrier bag that had spilled its contents had a broken handle, Louisa asked where Zoe was parked.

'In the main car park,' she said, indicating the way ahead.

'That's where I'm parked; I'll walk with you.'

'There's no need.'

'You're right, there isn't,' Louisa said, 'but that doesn't mean I can't do the decent thing and help you to your car with your shopping.'

Zoe gaped at her. 'Why on earth would you want to do that?'

Good question thought Louisa, as she hefted the carrier bag with the broken handle onto her hip and picked up her own shopping. A very good question. But then the answer came to her. 'If my daughter were in your shoes, I'd want her to be treated kindly.'

'Even if she'd hurt people?'

'Yes. Even if she'd done that.' Then: 'Come on,' Louisa said briskly, 'it's too cold to stand around like this, let's walk.'

But still Zoe hesitated.

'I promise you I'm not going to take you to task or say anything nasty,' Louisa said.

'Nobody would blame you if you did.'

'Would it make you feel better if I did? I can't say it would do anything for me, and besides, I think you've probably suffered enough as it is. You might not believe me, but I feel sorry for you.'

Zoe pulled a face. 'Your pity is the last thing I need.'

'I'm not offering you pity. Far from it.'

'When you heard the news that Kip had dumped me, wasn't there a part of you that was secretly pleased?'

'No. I was ashamed of him for treating you so cruelly. But I confess to not being surprised. He came to me the evening of Arabella's accident and after you'd told him you were expecting twins, and I knew then that something was wrong with him.'

'Did you encourage him to leave me?'

'Certainly not! I told him he had to do the right thing by you.'

'Maybe he did.'

'Only you will know if that's true.'

This time Zoe did fall in step with Louisa when she started to walk in the direction of the car park.

'Are you going to forgive him and take him back?' Zoe asked. 'Is that why you're behaving so magnanimously towards me, because you won in the end?'

Louisa shook her head. 'I think we can safely say there are no winners in this.'

'You didn't answer my question though. Are you going to forgive him? I would imagine that's exactly what he wants you to do so he can have his old life back and for everything to be as it was before I ever swirled into your family's orbit.'

'Well, nothing can ever be as it was.'

They both stood to one side on the narrow pavement as a young mother with a pushchair came towards them.

'So how's your pregnancy going?' Louisa asked when they walked on.

'I'm told that everything is fine. I had my second scan last week.'

'Does that mean you know the sex of the babies?'

'A boy and a girl.'

'That's nice, just like I had.'

Zoe sighed and slowed her step. 'Are you always this fair-minded and positive?'

'Not always, no. I'm as human as the next person and just as prone to anger and tears. And if you'd told me earlier this year that I'd be here talking to you, I wouldn't have believed you.'

'The same goes for me,' said Zoe. 'But surely you can appreciate why I would be wary of you? I'm the woman your husband had an affair with and the mother to his second unwanted family.'

'True,' said Louisa as they now waited for a car to pass and then crossed the road, 'but technically, he's just become my ex-husband as a few days ago the decree absolute came through.'

'I'm sorry,' Zoe said. 'If it wasn't for me, you'd still be happily married.'

'I might well still be married,' Louisa said, sounding more matter of fact than she actually felt, 'but would Kip have been happy? When he left me for you, he claimed he hadn't been happy for some time, that he wanted more than our marriage was giving him.'

'But what about you, was your marriage giving you what you wanted? Were you happy?'

It was a question that Louisa had been forced to ask herself time and time again, and as honestly as possible. 'I thought I was happy,' she said, 'but with hindsight perhaps I made the mistake of taking happiness for granted and assuming Kip was happy too.'

'I guarantee he was happier then than he is now. He convinced himself that being with me was the answer to everything. But it wasn't. Whatever it was he was searching for I couldn't give it to him. Instead, I've made everything worse.'

Louisa heard the sad regret in Zoe's voice and despite every bitter or angry thought that she had harboured towards this young woman since Boxing Day last year, she couldn't help but feel sorry for her. She even wondered if she felt a degree of empathy for her because they had both been rejected by the same man whom they'd loved.

'I don't think you should take all the credit for what's happened,' she said. 'Kip played his part too.'

They had reached the car park now and, taking Zoe's lead, Louisa followed her to where she'd left her car. It was with some relief that she relinquished the heavy carrier bag of shopping and gave it to Zoe to put in the boot of her Mini.

'Thank you,' Zoe said. 'It was kind of you to help.'

'It was no trouble.' She was about to turn away, when she said, 'I hope you'll be okay. Do you have anyone supporting you during your pregnancy and the birth?'

'I have a friend at work who has volunteered her services.' She smiled ruefully. 'I doubt that Phoebe knows what she's letting herself in for. I know I don't.'

'Nobody does. But I'm glad that you have someone.'

Once more Louisa was about to turn and go when Zoe said, 'I should have said before, but I was sorry to hear about Arabella losing her baby. How is she now?'

'A lot better than she was,' replied Louisa.

'The last time I heard from Kip, he said that Arabella and Giles had split up and that he'd gone back to his first wife.'

'Sadly, that's true.'

'And . . . what about Angus,' asked Zoe, surprising Louisa with the question. 'Is he well?'

'He's extremely well.'

'And is there anyone special in his life now?'

Every ounce of the protective mother in her made Louisa want to say, *Yes, and she's a much better girlfriend than you ever were to my son!* But all she said was, 'There is.'

'I hope it works out for them both. He deserves to be happy.'

'He certainly does,' agreed Louisa, recalling how cheerful and relaxed Angus had been when he'd arrived at the mill with his new girlfriend last Saturday afternoon. CeeCee's sunny demeanour acted as the perfect foil to her youngest son's propensity for introspection, and Louisa could tell they were a good match. She was also convinced that CeeCee was going to be a welcome addition to the family. Not that she'd said that to Angus, she hadn't wanted him to think she was too eager to have him happily settled.

'Have you seen Kip recently?' Zoe asked.

'Not for some weeks,' Louisa said, 'he's been keeping his distance. I think he finds it hard to face the family.' She hesitated before saying, 'It's none of my business, but I presume he is going to support you financially?'

'There hasn't been a serious discussion along those lines yet.'

'You should instigate one. These are his children, and he needs to take responsibility for them.'

Zoe's gaze on her intensified. 'I underestimated you.'

'In what way?'

'In every way. You're a far better person then I could ever be. I never thought I'd say this, but Kip's a fool. He should have appreciated what he had.'

We're all guilty of doing that, thought Louisa, *of taking for granted what we have and then losing it because we didn't take better care of it.*

'And I want you to know,' Zoe continued, 'that if I could turn back the clock, I would. I'd do it in a heartbeat.'

Chapter Forty-Five

It wasn't often that Ashley found himself at odds with his wife, but in bed that Sunday morning, he was.

With Peggy still fast asleep, and with the pleasurable thought of making love to Caro uppermost in his mind, she killed the mood dead by telling him that it wouldn't be just Arabella and Heidi coming for lunch that day, but his father would be joining them as well.

'I wish you hadn't done that,' he said.

'Kip is my father-in-law, so in my book that gives me every right to invite him here for lunch.'

'But you knew how I felt.'

'And I felt that you were wrong. Wrong too for making such a fuss about it now. He's your father, Ashley, and no matter how stupid or selfish he's been, he's still your father and you're still his son. Nothing's changed between the two of you.'

'That's just the point, everything's changed between us, he's a stranger to me now.'

Out of bed and wearing one of his old Radiohead T-shirts, Caro stood looking down at him with her hands on her hips. 'Are you taking Zoe's side over your father's?'

'Of course I'm not, but it's not as simple as you'd like to think it is. And apart from anything else, I'd have thought you'd have more sympathy for Zoe.'

'Why, because she's a woman and therefore my loyalty must belong to her? You couldn't be more wrong. To be honest, I'm disappointed in you, Ashley, I thought family was the most important thing to you. Isn't that what you've always said?'

'It is!' he remonstrated. 'That's why I'm so cross. My father's done the unthinkable, he's—'

'*Shh!* Keep your voice down or you'll wake Peggy. And for heaven's sake can you stop sounding like something out of a Victorian melodrama! We all know what Kip's done is outrageously wrong, but for all we know, maybe he just needs time to come to terms with the situation he's created and perhaps with some encouragement we can help him to see things with a fresh perspective.'

'I doubt that very much. Ever since he left Mum, he's refused to admit he's done anything wrong. He just goes blithely on ruining other people's lives.'

'That's an exaggeration. He's made two mistakes.'

'That we know of. What else has he kept hidden from us? For all we know there might be a trail of children he's fathered who we know nothing about!'

'Now you're being absurd.'

'Am I? Not so long ago it would have been absurd to imagine that my parents would be divorced, and my father's mistress be unceremoniously ditched because he's got her pregnant with twins. You couldn't make it up!'

'Well, it's where we all are, so we just have to make the best of it. Ostracising your father is not the answer. Which is why I've invited him for lunch. Your sister has made some sort of peace with him, so if she can do it, why not you?'

'Because—'

'It's not just your feelings that matter,' Caro interrupted him before he could finish, 'it's Peggy's as well. She's been asking where Grando has gone. She even asked me the other day when I was putting her to bed if he was dead.'

Ashley was shocked. 'Why would she think he was dead?'

'You tell me. But children pick up on the slightest bit of tension and interpret things in their own way based on what knowledge they have. They have an uncanny knack for filling in the blanks when they're not given the whole picture.'

'Did she seem upset when she asked you that?'

'Not particularly. But the very fact she asked the question means we need to change the status quo.'

The thought that their daughter's mind had been led down this disturbing route told Ashley that his wife was right. Which was why, when some hours later and after Arabella and Heidi had arrived, he opened the door to his father and forced himself to treat him normally. Or whatever passed for normal these days in their family.

He came with several bottles of claret and two large parcels for the girls. As icebreakers went, it was a good move on his part as it meant that they all stood by and watched Peggy and Heidi frantically rip at the paper to reveal two boxes containing a matching pair of dolls that resembled scarily realistic babies. The children's reaction was one of sheer delight and the demand for somebody to help free the dolls from their coffin-like packaging. But at his side, as Caro went to fetch a pair of scissors from the kitchen, Ashley sensed his sister stiffen and regarding her, he saw the contorted expression on her face. In a flash of understanding, he realised why.

'Could you have been any more insensitive, Dad?' he muttered.

'What?' his father said. 'I don't understand, I thought the girls would . . .' But then looking at Arabella, he must have grasped what the problem might be. 'Oh God, I'm so sorry, I didn't think. I didn't—'

'That's your trouble all over, isn't it, Dad,' Ashley said under his breath. 'You don't think. You don't think of anyone but yourself.'

'It's okay,' Arabella said, as Heidi and Peggy looked at the three of them, plainly sensing that something was wrong. 'It's not a problem,' she added. Then perching on the footstool so that she was now on the same level as the girls, she said, 'What beautiful dolls, aren't you both lucky? Are you going to say thank you to Grando?'

'Thank you, Grando!' they chorused, just as Caro returned from the kitchen, a pair of scissors in hand.

'Kip,' she said, 'perhaps you'd do the honours for the girls while Ashley sorts out drinks for everyone. Arabella, are you comfortable on the footstool, or would you prefer the armchair nearer the fire. There's quite a chill in the air today, isn't there?'

'I'm fine, thank you, Caro.'

By the time Ashley had poured out drinks, the dolls had been released from the packaging and the girls were cradling them with all the expertise of seasoned mothers. How did that happen? he wondered. How did girls, even as young as Peggy and Heidi, always seem to know how to hold a doll as though it were a real baby? And why in God's name hadn't his father thought more when he'd been buying presents for his granddaughters? Or was Ashley, as Caro would probably say, overreacting?

No, he thought, thinking of the pained look on his sister's face, he wasn't overreacting. But perhaps it was enough that his father now realised his mistake. There was no need to make things worse. After all, Arabella had recovered and was now playing happily with the girls.

Passing the glasses round, he decided to do as Caro had suggested – engineer a situation whereby he and his father could spend some time on their own. 'Dad,' he said as casually as he could, 'how about you help me in the kitchen with lunch? Those spuds and parsnips won't peel themselves.'

'Sure,' his father replied with equal nonchalance. 'Put me to work.'

But once they were alone in the kitchen with the door closed and Ashley had given his father a peeler and a bag of potatoes, there was nothing remotely nonchalant about him.

'Okay, Ashley,' he said, 'let's get this over with, shall we?'

Feeling wrongfooted that his father had taken the initiative and had gone in hard and fast, he said, 'In that case, why don't you go first?'

'Fair enough. I know you're disgusted with me and that I'm only here because Caro invited me. Were you very annoyed when you knew I would be joining you?'

'Yes. Very annoyed. Caro only broke it to me this morning.'

'Would you have preferred I stayed away, and would that have helped?'

'I don't know. What I do know is that I can't believe how selfish and callous you've become. You're not the man I've always admired and respected.'

'I'm sorry. The truth is, I'm not the man I thought I was either.'

'Then do something about it.'

'Such as? How can I ever put things right?'

'What are you, a child now that you can't figure this out for yourself? You've ruined Mum's life and now you've ruined Zoe's life. How the hell do you sleep at night?'

'Hardly at all, since you ask. But none of what's happened was deliberate, Ashley. None of it.'

'Please don't try saying this had nothing to do with you and the choices you made.'

'I'm not, but I never meant for it to end this way.'

'It hasn't ended, it's just the beginning for Zoe and the children she's expecting. Don't you have any sense of responsibility for her?'

'Of course I do, but . . . but this wasn't what I wanted. I didn't want to be a father all over again at my age.'

'No, you just wanted to believe you were in love, that you weren't getting old.'

'Yes, if you must know that was part of it.'

'And then Zoe delivered her bombshell and suddenly you weren't in love anymore and you were just another pathetically selfish man who'd thought he could kid himself he was young again. No doubt you wanted Zoe to have a termination to make the problem go away, didn't you?' Ashley knew that he was being brutally tough on his father, but he didn't care. He wanted him to know just how profoundly he had hurt and betrayed them as a family.

'What I wanted was for Zoe not to be pregnant in the first place,' Kip said quietly.

'Then you should have been more careful!' Ashley fired back. 'For pity's sake, I never thought I'd be saying that to my own father!'

'I'm not trying to shift the blame, but Zoe was the one who had taken charge of that side of things. Put yourself in my shoes, imagine how you'd feel.'

'This isn't about me.'

'Haven't you ever done anything that you've seriously regretted?'

'Not on the scale you have. What was it you used to tell us when we were children and had done something wrong? Oh yes, actions have consequences.'

'I had no idea you could be so bloody pompous,' his father muttered, turning his back on Ashley and slashing away at a potato.

'Yeah right, well I had no idea you could be such a bastard!'

The shocking words, something he never dreamt he'd ever say to his father, hung in the air between them and as Ashley waited for a response, perhaps even a telling off, as though he were a naughty child, the inconceivable happened and his father staggered forwards against the worktop and then back, a strange gasping sound coming from him.

Instinctively, Ashley reached out and then found himself

bearing the full weight of his father. 'Dad,' he said, alarmed, 'what's wrong?'

'It's . . . it's nothing.'

'Here, come and sit down.' He guided his father to the nearest chair. 'Dad,' he said, crouching on the floor in front of him and trying to remain calm, 'what is it, is it your heart? Shall I call for an ambulance?'

'*No!* No ambulance. I'm okay. I just need . . . I just need to catch my breath.'

He seemed anything but okay to Ashley – his face was flushed, his breathing was laboured, and his eyes were glazed. 'I think I should call for an ambulance,' Ashley said firmly. 'Or take you to A and E myself.'

His father shook his head. 'No . . . it's nothing serious. It's . . . it's just a panic attack.'

'Are you sure?'

'It's happened before.'

'Since when?'

'For some time. Can I have a glass of water, please?'

Ashley stood up and went over to the cupboard where they kept the glasses. He quickly filled one with cold water.

'There you go,' he said, giving his father the glass. He then watched his father closely, full of alarm that his face was still flushed, and his breathing was just as erratic and laboured. The hand that held the glass was also visibly shaking. 'How often has this happened?' Ashley asked.

'I've lost count.'

'What does the doctor say?'

'I . . . haven't seen a doctor.'

'Why in hell not?'

'Please don't fuss.'

'I'm not fussing, but if you haven't seen a doctor, how do you know it's panic attacks you're suffering?'

'I just know. I've looked it up.'

Before Ashley could respond, the door opened and Caro came in. 'How are the workers doing then?' She broke off, looking first at Ashley and then his father. 'What's happened?' she asked. 'Are you okay, Kip?'

'No, he's not,' Ashley said. 'He says he's having a panic attack, but I'm not so sure. I think I should take him to A and E.'

'*No!*' his father said, banging the glass down on the table beside him. 'Please, Ashley, just listen to me, will you? You're making it worse. If you'll only stop making a big deal of this I'll be fine, I just need—' His voice cracked and he turned from Ashley to look at Caro. Please,' he said breathlessly, 'I just need to be given a moment of quiet.'

'Ashley,' Caro said, 'why don't you go and keep your sister company with the children, and I'll handle things here?'

He opened his mouth to say he wasn't going anywhere when his father said, 'Please, Ashley, give me ten minutes and if I'm not feeling any better, then you can take me to A and E. And,' he added with a shuddery gasp of breath, 'not a word to Arabella, she doesn't need this extra worry.'

Chapter Forty-Six

Barely able to get the words out, Kip thanked Caro.

'No need to thank me,' she said, 'just take it easy and let's see if we can get your breathing under control. Focus on my eyes and voice, and cup your hands around your mouth and breathe in as slowly and as deeply as you can. And then out. That's it, that's good. If you'd prefer, I can find you a bag to breathe into.'

Listening to Caro's calm, almost hypnotic voice, he did as she said and gave a small shake of his head. It was the best he could do as he suddenly didn't trust himself to speak, worried that if he did, he might fall apart altogether.

He was mortified at the scene he'd caused, and that Ashley had seen him in such a pitiful state. He'd always been the strong one of the family, or so he'd liked to think, but now he'd been brought about as low as he could go, stammering over his words, scarcely able to breathe, and incapable of standing. And all because he'd felt under threat from his eldest son, as though once again he was having to defend himself.

But then most of the time he was desperately trying to defend himself to himself. Yet no matter how elaborately he laid out all his reasons for what he'd done, he ended up backed into a corner of shame and self-loathing. Hearing Ashley accuse him of all the things he knew he was guilty of had been like a series of hammer blows hitting their target with lethal accuracy.

The disgust on his son's face had been the final straw and had let loose the panic attack which he'd been fighting from the moment he'd entered the kitchen. With the sensation of the walls suddenly closing in on him, he'd felt as though a quake of trembling was about to erupt from him and with his pulse racing and his arms and fingers tingling as though an electric shock was passing through them, his ribcage had seemed to press hard against his lungs, squeezing the breath out of him.

It had happened so quickly and with such a virulent force he'd felt overwhelmed with the need to cry out. The humiliating fear of doing just that, of losing complete control, only added to his struggle to fill his lungs with air.

Realising that he was now breathing normally, and that his pulse had settled, and the tingling sensation had passed, he summoned the courage to speak. 'I'm sorry for being a nuisance,' he said.

'You're not being a nuisance,' Caro said. 'But if these attacks are a regular occurrence, you need to seek professional help.'

'It'll pass. When life calms down.'

'And if it doesn't, what then?'

'Don't say that. I need to believe that things will get better. Not just for me, but for everyone I've hurt. Do you think Ashley is ever going to forgive me?'

Caro nodded. 'In time, yes.'

'But I have some work to do, don't I?'

'You must know that all his life Ashley's been so proud of you, put you on a pedestal as the perfect father and then—'

'And then I went and destroyed everything he ever believed about me. What about you, Caro? Will you forgive me in time?'

'It's different for me, Kip. But I'd be lying if I said I wasn't disappointed in you for the way you've treated Zoe.'

He swallowed at the candour of his daughter-in-law's response. 'I'm sorry.'

'It's not me you need to apologise to, it's Zoe.'

'I have. Or rather I've tried to, but she's not interested in anything I have to say. What more can I do?'

'Oh, Kip, that's disingenuous of you. You know what you need to do, you must find a way to talk to Zoe so you can share the responsibility of what lies ahead. She's not a child, and nor are you, so you both need to accept the situation and stop running away from it. And from one another.'

Reaching for the glass of water which Ashley had given him, he raised it to his lips and thought that taking responsibility was what he'd done since as early as he could remember, right back to those days when he'd begun financially supporting his parents. From there he'd gone on to marry and have a family and start up his own company, and it had all been about keeping everything going as he took on yet more responsibility. Now he just wanted to run from any form of duty and obligation. He was so very tired of it.

In the initial weeks and months of his affair with Zoe that was how he had felt: as though he had run away and was liberated from everything that had gone before. Answerable only to himself, he'd felt utterly free and for the first time in his life he'd relished the sense of having thrown caution to the wind. Then from nowhere the shackles had been put on him again and he was effectively back where he'd started. Except it was worse than it had ever been before. So much worse.

Every day when he went into work, he conducted himself in as convincing a manner as he could that he had everything under control. When he left the office and drove the short distance to the house in Bury St Edmunds he was now renting, it was a different story. Alone in that depressing house, there was no escape from the misery of his situation. For a while he drank his evenings away, but then he'd given himself a stern talking to when he'd seen his ravaged self in the mirror one morning and not liked what he'd seen.

'I know what you're thinking,' Caro said.

Kip looked at her. 'You do?'

'That I must view you as just another selfish man who'd wanted more than his fair share of cake and eaten every scrap of it. But really, isn't that what everyone wants, the best bits of life without the bad? We're all guilty of that.'

Kip had always been extremely fond of his daughter-in-law, but never more so than in that moment. 'My son's a very lucky man,' he said.

She smiled. 'He knows how lucky he is because I regularly remind him of his good fortune.'

Somehow Kip managed to dredge up a smile for his own face. 'Oh Caro, I've made so many bad choices, some of them I can defend, but others I can't.'

'Well, for the sake of keeping things on a positive footing, why don't you tell me a choice you've made which you feel you can defend.'

'Okay, and not to over-dramatise what happened, but that day of Arabella's accident I was effectively faced with the eternal question of what I would do if my house was on fire – who would I save, my daughter or my girlfriend? In other words, did I go with Zoe for her first scan, or be with Arabella in A and E? Naturally I chose Arabella and not Zoe. That's when it all came apart, when I realised, as did Zoe, that no matter how much I loved her, my family would always come first.'

'Come off it, Kip, that's a fatuous argument. Are you saying that if I had to save Peggy over Ashley, that would mean I didn't love my husband, or didn't love him enough? Neither of which is true. I would reason that Ashley would save himself and that Peggy needed my help. That's all you did that day when you rushed to the hospital. You had a perfectly simple decision to make and absolutely made the right choice. Zoe might have been upset at the time, or even overreacted to it, but that's the prerogative of a pregnant woman. And a postnatal woman, I might add. I can remember saying some dreadful things to Ashley after Peggy was born, really hurtful things. I was a total manic bitch in the first months of our daughter's life.'

'If that's even half true,' Kip said with a frown, 'that's different, you were at the mercy of your hormones. What excuse do I have?'

'I'd say the fear of feeling trapped would be a plausible excuse.'

Kip shook his head in despair. 'But not a justifiable one,' he murmured.

'On the other hand, fear is just something to be conquered, isn't it?' said Caro.

He looked at her doubtfully. 'You make it sound so easy.'

'I'm a great one for simplifying things. Which I know infuriates Ashley at times because he tends to see problems when I don't.'

'You probably see challenges, don't you?' he suggested.

'Something like that,' she said. 'Now then, are you feeling well enough to join the others in the sitting room, or would you prefer to stay here and help me get on with preparing lunch?'

His mind still playing over so much of what Caro had said, he placed the glass of water on the table and stood up. 'I'm more than happy to resume potato-peeling duties,' he said with a show of spirit and renewed energy.

'Good,' she responded in her pleasantly capable voice, which unexpectedly reminded Kip of Louisa and filled him with profound sadness.

Chapter Forty-Seven

'What do you mean Dad's having a panic attack and that Caro's taking care of him?'

'*Shh!*' her brother said, throwing a glance over his shoulder to where Peggy and Heidi were playing with their dolls.

'Are you mad?' Arabella hissed incredulously. 'Our father is ill and you're telling me to *shh*?' Shocked at what Ashley had just told her, she started to move towards the hallway and the kitchen beyond, but Ashley stopped her.

'No,' he said, 'I've a feeling our presence will only make things worse. Especially as he didn't want me to tell you. Let's just give it a few minutes longer. Yes?'

'But why didn't he want you to tell me?'

'Because he didn't want you to worry. Now come over here.'

Reluctantly Arabella allowed her brother to lead her across the room to the French windows where there was less risk of Peggy and Heidi overhearing their conversation.

With their backs to the children and facing the garden where the November wind was ripping the leaves from the trees, Arabella said, 'Two minutes, and then I'm going in that kitchen and nothing on earth will stop me, not even you, Ashley. Now tell me what the hell's going on. And then explain why Caro is with him and you're not.'

'My presence wasn't helping.'

'Why, what were you doing?'

Ashley sighed. 'It was what I'd just done. I'd had a massive go at him about Zoe and everything else and the next thing he . . . well, he seemed to crumple and then he couldn't breathe. From nowhere he was like an old man.'

'And what, you just stood there?'

'Of course I didn't! I was all for calling an ambulance, I thought it was his heart, but he was adamant it was a panic attack and that it had happened to him before.'

The thought of her father being ill, of him suffering and not telling them, made Arabella want to shove Ashley out of the way and be with her father, just as he had dropped everything and come to her when she'd had the accident. When he'd sat by the side of her bed in the hospital, she had felt the love that she always had for him before he'd left Mum. Suddenly she didn't care what he'd done, all that mattered to her was that he was there for her, just as he'd always been.

'If this is what you're sure you really want to do, you won't be on your own, love, you'll have the family to help and support you,' he'd assured her when she'd told him and Mum that she'd decided she didn't want to stay married to Giles.

Giles's return to his ex-wife was a humiliation that Arabella was determined to overcome, regardless of the effort it took, or the lies she had to tell to convince people that as far as she was concerned, Jen was welcome to have Giles back. If the woman was mad enough to trust him again, then good luck to her! What she was determined to keep from everyone was just how utterly broken she felt. Not so long ago she had loved Giles so much and had never once doubted the strength of their relationship.

In the weeks since he'd gone, Arabella had tortured herself with a variety of reasons why their marriage had come apart.

Maybe she had never been anything more than a diversion for Giles when his first marriage had been going through a rocky patch.

Maybe he was one of those men who was incapable of monogamy for any length of time.

Maybe Arabella had just been an excellent bit on the side but a rubbish wife who made too many demands on him.

Maybe it had never really been love between them, not a true and lasting love that could weather the inevitable storms of life.

Maybe she had never truly known Giles but had created him in the image of the man she'd wanted him to be – a man like her father.

The list in her head, especially when she couldn't sleep at night, was never-ending and taunted her mercilessly. But it was nothing compared to the distress of letting Heidi spend time with her father, because it wasn't just time with him, it was time with Jen and Lexi too. She tried to prevent herself from imagining one scene in particular that might be playing out over in Ely, of Lexi manipulating Heidi against her, and it drove Arabella to the point of irrational despair. She knew it was a sort of madness she was succumbing to in those moments, but she was powerless to stop it.

'It will give Heidi a sense of continuity seeing Lexi again,' Giles had said when Arabella had protested. 'They are half-sisters, after all.'

'It's too soon for you to start playing happy families with her in that way,' Arabella had insisted.

'Why not?' he'd countered. 'You play happy families all the time with yours and exclude anyone considered an outsider into the bargain.'

'What the hell is that supposed to mean?'

'Your family never really approved of me. Or Lexi.'

'That's simply not true. Everyone has always made you and your daughter feel welcome. What more could they have done?'

'They could have treated Lexi more kindly and not ganged up on her.'

'One isolated incident when Lexi was so clearly in the wrong,' Arabella had said, appalled that he could drag up the day of her mother's ill-fated birthday and still hold it against her, 'and you're condemning my family?'

He made no attempt to substantiate the accusation he'd made, but said, 'You're the one who made this happen, Arabella, so you must take the consequences.'

The downright delusional self-righteousness of his statement made her wild with anger. 'You were the one who packed your bag and moved out under the pretence of wanting time apart to think!' she flung at him.

'But you were the one who pushed me away and then demanded a divorce!'

'Any sensible woman in my shoes would have done the same!'

So many of their exchanges left Arabella in floods of tears which she tried her best to hide from her daughter, but often it just wasn't possible. On one occasion Heidi had gone in search of the tissue box and returned with a clump of tissues in her small hands. 'Mummy, better now,' she'd said, pressing them to Arabella's eyes. Which had set her off crying even more.

Snapping herself out of her thoughts, Arabella heard her brother saying, 'It must be the stress of the whole Dad and Zoe situation that's brought these panic attacks on. Do you think we should tell Mum?'

'Of course we should,' Arabella said. 'She'll want to know. But right now, I'm not going to stand here a second longer. Caro might have appointed herself chief medical officer for the day, but he's our father and I want to be with him.'

'Going in there and fussing over him won't help,' her brother said with a pained expression on his face, 'that's probably why he was happy to let Caro stay with him, you know how totally unflappable she is.'

'I'm sorry,' Arabella said in a softer voice, knowing that she had just broken the cardinal rule, that of criticising Caro to Ashley. Putting aside her jealousy that she could never be as wholesomely capable as her sister-in-law, and knowing how kind Caro had been to her since her miscarriage, she placed a hand on her brother's arm. 'I promise I won't make a fuss, but I need to see with my own eyes that Dad's okay. Come on, let's go together.'

'All right, but no big scene. Yes?'

Arabella wasn't entirely sure what she had expected to see when she pushed open the kitchen door, but it wasn't her father standing at the breakfast bar with a chopping board and bag of potatoes in front of him and a peeler in hand.

'Hello love,' he said cheerfully, perhaps just a little too cheerfully, 'have you come to help?'

Arabella stared at him and then at Caro who was pulling a large roasting pan of partially cooked pork out of the oven.

'So you're feeling better, Dad?' Arabella said.

'As right as can be,' he said, flashing her a smile, but giving Ashley a reproachful look.

Arabella frowned. 'Is this going to become the elephant in the room then?' she asked. 'You having panic attacks and not talking about it to us?'

'It's nothing to worry about,' he said mildly.

'Dad,' said Ashley, 'please don't try to fob us off, not when we're so worried about you. I saw what happened to you and how debilitating it was.'

'Just tell us what's really going on,' Arabella said, going over to him. 'And while you're about it, why not leave those potatoes to me and you sit down and rest.'

He shook his head. 'No, and that's exactly what I'm afraid of, you treating me like an invalid. Or worse, an old man.'

At the sound of raised voices and something getting out of hand in the sitting room between Peggy and Heidi, Caro hastily slid the roasting pan back into the oven. 'I think I'll leave you to it,' she murmured, 'and go and see what those two monkeys are up to.'

When she'd made her diplomatic exit, Ashley said, 'Dad, I'm sorry for what I said earlier, I was out of order. If I'd known how it would affect you, I wouldn't have—'

'That's just my point! Now you're going to start handling me with kid gloves and not speak your mind. Suddenly I'm no longer me!'

'Would that be such a bad thing?' asked Arabella, 'us looking out for you? 'We care about you. We care a lot.'

'A few months ago you didn't, did you? You probably hated me for leaving your mother, and you'd have had every right to do so.'

Arabella put her arm around her father. 'We were cross, Dad, and upset for Mum, but we never hated you. How could we?'

'Well, I hate myself. I hate what I've done to you all.'

Worried that he might work himself up into another panic attack, Arabella hugged him. 'Don't talk like that. Didn't you always tell us we weren't allowed to say we hated one another when we argued as children?'

'But I'm not a child, I'm a grown man who's ruined everything and if you carry on being so nice to me, I might let the side down again and lose it altogether.'

'Then you'll have me sobbing too,' she said. 'And to be honest, I've done enough of that recently.'

Joining them at the breakfast bar, Ashley put a hand on their father's shoulder. 'You need to be honest with us, Dad, so we can be there for you. How can we help when we don't know what's going on with you?'

'How can I be honest with you when I'm not sure I can be honest with myself?'

'Sounds to me like you are, given how you're beating up on yourself,' responded Ashley.

'It's easy to pile on the blame and hold oneself accountable, just not so easy to admit to others the hows and the whys.'

'Not even to us?' asked Arabella.

Her father turned from Ashley to look at her and she saw an expression of such profound sadness in his eyes, it was hard to maintain eye contact. 'Especially not to you, children,' he said quietly. 'I've disappointed you all enough. And Arabella, I'm so sorry about those bloody awful dolls I gave Peggy and Heidi, I just didn't think.'

'They're not awful and reminders like that of what happened is just something I have to learn to get over.'

As convincingly as she said the words, Arabella knew it wasn't true. Her miscarriage wasn't something she would ever get over; it would stay with her forever. The heartbreaking pain of losing her baby was as raw today as it had been when she'd lost it. The fact that the baby had never had the chance to live was not something she ever wanted to put behind her. And as desperately as she had wanted a brother or a sister for Heidi, she had to accept that it was probably never going to happen now. But at least her daughter would always have Peggy; for that Arabella would be forever grateful.

After lunch, Caro suggested that she and Arabella take the girls down to the small play area in the village so they could burn off some of their excess energy, leaving Ashley and Dad to deal with the dishwasher.

With some trepidation, Arabella trudged alongside Caro while the children ran on ahead chasing leaves being carried along by the blustery wind. She had an inkling that her sister-in-law had something to say to her, which was why she had engineered things as she had.

They hadn't made it as far as the play area when Arabella's suspicion was proved spot on.

'It struck me over lunch,' Caro began, 'that it might be a good idea for Kip to move in with you for a while. That rental he's in was only ever a short-term let, and he doesn't seem to have done anything about buying anywhere yet. It's as if he can't bring himself to look too far into the future. There are also the panic attacks to factor in, suffering those when you're alone can be quite scary.'

There was a lot to absorb from what Caro had just said, so Arabella took the last point first. 'I should have thanked you before for helping Dad to recover from the attack. How did you know what to do?'

'I did a course at work. In HR we're practically paramedics these days.' Caro gave a small laugh. 'I exaggerate, but I was asked if I'd like to do the course, and I thought, why not?'

'And before today, did you ever have to put your expertise to use in the office?'

'A couple of times. Anyway, what do you think to my suggestion about Kip moving in with you?'

'I don't know how Giles would react to that,' Arabella said doubtfully, 'seeing as it will only be a matter of time before he insists the house will have to be sold.'

'Even if the house was put on the market tomorrow, it would still take time before the sale went through, just as it did with Charity Cottage. You really shouldn't be afraid to dictate some of the terms of your divorce to Giles, so if you want your father to live with you, just tell him that.'

'From my perspective I like the thought of Dad being with me,' she said, wondering why she hadn't thought of it herself, 'but he might view it as a retrograde step, moving in with his daughter. It might make him feel even more desperate about his situation.'

'Then dress it up by saying he'd be doing you an enormous favour by moving in as you need the emotional support. How could he say no to that?'

Pushing at her hair which the wind had whipped into her eyes, Arabella knew that Caro was right, her father wouldn't say no to helping her. She also had to give Caro credit for coming up with such a good idea; it was perfect in every way.

They had reached the play area now and with no one else about, the children made a beeline for the climbing frame.

'Can I ask you something?' Arabella said when she and Caro stood guard ready to help the girls should they need it.

'Of course.'

'Did you think my marriage would come unstuck the way it did?'

Caro looked at her. 'Honest answer?'

'What an odd thing for you to say.'

'Why?'

'Because you're always honest.'

'Wow, and there was me thinking I was guilty of sitting on the fence when it came to my opinions.'

Catching the smile on Caro's face, Arabella smiled too.

'I had my doubts,' Caro said. 'But I didn't think you would be the one to end your marriage.'

'Why, because you thought I was too weak and pathetic to do that?'

'Not at all! Quite the reverse. I saw you as being strong enough to stay married no matter how bad things were.'

'That doesn't sound strong to me, it sounds cowardly.'

'Wrong. It takes guts to stay in a bad situation. Millions of women do it all the time, making compromise after compromise. Let me ask you this, did Giles ever compromise or make allowances for your benefit?'

Arabella thought of his angry reaction when she'd told him she was pregnant and how worried she'd been about breaking the news to him. 'Not that I can recall,' she murmured.

'He didn't need to, not when you were prepared to do it all the time. He knew that and took advantage of it.'

'Now you make me sound like the worst kind of fool that I repeatedly bent over backwards to please him.'

'That's not my intention. Like I say, you were strong enough and perhaps you loved Giles enough to try and make it work. Which is more than he did. You should applaud yourself for that and for having the strength to walk away when you did.'

'So you don't have a shred of doubt that I'm doing the right thing?'

'Why, do you doubt the decision you've made?'

'No!'

'That's all that matters then.'

'Does that mean *you* doubt that I'm doing the right thing?' Arabella said apprehensively.

'Absolutely not. I'd have done exactly the same thing.'

Receiving this previously unimaginable validation from her sister-in-law made Arabella inexplicably want to throw her arms around Caro and thank her. Not knowing how such a gesture would be received, she held herself in check.

But later, when they walked home with the children once more running on ahead, Caro linked arms with Arabella, something that had never happened between them before.

It felt good, this unexpected closeness, as though finally they had found a way to bridge the gap that had always existed between them.

Chapter Forty-Eight

Sunday evening, just after six o'clock, and with darkness complete, Angus drove slowly along the street where he had parked so many times before during what he now regarded as that *other life* when he and Zoe were a couple.

He pulled into a space directly behind Zoe's car and, switching off the engine, he looked up at her house, specifically to the front bedroom which he had so often shared with her during their visits from London. He forced himself to picture himself in bed with Zoe, to see if the memory still had the power to affect him. But he felt nothing. Which was good. It gave him hope to believe that coming here really was the right thing to do.

After spending the day with his mother helping her redecorate her bedroom, he should have been driving directly on to Lincoln and the hotel he was booked into for the latest assignment he was working on, but he'd taken this detour.

He hadn't told his mother what he planned to do and in many ways it was down to her that he'd made the decision he had. She had told him how she'd bumped into Zoe yesterday in Chelstead and how, as bizarre as it sounded, she'd helped Zoe to her car with her shopping.

'I know you'll think I must have a screw loose or something,' Mum had explained, 'but I couldn't help but feel sorry for the girl. Her life has been turned dramatically upside down and will never be the same again. Kip might be able to fool himself that he can walk away from her, but I can't.'

'But you didn't do anything to her, Mum,' Angus had said, 'so how can you possibly feel any sense of responsibility?'

'It's not that exactly, more a case of understanding what it's like to give birth to twins, the constant chaos of it all and the physical and mental toll it takes on a new mother. And then there's the matter of those babies being related to you and your brother and sister, to Peggy and Heidi too. As a family I don't feel it would be right to turn our back on her.'

'What if Zoe doesn't want to have anything to do with us?' he'd reasoned. 'She wasn't too keen on being swallowed up by the Langfords in the first place, she made it very clear to me that she felt overwhelmed by us.'

'True. But she might well think differently when she's at her wits' end trying to feed two screaming babies. With no family of her own, who will be there for her?'

'That's a question Dad should be asking, not you.'

'Zoe told me she hasn't seen him in a while.'

'That goes for all of us, doesn't it?'

'Well, he's spending today with Ashley and Caro and your sister. I only know that because Caro told me that she'd gone behind Ashley's back and invited Kip. She'd decided it was time to get them together again.'

'Why weren't you invited?' Angus had asked. 'Or me for that matter?'

'Because I was there only a few days ago and Caro knows that, like your brother, you're still cross with your father and she didn't want the two of you ganging up against him at the lunch table.'

Angus had to agree that Caro probably had made the right call.

Still sitting in his car staring up at the house, he wondered what CecCee would think of him coming here. Did she even need to know? Yes, she did, he told himself sternly. There would be no deceit or opaqueness to his relationship with CeeCee, not when he knew it was the real deal this time. Besides, he was sure that she would understand why he felt this was something he had to do. He supposed it was some kind of closure he needed to initiate.

It had been niggling at him ever since that telephone conversation he'd had with Zoe the day of his sister's accident. Someone else in his place might have derived satisfaction from hearing an ex-girlfriend sound so despondent, or maybe felt that justice had been served on her, but he'd experienced no such emotion, only a depressing awareness of the monumental shitstorm his father had created.

Zoe opened the door to him in pyjamas and an unbelted dressing gown. To his inexperienced eye she looked alarmingly ready to go into labour any moment.

'Angus!' she said, her shock at seeing him written all over her face.

'Yeah, I know,' he said with a shrug, 'I'm the last person you expected to see on your doorstep, and I promise I haven't come to cause trouble. I won't stay long, I just wanted to . . . well, point of fact, I'm not entirely sure what I wanted to say.'

'You'd better come in, then.'

The door closed behind him, he followed her down the narrow hall and into the sitting room. The last time he'd been here they'd watched the final episode of some Netflix series they'd been addicted to. For the life of him he couldn't remember what it was.

'Sit down,' she said, indicating the sofa. 'Can I make you a drink?'

He shook his head. 'No thanks. I'm on my way to Lincoln.'

'And that rules out tea or coffee?'

'I'm full of food and drink from being at Mum's.'

Zoe sat in the chair next to a small table where there was a book placed faced down alongside an empty mug and a plate. He imagined that she must have been sitting here quietly reading before he'd knocked on the door.

'Presumably your mother told you about our little chat yesterday.'

'Yes,' Angus said. 'She meant well, you know. I hope you didn't think she was interfering in any way. It's just how she is. She's a great one for fairness and for treating people decently.'

'Relax. I didn't think anything bad about your mother. I thought she was kind, if a little unnervingly so. So what's happening in Lincolnshire?'

'Another assignment. This time with a frozen food manufacturer. Their current logistics system was installed back in the Dark Ages and . . . but I'm sure you don't want to hear about that.'

'How does your new girlfriend like you spending so much time away? Your mother told me how lovely she is.'

Was it his imagination or had Zoe deliberately put an emphasis on the word 'lovely' as if to imply something by it? 'I'm totally biased,' Angus said, 'but I'd have to agree with Mum, CeeCee is great, and not just because she doesn't seem to mind me spending time away. Although to be honest, I'm beginning to tire of it. It might be time to look for a new job.'

'Did you meet through work?'

'No, she lives in the same apartment building as me. She's a paralegal assistant by day and plays the cello in a quartet in her free time and is always off on some gig somewhere. Ideally that's what she'd like to do full time.' *TMI*, he thought to himself. *Way too much information.*

'Then my advice to your girlfriend is to do it because who knows what's around the corner?'

There was no ambiguity this time in what Angus heard coming from Zoe; her words were heavily weighted with regret and resignation.

'Did your mother tell you how we actually met yesterday?' she then said.

He nodded. 'Yes, you'd fallen over, and she helped you with your shopping that had gone everywhere.'

'I don't think I've ever felt more unworthy of anybody's help than I did in that moment.' Zoe puffed out her cheeks and rubbed her hands over the basketball swell of her abdomen.

'You okay?' he asked anxiously.

'I'm fine. Don't worry, I'm not about to go into labour; the two of them are kicking away like crazy in there.'

He hoped she wasn't about to ask if he wanted to put his hand on her stomach to feel the babies moving around and was relieved when she said, 'Your mother has to be one of the strongest people I know.'

'She is,' he said simply. 'And I suspect that if you needed help in any way, she'd willingly be there for you.'

'I don't mean to sound ungrateful, but why? Why on earth would she want to help me?'

'Because that's what she's like, and I know you hated feeling swallowed up by my family, but the thing is, you're connected to us now by virtue of the children you're carrying. Does that freak you out very much?'

Her expression softened. 'This might surprise you, but no. As an only child I know that I missed out on a whole load of stuff and very likely it made me the person I am, good and bad, but I'm glad that having twins means they'll always be company for one another.'

'Have you spoken to my father?' asked Angus.

'No,' she said flatly. 'There's been no contact for some time.'

'But he has to be involved. He can't just stick his head in the sand and kid himself that this will magically go away.'

'Perhaps we both need more time before any decisions can be made.'

He wondered if Zoe was also sticking her head in the sand. 'From what Mum said you're more than halfway through the pregnancy, so wouldn't it be better to start making those decisions now? Do you need someone to . . .' he hesitated, 'to mediate in some way?'

'Are you offering to do that?'

'I'm not sure I'd be that good at mediating as I'm still not really speaking to my father.'

'That, if you don't mind me saying is just plain silly. If you can sit here and talk normally with me, surely you can do the same with Kip?'

It was a good point and one that stayed with Angus when he was back behind the wheel of his car and on his way to Lincoln.

He was just contemplating calling his father when his mobile rang. It was Ashley, and what he said shocked Angus.

'Dad having panic attacks, you're joking?'

'I wish I was. It's been happening to him for a while from what we understand, but he hasn't done anything about it. It's stress, of course. And look, I know we're both still mad as hell with him, but I think the time has come when we need to put aside our own feelings and support him. It's possible he might then do the right thing by Zoe.'

'Funny you should say that, but I've just been to see her.'

'You have? You're not thinking of getting back with her are you, I mean, that would be seriously off-the-chart weird.'

'No, nothing like that. But I wanted to see for myself that she was okay.'

'And is she?'

'Staring down the barrel of her future with a stoicism that borders on stubborn determination. I have to admire her for that.'

'She's not bitter, then?'

'I didn't detect that in her, no.'

'It was good of you to go and see her. What brought that on?'

'I did it on impulse and it's difficult to pin it down really, other than to say it felt the right thing to do in the circumstances.'

'So, when are we all going to meet this new girlfriend of yours?' Ashley then asked. 'Mum's met her, but not the rest of us.'

'I didn't feel like dropping CeeCee into the whole family at a time when we're not exactly at our best.'

Ashley made a noise that was halfway between a cough and a laugh. 'Who knows, this might be us at our best. It could all get a hell of a lot worse for all we know. By the way, if you're going to speak to Dad, maybe not tonight as I think he'll still be feeling a bit put under the microscope by what happened here earlier. He hated me seeing him the way I did today. If you think about it, when we were kids, he was our very own invincible Super Dad and in his mind losing that status must be tough for him.'

'I guess so. By the way, why didn't you make it a full family lunch today?'

'That was down to Caro. I didn't know Dad was coming until she broke it to me this morning. I thought it was just Arabella and Heidi coming for lunch. Would you have come if Caro had invited you?'

'I'd already arranged to see Mum.'

'Well, there you go. No harm done. But I take your point, in future we need to make sure no one feels left out. That's the trouble with divorce, it creates a fault line.'

'Only if it's allowed to happen. And talking of divorce, how's Arabella?'

'Good days, bad days would be a fair assessment.'

'Did you ever really like Giles?' Angus asked. 'Or did you tolerate him for Arabella's sake?'

There was a brief pause before Ashley said, 'I always suspected that he resented us as a family. He certainly didn't try to fit in as well as Caro has. But look, never mind Giles. Do you agree that we need to help get Dad back on track so he can start thinking straight about the future?'

'Of course. What's your end plan, Dad and Zoe together again?'

'Actually, I was thinking more Mum and Dad back together again.'

Chapter Forty-Nine

Monday afternoon and as the rain came down and was lashed by the ferocious wind against the panes of the two small windows in her bedroom, Louisa was busily putting everything away after Angus had helped her decorate it over the weekend.

It had been a spur of the moment decision to repaint the walls a colour that was called *antique cream*, which years ago would have been called plain old magnolia, but at some point the word magnolia had become synonymous with boring blandness so a rebrand was born. Perhaps there was a metaphor in that, that everyone at some stage in their life should give themselves a rebrand to avoid the accusation of being dull. Or of feeling dull.

Ironically, she had never had cause to ponder whether she was dull or boring, and that wasn't down to arrogance or an overly inflated ego, more a matter of simply being herself all her life and happily accepting who she was. But then Kip had ripped the rug from beneath her feet and she had been forced to question if she hadn't been too complacent. He had obviously decided that she was indeed very dull and not what he wanted anymore.

Doubtless she was just one of millions of ex-wives who had asked themselves the very same thing when traded in for a younger and more exciting model and while there was no easy answer, Louisa was determined not to shoulder all the fault for Kip looking elsewhere for his happiness. Nor would she torment herself with anxious self-scrutiny and the recrimination that she could have done better. Frankly, the person who should be doing that was Kip.

With a final burst of energy, she pushed the large chest of drawers, the last piece of furniture that had to be put in place, against the wall between the two windows. Standing back to admire the fresh new look for her bedroom, she felt a sense of pride and achievement. It was the first room in her new home on which, and with Angus's help, she had placed her own stamp. It felt good and was another small step in the right direction.

Or, as her sister would have it, it was another example of Louisa indulging in an act of displacement activity, busily occupying herself to stop her dwelling on things she didn't want to think about. Stephanie was so quick these days to categorise anything Louisa did by pigeonholing it to fit a narrative which she thought would be insightful and helpfully revealing.

'I'm just trying to hold the mirror up to you,' Stephanie had said on the phone last night not long after Angus had left, 'so you can see how your behaviour might look from an external perspective.'

Try holding it up to yourself, Louisa had wanted to say, but instead she had let her sister prattle on with her so-called words of wisdom, which covered all manner of subjects, including Louisa's financial situation now that the divorce was finalised.

'If things become tight, which I don't think they will, I could always go back to teaching,' Louisa had assured Stephanie, 'and my miniature work is keeping me in pocket money,' she'd added.

'A return to teaching at your age?' Stephanie had said in a tone that implied Louisa had just expressed a desire to take up lap dancing to pay the bills.

From quizzing her about her pension and the division of savings and investments, Stephanie had then informed Louisa that what she now needed was to meet a man by joining an online dating site.

'There's no stigma to it now, everyone is doing it.' The very fact that her sister had felt the need to say there was no stigma attached to meeting a man this way inferred that there was.

'I have zero wish to meet anyone,' Louisa had said irritably. 'I really don't have the time.'

'What precisely is keeping you so busy?' Stephanie had asked.

'My work, organising my new home, the family and in particular helping Arabella,' Louisa had replied.

'There you go again, frantically filling your days with activity rather than giving yourself time to let go and think, or perish the thought, give yourself time to enjoy life.'

Louisa had very nearly made the mistake of blurting out that she was far too busy to enjoy life but managed to stop herself in time.

There was, of course, sufficient truth to her sister's comments to leave Louisa bristling with defiant indignation long after their chat was over, because hadn't she done just that for most of her life, filled her days with busyness because that's who she was – busy, competent Louisa? And never more so since Kip had left her, when she convinced herself that her broken-hearted self would be healed and made whole so much the quicker through constant effort on her part.

Her coping strategy had been a combination of determined resourcefulness and quiet acceptance. It had been important to her to save herself from any further pain and humiliation by acquiescing to Kip's wishes for a divorce and the sale of Charity Cottage. Yes, there had been plenty of tears and anger, but ultimately she had faced the ordeal by rolling up her sleeves and getting on with it.

Now though, she questioned whether she hadn't been too quick to give in to all of Kip's demands. What if she had dug in her heels and refused to agree to the divorce so readily? Had she done that, might she have saved Kip from himself?

The ring of the doorbell saved her from pursuing the thought any further and going downstairs, she wondered if it was her lovely neighbours from up the road bearing gifts as they often did.

It wasn't Jim or Maggie, but a stranger.

'I'm sorry to disturb you,' the man said, peering out from beneath the hood of one of those huge dark green waxed coats that reached almost to his ankles; behind him and parked alongside her car was a large four-by-four. '. . . but I had the idea that the latest new owner of the mill might like this.'

From the depths of his coat, he brought out a framed picture approximately twelve inches by twelve. 'I was given it when I lived here some years ago,' he explained, 'and I'm currently having a sort-out and found the picture in the attic, but I couldn't bring myself to chuck it away. Not when it belongs in the mill really.'

'Oh,' she said, taken aback, 'that's so kind of you. Would you like to come in? I'd love to know more of the mill's history. I never met the previous owner so didn't have the chance to learn any of its backstory.'

'Are you sure?' he asked, peering out from beneath the hood of his coat as the rain pattered noisily against it.

'Quite sure,' she said, stepping aside to let him in.

Once he was in and the door shut against the wind and rain, and she'd taken his coat from him and hung it up, she led him through to the warmth of the kitchen.

'That looks interesting,' he remarked, going over to the table, and bending his tall frame to take a closer look at the 12th scale lady's desk and chair she had completed that morning. 'The detail is extraordinary,' he said, peering at the green and gold paintwork delicately overlaid with roses. She had reupholstered the chair with pale green silk and painted clusters of roses onto it to match the desk. She hoped the customer would be as pleased with the finished items as she was.

'Did you make the pieces as well as paint them?' he asked.

'No, I buy cheap stuff online and upscale it depending on what the customer wants. Or I do whatever I fancy doing at the time.'

'You clearly have a talent for it,' he said with a smile. 'I'm a carpenter by trade but couldn't paint like that to save my life.' He straightened up and indicated the wooden kitchen cupboards that lined the sloping curve of the circular walls. 'I made and installed all those,' he said. 'It's good to see they're still going strong.'

'Did you make the fitted cupboards in the rooms on the other floors as well?'

'If they're the same ones I put in when I lived here, then yes. I bought the mill as a bit of project with the plan to convert it into a residential property.' He gave a small deprecating laugh. 'It proved to be a lot more than that, more like a nightmare of a battle with the planning department, but I got there in the end.'

'How long ago was that?'

'Over fifteen years now.'

'What made you leave such a magical home after putting so much into it?'

'Usual story,' he said with a shrug, 'divorce meant my wife and I had to sell and divide everything up.'

She could have kicked herself for being so clumsy. Given her own situation she should have known better. 'I'm sorry,' she said, 'that was none of my business.'

'It's not a big deal,' he said lightly, 'all water under the bridge from a long time ago now. These things happen.'

Don't they just, she thought.

'Anyway,' he went on as though remembering why he was here. 'If you'd like the painting, it's yours. But I can see it's not up to your high standard of workmanship.'

She took it from him and looked at the watercolour properly. It was no work of art, but it had a certain charm in its simplicity and was part of the mill's history. 'Thank you,' she said, 'I'd love to have it. But I ought to give you something for it.'

He pulled a face. 'No, there's no need for that. I'm just happy it's back where it should be. Are you and your husband happy here?'

'I'm very happy here,' she said, 'but there is no husband. I'm newly divorced.'

'Right,' he said with a roll of his eyes, 'so that makes us even when it comes to blundering in.'

'Like you say, these things happen.' Putting the painting down, she said, 'If you won't accept anything for the picture, the least I could do is offer you a drink while you tell me some more about the mill.'

'That would be nice, but only if I'm not keeping you from anything.'

'I'd just finished what I was doing, which was moving furniture around upstairs.'

'If there's anything else you need moving, I'd be happy to give you a hand.'

'All done now, but thank you. What would you like to drink, tea, coffee or perhaps a glass of wine? Or is it too disgracefully early for that?'

'I'd love to be disgraceful, but since I'm driving, I'll stick with tea please. By the way, my name's Si. Not as in a deep sigh, but as in short for Silas. Yeah, I know, imagine growing up with that name?'

Thinking that she quite liked the name, she introduced herself. 'I'm Louisa.'

'Well, Louisa, I'm very pleased to meet you.'

Likewise, she thought as she went over to the kettle to fill it and quickly set about the business of making tea. As she did so, she couldn't resist surreptitiously appraising the man now looking at a framed photograph on the wall. He was a good deal taller than Kip, and had perhaps an inch or two over Angus who was the tallest of her sons. Without the all-enveloping coat, she could see that his build was that of a man who would have had no trouble moving any of the furniture upstairs. He had a good head of hair which was a pleasing mix of silvery-grey that was almost collar length and swept back from a broad forehead. His moss-green woollen jumper was worn thin at both of the elbows and his jeans were well-worn and stained in places with what she guessed might be wood stain or polish. She put him a year or two younger than her.

'Your family?' he commented when the kettle had boiled, and she'd filled two mugs.

'Yes,' she replied. Kip had taken the photograph of them all together two Christmases ago when Heidi and Peggy were babies. It was a rare photo of the family in which Kip didn't feature, which was why she had chosen it to put on the wall.

'Milk and sugar?' she asked.

'Just milk, please,' he said, moving away from the photograph.

When she brought the mugs over to him, along with the biscuit tin, and they both sat down – he in the chair that had always been Kip's place at the table – she asked him to tell her all about the mill. 'I've googled it, but found out only the bare bones, that it was used to grind wheat for flour.'

'That's right, it was. You know, I have a file of information at home which I could let you have, if you'd like,' he said.

'Are you sure you don't want to hang on to it?'

'Some things you have to let go. I'm on the move again, that's the hope anyway, so I need to jettison stuff I've hoarded for sentimental reasons. That's one of my failings, being too much of a sentimentalist.'

'There are certainly worse things one could be guilty of,' she said with a smile. 'But I do understand, as I've just experienced something similar when leaving a house that had been home for a very long time. Once I started on the task of getting rid of stuff, mostly old junk, the process became quite cathartic.'

'That's one of the challenges in life that we all need to learn,' he said, 'discerning what we really need as opposed to burdening ourselves with stuff we don't need. As life goals go, a simpler life is invariably a happier and better life.'

Louisa sipped her tea thoughtfully, thinking that having been forced to simplify her life and shed so much of her old self there were definitely moments when she felt a lightness of spirit and a sense of hope and peace for the future.

Which was perhaps a lot more than poor Kip could say after everything he had inflicted on the family and himself. Was it cruel of her to think that of the two of them, she had come out of their wretched divorce the stronger and better able to cope with the situation in which they now found themselves?

Chapter Fifty

Close up, Zoe was shocked by the change in Kip. He'd lost weight and his skin had taken on an almost greyish complexion. From the look of the puffiness beneath his eyes she guessed he was sleeping even less than she was. It pained her to admit it, but he looked his age, if not older. Yet as changed as Kip was to her, he had to be more shocked by the sight of her. She certainly was every time she looked in the full-length mirror in her bedroom, something she tried to avoid doing as much as she could.

It was the end of November, and she couldn't imagine how her body could go on expanding at the rate it was. When she'd voiced this at her last antenatal appointment, she'd been told that she was doing just fine and that it was all perfectly normal and that it was extraordinary what the human body could cope with.

What wasn't normal was standing here awkwardly in line in the queue of the on-site café with Kip. 'Hi,' she said, 'how's it going?'

Other than a fleeting sight of him coming and going from the car park that served the offices on the business park, this was the first time Zoe had seen Kip properly since they'd parted so acrimoniously. As pathetic as it was, until today she had avoided using the café, opting to bring her own lunch and drinks to work. Occasionally Phoebe would fetch her a decaf coffee or more recently, with the onset of the colder weather, a cup of hot chocolate. The latter had become something of a craving for Zoe and with Phoebe off work this week, and suffering with a desperate need for a hit of strong hot chocolate and a squirt of cream on the top – never mind the calories! – Zoe had risked a visit to the café. For all she knew Kip had probably been doing the same thing and had also given the café a wide berth.

'Not so bad,' he said hesitatingly, 'how about you?' His gaze dropped from her face down to what had once been her waistline and then darted back up again as though scared to let his gaze linger any lower.

'I'm surprised you were able to recognise me,' she said.

Once again, his gaze dropped as though he was powerless to stop it, then back up but he wasn't quite able to look her in the eye. 'Is that meant as a barb?' he said in a low voice that resonated with defensiveness.

'No. I just meant that I'm so gigantic I could easily be mistaken for a very large inflatable Humpty Dumpty.'

He stared at her but didn't respond to what she'd hoped was an attempt to lighten the mood. 'So . . . are you keeping well?' he asked falteringly.

'Pretty much,' she said. 'All things considered.'

He seemed to register her reply as another slight, and possibly he was right to do so. Why should she pretend that she was fine without a care in the world? Why shouldn't he know that she suffered sleepless nights worrying how caring for twin babies was going to impact on her life, or the not so small matter of supporting herself in the years to come?

When Angus had visited, he'd made a big deal of her holding his father to account when it came to helping to support her, insistent that Kip had a duty to do the right thing. A few days later she had received a letter from Angus's mother, in which Louisa said that she didn't want Zoe to feel that she was interfering, but she wanted her to know that she didn't have to go through the coming months alone, that if Zoe needed help, she had only to ask.

The Zoe of before – the independent Zoe who had held on fiercely to the right to do things her way and on her own – would have balked at such an offer and from of all people, the ex-wife of her ex-lover. *That* Zoe would have hated the thought of Louisa muscling in to play the prospective grandmother card; she would have said, if only to herself, *'These are my babies, not yours!'*

There was still a part of her that felt the pull of needing to go it alone, to stand firm and refuse to be sucked into the Langford family. But the pull of Louisa's sincerity was greater and using the mobile number Louisa had provided in her letter, she had messaged to thank her for the offer of help.

In stark contrast was the radio silence from Kip. But then she was to blame for that as much as he was. She could so easily have contacted him by phone or email, or faced him in his office, or even lain in wait to bump in to him here in the café.

Now though, the time had come for her to show the kind of strength that Louisa had shown so she could find a way forward with Kip. Because they really couldn't shut each other out the way they had.

'We should talk,' she said, moving forwards in the queue as she realised there was only one customer ahead of her now. She was also conscious that just about every pair of eyes in the café was glancing their way and pretending not to. Inevitably, just as word had gone round about their relationship once they'd gone public, so too had their split and her pregnancy. How could it not in a community of office workers who loved nothing more than a good gossip over their lunch or coffee break?

'I suppose we should,' Kip muttered. 'But not here.'

'No,' she said, 'here wouldn't be appropriate. When would be better for you?'

The look he gave her said *never. Never this side of never ever.*

'How about after work this evening?' she said firmly and after she'd placed her order for a take-out cup of hot chocolate. 'My place, six-thirty.'

At twenty-five minutes past six and pacing restlessly around her sitting room, Zoe had no idea if Kip would show up. She didn't really know what could be achieved if he came but still felt the way he did when he was last here. More importantly, what did she want from him?

At six-thirty-nine she poured herself a glass of water and sat down in the kitchen. But the babies inside her weren't having that. Her anxiety must have set them off as they suddenly started tussling like a pair of sumo wrestlers, making it uncomfortable for her to sit down.

'Easy there,' she said, rising to her feet placing a hand on the beachball of her stomach. 'Play nicely you two.'

At three minutes to seven, now back in the sitting room and lying on the sofa having given up on Kip, she heard a car door slamming out on the street. She hauled herself to her feet and went to the window and sure enough, there was Kip.

'Sorry I'm late,' he said when she let him in, 'but there was a problem at work. And I stopped for these,' he added, passing her a bunch of vibrant yellow and ochre chrysanthemums.

'Thank you,' she said, leading him through to the sitting room. Inviting him to sit down, she asked if he wanted a drink.

'I don't want to put you to any trouble,' he said.

She could have laughed out loud at the absurdity of his words – she was in trouble up to her neck!

'I don't have any wine, but I can manage to rustle up a coffee, or tea if you'd prefer. Or,' she said, 'I think there's some whisky of yours in the kitchen cupboard which you left behind.'

'A small glass, then,' he replied. 'I could get it if you like?'

'No need, pregnancy doesn't mean I can't fetch you a drink.'

'I'm sorry, I'm just trying to be helpful.'

Seeing the anxious expression on his face and noting how, if it were possible, he looked even worse than he had earlier that day, she said, 'I'm sorry too. Let's put it down to us both being on edge, shall we? Stay there and I'll put these flowers in water and pour you a drink.'

How calm and in control she sounded, Zoe thought when she disappeared to the kitchen and grabbed the first vase to hand and filled it with water and plonked in the flowers. Next, she poured a measure of whisky into a tumbler, and as the amber liquid splashed into the glass, its aroma rose up and filled her with sudden sadness. The rich peaty smell was synonymous with the man she had fallen in love with and breathing it in reminded her how happy she and Kip had been together. If only they could recapture what they'd once had, she thought sadly. Their love had been so real and even after all that had been said and done, she knew that she still loved him.

Taking a steadying breath, she went to rejoin Kip. But he wasn't sitting on the sofa where she'd left him just minutes before, he was on his feet and holding the ultrasound scan photo of their son and daughter which she'd framed and placed on a shelf on the bookcase. He seemed unaware of her presence, so she stood very still and observed him. What was he thinking as he held that small, grainy black and white photo that showed two miraculously well-formed babies? She knew what she felt whenever she looked at it; an intensity of love that took her breath away. She had never imagined it could feel like that, so overwhelming and profoundly life-changing.

As she continued silently to observe Kip, she realised her hands were empty – she'd left his drink on the worktop in the kitchen. Pregnancy brain, she thought with a half-smile, going back to the kitchen. While she was there, and feeling hungry, she opened a bag of Thai chilli-flavoured crisps. Tipping them into two bowls, she had just placed them on a tray with Kip's whisky when she heard what sounded like the front door closing. Thinking she must have misheard, she went through to the sitting room, but the room was empty: Kip had gone.

She rushed to the window and in the light cast from the street lamp, she saw Kip unlocking his car and sliding in behind the wheel. She briefly considered going out to him, but what good would it do? If he couldn't face talking to her, what was the point? She watched him drive away, then drew the curtains with a swish of finality. *That was that, then.*

Crossing the room to the bookcase, she picked up the framed scan of her unborn twins. There had been so much she had wanted to share with Kip this evening, but mostly she had wanted to tell him that she understood that this wasn't what he'd wanted, that he felt cheated, tricked into parenthood all over again. She'd wanted to explain that it needn't be like that, that they could find a compromise that would suit them both. But to do that they had to talk, and that was something he just didn't seem able to do.

Chapter Fifty-One

His head spinning, his mouth dry and his chest as tight as a drum and choking off his breath, Kip drove away as fast as he dared. He'd seen Zoe at the window, and he could only imagine what she must think of him. Yet however much she despised and hated him, it couldn't come close to what he felt for himself. Each time he thought he couldn't behave any worse, he proved himself wrong.

He'd turned up at Zoe's with all the right intentions, determined somehow to put things straight, or as straight as they ever could be between them. He'd wanted to listen to what she had to say, he owed her that much, but then he'd seen that framed baby scan photograph, and suddenly, as though a switch had been flicked, everything had spun out of control, and he'd felt his body slipping away from him. The fear that he was about to lose himself to another attack that would lay him bare again, and this time to Zoe, had ramped up the intensity of the crushing pain in his chest and the tremor already building in him. By then he had only one thought in his head: escape.

He knew he wasn't in a fit state to drive, but the need to escape overruled any notion of road safety and he drove on, his chest tightening even more, his fingers tingling so much he could scarcely feel the steering wheel. Rounding a corner too fast, the tyres squealing in protest, he thought that maybe death was the answer. A quick and easy fatal accident would solve everything.

He would be released from living with one foot in hell and the other in purgatory. His family would mourn but they'd be spared anymore angry shame at what he'd done.

But the thought of causing his children yet more distress on top of everything else brought him to his senses and now speeding along a quiet country lane and spotting a place up ahead where he could pull over, he jammed his foot down onto the brake pedal and swerved in. With a violent jolt, he brought the car to an abrupt stop, the seatbelt digging into him as he lurched at the windscreen. At the same time a car flew by blaring its horn and flashing its lights and in shock he realised he hadn't even registered that there had been a vehicle behind him.

Adrenaline pumping through him and his heart racing, he put the car in neutral and releasing the seatbelt, he rested his forehead on the steering wheel, and then, very slowly, he raised his head before crashing it hard against the wheel, again and again until the pain was too much. Then gripped in a state of God knew what, he flung himself back against the headrest, shaking his head from side to side and with tears running down his face, he let out a loud howl of torment.

It came from deep inside him, from a childhood place of unspoken fear and suppressed memories which he rarely allowed himself to think about, having slammed the lid down tight on the dread with which he'd lived as a young boy.

Life for him and his family had changed radically after his father's accident and what followed was a common enough story then, just as it was now in these economically tough times, when a perfectly ordinary family could go from relative comfort and security to being in debt and living in fear of losing their home. That was the great fear for his mum and dad, and it was why Kip readily took on the mantle of responsibility by relinquishing his childhood to be the man of the house, to keep them from being homeless.

But that wasn't his real worry. No, he knew what happened to families who couldn't cope: the children were taken into care. It had happened to a boy at school; his father had died, and his mother hadn't been able to cope with the four children she had been left with to bring up on her own and one by one they were taken away and put into care. That became Kip's biggest fear and night after night he had terrifying dreams of being dragged off to a children's home, never to see his parents again. He told no one of his fear and it became a way of life for him, of living constantly looking over his shoulder as though any second somebody would appear to snatch him away. His anxiety became so bad that he couldn't eat properly or concentrate on his work at school.

But one day, he realised that the answer to overcoming his fear was to do better at school so the teachers wouldn't show any concern about him or have their suspicions raised that all was not well at home. He then decided that he had to find a way to earn money, and as much as he could. So he washed cars, did a paper round, dug neighbours' gardens, carried out odd jobs for the elderly and fetched their shopping.

Eventually, when he was legally no longer a child, the risk of being taken from his parents and put in a children's home passed, but the fear he'd lived with never really left him. And nor did the desire to be financially secure and make his parents' lives better. He knew no other way to be.

That was the trajectory of his life forever on, always striving to help and do his duty, and do the right thing for those he cared about. True to his commitment to his parents, he helped them financially right to the end of their lives when his dad died some twenty years ago and then his mum just a few years after.

Now every good thing he'd ever done was trashed by his having thrown away the playbook of his existence to do something entirely for himself, something that was wholly selfish by following his heart, and not his head.

That wasn't to say he hadn't followed his heart with Louisa when they'd met, but it had been different back then; at the age they'd been, their relationship had had a natural linear path leading directly to marriage and children.

With Zoe, there had been no end point in sight, other than the simplicity of being together and of him relishing the freedom his relationship with her gave him. It had given him the chance to reinvent himself, to be someone other than good old Kip Langford.

'Well, guess what, Kip Langford,' he yelled at the top of his voice and with tears streaming down his cheeks, 'you have yourself a new identity as the dumbest, most selfish man that ever lived!'

An approaching vehicle, with its lights on full beam briefly filled his car with a dazzling brightness before leaving him in darkness again, and with the sense of being completely alone and cut off from the rest of the world.

Yet as alone as he felt, the eruption of emotion had subsided, and the vice-like grip on his chest had relaxed to allow his breathing to level out to a more normal steady rhythm. In place of the panicky fear was a weary emptiness and a sense of loss, as though he were grieving not just for losing everything that truly mattered to him, but for losing himself.

Staring into the darkness, he thought of the concern his family had recently shown to him since he'd been forced to admit that he was suffering panic attacks. He had promised them that he would see a doctor, but when he'd rung the surgery, he'd been told he'd have to ring back at eight o'clock the next morning. He'd done that only to be told the same thing and the following morning he was informed there were no appointments for another ten days, not unless it was an emergency. 'Is it an emergency?' the receptionist had enquired.

'No,' he'd said.

Arabella had been furious and told him that he should have lied and said that it was most definitely an emergency.

Louisa had also added to the chorus of voices expressing concern for his wellbeing. He'd felt thoroughly humiliated when he realised the children had involved their mother, but she'd been her usual practical and concerned self on the phone when she'd contacted him.

'It's really no big deal,' he'd said in an effort to play things down, 'I'm just a bit wound up, that's all. It'll pass.'

'But there'd be no harm in seeing a doctor, would there?' she'd said, 'just in case it's anything more than that.'

'Easier said than done,' he'd muttered.

She'd then gone on to ask how he was settling in with Arabella.

Their daughter's suggestion that he move in to keep her company hadn't fooled Kip for a minute, he'd known full well that it had been a plan devised to keep an eye on him, but he'd been happy last week to leave the miserable rental he'd been staying in to be with Arabella and Heidi. Superficially being with them helped to lift his spirits, you couldn't be around a small child like Heidi and not feel cheerful, but it hadn't resolved anything; every morning he still woke to the same ugly barbs of truth of what he'd done, lethally sharp hooks digging into the flesh of his guilt and self-loathing.

After encountering Zoe in the café that morning he'd spent the rest of the day psyching himself up for seeing her in the evening. He'd almost been relieved when a late phone call had come in from one of the house owners in Corfu and he'd been duty bound to deal with it. If the owner had wanted to talk with him for the rest of the evening, he'd have willingly done so; anything rather than face Zoe.

When he had made it to her house, he'd held it together pretty well until he'd seen the framed baby scan. That had been too much. The sight of those tiny babies bound together in an embrace, as though protecting each other, had reminded him so much of seeing the scan image he and Louisa had treasured of Ashley and

Arabella. They'd had one of Angus too, of course, but there had been something just so uniquely special about seeing the black and white evidence of their first two children, like two perfect little peas in a pod. The bond created in their mother's womb had never once been threatened, it was as strong today as it ever had been.

Before that moment of holding Zoe's scan photo in his hands, and as callous as it sounded, he had fought hard to detach himself from the two lives he had helped create. So long as he could avoid seeing Zoe, he could go on telling himself that those children had nothing to do with him. They were hers. They were her problem. It was what she had wanted.

Thinking of that grainy black and white image now, he could feel the swell of his emotions again and a tightening in his chest. He closed his eyes and focused on breathing slowly and steadily, one breath at a time, just as Caro had instructed him.

Tomorrow, he promised himself, he would try and make an appointment to see a doctor and if needs be, he would lie in order to see one. A few tablets might be all he needed to put him back on an even keel and then he'd be more able to cope with what had to be done.

For now, and although he knew by rights he should do a U-turn and drive back to Zoe and talk, he felt the pull of somewhere else.

Or rather, the pull of someone else.

Chapter Fifty-Two

Louisa was enjoying herself immensely.

Earlier that evening, and as arranged, Si had returned with a box file of information about the mill and they'd spent an age at the kitchen table going through the old black and white photographs and documents, some of which went as far back as the 1800s. There were also newspaper articles written about the mill when it was abandoned in the 1970s, and then how it was put up for sale in a poor state of disrepair and changed hands several times, including a period when it was owned by a consortium of investors who had hoped to return it to its original use as a working mill combined with being a tourist attraction. But the project had failed because they couldn't raise the necessary funds to get the scheme off the ground. Once again, the dilapidated mill was put up for sale and Si, in his own words, took a mad punt on it.

'It was the maddest thing I ever did and sadly, that's what killed my marriage,' he admitted ruefully. 'I spent too much time and money converting the mill into a home and not enough on my wife. I had only myself to blame.'

Now, and having poured two glasses of wine which they'd carried upstairs to the top of the mill, at Si's request Louisa was showing him her workspace. She would be a liar if she said she wasn't flattered by his interest in her miniature work. He was particularly fascinated by her collection of doll's houses, especially her oldest one with which her parents had surprised her on her ninth birthday. She had loved it so very much and had enjoyed decorating it in her ham-fisted childish way, using offcuts of wallpaper and carpet, the scale of which had been hopelessly wrong.

Since then, she had refurbished the doll's house many times over and, in the process, had learnt her craft. She had, of course, given her granddaughters a doll's house each and an assortment of child-friendly unbreakable furniture to play with. She looked forward to the day when they were old enough for her to teach them some of her skills.

'Do the lights actually work?' asked Si.

'Absolutely,' Louisa replied with a smile. Putting her wineglass down, she reached round to the back of the doll's house, flicked the switch, then watched his expression. The instant smile of appreciation on his face didn't disappoint.

'Hey, that's amazing!' he said, peering closer still into each room, the roseate glow from the miniature lights and lamps illuminating the contours of his face.

'I know some people think it's infantile and something we should grow out of,' she said, 'as though we miniaturists are playing with what most would think was just a child's toy, but it really is so much more than that.'

'There's no need to justify any of it to me,' he said, standing up to his full height now. 'I'm in awe of the workmanship. And if a hobby brings you pleasure, then I say enjoy the hell out of it! What's more, none of what you've shown me is a toy. I can see that everything is a mini piece of art in its own right. I mean, just look at the detail here.' He pointed to another doll's house, and its tiled floor which she'd made from cutting up card and then painstakingly painting each small square to resemble a stone tile. It had taken her weeks to do that. 'I feel like I've entered a parallel universe,' he said with a happy laugh.

'For me, and for many who pursue the hobby, that's what we

do,' she said, 'we create alternative worlds in which people can lose themselves. We all need to escape at times, don't we?'

'We certainly do. The shame is so many people don't realise that, or don't have the opportunity to lose themselves in something creative and absorbing. When I'm not doing the bread-and-butter work of making wardrobes, bookcases, or kitchen cupboards for customers, I do woodturning as a creative outlet.' He gave another laugh. 'You won't believe it, but I've developed quite a following on Instagram with my hobby. And before you say it, no, I'm not posting videos of naked woodturning, or anything else so salacious! Although come to think of it, it might not be a bad way to increase the number of followers I have. There again, at my age, it might put the punters off!'

She laughed too as an irreverent thought popped into her head of strategically placed chisels and mallets and whatever other tools Si might use.

Just as she was chasing this amusing thought from her mind, Si said, 'I ought to be going, I've taken up far too much of your evening.'

'Not at all. It's been lovely chatting with you.' She immediately regretted what she'd said, worried that she might be giving the wrong impression, that he'd either think she was a lonely divorcée desperate for company, or was—

Or was what? Demanded the prim voice of her inner married woman – *Embarrassing yourself by throwing yourself at him?* And so what if he did think that? Her inner married woman was a thing of the past, those days were behind her. She could behave just how she wanted to!

'If you don't have anyone expecting you home,' she said, 'I could rustle up a couple of pizzas and some salad if you'd like to stay for supper.'

He smiled. 'No,' he said, 'there's no one expecting me home, so if you're sure it's no trouble, a pizza would be good. But,' he added, 'only if you'll allow me to repay your hospitality with a meal out some time.'

Liking the sound of that, she said, 'I think I can accept those terms.'

Downstairs in the kitchen, and while Si tidied away the photos and papers they'd been looking at earlier, Louisa opened the freezer and dug out two pizzas and put them on baking trays and slid them into the Aga oven.

'Does it feel strange being here?' she asked, turning around to face her guest. 'I think I'd feel a bit odd if I were back at my old house as a visitor.'

'I know what you mean, but it's strangely nice, if that doesn't sound too weird. It's the familiarity of it, but combined with a fresh take.'

'Was it a happy home for you, for the most part?'

'Until things went wrong, yes. What about you and the house you left?'

'It was the perfect family home,' she said, her voice suddenly tight with sadness, 'or so I thought. Obviously, it wasn't for my husband.'

'It's not a house that makes a home though, is it, it's the people in it? Bricks and mortar are just that, bricks and mortar.'

She nodded. 'Which was the conclusion I reached when I realised I had no choice but to agree to sell Charity Cottage. Initially I wanted to fight it tooth and nail.'

'That's understandable, but was there no way you could have stayed there without your husband?'

She shook her head. 'Financially it was an asset that had to be divided up. You know how it is.'

'Yup,' he said, 'I do. But as big a wrench as it must have been for you to sell up, I can see that you've made yourself very comfortable here. Does your family like it?'

'My youngest son loved the mill on sight and encouraged me

to buy it, but my eldest two, the twins, needed convincing. They probably thought I was bonkers for wanting to live here. There were mutterings about my age and being on my own, and what about the future and all the stairs. I can tell you I wasn't best pleased at their attitude!'

'I guess they were just looking out for you. But presumably they've seen how happy you are here and have come round to the idea?'

'Yes,' she said with a smile, thinking how intuitive he was. 'Do you have any children?' she asked.

He shook his head. 'It never happened for us. I think that might have been a contributing factor for things going wrong the way they did. What about your ex-husband, is he happy now?'

Where to start, she thought. Poor Kip, he was in a far from happy state. When Ashley rang her to say he was concerned about his father and explained why, Louisa had been shocked. And worried. How could she not be when they'd been married for so long and after everything they had shared together?

'He left me for another woman,' she said, 'a much younger woman and let's just say things haven't worked out for him the way he thought they would.'

'Love's young dream not quite the dream he imagined it would be?'

'Something like that,' she said vaguely.

'Do you think your husband regrets what he's done? And sorry if I'm speaking out of turn, but if he does, is there any chance you could forgive him and the two of you patch things up?'

How easy he made it sound, as though a needle and thread were all that was required to repair the damage Kip had caused. All her life she had been able to fix most things, but even if it were in her power, did she want to fix Kip and their shattered marriage?

She recalled just a few weeks ago when she'd thought that if she had behaved differently, might she have been able to save Kip from himself? It had been a conceited thought on her part, that she regarded herself so highly as to be capable of doing that. Who did she think she was, Kip's personal saviour?

'It's gone way beyond the patching-up stage,' she said in answer to Si's question. She was wondering if there was a specific reason why he had asked her what he had when she heard a car on the drive outside and a flash of light shone in through the un-curtained window.

Si heard the car too. 'Perhaps I should be going after all,' he said, 'if you have company.'

'There's no need for you to leave,' she said, glancing at the kitchen clock – it was a few minutes after eight o'clock – 'I'm not expecting anyone.'

She had just made it to the door and opened it when, and in the brightness of the security lights that had come on, she saw a car disappearing at speed down the lane. She recognised the car and numberplate immediately: it was Kip's.

Chapter Fifty-Three

It was two weeks until Christmas and at the first sight of snow falling, Arabella was reminded how she had been fooled by an older girl at infant school into believing it was frozen angels' tears falling from heaven whenever it snowed. At home she had proudly announced this newly acquired fact to the rest of the family and Mum had said, 'In that case there must be a lot of very sad angels in heaven.'

From then on, unlike other children who used to whoop and cheer at the first sight of snow, Arabella had always felt a little sad. Even when she had long since outgrown the silly notion of weeping angels, that old sadness would make itself felt.

She experienced it now as she stared out of the car window while her father attended his first cognitive therapy session. She had driven him here, to the very same place where she had come for her one and only couples therapy session and which had ended so disastrously with her driving into the back of the car in front of hers. A moment's lack of concentration and she'd lost the baby she had longed for. It had been nobody's fault but her own. Oh yes, she'd wanted wholeheartedly to blame Giles for the accident, for making her do something she hadn't wanted to, but in the weeks that had passed she had accepted that the responsibility for what had happened was her own.

If she had learnt one thing in the last few months, it was that blaming others for something going wrong was a cop-out and resolved nothing. Being an adult meant owning up to your mistakes. With this in mind, and wanting to be the best mother she could be to Heidi, she was determined to follow Mum's example and not let any ill-feelings towards Giles blight her relationship with Heidi. But as resolute as she was, it wasn't easy. Her natural default setting was to bare her claws when feeling vulnerable and under attack, and every time she spoke to Giles that was just how she felt, her claws ready to defend herself and at the same time puncture his infuriating puffed-up air of him being in the right and her firmly in the wrong.

Not wanting to dwell on her own problems, she switched her thoughts back to her father, imagining that he would be feeling horribly vulnerable and under attack now as he subjected himself to a process he had resolutely opposed, just as she had. She still couldn't believe that he had agreed to keep the appointment. She had expected him to bail out at the last minute with some excuse about not feeling well, or there being something at work which only he could deal with; or worse, the fear of the session inducing a panic attack. But that morning he had appeared at the breakfast table washed, shaved, and dressed and looking startlingly very nearly his normal self.

'Don't look so worried,' he'd said to Arabella while helping Heidi open the door on her chocolate Advent calendar, 'I'm not going to let you down.'

'Why would you think I'd be worried that you'd let me down?'

'Oh, sweetheart, it's written all over your lovely face. Just as it was last night. You're concerned that I'm not going to go through with the appointment, and I know how desperate the family is to see me helping myself to get well.'

'You mustn't go through with it just to please us, Dad, it must be because you want to do it. But I do understand how much you hate the idea of talking to a complete stranger about, well, you

336

know . . .' She'd left the rest of the sentence hanging, anxious not to say the wrong thing. Which she knew only made it worse, her father could see right through her attempts to go easy on him and he didn't much like it.

'That I've totally messed up and ruined everything that was good in my life,' he'd finished for her. 'And to prove that I know just how low I've fallen I'm agreeing to see a therapist in the mistaken hope that a magic wand will be waved, and all my problems will go away.'

Arabella hated it when her father spoke about himself this way, putting himself down with such obvious self-loathing but at the same time trying to make light of it. That wasn't her father. Dad had never been like that. He'd never once displayed self-pity before or been anything other than a tower of supportive strength and confident optimism.

After finally managing to see a GP – an appointment Arabella made, having kicked up an almighty fuss at the surgery – her father had been advised to take some time off work and to the family's amazement, he had done just that. No one could remember when he'd last taken a sick day, or for that matter been ill with anything more than a common cold. He hadn't cut himself off entirely from work, he'd kept in touch now and then with his team via Zoom and email, but Arabella had made it clear to those in the office who worked most closely with him that Kip was ill and needed to rest.

Initially, after Arabella had put a stop to any more meetings and phone calls, he had busied himself with doing jobs around the house for her – jobs which Giles had never found time to do. He bled the radiators, replaced a washer on the tap in the downstairs loo, reapplied the sealant around the bath, fixed the leaking gutter above the back door and even cleaned out the wheelie bins with a pressure jet hose. He did it all in a frenzy of activity, as though up against the clock with not a minute to be lost.

When he'd run out of things to fix, he'd mooched about the house much like Lexi used to when she had nothing to do, and then he seemed to withdraw and give up altogether; he stopped shaving and some days he didn't bother to dress. More than once after dropping Heidi off at nursery Arabella would return home and find her father practically comatose on the sofa in his dressing gown. It had upset her to see him like that, so lacking in energy and drive. His behaviour, the family decided, was a mark of how stressed and close to the edge he must have been.

Mum had wanted to call in to see if there was anything she could do to help, but when Arabella had told her father, he'd begged her to keep everyone away. Especially Mum. 'I couldn't bear for her to see me this way,' he'd said, his eyes dark pools of misery.

The sight of him at breakfast this morning looking better than he had in days had reassured Arabella; it had given her hope that her real father – the man she had always loved and admired – was still there inside somewhere. It was while they were in the car coming here, and after dropping off Heidi at nursery, that he had explained why he agreed to see a therapist. 'It was the lesser of two evils; either I sit for an hour every week with a so-called expert, or I take handfuls of mind-numbing anti-depressants as the doctor wanted me to.'

'Neither of the options need be as bleak as you think they might be,' she'd said, knowing that given her resistance to the idea of therapy to save her marriage, her father would have every right to accuse her of hypocrisy. 'If the session and any future sessions help, just in some small way, wouldn't it be worth it?' she'd said.

Her father had said nothing in response and had remained silent until she'd parked the car. Twisting round in his seat, he'd kissed her on the cheek. 'Wish me luck,' he'd murmured.

'Tons of luck and love to you, Dad,' she'd replied, giving him a fiercely protective hug.

She'd watched him cross the road as fat flakes of snow slowly drifted down from the pewter-grey sky. His shoulders hunched, his hands pushed deep into his coat pockets, her heart had squeezed with love for him. He looked so lost, so vulnerable and uncertain of himself. 'Oh Dad,' she'd said softly, 'if it's possible, please find the person you always used to be. I want the old you back.'

Now, and with her gaze fixed on the attractive four-storey Georgian building her father had entered thirty minutes ago, she contemplated making a start on the Christmas cards she'd brought with her to write. But it was not a job she had any eagerness to undertake. What kind of message could she write in the cards to those friends who didn't already know the hellish year she and her family had experienced?

Putting the job off, she messaged her brothers, letting them know, as she'd promised she would, that their father was right now undergoing his first therapy session. She then messaged her mother.

She was about to put the mobile back in her bag when it buzzed. It was a message from Caro asking if Kip had made it to see the therapist.

Arabella would have liked to ring Caro, but since her sister-in-law was at work, she settled for a message instead. *So far so good. Will let you know more later today.'*

Caro replied with a thumbs-up and a smiley face.

This was a new thing from Caro. She had never been one for smiley emojis in the past and Arabella had always avoided using them with her sister-in-law for fear of appearing silly or immature. But things had changed between them recently, and for the better. Instead of Arabella always feeling intimidated by Caro, she now regarded her as an ally, someone to whom she could turn for help or an honest opinion. It had been that moment in the play area – the day they'd discovered how unwell Dad was – that Arabella had begun to see her sister-in-law differently. Whereas previously she had often been irritated by Caro's no-nonsense manner, she now valued it, appreciating the straightforward advice, seeing it as something she could trust. She knew that this shift in their relationship pleased Ashley, and that made Arabella happy too.

In one of the upstairs windows overlooking the street that was now covered with a layer of snow, and with the light fading although it wasn't yet midday, a lamp came on and Arabella wondered if that was the room in which her father was being encouraged to share his innermost feelings.

Chapter Fifty-Four

'I know it sounds crass, and you might not believe me, but I never meant to hurt anyone.'

'Seldom does anyone go out of their way to do that, but who do you think you've hurt the most?'

Dubious as to where the question might lead, Kip stared blankly at the cognitive behaviour therapist sitting opposite him. Climbing the stairs up to this high-ceilinged room with its sash windows and fresh smell of paint, he had expected to be greeted by a woman, because in his head, doubtless based on stereotypes he must have seen on the TV or read about, therapists were always women. But the one to whom Kip's GP had referred him fitted no such stereotype.

His name was Paul Read and at a guess Kip would put him in his late forties. He was broad-shouldered with a thick neck and dressed in a pair of jeans and a white T-shirt with a blue-and-white plaid flannel over-shirt. His feet were firmly planted on the carpeted floor in a pair of well-worn Timberland boots and on his right wrist was a brown-coloured leather bracelet of some sort with two black beads attached. On his other wrist was a Smart watch very like the one Kip had recently started to wear. It had been Ashley's idea to have the watch so that it would monitor Kip's heartbeat and alert him to any irregularities. He didn't need to look at the watch to know that right now his heart was racing at full tilt.

Leaning forward, the therapist reached for the mug of coffee on the glass-topped table between them. He'd made them both coffee but so far Kip hadn't been able to drink any of his; he didn't dare risk picking up the mug when his body was thrumming with an explosive amount of adrenaline and the threat of a panic attack that could happen at any moment. For the last thirty minutes, and while submitting to the pain of confessing his crimes – though not the one about betraying Zoe when he'd been at the trade show, he couldn't bring himself to do that – he'd kept his arms rigidly folded across his chest as though preventing his heart and lungs from bursting through his ribcage.

Watching the other man sip his coffee, Kip forced himself to answer the question. 'Obviously Louisa and Zoe are the ones I've hurt the most. I've treated them abominably.'

'Isn't there one more person you've hurt just as badly? What about you? Aren't you hurting?'

Kip sucked in his breath and clasped his arms even more tightly across his chest. But he said nothing.

'From what you've told me,' the therapist went on, and in what he probably thought was a meticulously pacifying and neutral tone, 'the two women you've hurt appear to be coping and moving on, but you aren't.'

Kip swallowed. 'How can I? Or more to the point, why should I be able to do that after everything I've done?'

'Everyone deserves to be happy.'

'But not at the expense of somebody else's happiness,' Kip said.

'That's one way of looking at it. But in general, it's not healthy to keep a logbook on who is worthy and who isn't. Do you want to be happy?'

With a powerful surge of adrenaline causing his heartbeat to pound even faster, Kip sought to find the right answer from the confusion of thoughts scrambled inside his head. Say he wanted to be happy, and it made him look like he didn't care a damn about what he'd done. But say no, and he'd come across as a wreck of a man and he'd have to come here every week for God knows how long! Effectively it would be a life sentence, he'd never be free of the endless questions. Or the guilt. Every session would be like scratching the scab off a sore that could never heal.

'I'm sorry,' he said, feeling his muscles coiling in his body, a reaction to his brain demanding he was anywhere but here. Unfolding his arms, he rose hastily from the chair. 'It was a mistake coming here. It's a waste of time for you and me.'

With not a flicker of surprise on his face, and putting his cup down on the table, the other man stood up too. 'It's a great shame you feel that way as rarely in my experience is it ever a waste of time to talk to someone about what really matters.'

'Look,' Kip said irritably, 'I just want the panic attacks to stop. That's why I came here. Happiness doesn't come into it.'

The therapist levelled his gaze on Kip, somehow making it impossible for him to look away. 'It's perfectly understandable that you're finding this challenging, especially if you're here under sufferance, but I can assure you it's the same for everyone. Nobody relishes a stranger asking a lot of seemingly intrusive and pointless questions. The whole process probably feels counterintuitive, doesn't it? Why open Pandora's box when you can toss it away and forget about it? And perhaps you've decided you're beyond help. That's also a very common reaction. Or the opposite can be true, you don't believe you need any help, that you can sort this on your own. Because that's what you've always done. Am I right?'

Some of the tension dissolving from his body, Kip breathed in deeply. 'I know what you're doing.'

'Good. Transparency is always preferable. And what if I told you I've never yet had anyone walk out on me and so I would value you staying at least to the end of this session, so I keep that record intact? You've made it to the halfway point, why not see it through to the end of the hour? How does that sound?'

'It sounds like a negotiator talking a terrorist round.'

'Funny you should say that,' the therapist said with a smile, 'that's what my children say. "Dad," they say, "we are not terrorists, so put away your tedious negotiating voice."' He laughed. 'They see through me every time, as does my wife. That's the thing about those who care about us, they know how we operate. They sometimes know us better than we know ourselves.'

Kip thought of his own children and how worried they were about him and how much they desperately wanted him to seek help. He thought of Ashley presenting him with the Smart watch and of Angus's regular phone calls, then he thought of Arabella sitting outside in the car and how anxious she was for him to be well again. She had so many problems to deal with herself, yet every day she prioritised his problems over her own. Didn't he owe it to her, as well as his sons to talk to this therapist? What harm would it do? Other than make him feel even more humiliated than he already felt and bring on a panic attack. It was a small price to pay in the big scheme of things if ultimately it helped. If it set him free.

He flinched at the word. Setting himself free had been what had precipitated this whole sorry mess.

'I'm sorry,' he said to the therapist, 'I've been rude to you, and you didn't deserve that.'

'Not rude at all. A little overwhelmed maybe and that never brings out the best in us. Shall we sit down again and then you can tell me what made you want to leave so suddenly?'

Kip did as instructed, and this time made himself sit with his arms either side of his body in what he hoped was a less hostile and more openly receptive stance. 'You asked me if I wanted to be happy,' he said after a long and difficult pause while teasing out the reason for his response to such an innocuous question.

'And what emotion did that induce in you? Not that it need be just the one emotion, it could be any number.'

Kip looked out of the window at the snow settling on the nearby rooftops. It was coming down thick and fast now and knowing how Arabella disliked driving in the snow, he would suggest that he drove them home.

'I think it was mostly anger I felt,' he said eventually.

'And can you tell me when you last felt genuinely happy?'

Again, it seemed such an innocuous question, yet it was anything but for Kip. He rubbed his chin, then cleared his throat. 'Um . . . it was . . . it was before Zoe announced she was pregnant . . .' He hesitated before adding, 'But if I'm truthful, I was happiest when I'd just moved in with Zoe. That was when I felt the freest I'd ever been.'

'When you'd let go of everything from your old life and were starting out on an exciting new one? Is that how it felt?'

Kip nodded. 'It sounds pathetic, doesn't it?'

'Not at all. I've yet to meet anyone who doesn't want to be free of the stresses and strains of everyday life. It's why we go on holiday, isn't it? It's escapism for a week or two, or longer if we're lucky.'

Kip shook his head ruefully. 'I'd have been better off booking the holiday of a lifetime for my wife and me, wouldn't I?'

'But very likely you would have returned to the very same thing you were trying to escape.'

'With hindsight I wish that was exactly what I had done. It would have saved the pain and disruption I've caused for everyone else.'

'For yourself too. Don't lose sight of yourself in all this. You're at the centre of things and the hurt you're feeling is just as valid as anyone else's pain. You need to accept that and own it.'

Kip cringed. 'We're told that all the time now, aren't we, to own our truth and our emotions.' He exhaled deeply. 'I'm sorry, but it just seems like a load of bull—' He stopped himself short. 'Nonsense,' he said.

The other man smiled. 'The expression is helpful for some people, but not for others. But you know, you are allowed to feel what you feel because denying your emotional response to something is what ultimately erodes the self.'

'Don't you think that we've all become obsessed with the self, that we're convinced it's our right to have it all?'

'That's a very good point. But life isn't as simple as that, which means we need to perform a tricky balancing act to satisfy both the self and the expectations of others. And there's even the expectations of society we feel compelled to factor in. It's never solely about ourselves.'

'So what are you saying, that I failed to perform the balancing act when I chose to have an affair and left my wife? I might not look the smartest guy, but even I can figure that one out.'

'What did you hope to obtain by having an affair with Zoe? Freedom? Excitement? A sense of adventure? Feeling young again? Happiness?'

Embarrassed to admit it, Kip looked once more out of the window at the snow. 'All of those things,' he muttered. 'And love. Passion too.'

'What about peace of mind, wasn't that something you wanted?'

Kip frowned. 'I had it with Louisa and I threw it away.'

'Not necessarily. It's hard sometimes to analyse exactly what peace of mind really is. If you'd genuinely had it, do you think you would have been attracted to Zoe?'

'I don't know. It's so hard now to re-evaluate the situation after everything that's happened.'

'I can see that would be the case, you doubt every decision you made and can't trust what you felt then or subsequently.'

'All I can be sure of is that I feel guilty about every damned thing I've done, and that I have no right to be happy.'

'How does that make you feel, saying it out loud?'

'Angry with myself and ashamed,' Kip replied without thinking.

'You mentioned before that you financially supported your parents for many years, and then of course there was your responsibility to your own family, followed by those who work for you. Did any of that make you at all angry?'

'*No!*' Kip said vehemently. 'I did it because I wanted to, because it was what any decent person would do.'

'But you felt constrained perhaps, or maybe trapped by being the person you expected yourself to be, and how others expected you to be?'

Kip nodded. 'Not as trapped as I now feel.'

'By the thought of taking on yet more responsibility? Has Zoe demanded that of you?'

'No, but I have to do it, don't I? I can't turn my back on her and those two children. I'm their father.'

'So what's stopping you from doing that?'

'Selfishness. It wasn't what I planned on getting into. But then it wasn't what Zoe had planned on either.'

'When our plans go awry it can take some readjustment of the mind. Can you tell me what your initial reaction was when Zoe broke the news to you that she was pregnant?'

'Shock. Total shock. And then I was angry because she froze me out of the decision-making process.'

The other man fiddled with the two beads on the leather bracelet on his wrist before saying, 'That must have been hard for you when you've always been used to making all the decisions.'

Immediately on his guard, Kip frowned. 'I'm not sure I like what you're implying. If you're suggesting that my wife didn't play an equal part in our marriage, then you couldn't be more wrong. We shared all the decisions.'

'A well-balanced marriage, then. But Zoe didn't play by the same rules?'

'It was her right to make the decision she did, I know that, but it didn't feel fair. She didn't even want to discuss it with me.'

'Did that make you feel sidelined, as though you didn't count?'

'Something like that, yes.'

'And angry?'

Not caring now how his answer might be interpreted, Kip nodded. 'Very angry.' It was the first time he'd admitted this aloud.

'What do you normally do when you're angry about something?'

Thoughts of when he'd lost his temper with his children when they were young and driving him and Louisa to distraction sprang to mind. 'I've never seen myself as an angry person,' he said, 'but in common with most parents I've had my moments when I hit the roof over something my sons and daughter did when they were children, but it was always short-lived.'

'Ah yes, nobody pushes our buttons more than our kids. And so apart from those episodes, you tend to contain your anger? Would that be a fair assessment?'

'I've never really thought about it before, but yes, I probably do. But isn't that what we all learn to do, to control our tempers? It's part of being an adult.'

'Indeed it is. However, internalising that emotion, or suppressing it, is all well and good until enough is enough.'

Kip reflected on this. He thought of the level of self-control he'd demanded of himself ever since he could remember and how when Zoe came along, he let go of it all and revelled in the heady rush of being in love and of not giving a damn about the consequences of his actions. But then he thought of the anger he'd felt when that was no longer the case, when suddenly the consequences very much mattered.

'Are you saying I've been suppressing years of anger and that's what's brought on the panic attacks?' he asked disbelievingly. 'Surely it can't be as simplistic as that?'

'Yes and no, but it might be something worth thinking about.'

A silence settled on the room and then the other man glanced at the clock on the wall above the blocked-off fireplace. 'We're nearly out of time now,' he said, 'but in the hope that I'll see you again next week, which will be our last session before the Christmas and New Year break, there's a real positive I want you to take away. For the whole hour you've been here, and no doubt feeling under threat by my questions, you haven't actually experienced a panic attack.'

And nor had he, thought Kip with surprise and relief when he took the stairs down to the ground floor, pulled on his gloves and tightened the scarf around his neck and then heaved open the heavy door onto the snow-covered street. He looked over to where Arabella was sitting in the car waiting for him. She caught sight of him and waved.

Raising a gloved hand in response, he stepped off the pavement onto the road and immediately slipped on the snow and lost his balance. His arms comically flailing and his legs going every which way, he somehow managed to keep himself from falling just as a large truck approached.

Was that a sign, he wondered as he made it safely across the road to where Arabella was now out of the car, a worried look on her face, that maybe as perilous as the way ahead was, he might just about survive it?

'I hope you approved of the floor show,' he said to his daughter. 'Anything for a bit of light relief.'

'It was rather spectacular. You didn't hurt yourself, did you?'

'Only the remains of my tattered pride as I made a right Charlie of myself. Shall I drive? I know how much you dislike driving in the snow.'

She handed him the car keys. 'Be my guest. And then you can tell me all about your session. That's if you want to,' she added.

The pair of them inside the car now, and with their seatbelts on and the windscreen wipers swishing away the snow, he said, 'I very nearly walked out at one point.'

'What made you stay?'

'Let's just say the therapist was quite persuasive that I should remain there for the full hour.'

'Was she good?'

'*He*. He was . . . good at digging.'

'Was it helpful?'

'I'm reluctant to admit it, but maybe it was. But don't worry, I'm not getting ahead of myself and thinking that a single therapy session has resolved all my problems.'

'But it's given you cause to hope?'

'It hasn't made me feel any worse. And amazingly I didn't suffer a panic attack while I was there being interrogated. It was what I dreaded most, losing control in front of a stranger.' And there it was again, he thought, his need always to be in control, to be seen in a certain way.

'I'm glad things went well for you,' Arabella said.

'Thank you, sweetheart. And thank you for everything you've done to help me reach this point. Especially when you have so many problems of your own to deal with.'

'You've always been there for me, Dad, so this has been my time to be there for you. It's the same for Ashley and Angus. They feel the same way. Mum does as well, she called me just before your session ended.'

'And?'

'Don't look so worried, she just wanted to know if you'd made it to the appointment. She also wanted you to know that she was thinking of you.'

'That was thoughtful of her,' he said, recalling the night some weeks ago when he'd been in that terrible state after going to talk with Zoe and he'd seen the ultrasound photo of the babies he'd fathered. Ignoring the fact that he wasn't fit to drive, he'd found his way to Louisa. He'd wanted the comforting familiarity of her matter-of-fact calmness. But after bumping his way down the narrow lane to the mill, he'd seen the vehicle parked next to hers and he'd suddenly come to his senses and seen how stupid and selfish he was being. Why would his ex-wife want to speak to him? She was getting on with her new life; she didn't need him pestering her for help or advice.

'Mum also had something else to say,' Arabella said, 'she wants to address the elephant in the room.'

'Which particular elephant would that be?'

'Christmas. She wants us all to go to her on Christmas Day. Including you.'

'Me?'

'Yes, you.'

'But I thought you said—'

'I know I'd suggested that the three of us, you, me and Heidi could have a quiet, stress-free Christmas on our own, but I only said that because I thought it would be easier on you.'

'Now you think differently?'

'I think Mum's right, we should all be together. Angus's girl-friend is going to come too.'

'But not Giles, I presume?'

'Er no, that's a total given. I'm not making nicey-nicey over the turkey and crackers with him. That would be too much for me right now. So, what do you think, shall I tell Mum we'll be there? Or would it be too awkward for you, too much too soon? If there's a danger it will, you know, bring on a panic attack, I'm sure she'll understand if we say no.'

'Knowing your mother, I know she will,' he said, conscious that just the thought of being together again as a family was making his breath quicken and his hand grip the steering wheel more forcibly. He breathed in deeply, then exhaled slowly.

'Dad, are you okay?'

'Yeah, I'm fine,' he said. 'It's just you've taken me by surprise. Or rather your mother has. I probably need some time to adjust to the idea of Christmas Day spent with everyone.'

But as he concentrated on keeping a safe distance from the car in front, he told himself it couldn't be any worse than last Christmas when he'd spent the day secretly preparing to break the news to Louisa that he wanted a divorce.

Chapter Fifty-Five

The heavy fall of snow ten days ago might have long since melted, but the festive season had well and truly arrived at Melbury Mill that Saturday afternoon.

With only four sleeps until Christmas the decorations were up, carols were playing in the background, the kitchen was fragrant with the spicy aroma of mince pies baking in the Aga and Louisa was icing the Christmas cake. On the other side of the table from her, and wearing their cute pinnies, Peggy and Heidi were rolling out lumps of green fondant icing on chopping boards to make the holly leaves which would then be stuck on the cake, with a little help from her if they'd allow it. They'd already made the red berries and as a result both girls had startlingly red hands and a few tell-tale red stains around their mouths.

Normally Louisa would have the job of icing the cake done much earlier than this, but the days had run away from her as she'd rushed to fulfil a flood of Christmas commissions that had come in. The fiddliest and most time-consuming commission had been hand painting an entire 12th scale dinner service based on a Royal Worcester design, the detail of which had to be a perfect match to the customer's full-size dinner service. She should never have promised to make the Christmas deadline, but that was her all over, she didn't like to let people down.

Kip was the same; he'd always had the need to please people, to help them as much as he could. It was one of the reasons they'd been such a good team, their value systems were so closely aligned. It was also one of the things that had attracted her to Kip when they'd met. But then who wouldn't be charmed by an engaging and good-looking man who, as ambitious as he was – although not in an arrogant, self-absorbed, or overly competitive manner – liked to put others first? Being the best he could possibly be, and being well thought of, had been so very important to him.

From what Louisa knew from the children and the reports they'd given her of the two therapy sessions their father had so far undergone, and based only on what he had been prepared to share with them, Kip was discovering that he may have pushed himself too far in his pursuit of this goal to be the best he could be, and it had left him wanting to rebel and be anything but the man he'd striven to be.

Louisa struggled to believe this could be true. If it was, it meant that for most of his life Kip had suppressed who he really was and that he was only now discovering the real Kip Langford. Apparently, even the fact that his real name of Christopher had been concealed by a made-up name was a sign that from an early age his true self had been denied in his desire to please others.

But couldn't it be true of everyone when the outer layers of their circumstances, experience and surrounding were stripped away and they were left with the raw self of their being? Could Louisa claim that she could have been an entirely different woman if she hadn't met Kip?

The big difference between her and Kip, she supposed, was that she had never reached a point when she questioned who she was or what might have been. Was that a fault in her, that she was too easily pleased and too content to go with the flow and had assumed that Kip felt the same way? Had she been too wrapped up in her own complacency that she hadn't realised the strain he was putting himself under to be the ideal husband and father?

She thought of all those times in the early years of their marriage when her friends had told her that she really couldn't have found herself a more ideal man. Initially she had basked in their approval of Kip, but then when the opinion was aired just a little too often it had rankled with her. Why didn't her friends say that it was Kip who had been the lucky one to find *her?* The truth was, they had been lucky to find each other and had created their own luck together throughout their marriage.

Another truth was that if Kip had died and not left her the way he had, she would have had nothing but cherished memories of all the good times they'd shared. But the tragedy of divorce was that it had the power to rob one of the ability to treasure what had gone before, to convince one that nothing was as it once seemed, the memories sullied with angry bitterness. It took a will of iron to hang on to what had once been so good about the relationship.

Arabella was presently going through the stage of believing everything about her relationship with Giles was tainted or an outright lie now that it was seen through the lens of her anger and pain. She had lost sight of all the good times, even the reason she had married him.

Louisa wasn't so naïve as to overlook that part of Giles's initial appeal for Arabella may have lain in him still being married and her wanting something that was strictly speaking out of bounds. He may have been separated, so Arabella had wanted them to believe, but there had been no getting away from the fact that he was still married and with a young child. There was also the appeal of her wanting to be the real love of his life, the only person who would heal the damage inflicted on him by his uncaring and unloving first wife. Very likely Zoe had experienced something similar with Kip, in that she'd seen herself as saving him from a loveless marriage and she would make him whole again.

It was, so Louisa's sister had informed her during a long chat on the phone a few nights ago, a common enough trait amongst women.

'Women are natural comforters and healers,' Stephanie had said – not something Louisa would have ordinarily associated with her sister – 'it's our default setting, so it's only to be expected that a woman will fall for the oldest trick in the book when a man claims his wife doesn't understand him. What woman doesn't want to prove for all she's worth that she's the one who will understand him? I'm afraid to say,' went on Stephanie, 'poor Arabella fell hook, line, and sinker for that when she met Giles. That might even be what hurts the most for her, knowing that she betrayed herself in believing the lie in the first place.'

This was one of those rare occasions when Louisa thought her sister might have made a very valid point. But whatever the foundations upon which Arabella had built her marriage, it didn't lessen the pain she was going through now, and Louisa knew from bitter experience how painful it was to lie awake in bed at night rummaging tearfully through the memories and wondering if any of them had been real.

Only now, almost a year on from when Kip had left her, was Louisa beginning to accept that he hadn't destroyed everything good they'd shared together. She hoped that one day Arabella might reach the same point.

Louisa hadn't told her daughter, but she had sent Giles and Lexi a Christmas card. How could she not when he was Heidi's father? It had been a difficult card to write when Louisa was still cross with him for the way he'd treated her daughter.

Ashley was convinced that Giles had checked out of the marriage some time ago, and maybe that was why he'd been so against them having another child. Yet for all that, Louisa knew that she and the rest of the family would have to find a way to keep the peace with Giles so that Heidi would not be adversely affected by the divorce.

Recalling how challenging it had been to get the wording right in her card to Giles, Louisa thought of all the other cards which she hadn't sent and never would, not when it was now only four days until Christmas. What could she have written in the cards, other than a simple *I hope this card finds you well*? Honesty would have been too much, because it was bad enough to share that there had been one failed marriage in the family, but to report two, as Oscar Wilde might have said, looked like carelessness.

Close friends knew about her and Kip, but as far as she knew, the wider circle, those on the periphery with whom contact was invariably only at Christmas, were unaware. If they did know they certainly hadn't been in touch with her. Maybe they had with Kip.

There had been a surprise card in the post yesterday from Zoe. She had written to wish Louisa well and to apologise again for the part she'd played in breaking up her marriage and for the distress she'd caused the family. Louisa didn't doubt the sincerity of the message and it provoked in her the need to contact Zoe to make sure she was okay. She couldn't help but wonder how things stood between her and Kip now and what she would be doing over Christmas. And why did she even care? *'Because,'* she heard her sister's voice say, *'women can't help but be comforters and healers.'*

Wasn't that why Louisa had invited Kip to come here for Christmas Day? She had discussed with Angus and Ashley the idea of inviting their father and they'd both readily agreed that he should be included.

'In the circumstances, how can he not be with us on Christmas Day?' Ashley had asked.

'The same goes for Arabella and Heidi,' Angus had added, 'we should all be together, nobody should be left out.'

They had briefly discussed whether Christmas Day should be hosted by Ashley and Caro, but Louisa had said she wanted to spend her first Christmas here at the mill, it felt important to her to pass this milestone of her new life in her new home and to have the whole family with her. Caro had then volunteered to do Boxing Day for them all. So everything was organised.

As was her night out this evening; Si was taking her for dinner over in Dedham to a restaurant she hadn't been to in a long time. It was a massive understatement to say that it was also a very long time since she'd been out for an evening with a man who wasn't Kip and she had to quell her nerves at the thought of what Si might be expecting of her. Or was she getting ahead of herself? He might not be expecting anything more than a pleasant evening out by way of thanking her for the pizza supper she'd given him some weeks back.

Having asked for her mobile number that evening, he'd since texted to ask if she was free to have the meal he'd promised her. After two hours of dithering, she had finally plucked up the courage to reply.

When are you thinking?

Whenever suits you.

Ten seconds later he'd called her to fix a date. 'I thought it would be easier this way,' he'd said, 'save all that tapping back and forth.'

She hadn't told any of the children about Si because really what was there to tell? He was someone she'd met who had asked her to go for dinner with him. That was all.

Oh, how we deceive ourselves she thought as she finished smoothing the surface of the icing on the Christmas cake. She hadn't mentioned Si to the family because she was worried how they might react. They had enough going on as it was without worrying that she might be getting involved with a man they knew nothing about.

Angus had let slip that Ashley harboured the notion of her and Kip getting back together again, which of course was never going to happen. But then Ashley had always been the more sentimental of her children and she could quite imagine how he might hang on to that hope and make the last twelve months disappear so everything could return to how it used to be.

But how could it when she had been forced to move on and rebuild her life? Maybe this was her finding her real self, just as Kip was trying to do?

Sensing her granddaughters were growing bored of rolling out the green icing and were more interested in eating large chunks of it, she said, 'Come on you two, time to do the exciting bit now and start cutting out the leaves.'

The girls gave a whoop of delight and immediately flung aside their mini rolling pins and with their hands stained with green as well as red now, they took the cutters from her.

At the sound of the timer going off, she went over to the Aga to take the mince pies out of the oven. When she'd done that, she filled two plastic beakers with a 50/50 ratio of apple juice and water and then peeled two clementines. Caro was a stickler for healthy snacks and as much as it was a grandparent's prerogative to spoil a grandchild, Louisa knew better than to flout her daughter-in-law's wishes. Which meant that, given the quantity of fondant icing that had been consumed at the table, Louisa had better scrub the girls' faces clean before Caro and Arabella came to fetch their daughters after spending the day Christmas shopping together.

But Caro and Arabella didn't come for the girls, instead Ashley and Kip had been despatched in their place.

Seeing her father, Peggy broke off from watching *Paw Patrol* with Heidi and hurled herself at him with a happy cry of '*Dada, Dada*, look what we made!' She pointed proudly to the Christmas cake on the table which was now decorated with a ribbon and a higgledy-piggledy arrangement of leaves and berries, and an oversized snowman fashioned out of the remains of the white fondant icing.

'That looks amazing,' Ashley said, 'did you and Heidi do that all on your own?'

'Yes,' she said solemnly.

'And are we allowed to eat some of it now?'

'No!' she cried. 'It's for Christmas and when Santa comes!' Peggy then scooted off back to the television.

'You've kept them busy, then?' Ashley said.

'I think they've kept me busy,' she said with a smile, while trying not to scrutinise Kip too obviously as he stood awkwardly to one side of Ashley.

She was glad to see he looked better than when she'd last seen him. He didn't seem so pinched and overwrought, or so weighed down.

'And in case you're wondering why it's us on taxi duty,' explained Ashley, 'Caro and Arabella decided to treat themselves to afternoon tea at the Swan in Lavenham after a hard day's shopping.'

'Good for them,' Louisa said. 'Well, how about you two, can I tempt you into having a drink and a mince pie fresh out of the oven, or do you have to rush off with the girls?'

'Have you ever known me to turn down one of your mince pies?' Ashley answered without a moment's hesitation.

When they were settled at the table, Louisa watched Kip looking over to where the six-foot-tall Christmas tree stood with its multi-coloured lights twinkling cheerily. If she were honest, she'd gone a bit crazy with lights and foliage, draping as much of it as she could along any available surface. She liked the Santa's grotto effect which she'd created in this room, which was essentially the heart of the house, just as the kitchen at Charity Cottage had been. She'd decorated the sitting room upstairs too, but with a touch more restraint.

'You've decorated this room beautifully,' Kip commented, uttering his first words directly to her since arriving, 'but then you always did Christmas so well.'

'Thank you,' she said, wondering what he was really thinking. Was he thinking of all the happy Christmases they spent together as a family, or maybe thinking of last Christmas when everything changed. 'The girls helped me put the finishing touches to the tree,' she said, 'so I can't take all the credit.'

'But you can take the credit for these,' Ashley said, wolfing down the last bite of a mince pie, 'definitely up to your usual high standard. Aren't you going to have one?'

Louisa shook her head. 'I'm eating out tonight.' The words flew from her lips before she'd realised what she was saying.

'Oh?' said Ashley. 'Where are you off to?'

'Nowhere special. Another mince pie?' she said, pushing the plate towards Ashley and then Kip, hoping to distract them. They both took one, but Ashley was not to be deflected.

'Where are you going? And who with?'

'Just someone.'

'That sounds very—'

'Ashley,' said Kip, 'maybe your mother doesn't want to tell us. She's entitled to her privacy.'

'Privacy,' Ashley repeated as though he didn't fully comprehend the word. 'What do you mean?'

'I mean, if your mother is going out, we should eat our mince pies and then take the girls home.'

'It's no big deal,' Louisa said, seeing the puzzled expression on Ashley's face. 'It's just a meal out with somebody who used to live here. He was the one who converted it into a home when it had been abandoned. He turned up here one day with a painting of the mill and wondered if the new owner might like it. I've hung it on the wall on the top flight of stairs. You should go up and take a look.' At last she fell quiet, feeling foolish for having rattled on for so long.

'I hope he's taking you somewhere nice,' Kip said, 'you deserve the best. Don't you agree, Ashley?'

But Ashley didn't look like he agreed at all. Louisa's heart sank. It was just as she feared it would be.

Chapter Fifty-Six

'I still can't believe it,' Ashley said. 'Mum going on a date, and with somebody we don't even know.'

'Dinner,' said Caro, 'does not necessarily a date make, and anyway, you should be pleased your mother is making new friends.'

They were in the kitchen where, after putting Peggy to bed, Ashley was grilling himself a steak to go with some oven-cooked chips. Caro had arrived home a few minutes ago from her day with Arabella saying that she couldn't eat another thing after the tea they'd enjoyed at The Swan. She was now pouring herself a glass of merlot from the opened bottle on the side; he was already onto his second glass.

He'd downed his first while waiting for Caro to come home, bristling with the need to offload. He'd tried ringing Angus, but there'd be no answer from his brother. So he'd waited as patiently as he could for Caro to arrive back and then just as patiently listened to her tell him what a good time she and Arabella had had together.

He was pleased that his sister and Caro were so much closer now. Arabella had recently confided in him that she had begun to see Caro in a new light. 'It used to annoy me that she always seemed to have all the answers,' she'd admitted, 'but now I appreciate how straightforward and pragmatic she is. But tell her that and I'll never speak to you again!' Arabella had added with a laugh.

Ashley suspected he was in for his own share of pragmatism from his wife with what he was about to say. 'What would you call it then, Caro?' he asked. 'And don't overlook how embarrassed my mother was to admit what she was up to.'

'*Up to*,' repeated Caro, looking at him as she replaced the screw top on the bottle of merlot. 'Oh Ashley, I love you dearly, but please listen to yourself, you sound ridiculous. Your mother is entitled to have dinner with whomever she wants and if she was reluctant to tell you what she was doing, it was because she knew you'd react like this.'

'I'm reacting in the way any son would. She scarcely knows the guy. He's clearly trying to impress her by taking her to Le Talbooth. I mean, come on, it's hardly cheap there, is it? What's he expecting in return?'

'Are you saying you'd rather he took her somewhere cheap and nasty?'

'No,' he said with a frown of frustration. 'But what if this is his MO and he picks on vulnerable woman and flatters them and then—'

'Louisa is not vulnerable. She's a strong and very capable woman who is not short on intelligence, so cut her some slack.' More softly, Caro added, 'I know you wanted your parents to get back together again, and you think a new man on the scene will put paid to that, but realistically the best you can hope for is that your mother will forgive Kip and they'll be friends.'

'Couples do make it work second time around,' he said obstinately. 'I know it's a long shot, but I can't help but want to believe that all those years of building a life together might mean something to them, that it was worth saving.'

'Those years still happened, Ashley, nothing can take that away.

But the past is the past, and now what counts is the present and the future. A future that includes Zoe and two children.'

'She might not want to have anything to do with us.'

'Is that wishful thinking on your part?'

'No. Not at all.'

He slid the grill pan out to put the steak on a plate he'd put ready. Then he tipped the chips on the plate, added salt and pepper and a dollop of mustard, grabbed a steak knife and a fork, and carried his supper over to the island unit where Caro was now sitting.

He took a long swallow of his wine and reluctant to let go of the subject, he said, 'Mum seeing another man couldn't come at a worse time for Dad.'

Just as Ashley knew she would, Caro helped herself to a chip from his plate. 'How so?' she asked.

'At this crucial stage of his recovery. The panic attacks are lessening, and he says that contrary to all his expectations, the therapy is helping. But what if the thought of Mum seeing another man sets him back?'

'Your mother can't put her life on hold to avoid upsetting your father, not after everything he's done. I'm hugely fond of Kip, you know that, and I'm as keen to see him well and happy again as you are, but I also want Louisa to be happy. Rather than waste any energy on thinking about what his ex-wife is up to, Kip needs to sort out his relationship with Zoe. He can't go on shirking his responsibility there.'

'But what exactly is his relationship with Zoe now?'

'He's the father of the children she's expecting, and nothing is ever going to change that.'

'You sound as though you're judging him.'

'Eat up,' Caro said, while helping herself to another chip and wagging it at him.

'Hey, I thought you said you couldn't eat another thing?'

She smiled. 'Chips don't count.'

He cut into the steak, then chewed on a piece. 'So *are* you judging my father?'

'Yes and no. The clock is ticking for Zoe and as far as we're aware she's not putting any pressure on him, but sooner rather than later Kip has to face up to the situation.'

'I'm sure he knows that. Which is part of the problem, it terrifies him.'

'Not as much as giving birth to twins must be terrifying the life out of Zoe, or the thought of looking after them on her own. What if she suffers with postnatal depression like I did? Who will be there for her? I had your support every step of the way and I dread to think what could have happened if you hadn't been so understanding and protective of me.'

It wasn't often Caro referred so openly to her nightmare struggle in the early stages of motherhood and it took Ashley by surprise. Seeing the woman he loved in such a dark place and so vulnerable to the change in her hormones and emotions had been the worst time for them both. He'd felt powerless to be of any real help to her; all he'd been able to do was keep her from plunging any deeper into the abyss and pray that she would recover. Which thank God she did.

He then thought of Arabella and the heartbreak she had suffered and was still suffering after her miscarriage, coupled with the end of her marriage. Through it all though, she'd had the family to turn to; they had all been there for her. Including Dad.

Who would Zoe have? And was it their problem to help solve?

Chapter Fifty-Seven

Sunday afternoon and Angus was wrapping Christmas presents. He just had two left to do, both books, so they were nice and easy.

It was a job he invariably left to the last minute, because invariably he left his Christmas shopping to the last minute. But not this year. This year he was fully prepped and enjoying the task while listening to the faint sound of CeeCee playing the opening bars of Elgar's Cello Concerto in her flat below his.

This unheard-of efficiency on his part was down to CeeCee, who had been preparing for Christmas from the moment she'd opened the first door of the Lindt chocolate Advent calendar he'd surprised her with. She had then jumped into overdrive with decorating her flat and enlisting his help to buy the perfect Christmas tree. No ordinary tree would do, it had to meet CeeCee's very exacting requirements, a mysterious process which involved her staring thoughtfully with her head tilted to one side and a finger pressed to her chin as he stood holding the tree for her inspection.

Her enthusiasm for Christmas had rubbed off on him and he'd even put up a few decorations in his own flat. Yesterday she'd surprised him by taking him ice skating at the outdoor rink at Somerset House and he'd watched in awe as she'd glided gracefully around the small rink, weaving her way through the other skaters, most of whom were rubbish like him. He hadn't actually fallen over, but then that was thanks to CeeCee keeping a firm hold of him.

Later that night when they'd returned home, his mobile had pinged with a message from Ashley: apparently their mother had been out on a date that evening. Angus could tell from the curtness of the message that his brother was expecting an immediate response – one of shock, maybe even outrage. But he felt neither of these things. His mother was entitled to do as she pleased. He'd shown CeeCee the message and she'd smiled. 'Good for your mum, she deserves to have some fun.'

Angus agreed with the sentiment, but he sympathised with his brother, knowing that Ashley had harboured the hope that Mum and Dad might be able to put the last year behind them and be together again. Not for one second had Angus thought there was a chance of that kind of happy-ever-after happening. He just couldn't see it.

Besides, there was Zoe to think of. He'd been in touch with her every now and again by text, just to make sure she was okay and to let her know how his father was doing now. She'd been shocked when he'd told her that his father had been suffering with panic attacks and that after finally making an appointment to see a doctor he was now undergoing therapy sessions, which so far, and it was early days, seemed to be helping.

'I think he's been running away from himself for some time but without realising it,' Angus had explained, 'if that makes sense.'

'It does,' she'd said. 'It explains a lot.'

Angus had told CeeCee that he'd gone to see Zoe back in November; he didn't want her to think he was hiding anything from her, and after discussing the idea with her, she agreed that he should keep Zoe in the loop on his father's progress. It was another reminder to Angus just how fortunate he was to have CeeCee as his girlfriend. She could so easily have been jealous of him having any contact with an ex, but she wasn't.

Her fair-mindedness made him ashamed of the way he'd acted towards his father and Zoe for much of this year when all he could focus on was their selfish deceit. But like his mother, he had somehow found a way to be at peace, perhaps more with himself than anyone else. Again, that probably had a lot to do with being with CeeCee; he was happy with her, the happiest he'd been in a long time.

It was why he'd gone to the trouble he had to organise the best possible Christmas present he could for CeeCee, he wanted her to know just how much she meant to him. For weeks he'd wracked his brains trying to think of something she'd really like and then inspiration had fallen into his lap when he'd seen her reading an article about a series of concerts Yo-Yo Ma was giving in the States. In secret, he'd gone online and scored tickets for the concert her hero was giving at the Lincoln Centre in New York next February. The tickets cost more than the two return flights he'd then paid for, but he didn't care. He couldn't wait to see CeeCee's face on Christmas morning when they woke up together and she opened the box inside of which was the itinerary for their long weekend away, which just happened to coincide with Valentine's Day.

Spending Christmas Day with him at Mum's was going to be the first time CeeCee met his family *en masse*. He wasn't worried, though. He knew that she would fit in and that everyone would love her. How could they not?

It would also be the first time in ages that he would see his father and while he knew there could be some tricky moments, he wouldn't be the cause of them. There had been enough bad feeling and hostility to last them a lifetime, and he wanted no more of it.

From downstairs, Elgar's Cello Concerto came to a sudden stop. Angus waited for the music to resume, but it didn't.

About twenty minutes later the doorbell sounded.

'Forgot your key?' he asked when he went to let CeeCee in.

'I didn't want to spoil your surprise you have for me,' she said, peering around him at the now wrapped pile of presents on the sofa.'

'And what surprise would that be?' he asked, pretending to block her view.

'Oh, you know, maybe you've bought me something wildly extravagant, like the Duport Stradivarius cello, or the Paganini Stradivarius. I'd be happy with either.'

He knew the value of both instruments because she had educated him on the subject of these priceless cellos. 'Good to know,' he said. 'Luckily I still have a few days to hit the shops.'

She laughed and gave him a hug. 'I knew you wouldn't let me down. By the way, my mother just called to remind me yet again about our visit.'

'Anything new to report?'

She shook her head. 'Just a rerun of all the existing plans.'

He smiled. 'Well, as you know I'm a great one for planning too, so your mother has my full backing.'

At her parents' invitation, he and CeeCee were going to stay with them in Paris, where, so he'd only just learnt, they owned an apartment in Montmartre. He was looking forward to the trip, even though he would doubtless be under close scrutiny from CeeCee's father.

He watched CeeCee go over to look at the presents he'd wrapped.

'Checking to see if there's something that resembles a priceless cello there?'

'No, I'm doing some quality control on your gift wrapping.'

'Marks out of ten?'

'I'll give you a nine.'

'Very generous.'

'And what mark do you think your father will give me when I meet him?' he asked.

She gave him a long assessing look, much like the one she gave when they were hunting for a Christmas tree with her head slightly tilted to one side. 'Now where did that question come from?'

'It stands to reason that he's going to have an opinion on the stranger who's captured his only daughter's heart.'

'Two things, Fan Boy, you're not a stranger and who says you've captured my heart?'

'Hmm . . . let me think about that. Ah yes, it was the girl herself.'

She tutted. 'That girl, she never knows when to keep quiet.' She came back to him and put her arms around his shoulders. More seriously, she said, 'Don't go underselling yourself, my mother thought you were great, and my dad is going to think you're the best, and you know why, because you are. Simple as.'

That was another thing he loved about her, how she saw every situation so simply, not in a superficial way, but by disregarding all the trivial stuff. She could cut through to the only thing that mattered.

Later, when they were in bed and CeeCee was fast asleep, Angus thought again of her parents, in particular Sabine who had given her opinions so freely to him that evening at the charity concert during her brief stay. She had spoken of the need for everyone to experience some kind of adventure and had advocated his mother finding herself a lover. As unlikely as that prospect had sounded to Angus at the time, and if Ashley's message last night was to be believed – a message he had yet to reply to – it seemed their mother might well be taking a step in that direction.

Sabine had also suggested that Angus should surprise CeeCee with an adventure. Did planning a surprise trip to New York count?

But what had really stuck in his mind following that conversation with Sabine was her apparent regret that her daughter had played it safe by opting for a routine job and settling for being an amateur musician, instead of aiming for more. In Angus's humble opinion, there was nothing amateurish about CeeCee's musical prowess, but then as she would no doubt say his opinion was completely biased. And she'd be right.

But. And it was a huge but. But what if there was something he could do to help CeeCee spend more time doing what she really loved?

Chapter Fifty-Eight

Even though he'd only had two therapy sessions, Kip was hopeful that he was on the road to recovery.

It was more than three weeks since he'd experienced a full-blown panic attack, and though he knew, just as the therapist had warned him, that that could change at any moment, he was feeling less like he was standing in the middle of a frozen lake, petrified that the surface of it was about to crack beneath him.

During the last session he'd forced himself to confess to the therapist that he'd been unfaithful to Zoe. It had been gut-wrenchingly hard to get the words out and he'd made no excuses for his shameful behaviour. There had been no sign of surprise, disapproval, or any judgement on the other man's face, but he had asked if Kip had felt worse about cheating on Zoe than he had when he'd done the same to Louisa. Kip had told him that it had felt far worse.

'And why do you think that is?' the therapist had asked.

'Because I love Zoe.'

The admission had slipped from Kip's mouth without him giving his answer a second's thought. It was all he could think of when he drove back to Arabella's and it had been on his mind ever since.

Whether it was down to those two sessions with the therapist, or taking the time off work, or maybe the combination of the two, but he was now feeling more like his old self, as if his energy reserves had been refuelled. With that renewed energy came the ability to think straight and to see things more clearly. With that clarity of thought came a powerful awareness of his feelings for Zoe, that he loved her as much as he ever had.

Which was why he was now on his way to see her, but with each mile that drew him closer to her house his concern grew.

This morning had been his first day back at work and he'd fully intended to speak to Zoe as soon as he could. He could have texted or rung her, but he'd wanted to make the initial approach face-to-face so they could arrange a time when they could sit down together and talk.

But there'd been no sign of her Mini in the car park. It was possible, he'd told himself while looking out of his office window and once again scanning the car park, that given how close it was to Christmas – tomorrow was Christmas Eve – she might have started the holiday early. Yet the doubt that something was wrong wouldn't leave him, which was why he had gone over to her office after lunch to find out if she was there.

The first girl he spoke to was unwilling to say anything, but then another girl appeared in the small foyer and while she had been discernibly disapproving of him, she had been more forthcoming. He'd recognised her as Zoe's friend, Phoebe, and after what she'd told him, he'd gone back to his office and grabbed his car keys.

He had no idea how she would greet him, or if she would even let him in so they could talk. But they had to talk. They couldn't go on as they were. He knew he was at fault. He'd done everything wrong and he couldn't be more ashamed.

His shame was compounded by something Arabella had done last night. She had brought out a photo album which Louisa had made for her. It was one of those albums you make online by uploading photographs and then a few days later a beautifully presented keepsake book arrives in the post. He could remember Louisa trawling through the hundreds of photographs they had taken of their granddaughters during the first year of their life and selecting the best to go in two albums as Christmas presents for Arabella and Giles and Ashley and Caro. She had also added several old photographs of Arabella and Ashley as newborn twins at the back of the albums.

Seeing those old photographs had brought back a deluge of memories for Kip and reminded him just how small Ashley and Arabella had been when they were born four weeks early and weighing in at 5lbs 7oz and 5lbs 6oz – Ashley being the heavier. In comparison when Angus was born, he'd seemed such a sturdy whopper of a baby. But the twins had been so tiny and vulnerable, their hands barely big enough to wrap around his thumb, their fingernails not even as big as a chilli seed, their skin almost translucent. It had been love at first sight for him, and he'd been so in awe that he and Louisa had created these two perfect little beings. Of course, all parents feel that way, in awe and wonder at the miracle of life for which nothing really prepares you, but at the time, your entire world is focused on this wholly transforming moment and the unshakable belief that your baby is the most perfect ever to be born.

He could still remember the fierce protective love he'd experienced when he'd first held Arabella and Ashley. He'd felt it for Angus too, and with Peggy and Heidi when they were born.

In bed last night, and unable to sleep, his thoughts had constantly circled the one undeniable truth: Zoe would soon give birth to two vulnerable babies who deserved to be loved and protected. How could he not be a part of their lives? And Zoe's too.

But was it too late?

He was just turning into Zoe's road and anxiously preparing what he was going to say to her, when he spotted a silver Volkswagen Polo up ahead pulling away from the kerb and driving off into the distance. For a mad moment he thought it was Louisa's car, and if he hadn't been so preoccupied, he might have clocked the numberplate

374

and known for sure that it wasn't her. Of course it wasn't, he told himself, silver was the most common colour for a car, it could have been anyone. What would she be doing here anyway?

He stopped the car well before he reached Zoe's house, not wanting her to see him from a window. He needed time to staunch the flood of adrenaline that was suddenly coursing through his body. Now was not the time to lose his nerve or for his anxiety to get the better of him. And remembering the relaxation technique the therapist had recommended he employ when he felt a panic attack coming on, that of visualising himself somewhere special and tranquil, he closed his eyes and pictured himself lying on a gentle rise of sun-baked grass, the hot rays of sunshine warming his fingers, then the palms of his hands, followed by his arms, neck and chest. Next, he imagined the heat working its way through his feet, ankles, legs and up through his pelvis to his stomach and then his chest where it settled, and all the tension and anxiety began drifting away.

It was a fond memory from his childhood, when during the summer holidays he would set off on his bike with a cheese and pickle sandwich wrapped in a piece of waxed paper from a cereal packet, and pedal for all he was worth to his secret place he liked to go to. He never told anyone where he went or invited any of his school friends to join him. This was something he did entirely for himself. It was what he did to escape home, which was selfish of him, but sometimes he needed to be free of the shadow that hung over the house since his father's accident.

He'd once told Louisa about his solitary cycle rides as a boy and how much he'd enjoyed them, and she'd suggested he buy himself a bike so he could do the same as an adult. He never did though. He'd felt it wrong to do something so selfish when they had three young children to look after, a new business to build up, and Charity Cottage to turn into their new home.

Conscious that his body was no longer tingling with the rush of adrenaline and that he felt quite normal again, he opened his eyes. Each time he carried out this simple technique to stop the threat of a panic attack in its tracks, he marvelled that it actually worked. As incredible, even mysterious, as it was, being able to help himself this way represented an important step in the right direction for him.

It was an echo of something similar which he'd said to Ashley after they'd learnt that Louisa was going on a date. 'It was bound to happen,' he'd said. 'Your mother is moving on in a new direction, as is only right and proper.'

'But isn't it too soon to take this kind of step?' Ashley had asked.

'It's for her to decide what she does and who she sees. No one else has the right to tell her what to do, not you, and certainly not me.'

He was going to have to employ the same understanding with Zoe. He could apologise profusely and tell her that he still loved her, but only she could decide what would happen next.

Chapter Fifty-Nine

'Two unexpected visitors in quick succession, it must be my lucky day,' said Zoe, trying to conceal her surprise at seeing Kip.

'Is it a bad time?' he asked.

She heard the apprehension in his voice and saw it in the unnaturally rigid way he held himself, as though he was holding his breath or nursing an injury and trying to avoid inflicting any more pain on himself by moving.

'Not at all,' she said, stepping aside to let him in.

But he hesitated, one foot placed on her side of the threshold, the other still outside on the doorstep. 'You're sure I'm not putting you to any trouble?'

It's a bit late for that, she thought as the twins chose then to start squirming inside her ever-expanding womb. It was as if the sound of their father's voice had roused them from their slumber. *Wake up*, she imagined one saying to the other, *this should be interesting*. More likely, their fidgeting had been brought on by the surge in her pulse at the sight of Kip which might have pushed up her blood pressure.

'Come in before we both freeze to death,' she said, as the wintry cold air blasted in, and Kip continued to stand as if frozen in time with one foot still outside on the doorstep. Was that an indication of how things were going to be in the future, a half-in and half-out father?

To make it clear that he really was welcome, she offered to

take his coat and placed it on the newel post at the foot of the stairs, followed by his scarf. It was, she noticed, the green and blue cashmere scarf she'd bought him last Christmas.

Standing as close as they were in the narrow hallway, she caught the familiar smell of his aftershave and at once it filled her with the memory of falling in love with him. She had never known a feeling like it when she'd realised that she loved him, and he loved her. It had made her feel invincible, as if anything and everything was possible for her. She had been utterly convinced that whatever difficulties lay ahead for them as a couple with Kip's divorce and his family, they would cope because they were protected by their happiness and an impenetrable shield of love. In those early weeks and months of feeling complete, she had wanted everyone to have what her heart was filled with, the euphoric state of knowing she was loved by a man who wanted to spend the rest of his life with her. She had been sure that there was nothing that could spoil things for them.

Except there had been.

'You're looking well,' he said.

'I'm looking ginormous, you mean,' she said with a short laugh. 'Would you like a drink?'

'That would be great, thank you.'

'Tea or coffee? Or hot chocolate. I can't stop drinking it myself. That might be why I'm so big.'

'Coffee please,' he said. 'Just instant though. Don't go to any trouble.'

Relax, she wanted to say. *Stop being so awkward or scared of me.*

They went through to the kitchen. 'Sit down and I'll put the kettle on.' While she selected mugs and tipped a sachet of powdered hot chocolate into one and spooned instant coffee into the other, he surprised her with a question.

'You said you'd had a previous visitor. I know it's none of my business, but who was it?'

A teaspoon in her hand, she turned around. 'It was your wife. I mean your ex-wife.'

'Louisa?'

'Yes, unless you have another ex-wife I don't know about.'

Her comment had come out more sharply than she'd intended, and he frowned.

'Sorry,' she said, 'that was a silly thing to say.' She was suddenly as nervous as he looked. They both needed to relax, or nothing would be achieved in him coming here, because plainly he'd come here with a purpose. Good or bad, she needed to know where she and their children stood with him. What was more, it was time for her to have the chance to be honest with him. And hopefully without him running away again.

'I thought I saw her car going off down the road as I was arriving,' he said, 'but told myself it couldn't be her because why would Louisa come to see you?'

'Believe it or not, she wanted to see how I was. She also had something she wanted to ask me.'

The kettle boiling now, Zoe turned away from Kip to make their drinks, resisting the urge to open the fridge for the calorie-loaded squirty cream to top up her hot chocolate. She took their drinks over to the small table and sat opposite him.

'So,' she said, 'what brings *you* here? And how did you know I was at home and not work?'

'Your friend Phoebe told me you were under doctor's orders to rest, that there was a complication.'

'You spoke to Phoebe?'

He nodded. 'I wanted to find you in your office so we could arrange to talk properly.'

'Why didn't you call me?' *Like any normal person would have*, she wanted to say, but didn't.

'I wanted to do things face-to-face.'

'You didn't seem keen to do that the last time you were here.'

He drank some of his coffee and stared at the kitschy snow-globe that was on the shelf directly opposite him. In what felt like a lifetime ago, she'd bought the snow-globe at a Christmas market in Prague when she'd gone there with a group of friends for a weekend of drinking, clubbing and general excess. How different she was now to that carefree girl in her twenties.

'I'm sorry for the way I ran off,' Kip said, his gaze back on her now.

'What made you do that? One minute you were okay, then you were gone.'

'It was seeing the framed ultrasound photo of the babies. It terrified me. I can't tell you how ashamed I am that I reacted that way.' He lowered his gaze and cradled his hands around his mug of coffee. 'But I wasn't myself. Which sounds like the most pathetic of excuses.'

She took a sip of her hot chocolate, followed by another, wanting to choose her words with care. 'I know you've been unwell, Kip,' she said gently, 'that you've been suffering panic attacks and are now seeing a therapist. I know it's been difficult for you.'

The frown returned to his face. 'Did Louisa tell you that?'

'We discussed you, yes, but it's Angus who's been keeping me up to date. About you and your family and how they all want you to be well again. They've been so worried . . . as have I,' she added. 'I hope you realise just how much they love you.'

He sighed. 'I do, and it's very humbling after everything I've done. It almost makes it worse as I feel even guiltier.'

'The way I see it, they've obviously forgiven you, so maybe you should try forgiving yourself.'

He stared into his mug of coffee then raised it to his lips. She waited for him to respond to what she'd said, but he didn't. Instead, he asked her a question.

'The complication which Phoebe mentioned . . . is it serious?'

Wondering what her friend might have told Kip – had Phoebe

deliberately exaggerated the situation for some reason? – Zoe shook her head. 'Not too serious. My blood pressure's up more than it should be, and my ankles swell as the day goes on, which is why I've been signed off. I doubt I'll go back to work in the New Year.'

'But you're feeling well in yourself?'

'Bored out of my mind if I'm honest. So bored I've been trying to teach myself to knit.' She placed a hand over her abdomen. 'Pity these two when they're born and wear anything I've made them.' She gave a clipped laugh.

'I'm sure they'll look fine in whatever they wear,' he said. 'That's the thing about babies, they can't help but look adorable.' His voice had taken on a note of soft tenderness. 'Do you know what sex they are?'

'Yes. Would you like to know?'

He swallowed. 'I would.'

'It's one of each.'

A smile of delight lit up his face and it made her smile too. 'That's wonderful,' he said. 'Although, of course, two boys or two girls would have been just as wonderful.'

'I know what you mean. But I like the idea of a girl and a boy.'

'Have you chosen any names?'

'Not yet. Do you have a preference?'

He looked startled at the question; the smile gone from his face. 'I don't think I have the right to have a preference,' he murmured, putting his mug down on the square coaster in front of him and moving it so that it was perfectly parallel with the edge of the table.

Wondering what he was thinking, she looked at him, really looked at him. He was frowning again as he ran his finger around the edge of the coaster, and she could see how the lines either side of his eyes and around his mouth were more pronounced than she remembered. There was a vulnerable intensity to his expression too, a desperate unhappiness that made her heart twist with love for him. Or was she reacting with sadness to what they had lost?

She wanted to believe that it was love that she felt, and that despite everything it had somehow survived the break-up of their relationship.

Still looking at Kip, she said, 'Let's go into the sitting room. We'll be more comfortable there.'

Without commenting, he stood up and followed her.

Once they were settled, he on the sofa and she in her usual chair which she'd moved nearer to the sofa to accommodate the Christmas tree, she pointed to the small table next to her and the evidence of her attempt at teaching herself to knit. 'See,' she said, 'I wasn't joking about the knitting.'

'What's it going to be?'

'It's supposed to be a jacket for a newborn, but at the rate I'm going it could be anything.'

'My mother taught me to knit when I was a child,' he said.

'Really?'

'I can't recall why, but I do remember following her instructions to the letter and being quite pleased with what I made.'

'What did you make?'

'A scarf for my father. Which I think he wore under sufferance.'

Trying to picture Kip as a young boy presenting his father with a scarf he'd made, Zoe said, 'This is going to sound like a clumsy segue, but I hope you're not here under sufferance.'

'I'm not. I came because . . . because I need you to know that I'm genuinely sorry for how I've treated you. Believe me when I say that if I could turn back the clock, I would.'

Remembering she had said the very same thing to Louisa, she said, 'But to when? Before we started our affair or when I told you I was pregnant?'

'Neither of those moments. I'm talking about when I failed

to love and support you in the way I should have when you said you were going ahead with the pregnancy. I let you down badly.'

'Yes,' she said simply. 'You did. But you acted honestly, there was no pretence involved.'

'There was pretence. You see, I was pretending to myself that the mess I'd made would somehow magically sort itself out if I walked away and hid from it. But life isn't like that. There are consequences to our actions and there can never be any hiding from that.'

Her mouth dry with nervous expectation, she said, 'Which leaves you – *us* – where exactly?'

'If you'll let me, I want to play a proper part in our children's lives. I want to be their father and I want them to know that's who I am.'

It was the first time she'd heard him say the words *our children* and it gave her a jolt. But a jolt of what? Relief? Happiness? Concern?

'Do you want to be involved because you think it's the right thing to do?' she said. 'If that's the case then I don't think playing a role as an act of duty is fair on anyone, least of all our children.'

He shook his head. 'That's not what I want, although I know I have no right to say what it is I do want, but I want to be properly involved as a real father because that's what I am. I'm their father and nothing will ever change that. But if you don't want me involved, then I must accept your wishes.'

'What's brought the change of heart on?' she asked.

'A combination of things,' he said. 'Being able to think straight again and realising that what I had felt for you hadn't gone, it was still there, but buried beneath the fear of letting everyone down, of letting you down by not being able to be the man you needed me to be.'

She stared at him confused. 'But you just had to be yourself,

Kip. That was all I needed. Just you being *you,* the man I fell in love with.'

'I'd lost sight of who that was,' he said quietly. 'Maybe I'd lost who I really was a long time ago. All I know now is that I miss you. I miss you so much.' He leaned towards her. 'I gave up my old life because I fell in love with you, Zoe, and wanted to spend the rest of my life with you and—'

'But you didn't give up your old life to be the father of yet more children, did you?' she interrupted him. 'That was never your plan, was it?'

'The best-made plans are seldom the ones which really make us happy. But I'd understand if you no longer want what we once had, especially as I probably destroyed it anyway.'

Resting her hands on her stomach, Zoe breathed in deeply. Was it possible what Kip was suggesting? Or would they be deluding themselves that they could pick up where they'd left off before she was pregnant? 'This has all come as such a shock,' she said, feeling a series of rapid movements beneath her hands as though the twins were having a fight inside her, elbows and feet pushing and shoving. *Play nicely!* she silently told them. 'I don't know what to say.'

'Then don't say anything. I'll go and let you think about what I've said.' He stood up abruptly.

'No,' she said, 'don't go. Not yet. Do that and I might think I imagined this conversation.'

The ghost of a smile passed across his face. 'I might imagine it too.' He stepped around the coffee table and came and crouched on the floor in front of her. He clasped her hands in his. 'I want to try and prove myself to you . . . if you'll let me. If it's not too late.'

His face so close to hers, it would have been the easiest thing in the world to lean nearer and kiss him. And she was suddenly so very tempted. Tempted to believe it could be as easy as that and to believe the pain they'd gone through had never happened, that they were the same Kip and Zoe. But they weren't the same. They'd changed.

But what if that was a good thing? Wasn't change the key to growth? If a person never changed then they'd stay the same, too scared to take a risk, too scared to make the most of life.

'Before we make any big life-changing decisions,' she said, 'I want to tell you something.'

'Go on,' he said anxiously.

'Don't look so worried, it's nothing awful. It was something Louisa asked me when she was here earlier. As unbelievable as it sounds, she's invited me to spend Christmas with you and your family.'

'She did?'

'The offer is meant well, I know, but as generous as it is, it's also completely terrifying.'

'I'll say.'

'So what do you think?'

'I think it's the first important step for us to take if we're going to make it work between us again.'

'I agree,' she said.

Chapter Sixty

Christmas morning and Louisa woke to the sound of laughter. It was coming from the bedroom above hers, where Angus and CeeCee were staying.

It was wonderful to hear her youngest son so happy and to see him so in love with CeeCee. It would be presumptuous of Louisa to say she knew that CeeCee loved Angus, but she had every reason to believe it was so. The glances they shared, the way they mirrored one another's movements and mannerisms without knowing it, and the easy rapport between them told Louisa all she needed to know: that they were a couple perfectly in step with each other.

Last night over supper they'd told her that CeeCee was going to rent out her flat and move in with Angus so she could give up her job to see if she could make music her full-time career.

'If it doesn't work out,' she had said, 'at least I'll be able to say I gave it my best shot.'

'You'll make it work, I know you will,' Angus had said.

CeeCee had given him a playful punch on his arm. 'Says the completely unbiased and totally objective boyfriend whose idea it was for me to move in with him.'

'Well, here's to new beginnings for the pair of you,' Louisa had said, raising her glass and chinking it against theirs.

Which had led to Angus teasing her about her own potential new beginning with Si.

There had been quite a few comments from her children about her 'date' with Si. Ashley had been slightly less jovial in his questioning of her, but she hadn't minded. She understood why he was resistant to the thought of her seeing anyone. He was just being protective. Arabella was more concerned as to when they would meet Si.

Louisa had made vague noises about them not rushing things. She said nothing about having suggested to Si that he could join them for Christmas, an invitation he'd turned down because he already had plans in place. It had perhaps been rash of her to ask him, but she'd decided that the new Louisa was going to be a lot more impulsive. Reckless even.

Going out for dinner with Si had felt wonderfully reckless. Who was this woman thoroughly enjoying herself with a man who wasn't her husband, she'd kept thinking. Everything about the evening had been perfect, from the moment Si had arrived to drive her to the restaurant which had been festively adorned with lights and a beautifully decorated Christmas tree. The food had been excellent too, every course a delight. Then there was Si sitting across the table from her dressed in a smart dark blue suit and an open-necked pale pink shirt and looking, she had to admit, rather gorgeous. She'd been glad she'd made plenty of effort with her own dress and make-up. It was a long time since she'd had to think so carefully about what to wear for an evening out.

Throughout the meal they'd chatted easily and made one another laugh with some anecdote or other. Remembering that when she'd first met him, he'd said he was having a clear-out with the intention of moving, she'd asked him if he was now ready to put his house on the market. He'd said he was waiting until the New Year to do that, but he had yet to decide where he really wanted to settle this time. She'd been on the verge of recommending Ashley to sell his house when she thought better of it. Perhaps mixing business and pleasure wasn't such a good idea. And anyway, Si knew that her son was an estate agent, he could join the dots up for himself.

Instead, she'd asked him about his past relationships and why he was still single. He'd laughed and then gone on to share with her a collection of humorous and some not so funny stories of online dating experiences. It sounded quite the minefield.

'It wasn't all bad,' Si had explained, 'I did meet a couple of nice women, but things just fizzled out between us. If it isn't right, it isn't right and it's better to accept that and move on.'

His comment had brought to mind what Kip had said to her when he'd been trying to describe how he felt about their marriage. He'd never said the words 'fizzled out' but as good as.

There had been no overt moves on Si's part during the evening to expect anything more from Louisa other than her company, which when he had dropped her off at the mill had been both a relief and paradoxically a disappointment. Had she been, and to use the modern-day parlance, 'friend-zoned' because she wasn't sexy or attractive enough to be considered anything more? Was she simply a good listener? Was that her appeal?

But the next morning a beautiful bouquet of flowers had arrived for her. Printed on an accompanying card were the words:

Thank you for a great evening, looking forward to the next time! Si. X

Maybe she hadn't been 'friend-zoned' after all. The thought had given her an unmistakable thrill of excitement and she'd immediately texted to thank him for the bouquet. His reply was to ask if she would be at home around midday as he had something for her.

It turned out to be an enormous box, about four feet tall and three feet wide and expertly wrapped in red and green paper, complete with a large silver bow. She was stunned and apologised for not having anything to give him in return.

'Nothing to apologise for,' he'd said, before asking where she'd like him to put the box.

'By the Christmas tree would be nice,' she'd said, feeling another thrill of excitement. What could possibly be inside such a large box? She loved surprises and Si certainly was proving to be a man of surprises.

'Do you have time for a drink and a mince pie, or a slice of Stollen cake?' she'd offered.

'I hate to say no,' he'd said, 'but I need to go and see somebody in Cavendish to measure up so I can give them a quote for a new kitchen.'

They were at the door and about to say goodbye when he'd said, 'I really enjoyed last night. I hope we can do something similar again sometime soon.'

'I'd like that too,' she'd said. Seized with an impulse, she'd then asked him what he was doing for Christmas Day.

'I'm going over to Woodbridge to spend the day with friends. Why?'

'It was probably a silly idea, but I was going to suggest you came here.'

'Doesn't sound silly to me, although I can't speak for your family. Wouldn't I be intruding in a big family get-together? And didn't you say your ex was coming?'

'Yes,' she'd said, 'that's why it was a silly idea.'

'I'll be back Boxing Day evening, so how about we talk then and arrange something?'

'I look forward to it,' she'd said.

That was when he'd leaned in and placed his lips against her mouth and kissed her. His hand had then moved to her cheek and the kiss had gone on for some seconds. Very gently, very tenderly. A part of her had felt the awkward need to adjust to the thought that it wasn't Kip kissing her, that it was another man, a rather lovely man. There was no doubting the happy sensation it left her with when she'd waved him off.

How's that for moving on? she'd thought.

Which had then led her to think of Kip and Zoe, but particularly Zoe. How was she? Would she be with friends for Christmas? Was that what she'd done last year when Kip was with the family and preparing himself to make his shocking announcement on Boxing Day? Or had she been on her own longing to see her lover?

Strangely, none of these thoughts had caused Louisa anywhere near the level of angry hurt they would have done just a few months previously. What she felt was sad regret. And if she felt sorry for anyone it was Kip and Zoe for the predicament in which they now found themselves. In contrast she had it easy. She had proved in a very short space of time that she could create a new life for herself and that she could even forgive Kip and Zoe. What she found harder to forgive was Kip treating Zoe the way he had. That wasn't the Kip she had known and loved, and she didn't doubt for a second that he knew deep down that wasn't the real him. He wasn't a cruel man.

So, the day before Christmas Eve, and with her sister's words playing inside her head – *Women can't help but be comforters and healers* – Louisa had felt compelled to go and see Zoe to make sure she was all right. She had probably known all along what she planned to say, but it didn't make it sound any the less bizarre when she'd invited Zoe to join them all for Christmas.

Zoe could not have looked more shocked.

'You just told me that you were planning to spend the day alone,' Louisa had said, 'and I think that's a real shame when you'd be most welcome to join us. Nobody should be alone on Christmas Day.'

'Do you have a habit of taking in waifs and strays?' Zoe had asked.

'Not at all. And you're not a waif or a stray, quite the contrary.'

'Does Kip know you're here inviting me to spend the day with you?'

'No, he'd be as shocked as you are.'

'He'd probably hate me showing up unexpectedly. It could only make things worse. He hasn't been in touch for so long, although I know he's not been well. But what about your family? What would they think?'

'That's not your problem, I'll deal with them. But the invitation stands. I could talk to Kip if you like, sound him out? Who knows, this might be the way to bring you two back together again. It is what you want, isn't it?'

Zoe had looked thoroughly bemused. 'I don't understand you. I'm the reason your marriage broke up and yet here you are trying to put things right between Kip and me. If I wasn't pregnant, would you still be doing this?'

'That's a very good question and I'm afraid I don't really know the answer. What I do know is that Kip has lost his way, and you might be the one to help him find himself again.'

Zoe hadn't looked convinced at that. 'You don't think I'm the cause of all his problems?' she'd said.

'It's possible that sooner or later he was always heading for a fall.'

'And you want me to be the one to catch him?'

'Wouldn't you have wanted to be the one to do that before things changed between the two of you?'

Zoe had chewed on her lip and without answering the question she had offered to make a drink for Louisa. Which she'd declined and said it was time she was on her way. Her parting words were to ask Zoe to give her invitation some serious thought.

'I will if you promise to speak to Kip yourself and see what he thinks,' Zoe had said. 'I really don't want to be the spectre at the feast and ruin everyone's Christmas.'

As it turned out there hadn't been any need for Louisa to contact Kip, he was the one to ring her that evening and he'd sounded better than he had in months. Almost as though he were his old self.

They were ten in all for Christmas lunch. It was a bit of a squash around the table but that just added to the fun of it. The noise of everyone talking at once made Louisa smile. Some things never changed, she thought, and not without a degree of relief.

There had been a moment last night when she'd been wrapping a few extra presents that she'd wondered if she'd been selfish in wanting to celebrate this first momentous Christmas in her new home. Had it been wrong of her to expect everyone to play along? Had they secretly been thinking that it was folly to try and replicate Christmases past? Would it have been better to relinquish the role she'd always played and pass the baton on to Ashley and Caro, or Arabella?

She had aired her concern with Angus while his girlfriend was upstairs having a FaceTime chat with her parents. 'Don't be ridiculous, Mum,' Angus had reassured her, 'nobody would ever accuse you of being selfish, everyone is coming here for Christmas because they want to, not out of a sense of duty.'

'Next year we'll do things differently,' she'd said. 'I promise.'

'After the year we've had who knows what next Christmas will bring us,' he'd said with a smile.

'Goodness,' she'd replied, 'let's not tempt fate!'

But she had tempted fate by inviting Zoe to join them and from what she could see, so far so good. At the other end of the table, Kip was in his customary position opposite Louisa but with Zoe seated to his right. She had looked utterly petrified when she'd arrived with Kip and Arabella and Heidi. 'Look, Grammy,' Heidi had said, 'Grando's nice friend has come with us!'

Oh, the innocence of children! Louisa had thought. 'Well, isn't that lovely?' she'd said brightly. 'And what did Father Christmas bring you?'

Now though, Zoe looked a little more relaxed, as did Kip and everybody else. She had warned everyone that Zoe would be joining them and while they'd been stunned by this latest turn of events, they had all said that if it was what she and their father wanted, they were fine about it.

Kip had most definitely wanted Zoe to be with them. Apparently, he had turned up at Zoe's house just as Louisa had left. He'd gone there, so he told Louisa when he rang her, to try and put things right with Zoe. 'She's giving me a second chance,' he'd explained. 'I'm not kidding myself that it will be easy, we'll need to take things slowly and I have to earn her trust, but I'm determined to prove myself to her and to be a good father all over again.'

'You'll do it, Kip,' Louisa had said, 'you were a great father first time round. You were a good husband too.'

'Don't,' he'd said hoarsely.

'Don't what?'

'Be so bloody nice and fair-minded.'

'How would it help either of us if I was nasty and vindictive?'

'You'd have every right to be like that.'

'Well, I've chosen not to be that way.'

Before they'd ended the call, Kip had thanked her for offering her support to Zoe when he'd failed to do so. 'All I did was imagine that it was Arabella in that situation and how I would want someone looking out for her.'

Turning to her left, Louisa helped to chop up a roast potato for Peggy and heard Arabella teasing Angus about something which made CeeCee laugh. She had such a happy unfettered laugh; she really was a joy to have around, and she fitted in so well with them as a family. Peggy and Heidi had been instantly charmed by her and had insisted she sit between them for lunch. In turn she was a good sport and happily pulled crackers with them and made sure the girls were the ones to win the trinkets. She helped them put on the paper hats, which inevitably kept slipping down over their faces which they both thought hysterically funny.

While all that was going on, Kip had carved the turkey just as he always had and Louisa had ensured that vegetable dishes and the platter of chipolatas and roast potatoes, parsnips, and chestnut stuffing were passed around, followed by two large jugs of gravy and bread sauce. The cranberry and port sauce was nearly forgotten, but remembered just in time.

'Come on, little bro,' Arabella said, 'tell us why you look so pleased with yourself.'

'I can tell you why,' CeeCee said, 'it's because he's earned himself a ton of brownie points for the present he gave me this morning. He surprised me with concert tickets for Yo-Yo Ma in New York.'

Caro looked at Ashley. 'Now why don't you buy me fabulous presents like that?'

'Because he's not as thoughtful as I am,' Angus crowed.

Ashley rolled his eyes but before he could come back with a suitable rejoinder, Arabella said, 'Talking of presents, I want to know what that enormous present is by the tree. Who's it for?'

'It's for me,' said Louisa. The grandchildren had opened most of their presents not long after they'd arrived, tearing at the paper, and squealing with glee at what they'd been given, but the rest of them were waiting until they'd eaten before tackling theirs. 'And before you ask,' she went on, 'it's from Si, and I have absolutely no idea what it could be.'

'Are you sure he's not hiding inside the box?' asked Angus.

'That would certainly be a surprise,' she said, glancing around the table to gauge the family's reaction. Everybody suddenly seemed more intent on eating than making any further comment or catching her eye, but it was Kip's gaze which locked with hers. After the briefest of moments, and with his wineglass in his hand, he raised it an inch or so towards her and smiled.

It was a gesture that reminded her of so many occasions in the past when they'd been at a dinner party, or some other social event when they'd catch one another's eye and raise their glasses with an imperceptible smile of complicit understanding.

Returning the gesture and then drinking from her own wine-glass, Louisa smiled back at him. It felt good.

Later, when they'd watched the King's Christmas Day message – it still felt odd it not being Queen Elizabeth on their screens – Peggy and Heidi insisted that it was time they helped Louisa unwrap her large present from Si.

They had the paper off in seconds flat and after prising open the cardboard box, Louisa peered inside and let out a cry of astonishment.

The girls demanded to see inside too and with Ashley lifting Peggy, Louisa did the same for Heidi.

'What is it?' they both asked, peering into the box.

'It's something very special,' Louisa said, putting Heidi down. Then with Ashley's help, they eased the present out of the box and placed it on the floor. Everyone crowded round to look at it.

'It's beautiful,' said CeeCee, kneeling on the floor with the girls.

'It certainly is,' agreed Angus.

'I can't believe he's gone to so much trouble for me,' said Louisa, joining CeeCee and the girls on the floor and admiring the skill that had gone in to making a 12th scale wooden model of the mill. 'And look,' she said to the children, 'it opens too. Oh, my goodness,' she exclaimed, 'he's actually made all the kitchen cupboards just as they are here. And the cupboards upstairs. It's a perfect replica.'

'So is this what he does, then,' asked Zoe, 'makes doll's houses?'

'No,' answered Louisa. 'He's a carpenter by trade, and this to my knowledge is the first time he's made anything like this.'

'In that case, big kudos to him,' said Angus.

'He must like you a lot,' said Ashley, 'to go to so much trouble and make you something so personal.'

There was no hint of a barb to Ashley's voice, but even so Louisa glanced up at him to check his expression. She was relieved to see he looked his usual self.

'Do you think he'll take commissions?' asked Zoe. 'It would be fun to have a replica of my cottage.'

'No harm in asking him,' replied Louisa, now on her feet.

'Here, Kip,' Zoe said, 'give me your hand so I can kneel on the floor to get a better look.' She laughed. 'Mind you, it's going to take two people to help me back up again.'

'No shortage of helpers here,' said Caro, offering her hand too as she knelt to get a better look.

And wasn't that the truth, thought Louisa when she stood to make room for Zoe and Caro. Observing her family as they admired the mini version of her new home, she thought how against all the odds, they had found a way to be the family they'd always been, a family that was loyal and always there to help each other. They had lost that for a while, just as Kip had lost himself, but here they were, moving on together. That was what counted as a family, being together and being able to count on each other no matter what.

Chapter Sixty-One

His heart filled with love, Kip held the small precious bundle closer to his face and rubbed his nose against the delicately smooth skin of his daughter's cheek. He had done it a few moments before, and he'd swear that in response Lara had smiled back at him.

She was only seven weeks old, so some might say it wasn't a genuine smile, nothing more than a case of wind or a simple widening of the mouth for no real reason. He was convinced it was a proper smile though and nobody would persuade him otherwise. But then he was a completely besotted father, just as he'd been first time round. The difference now was that he had none of the nervous butter-fingers apprehension he'd had all those years ago. He knew what to do this time and was better able to take on his fair share of looking after the twins. Zoe had done amazingly well with breastfeeding for the first four weeks, but with the twins demanding to be fed more and more, she had switched to using formula milk which meant that Kip could help a lot more, especially when it came to the night-time feeds when they would sit up in bed together each with a baby in their arms.

'Yes,' he said to the sweet face staring up into his and with a pair of unusually vivid violet-blue eyes. It was possible, of course, that the colour would change as the months passed, but Kip hoped it didn't alter too much. In contrast, Nathan, who was fast asleep in his Moses basket, had darker eyes, which Kip imagined would end up brown like his and Ashley's.

'Now do you think you're ready to sleep?' he asked Lara in a low voice, rocking her gently and moving towards her Moses basket. 'Do you feel sleepy? Just a little? Because I would deem it a great honour if you'd have a nap like your brother so I can go downstairs and start organising things for the family get-together this afternoon.

'There isn't that much to do as everyone is bringing food with them. Your Grammy Louisa is bringing a cake and two quiches, your big brother Angus and his girlfriend CeeCee are bringing a salmon mousse, probably from M and S because Angus would be the first to say he can't cook. Your other big brother, Ashley, and his wife Caro and your cousin Peggy are bringing sandwiches, nice dainty ones with the crusts cut off, and your big sister, Arabella, and your cousin Heidi are bringing those lovely little pork sausages everybody can't eat enough of and a selection of filo parcels. Yes, the silly ones that always make such a terrible mess scattering tasteless bits of paper-thin pastry onto the floor unless you put the whole thing in your mouth at once and then can't talk for fear of spraying the aforementioned paper-thin pastry at anyone standing within firing range.

'Party food, eh? And do you know why we're having this little party? It's to celebrate a very special day: it's Mothering Sunday. When you're older, you and Nathan will know what that means, but for now, take it from me, it's something worth celebrating.

'Now then, while I could stand here all day happily chatting with you, I need you to sleep. What do you think, are you ready for me to put you down now?'

All the while he'd been speaking, his voice at a low and steady tone, Lara's eyelids had fluttered and now finally they were closed, and she was asleep. Zoe teased Kip that he had hypnotic powers, that he could beguile the twins into sleep just by talking to them.

'You mean I'm boring them to sleep with my scintillating conversational skills?'

'Whatever it takes,' she'd said with a laugh.

After carefully putting Lara into her Moses basket and checking on Nathan, he left the bedroom quietly, placing each foot on the floor with infinite care, wanting very much to avoid any sudden noises. They'd only moved in to their new home last week and were still figuring out which floorboards to avoid stepping on.

Meadow View was a modern detached timber-clad house set in a large garden with far-reaching views of the surrounding farmland. A mile from Chelstead, with all its handy amenities, both he and Zoe had loved the house and its situation on sight. Their nearest neighbours were a short walk away and had already introduced themselves, bringing flowers and cards.

Ashley had alerted Kip to the property about to come onto the market in the New Year and they'd been first through the door. The following day Kip had offered the full asking price on the basis that the property wouldn't now be marketed. As a cash buyer and with the vendors prepared to move into rented accommodation for a quick and easy sale, things had progressed rapidly.

It had been a bright and sunny March spring day when they'd moved in last week. Coming so soon after the twins had arrived at the end of January, when Zoe had been thirty-four weeks, hadn't been ideal, but the family had rallied round and lent a hand with the immediate unpacking. Louisa had looked after Peggy and Heidi while Caro had kept the removal men fed and watered with tea and biscuits and Arabella had helped Zoe with the babies. She was still recovering from the C-section she'd undergone, and Kip was insistent that she be careful and take it easy. As easy as it was possible with twins to look after. Ashley and Angus had assembled the newly bought king-size bed for the main bedroom and then sorted out Zoe's double bed from her old house to go in the guest room. Apart from boxes of clothes, bed linen, books and personal items and all Zoe's furniture, and the things Kip had selected from Charity Cottage and put into storage, there wasn't a lot of heavy lifting to be done. Even so, it had been good having the family pitch in.

Zoe's cottage was now being prepared to be rented out. Last year Kip had been annoyed that she hadn't wanted to sell her place and the proceeds added to the pot of their combined finances, but he understood now why she had wanted to hang on to it. Angus had explained to him that as committed as CeeCee was to their relationship, she had no intention of selling her flat any time soon, not when it was such a sound investment in a sought-after area with excellent rental earning potential.

Zoe's house was also a sound investment in a popular area, but more importantly, as Kip had come to realise, she was more sentimentally attached to it than she'd cared to admit. Also, and he might not like it, but he understood that she needed to keep her house as a sign of her independence and as a safety net. After all, he'd let her down once before; who could criticise her for wanting an insurance policy in case something went wrong between them again? He hoped to God it wouldn't as it was his sole purpose in life to do everything he could to be the partner and father he was now committed to being.

'Two babies successfully delivered to the Land of Nod,' he said when he went downstairs to the kitchen where Zoe was removing feeding bottles from the steam steriliser. 'My guess is that we have an hour of quiet time before all hell breaks out.'

'If we're lucky,' she said.

He went over and kissed the nape of her neck. She leant back against him and sighed. 'Do that again, please.'

He did. Then putting his arms around her, he said, 'What would you like me to do next, or shall I just keep standing here kissing you?'

'A tempting offer,' she said turning around to face him. 'But with everyone arriving' – she checked her watch – 'in an hour and a half, I for one need to have a shower and clean myself up. I smell of milk and probably an awful lot worse too.'

He smiled. 'Why don't you take the chance to relax in a bath and after I've lit the fire in the sitting room to take the chill off the room, I'll bring you up a glass of wine.'

'That would be heavenly, even if it is a bit early,' she said, 'but—'

'Don't worry about Lara and Nathan, I'll listen out for them on the baby monitor. Go and pamper yourself.'

She was at the door when she said, 'I nearly forgot, while you were upstairs, Louisa texted to say that Si would be happy to come and give us a quote for fitting a new kitchen.'

'That's good.'

'And . . .' She hesitated. 'I suggested Louisa bring him this afternoon if he was free.'

'Good idea, the more the merrier. Now go and have that bath before you-know-who wake up.'

Once she'd gone, Kip went and lit the fire in the sitting room. Fortunately for them, the previous owners had left a generous supply of logs behind.

When he had the fire going, he put the guard up against it and went to look out of the French windows at the garden. The previous owners hadn't been keen gardeners and as he surveyed the expanse of lawn, he imagined planting his very own orchard. He might even have a go at growing vegetables. When Lara and Nathan were old enough that might be something they'd enjoy doing with him.

That was the thing about being a parent, you couldn't stop yourself picturing your children when they were older; it was always about the next stage, the next phase. But as much as he knew he was bound to do the same, he wanted to enjoy being in the moment with Lara and Nathan. He didn't want to wish their lives away. Perhaps because it would be wishing his own life away.

To a certain extent he was guilty of doing that first time round when he was working all hours to build up the business. He'd kept longing for the next stage which would surely be easier. It never was. Looking back on those days, he probably didn't see enough of the children and left Louisa to take on the lion's share of the parenting. He was determined not to make that mistake again.

Which meant he had to think very hard about the future of Uniquely You Villas. There had been several approaches over the years from a couple of competitors and maybe, if they were still interested, it was time to reconsider. If he did sell up, he would have to give Louisa her share, that was part of the divorce settlement, and rightly so.

But was he ready to retire? He didn't think so. A lighter workload, yes, that would be the ideal solution. It was what Arabella had been saying to him for some weeks now, ever since she'd started working for him. She was learning the ropes from Christine, who had been with Uniquely You Villas for ten years and was the all-important first point of contact for the villa owners if they had any problems. In her mid-fifties, she had decided she wanted to work reduced hours so she could spend more time with her young grandchildren. Knowing that Arabella was thinking about getting back into the job market now that Heidi was at pre-school, Kip had asked her if she would like to be trained up and then job-share with Christine. She'd jumped at the chance. It wasn't the first time Arabella had worked in the office, all three of his children had spent some of their holidays working at Uniquely You Villas in some capacity or other, in the mail room sending out brochures, or answering the phone; or in Angus's case dealing with IT problems, he'd always been the best in the family at that kind of thing.

Louisa used to say it was a pity that none of the children had wanted to go into the business with him, but it was only now that Kip wished at least one of them had as then he'd find it easy to delegate and hand over more of the day-to-day running of things. Who knew, maybe Arabella might yet be the one to be fully involved.

It was a great relief to Kip that Arabella was, and to use her own words, in a much better place now. She had been so impressed with Kip's progress following his sessions with the therapist, and which had proved so helpful to him – he still saw Paul Read once a fortnight – she had decided to give therapy a proper go herself. Giles had agreed to go too, which was a massive step forward for the two of them and from what Kip understood, they had both taken off the boxing gloves and were doing their best to get through their divorce in a civilised manner, if not for their own sake, then Heidi's.

Arabella still had the sadness of her miscarriage to deal with and maybe that was something that would never leave her. Kip sometimes wondered what was passing through her mind when she held Lara and Nathan. Was it very painful for her? He hoped not.

All credit to Giles, he wasn't hounding Arabella out of their house (unlike the shameful way Kip had with Louisa), but she was already talking to Ashley about selling it. 'It's a way for me to look to the future,' she'd said. 'It helped Mum, and I think it will be the same for me; it will give me a new beginning.'

He knew that she was right. Creating a new home here with Zoe and Lara and Nathan was the same for him. Together they were embarking on a new and exciting chapter in their lives. It wasn't going to be plain sailing all the way, he knew that wasn't possible. They had any number of challenges to face, not least Kip earning Zoe's trust again. As far as they had come since Christmas, he knew that there would be times when she would doubt his love for her. How could she not? There was also the age gap, which wasn't something he wanted to dwell on, but they had to face facts that when Lara and Nathan were in their twenties, he'd be in his eighties. That's if he made it that far.

'Which is true for everyone,' Zoe had told him when he'd voiced this concern. 'We none of us knows what lies ahead or when our time is up, so get a grip and put this high-grade weapon of destruction in the bin!'

Taking the foul-smelling nappy from her, he'd laughed and promised there'd be no more introspection when there were more pressing problems to deal with.

One problem they'd had to sort out, although in the big scheme of things it hardly mattered, was how Louisa should be referred to in relation to Lara and Nathan. Technically she wasn't related, but after Zoe had discussed it with her, they'd settled on her having grandma status.

If somebody had told Kip this time last year that he'd be a father all over again and Louisa would accept the role of grandmother to his second family, he would have accused them of lunacy.

Still staring out of the window, he wondered if Si, whom he'd yet to meet – maybe he would this afternoon – would become a fixture, and if so, would he become a grandfather figure to Lara and Nathan?

Paul – he was on first-name terms these days with his therapist – had asked Kip how he felt about his ex-wife seeing someone.

'I'm fine about it,' Kip had said.

'No jealousy? No desire to check out his prospects and intentions?'

Kip had smiled, but it was an attempt to conceal his real feelings. Of course he wanted to check out the man! Who was this stranger who had entered their lives? Because it wasn't just Louisa's life he was now connecting to, it was all of them.

Paul had warned Kip that it wasn't his job to be responsible for everybody else in this life.

'But as a father, grandfather, ex-husband and partner, it *is* my job to be there for them all.'

'A nice sentiment, but not altogether true. Each one of us must take responsibility for ourselves.'

'Is that what you tell your children?'

'Fair point,' Paul had said, 'but the time will come when it is down to them to take charge of their own lives.'

'I've never been an interfering or overbearing kind of husband or father,' Kip had said defensively.

'I didn't say you were, but letting go is always easier said than done.'

'But I don't want to let go of my family. Why would I?'

'Okay, then how about we substitute *standing back* for *letting go*, does that sound more acceptable? Because what I'm really trying to get at is you not being too hard on yourself. You need to accept that you can't always get it right, and that's okay. Nobody can operate at peak perfection all the time, it's simply not possible.'

Paul had then warned Kip again not to be surprised or disappointed if he experienced another panic attack. This had been the week before the move to Meadow View. 'You've done well to avoid one all these weeks, but pile on the emotional stress and guilt,' he'd said, 'and it could trigger an attack. But you know what to do now to help yourself; go to that secret place in your head, when you were a boy and lying in the sun on that hill.'

The nearest Kip had been to experiencing an attack had been on Christmas Day when he and Zoe had been on their way with Arabella and Heidi to be with Louisa and the rest of the family. He'd suddenly felt light-headed and his heart had begun to pound. He had tried not to feel apprehensive, telling himself there was nothing to worry about, that Louisa wouldn't have invited him and Zoe if she hadn't wanted them both there, yet the anxiety just wouldn't leave him. With Arabella driving, he'd been able to close his eyes and take himself off to that secret place in his head and bit by bit the dread and the fear of losing control had subsided.

Later, Zoe had admitted that she had been close to bottling it in the car as well. But as it turned out, the day had been an inordinately happy one. There had been no undercurrents of ill-feeling or disapproval. And no stress. Everyone had behaved as though they were a perfectly ordinary family enjoying Christmas in the usual way.

During that same therapy session Paul had suggested that all his life Kip had set himself too high a standard and that in the last year he'd been forced to acknowledge that he couldn't live up to that standard. 'You've seen it as a huge personal failure,' Paul had explained, 'which is perhaps what brought on the panic attacks in the first place. Would you agree with that as a possibility?'

'Yes,' Kip had replied. 'I hated knowing that I was fallible, it was anathema to me. It still is.'

'That's understandable. But you don't have hidden superpowers that make you better than anyone else.'

Pressing his forehead against the cool glass of the French windows, Kip thought how it was human nature to want to believe that we were all special. Yes, DNA proved we were unique, but that didn't mean special. Special put too much of a burden on us. He was happy accepting that he was just an ordinary man trying to do his best.

He would forever be grateful for all that he'd learnt about himself from talking to Paul. Without the therapist's help, he doubted he would have been able to unravel the mess he'd got himself into.

But here he was, the luckiest of men who had been given a second chance with Zoe, a chance to get things right. Not perfect, because that wasn't possible, but as right as they could be. That was all anyone could ever hope to do.

Giving the garden a final glance, he moved away from the French windows and, throwing another log onto the fire and replacing the guard, he listened to the baby monitor on the table in the hall and then went to pour a glass of wine to take upstairs to Zoe.

Acknowledgements

I spend a year alone writing a book but then the moment arrives when I must hand over my 'baby' and become part of a team. And what a stellar team I'm lucky enough to be a part of at HQ! Thank you to Kate, Lisa, Dawn, Becci and Rachael who, along with many others, make all things possible. As always, a huge thank you to the team at Curtis Brown, especially Jonathan Lloyd.

But the biggest thank you is for all my readers who have been with me for so many years, and if you're new to my books and took a punt on this one, I hope you enjoyed it and might be tempted to try another.

Captivated by *An Ideal Husband*?

Craving more from *Sunday Times*
bestselling author Erica James?

Why not try another of her uplifting
and compelling reads?

Available now.

Keep in touch with
Erica JAMES

For all the latest book news, exclusive content and competitions, visit Erica's website and sign up to her newsletter at

www.ericajames.com

Erica loves to connect with readers on social media.
Find her on:

🅕 @ericajamesauthor

𝕏 @TheEricaJames

🅞 @the_ericajames

PS. Want even more great reads, giveaways and book news?
Follow @HQStories
🅕 𝕏 🅞

ONE PLACE. MANY STORIES

Bold, innovative and
empowering publishing.

FOLLOW US ON:

@HQStories